VIKA'S AVENGER

Lawrence Watt-Evans

Misenchanted Press

Cover, illustrations & book design by Bradley W. Schenck

CONTENTS

Dedicated to my children,
Kiri and Julian

CHAPTER 1

The two men stepped into the roadhouse and stood blinking for a moment as their eyes adjusted to the dim interior. When Sart, behind the bar, saw them, he picked up a mug and gave it a quick polish with his apron – on a day like this, sunny and dusty and dry, it was a safe bet that this pair would want something to drink and would not want to wait for it.

He was reaching for a second mug when the taller, younger of the two travelers lowered the pack from his shoulder and tugged at the drawstring. Sart frowned; if this fellow pulled out a flask or water skin...

But he did not commit any such social blunder. Instead the young man pulled out two wooden boards bound together with black ribbon, boards about a foot wide and a foot and a half long. The older man watched as this bundle was carefully extracted from the pack, and then the two men walked side by side to the bar.

"Two pints of ale," the older said, holding up two fingers. He spoke Rogau, but with a decidedly rural accent.

Sart nodded and thrust a mug under the tap on the big barrel. The older man watched avidly as the beer flowed, but Sart noticed that the younger man, who must surely be just as thirsty, was paying no attention at all. Instead he had laid his boards on the bar and was carefully untying the two black ribbons. When Sart set the two mugs on the counter the young man carefully slid the boards well away from them, clearly concerned lest anything splash onto his precious cargo.

The older man took a healthy swig from his own mug, and then, as the younger finally got the knots undone and lifted the top board away, leaned forward toward Sart and said quietly, "We're looking for someone. Perhaps you've seen him."

Before Sart could ask for more details, some way to know just who they were after, the younger man pushed the lower board across the bar toward him. Sart glanced at it, then stopped and looked more closely.

What appeared to be a piece of birchbark was secured to the board. A man's face was drawn on the bark in grease and charcoal. It was no mere sketch, but a detailed and beautifully done portrait; Sart could see the gleam of light on the man's curly black hair, the scar on his nose, the cruel amusement in his smile, and the hard glint in his eye. For a moment Sart just stared; the image was astonishingly lifelike, and there was no mistaking the face.

"Well?" the older man asked.

Sart blinked and looked up. "Yes, I've seen him. He left this morning, headed east across the crater." His gaze fell back to the portrait. "That's a good piece of work. Who's the artist?"

"My niece Vika," the older man said. He nodded toward his companion. "The boy's sister. You said across the crater? Toward the city?"

"Yes, I'm afraid so," Sart said. He looked up again. "Why are you after him? What did he do?"

The two travelers exchanged glances.

"If he's crossing the crater, then he's headed for Ragbaan," the older man said to his companion, ignoring the barkeeper's question.

The younger spoke for the first time. "Then so are we," he said, in a surprisingly deep voice.

The elder frowned. "Tulzik, there are *millions* of people in Ragbaan. You've seen the pictures and heard the stories. We'll never find him there."

"We might," the youth replied. "We could ask around. Why would the city folk want to hide him? They'll point him out when we show them the picture."

"No, they won't. Why would they want to help us any more than they'd want to help *him*? And he can probably pay his hosts to keep quiet. Besides, I don't think you really understand just how many a million is, or how big the city really is. Just finding someone who's seen him could take years. In Ragbaan there are at least a *thousand* places like this one we're in, and he might have stopped in any of them – or none, if he has family there. He might go straight through and come out on one of the other roads, he might get on a ship and sail or fly somewhere. No, if he's gone into Ragbaan..." He shook his head.

"We'll *find* him, Uncle," Tulzik insisted. "We *must*. He killed Vika. He *killed* my *sister*. We'll find him, and we'll kill him for that. If we need to catch him before he reaches the city, then what are we standing here for? Let's go – maybe we can catch up to him in the crater, before he gets to Ragbaan."

Sart, following the discussion with interest, interrupted. "Not unless he's gone mad, you can't," he said. "He left early, said he wanted to take advantage of the cool of the morning. He's got a good six hours' head start on you, and it's only maybe seven or eight hours across the crater at a moderate walk, and stopping for more than a few minutes along the way can be very unpleasant, maybe fatally unpleasant, what with the heat and the bad air and the predators and all. He's probably climbing the far wall right now, up toward Slaughterhouse Pass."

"Well, what's beyond the Pass?" Tulzik demanded.

"Ragbaan," Sart told him. "The Pass opens directly onto the Old West Road, and that's in the city. The east wall of the crater is the city's western border."

"There, you see?" Tulzik's uncle said.

"Of course, he won't stop there," Sart said. "That part's all ruins. It's maybe another four miles before you reach the Peaks, and most of the buildings are still abandoned until you pass the Peaks and the High Piers. But there are a dozen routes open through the Peaks, and unless you can track him somehow there's no way of knowing which one he's taken."

"You see?" the elder said again. "I'm sorry, Tulzik. You know I loved Vika, but we'll never catch him. It's hopeless. We might as well give up and go home."

"You can go home if you want, Uncle Urushak," Tulzik said, his jaw thrust forward, "but *I* am going to Ragbaan, and I am going to find the worthless lying scoundrel who killed my sister, and I am going to kill *him*. He won't get away with it. Vika will be avenged."

"Tulzik – "

"I'm going *now*, Uncle, so he won't have time to get any farther ahead." He gulped down his beer, then started reassembling the protective wrapping around the birchbark portrait.

The uncle started to protest further, then glanced at Sart for support. Sart shrugged.

Tulzik paid no attention to either of them as he carefully retied the black ribbons and slid the boards back into his pack. He hoisted the pack.

"Boy," Sart called, as the young man started for the door, "a bit of advice."

"What?" Tulzik barked, pausing but not bothering to look back.

"When you get there, if no miracle occurs and you can't find him, you might want to talk to some of the natives and see if you can hire them to help. They have their magic – I'm sure you've heard all kinds of tales, and while half of it is lies and trickery, it's not *all* just stories. Some of it is real, and if they aren't the great *tek* wizards of old, some of the folks in Ragbaan still know how to use some of the crumbs that fell from the wizards' tables. I'm sure you've seen some *tek* back home, but there's far more in Ragbaan, and it can do things you'd never have thought possible. It can probably find this man you're after."

"I don't – "

"The place to ask is the north arcade in the great hall of the Imperial Palace," Sart continued. "At least, that's a place to ask that an outsider can find. Now, go if you're going, so you can get safely down the crater's western slope before the sun gets any lower – the shadows can hide the trail when they lengthen."

Tulzik hesitated, then looked back over his shoulder at Sart.

"The north arcade in the Imperial Palace," Sart repeated.

"The north arcade. Thank you." Then he heaved his pack up to his shoulder again and marched out.

"He'd have been wise to eat first," Sart said, as the door closed. "Does he have any food in that pack of his?"

"A few biscuits," Urushak replied with a sigh. "Not the best thing out in the sun with no water."

"There's a safe stream that runs down beside the trail on the eastern side," Sart said. "There are supposed to be markers, if no one's stolen them. I assume he has the sense not to drink from the pool in the center, not when he sees its color."

"I hope so," Urushak said. "I'd hate to lose him, as well as his sister. As it is, *my* sister is going to have some unkind words for me, for letting him go on alone."

Sart grimaced in sympathy. "So the man in the picture really did kill your niece?"

"So it would appear." Urushak turned and leaned back, elbows on the bar. "He came through our village, flirted with her, then went off about his business, and poor little Vika ran off after him, and when we came to bring her back, or at least make sure she was being treated well, we found her dead in his room at the inn in Kalidar. Not a mark on her, so...well, Tulzik assumes it was poison, or that the bastard strangled her with something soft enough not to bruise."

"Maybe she took poison herself when he wouldn't marry her," Sart suggested.

"I thought of that," Urushak said, turning back to face the bar again. "It might be, but Tulzik won't hear a word of it. I'd be interested in hearing what this man Peval has to say for himself, and I'd be happy to see him hang if he *did* kill her, but whatever happens to him, it won't bring her back. That poor sad little fool, caught up in her romantic dreams of running off with a handsome stranger!" He shook his head. "I'm not going to chase halfway around the world after him – I must be more than a hundred miles from home here, and I need to get back to my farm and family. Tulzik's a young man, hot-blooded, absolutely sure this man raped and murdered poor Vika, but he'll come to his senses eventually. Let him search the streets of Ragbaan for a few days, see how hopeless it is, and he'll come home. When he comes back through here, give him a kind word, would you?"

"Pay me now for three beers instead of two, and I'll have more than a kind word for him," Sart suggested.

Urushak snorted. "And if he never *does* come back this way?"

"Then you've wasted the price of a beer, but bought yourself a little good will, maybe earned a blessing from some of the lesser gods."

Urushak smiled. "You've a quick tongue, don't you?"

Sart smiled back. "Comes with the job."

"I suppose it does." Urushak finished his beer and stared into the empty mug. "What you said about the Imperial Palace – what's that about?"

"Just a bit of advice. I hear things from my customers here, and I passed on something I'd heard, that's all. Many of the people who come through here tell me it's the best place to hire certain sorts of people."

"While I suppose there must be a few palaces in a city like Ragbaan, what makes that one 'Imperial'?"

Sart shrugged. "Built for an emperor, I suppose. Ragbaan's seen a few."

"Not for a dozen lifetimes, surely?"

Sart grimaced. "You've never been to Ragbaan, then?"

"No. Why is it so obvious?"

"Friend, in Ragbaan a dozen lifetimes is nothing. Didn't you hear me mention the High Piers?"

"I did," Urushak acknowledged. "I don't know what they are."

"They're *piers*," Sart explained. "Docks. Wharves. Except instead of on the bay, they're on the hillside above most of the city."

Urushak looked puzzled. "What, for airships?"

Sart shook his head. "No, no. At least, not originally. They were built thousands of years ago, in the Warm Years, when the sea was a hundred yards deeper than it is now. And they're still standing. Some of them even have *buildings* on them, mostly temples. If the people of Ragbaan built their ordinary *docks* well enough to last for millennia, do you think they'd do any less for their palaces? Those ruins I mentioned, beyond the crater wall? Some of them weren't even built by humans. You can tell just by looking."

"I know Ragbaan is big and old..." Urushak let his sentence trail off.

"Bigger and older than you can imagine, my friend," Sart said. "And stranger, too."

Urushak stared at him for a moment, then held out his mug for a refill. He took a swig, then turned to gaze out the door.

"I hope Tulzik will be all right," he said.

CHAPTER 2

Tulzik clambered up the final steep slope and paused, standing in the narrow gap in the stone at the break in the crater rim while he got his first look at the city – if what he saw there actually *was* part of the city. He was none too sure of that.

The sun was just below the western wall of the crater by now, and the sky was still bright; Tulzik had pressed himself hard to cross the broad bowl before dark, hoping to gain some ground on the murderer, and had made it in much less than the "seven or eight hours" the barman at the roadhouse had estimated. The rim had hidden everything east of the crater from him very effectively until he reached the breach in the wall, but now he gazed out, with the sun's light behind him, at...something.

He had seen ruins before, of course. The world was old, and humanity's days upon it had been long, so there were ruins scattered everywhere: old cellar-holes and broken walls and fallen towers, bridge supports that held up nothing but air, cracked pavements in the middle of nowhere, strands of plastic blowing in the wind, bits of tumbled stone where one face was a weathered carving of some sort, or where a few scraps of mosaic still clung to a surface. The barman had said there were ruins beyond the pass, and Tulzik had expected the same sort of scattered remnants he had seen in a hundred other places.

Instead, when he looked through the break in the crater wall, past the jagged stone barrier at the outer edge of the city, he saw what at first seemed a huge and irregular mass of gleaming color; it took him a moment to resolve it into an actual *shape*.

The walls weren't quite straight, the broken remains of the roof seemed to curl back from the eaves, and the empty doorways and window frames were all wrong. It stood perhaps thirty feet high and was primarily a deep, intense blue that seemed almost to glow in the sunset – at least, the part of it that stood higher than the crater wall, which Tulzik figured at ten or twelve feet. Streaks of rusty brownish red angled across the blue here and there in what was clearly a pattern of some sort, but not one that Tulzik could make sense of. The surface was not *painted* blue; instead it looked as if the entire facade were a single gigantic ceramic pot or tile, with the colors in the glaze. The finish was chipped in a few places, revealing a rough reddish-brown substrate.

The doorways were all wider than they were tall, and they weren't tall enough; even an average woman, let alone a man as tall as Tulzik, would have had to stoop to use them. The windows, also low and wide and oddly proportioned, had rounded corners at the bottom and square corners at the top.

It was, in short, the strangest, most inhospitable architecture Tulzik had ever seen, and although he had intended to hurry on past into the city proper, his curiosity got the better of him. As he emerged from the crater wall he left the main path and walked over to peer through the nearest glassless window.

He told himself it wasn't *just* curiosity; Vika's killer might have taken shelter in there after the long walk across the crater. He stooped and looked in.

The interior was thick with dust and debris and half-hidden in lengthening shadows, but he could see long-abandoned bird's nests, the ash and charcoal left by squatters' campfires, a few scattered bones, and innumerable broken bits of unintelligible machinery. On the far wall, about eight feet up, was a row of what were unmistakably meat-hooks, although they were shaped differently from any he had seen before, with a broad, straight shaft, then a second straight leg at an oblique angle, and finally an oddly curved, double-barbed hook.

This, then, was the slaughterhouse for which Slaughterhouse Pass was named. Tulzik wondered who had built so bizarre a place and how long ago for it to be so very peculiar. He glanced at a nearby doorway and wondered whether the builders had even been human – could it have been constructed by trolls or dwarfs or some other non-human race? He knew Ragbaan had seen its share of inhuman peoples in its long history.

Just what meat had been hung on those hooks, then?

Tulzik shuddered and stepped back from the window. There was no sign of his quarry in there. Nothing inside appeared to have been disturbed in years. He looked to either side.

The main road seemed to go to the left, around the nearer corner of the ruined abattoir, but the path to the right was clear, as well. The hard-packed earth and bits of exposed pavement gave no sign of which way his quarry had gone.

Logic did not provide an obvious choice. Peval would have no way of knowing he was being pursued by Vika's kin, so he would not necessarily be trying to disguise his path – he had taken the most direct route available from Kalidar to Ragbaan, with no dodging or delay. On the other hand, he surely must know that pursuit was *possible*, after he killed an innocent girl, so now that he had ruins to hide among he might start zigzagging about.

Tulzik did not know where Peval was headed. He and his uncle had not found any notes or records at the inn in Kalidar, or anywhere along the way, and no one they had spoken to had admitted to hearing Peval say anything about his intended destination, though several had recognized the portrait and pointed Tulzik and Urushak in the right direction. Was Peval's unknown goal somewhere in Ragbaan, or had he come here to board a ship bound for some distant land beyond the sea, or perhaps to board an airship headed over the mountains to the north? If he were going anywhere else in the vicinity, rather than Ragbaan, he would surely have gone *around* the crater, instead of across it, so Tulzik was certain Peval was going into the city – but the city was huge and was an obvious place to find either sea or air transport. There were still plenty of possibilities.

Thinking about the crater trail reminded Tulzik that he was tired and hungry and that the trickle he had drunk from on the climb up the east wall had done little but take the sharpest edge off his thirst. The light would not last much longer. He needed to move on quickly and find himself food, water, and shelter. Those would probably be easier to find along the main road. He turned left and strode around the corner of the slaughterhouse.

At his first glimpse of the Old West Road, he stopped again and stared.

The slaughterhouse was not a lone aberration. The Old West Road – and this road or street was broad and straight enough that he had no doubt it was indeed the Old West Road the roadhouse bartender had mentioned – was lined for at least half a mile with ruins just as strange as that blue enigma. All these structures had the broad, low doorways, the curled-back eaves – well, those that still had eaves of any sort – and the glazed, colored surfaces, though only a few were blue. Others were green or violet or a peculiar orange-brown, and almost all seemed to be artistically streaked with that rusty red-brown. Tulzik had wondered at first, given the nature of the big ruin, whether that might have been meant to represent dried blood, though it was not the right shade for any sort of blood he was familiar with, but that hardly seemed likely to make sense on *all* these buildings.

None of the others were as large as the slaughterhouse; most were a height that seemed to be about a story and a half, which made no sense – not unless they really were intended for something other than human beings.

Tulzik shook his head. The world was a big, strange place. He started to tell himself he had seen stranger things than these ruins, but then he caught himself. No, he had *not* actually seen anything stranger than these ruins, but all the same, they were just ruins, and he had needs to attend to, a murderer to catch, and a sister to avenge. He set out up the Old West Road at a trot.

The road sloped up; it was nowhere near as steep as the sides of the crater had been, but he was still climbing steadily. He came to an intersection where three streets crossed, and he could see that the strange, bright ruins extended in all six directions. He hurried on, past more intersections.

It was most of a mile before he finally reached more ordinary, obviously human-built structures of gray stone – but these, too, were ruins. Despite ornate and unfamiliar architecture they were recognizably shops and tenements, but the doors and windows were empty frames, the roofs gone, walls cracked or crumbled.

He wondered whether the entire city was ruined – had Ragbaan fallen in the last few weeks and word not yet reached the surrounding towns? But he could see light ahead – in fact, with the sun below the western wall of the crater and the sunset fading from the sky, the eastern sky was now brighter than the west, and that sky-glow could only come from a living city. He pressed on.

As the dusk thickened, and the road continued virtually unchanged straight into the east, the ruins on either side seemed ever more ominous; the empty doorways grew darker, the gloom within them deeper. Tulzik suppressed an occasional shudder when a particular opening appeared especially mouthlike or befanged, but he kept on, and in time, about a mile and a half from the crater wall, the road beneath him finally leveled out as he arrived in a broad, flat, and utterly deserted plaza.

At one time the square had been paved, but now it was largely bare earth, with scattered mossy outcroppings of red brick half-hidden in the dust. This plaza was fifty yards across and a hundred yards long, and the ruins surrounding it were taller and grander than any he had seen along the Old West Road, with carved pillars rearing up into the darkness overhead, their broken cornices black against the indigo sky.

Tulzik marveled that such a place could be so utterly lifeless and abandoned. The extent of the ruins, which he had initially accepted as merely impressive, had become overwhelming; how could so vast a city ever have supported itself? How could anyone stand to live huddled into the surviving portion of Ragbaan, surrounded by such great swaths of desolation? He paused in the center of the plaza and turned around slowly, taking in the shadowy remnants of vanished splendor.

As he finished his turn, he realized he had a problem. Not only was he hungry, thirsty, and exhausted, but he was lost. The Old West Road ended here. It came into the center of the west side, but did not continue east from the plaza. Two smaller avenues angled out from the eastern corners, instead.

He had no idea which was the better route into the surviving portion of the city, nor which route his sister's killer had taken.

The barkeeper at the roadhouse had said there were a dozen routes through the Peaks, and he had apparently been telling the truth. Tulzik sighed and chose the right-hand road.

A hundred paces from the plaza the ruins around him began to change; rather than largely intact buildings lining a clearly delineated street, he was now entering an area more like ruins he had seen elsewhere, where the ruins were not distinct and recognizable buildings, but rather a tangle of stones and fallen beams here, a cellar-hole there, an isolated column or broken wall to one side. The streets degenerated into winding paths between piles of rubble and across empty fields. Ahead he could see things the ruins had hidden before.

There was a line of large uneven mounds rising up from the ruins before him, black silhouettes stretching north and south as far as he could see, and everything on the near side of these mounds was dark; beyond them, though, the city's glow was clearer and stronger than ever. There were towers atop a few of the mounds – he counted five in all, though he was not absolutely sure of all of them, given the distance and darkness. One or two of the "towers" might have been natural rock formations, or even clusters of tall trees.

One of the towers had a light shining yellow in a high window, though – proof that the city was *not* entirely dead.

Well, perhaps not *proof*, he corrected himself.

The gaps between the mounds seemed to be glowing invitingly. These mounds, Tulzik guessed, were the Peaks. *Most* of the buildings west of them were abandoned, the barman had said – but perhaps not all, and if there were any still inhabited, wouldn't it make sense for one of them to be an inn, welcoming people like himself who came across the crater? He scanned for a light on the western slopes, but could see none.

He sighed, swallowed, and headed for the nearest gap in the Peaks, picking his way through the ruins.

By the time he finally reached that gap the sky overhead was black and riddled with stars. The sky-glow ahead had not faded noticeably, though; apparently the city-dwellers did not retire and douse their lights early.

Tulzik was ready to drop and was quite sure that it was more than the promised four miles from the crater wall to the Peaks – but ahead he could now see an illuminated signboard bearing the image of a foaming mug of beer.

Well, it was either a mug of beer or a mug of shaving soap, and Tulzik thought that even a barber would be welcome at this point, as at least he would have a comfortable chair to sit in, and the water intended to slick down hair should be good enough to drink.

When he reached the sign Tulzik found that it did indeed hang above a beer garden. Half a dozen small tables were arranged on a terrace adjoining a tavern, with a row of exotic trees along the north side and pots of flowers here and there, the whole thing lit by a score of oil-burning lanterns. It was open to the breeze, so it was a little cool now that the heat of the day was passing, but it was still pleasant enough. One table was occupied by a couple about Tulzik's own age, who were obviously far too interested in each other to notice his arrival; the others were empty.

Tulzik tumbled into a chair by one of the unoccupied tables, dropped his pack to the pavement, and simply sat for a moment, catching his breath, resting his feet, and taking in the view.

That view was something quite worthy of consideration. The eastern side of the terrace faced out over the part of Ragbaan that was still inhabited, and Tulzik stared at it in amazement.

This was not what he had expected after crossing miles of

ruins. He had assumed, after seeing so much desolation, that despite the stories *most* of the city must be empty, dark and abandoned, and that the inhabited portion could be no more than a large town. Now he saw he had been wrong.

The terrace was at the top of a long, irregular slope, a drop of a thousand feet or so in perhaps two miles, down to a coastal plain a mile or so in width, wrapping around a broad bay. The water appeared slightly phosphorescent, but its pale blue–green glow was largely lost in the city's much brighter illumination – or perhaps, Tulzik thought, the water was merely reflecting a little of the city's light.

There was certainly enough light for that. The city was gigantic, even without counting the deserted western areas he had already traversed. Because of the terrace's location and angle he could not see very far to the south, but Ragbaan extended as far in that direction as he could see, easily three or four miles. To the north the land curved eastward around the bay until it vanished in the darkness, and Tulzik could not see any clear end to the city, though the lights thinned away to nothing eventually. He guessed that the inhabited area reached at least a dozen miles from where he sat, and abandoned streets extended beyond.

The nature of the city was at least as astonishing as its size. Tulzik had seen several towns and a few small cities before, but he had never imagined anything like this. The pictures he had seen had not begun to do it justice. A jagged landscape of hundreds of towers and palaces rose from the streets to absurd heights. Some were ruined and dark, some were illuminated for their entire height, but most were lit for four or five stories, and dark, apparently abandoned, above that point. In some cases he could see broken domes, shattered spires, protruding beam–ends, and other clear signs of ruination atop structures where the lowermost levels were obviously still inhabited.

Any one of a hundred towers would have been the tallest structure he had ever seen, were it not for its neighbors. Any one of a hundred palaces would have been the largest and most grandiose he had ever encountered, if not for the others a few blocks away.

Nor were scale and number the only unusual features; a few of the towers, both lit ones and dark ruins, rose up out of the bay's waters, rather than standing on dry ground. It appeared that at some point the water level had been significantly lower, and these had been built during that period, and survived the eventual flooding when the seas rose. Tulzik had heard legends of the Dry Years, when the oceans shrank, and these towers presumably dated from that era – but that had been more than four thousand years ago, which would make those towers some of the oldest buildings he had ever seen.

Certainly, they were not of recent construction. Even at night, Tulzik could see that they were rounded and irregular, worn down by the centuries until their every sharp edge had been weathered away. If it had not been for the lights, and the ships and barges and even airships he could see moored to some of these towers, Tulzik might have mistaken them for natural formations of some kind.

Airships were tethered several other places, as well. Tulzik counted about thirty of them hanging above the city, their watch-lanterns and running lights aglow, lighting their colorful fabric. Hundreds of waterborne vessels of every size and shape crowded the docks and piers that lined the waterfront, as well.

A second line of stone piers was also visible from the terrace, but these were not along the water; instead they lined a break in the long slope below the terrace on which Tulzik sat, perhaps a mile and a half from the crest, halfway from the beer garden to the sea. Some of these piers were broken off short, or crumbled into ruin, but most were intact. Ornate domed buildings stood atop half a dozen of them, while two or three passed over a hundred feet or so of rooftops and then into the side of a tower or palace. One otherwise undistinguished pier in this row had three airships moored to it at various altitudes.

Tulzik might have taken these dry piers for broken bridges had they not been arranged along what was so obviously once a waterfront – presumably in the legendary Warm Years of twenty-five or thirty centuries back, when the seas that had retreated in the Dry Years came back, rising steadily for several lifetimes, until some people were said to have feared the entire world might be drowned.

Ragbaan had retreated up the slope, but had survived. The water level had stabilized in time and eventually dropped back to its current level, leaving those old docks behind. Those were undoubtedly the High Piers the roadhouse barman had mentioned, and as he had said, most of the city above them to the west was abandoned. Lights in these upper areas were scattered amid broad expanses of dark, empty streets, though here and there were clusters where entire neighborhoods still flourished.

Below the High Piers, though, the city was a great crescent of light wrapping the bay; ruined towers and domes punched dark holes in the glowing fabric, but every street between them was alive with light.

The sea of light was remarkable not only by its extent, but because only perhaps half of it was the natural yellow or orange of open flame; the rest was the intense glow of teklights in shades ranging from pure white to a hellish red, sick green, or hard blue. Tulzik had seen teklights often enough before, used as lanterns or reading lamps or even shop displays, but nothing like this. There were a dozen colors here he had never seen before, in teklights or anywhere else.

Nor were they all steady; instead many of them flickered and flashed in complicated patterns, so that the entire city seemed to be alive. The hovering airships and the vast phosphorescent bay sparkled with reflected teklight. Here and there a few dark winged shapes soared above the rooftops, adding more movement; Tulzik did not think all of these were birds, but he could not be sure.

The city's tableau was beautiful, and he wished Vika could see it. She would have wanted to draw it, to record what she saw on paper.

But Vika was gone. He swallowed, his throat suddenly tight.

The view was amazing and engrossing, but most of all, for Tulzik, it brought a surge of despair, a great sense of futility – how could he ever hope to find his sister's killer in so vast and complex a city? He had not expected anything like this. His uncle had been right – it would take a miracle to find Peval here. He slumped in his chair, his attention so focused on the glittering panorama below the terrace that he did not notice the waiter approaching.

"Can I get you something, sir?"

Tulzik started and looked up to find a young man in a black silk shirt and white apron standing by his shoulder, holding a pad and stylus. "Uh..." His voice cracked in his dry throat.

"A beer, perhaps? Brewed on the premises from the finest rooftop barley and the best imported hops."

"Yes," Tulzik croaked, as the prospect of relieving his thirst registered. "Beer." Then elementary caution returned, and he asked, "How much?" He had brought a moderate amount of money with him, by his standards, but he had not anticipated needing to search Ragbaan, or pay city prices, so he had serious doubts about whether his funds would be sufficient. He needed to husband them carefully.

"Well, sir, we have a fine selection..." The waiter paused, stylus raised.

Tulzik shook his head. "Plain beer, nothing fancy. And food. How much?"

"Would you like to see a menu?"

"No. What's cheap?"

The waiter managed to convey that he was suppressing a sigh without actually making any overt sound or gesture. "We have the house special – our own ale and a plate of *drash*, with three simple sauces. I believe that's the least expensive choice."

"How much?"

"Just a *fing*, sir."

"A what?"

"A *fing* – I'm sorry, you aren't from Ragbaan, are you? Twelve *jit*. *Fing* is the local slang."

Tulzik was in no mood to worry about local slang; the price was fair enough, assuming the *drash*, whatever that might be, was edible and nourishing. "That would be fine," he said. "And water?"

"Of course." The waiter bowed and hurried away.

Tulzik watched him go, then turned back toward the view to the east. A cool breeze ruffled his hair, and the leaves of the trees to his left rustled; the heat of the day was fading rapidly.

Somewhere down there, he knew, was the man who had called himself Peval, who had told Vika silly stories and paid her outrageous compliments, who had lured her away to Kalidar, and who had then left her sprawled dead across the narrow bed in an upstairs room of the Redbird Inn, wearing nothing but a lace nightgown bunched up around her waist. Somewhere, among those ruined towers and poly-chrome teklights below him, was Vika's killer.

But he had no idea where, and the city was vast and strange.

The sensible thing to do would probably be to follow Uncle Urushak's lead and go home, but Tulzik was in no mood to be sensible. Those thousands of teklights down there meant that this city was awash in old magic and that magic might help him find his quarry. The man at the roadhouse had said to go to the north arcade of the Imperial Palace; Tulzik could see *dozens* of buildings that could reasonably be called palaces.

Ah, but surely one of the locals would be willing to direct him to whichever was the Imperial one.

He stared down over the rail, wondering which it was – and what *drash* was, and how rooftop barley differed from any other sort, and why in the name of all the myriad gods the locals called a dozen *jit* a *fing*.

If he was to learn his way around Ragbaan well enough to find Vika's killer, he would probably need to learn all of that.

CHAPTER 3

The stuff on his plate was a sort of crumbly beige putty cut into cubes; it seemed to exude a pale fluid that pooled beneath it. A small separate tray held a folded napkin, three small bowls of liquid, and a pointed steel instrument that looked something like an ice-pick and something like a pen. Tulzik took a healthy swig of beer, then looked at the food.

"This is *drash*?" he asked. "How do you eat it?" He had noticed there was no fork, nor spoon, nor chopsticks.

The waiter pointed to the steel implement. "Use the pick to dip it in the sauces, sir, and then simply pop it in your mouth."

"Sauces."

The waiter indicated the three bowls. "Mushroom," he said, pointing to a creamy off-white goo in a red-and-white bowl. "Brewed soy." That was dark brown, in a blue bowl, and steamed slightly. "Penzerene hot sauce." That was red-brown with black and yellow flecks, served in a black bowl. None of the servings were generous.

Tulzik nodded. At any rate the beer was familiar and quite decent, and of course water was water – at least, when it was as clean as this. "Thank you," he said, picking up the pick.

"Will there be anything else?"

Tulzik hesitated and said, "I do have a few questions, if you don't mind."

"You're free to ask them."

The most urgent question was whether Peval had passed this way, but Tulzik did not want to rush matters – and he wanted to eat something. He speared a cube. "Can you tell me which of those is the Imperial Palace?" He gestured toward the city below.

The waiter blinked. "The *Imperial* Palace? I suppose that would be the big one over there." He pointed to the northeast, to an immense dark structure overlooking the curving corner of the bay.

That was farther away than Tulzik had hoped. "How do I get

there from here?" he asked, as he dipped the *drash* in the mushroom sauce.

The question puzzled the waiter. "However you choose, I'd say."

"There's no best route?" He popped the cube in his mouth and chewed and discovered that *drash* had only the very faintest taste of its own, a slight sourness. The texture was simultaneously oily and gritty.

The mushroom sauce, however, was excellent, and the *drash* seemed to absorb the flavor. The result was more palatable than he had expected.

"Not that I know of. Was there anything else?"

"Yes, there is. If you could wait a moment..." He put down the *drash* pick and reached for his pack. A moment later he had Vika's portrait of Peval out. "Have you seen this man?" he asked.

The waiter turned the picture this way and that, trying to catch as much of the lamplight as possible, then studied it carefully. At last, though, he shrugged and handed it back.

"I can't say I've *never* seen him, but I don't recognize him."

"He would have been through here earlier today. He crossed the crater this morning."

"Oh, well, I certainly haven't seen him *today*. I'm sure of *that* much!"

"Oh." Tulzik carefully returned the drawing to its place between the protective boards. "You're certain?"

"Absolutely, sir. No doubt at all. It's been a slow evening, and I'd remember if I'd seen him. You say he crossed the *crater*? Why would he do *that*?"

"Shortest route to Ragbaan, I suppose." Tulzik slid the boards back into his pack, then reached for the pick. "One last question, if I may?"

"Of course."

"Is there an inn or other inexpensive lodging nearby?"

The waiter blinked at him. His mouth opened, then closed again.

"I just want a roof over my head; I'm not looking for luxury," Tulzik added, as he stabbed a cube of *drash*.

"Friend," the waiter said, "look around you."

"I don't understand," Tulzik said, glancing about, unsure what he was supposed to be looking at.

"We are completely surrounded by abandoned buildings," the

waiter said. "If all you want is a roof over your head, and you don't demand a bed and sheets, then you can have your pick of a hundred. If you want a maid to fill the basin and light you to bed, then you'll need to find a hotel down in the city proper – there's nothing up here. No passenger ships dock this far up, and it's more than a mile down to the coast road; who'd put an inn here? Any hotel in Ragbaan will cost you a few *walu*. When a hundred thousand doors are standing open, those who can't afford to pay a good price pay none at all, and the lodgings don't try to lure them. They cater to those who don't mind some expense."

"Oh." Tulzik dipped the cube in the dark brown sauce and conveyed it to his mouth. The man made good sense. That was just as well; sleeping in the ruins would conserve his limited funds. He might need money later.

The soy sauce was surprisingly rich and tangy; he snagged another cube and dipped it in the same brew.

"Is that all, then?" the waiter asked.

"Thank you, I believe it is."

The waiter hesitated. "I take it this is your first time in Ragbaan?"

"It is."

"Are you familiar with the custom of..."

He did not need to finish the sentence before Tulzik dropped a five-*jit* coin into his open hand. The waiter bowed deeply and hurried away.

Tulzik was pleased with the soy sauce, but decided he should give the Penzerene a try. He dipped a cube of *drash* into the black bowl, then dropped it on his tongue.

He immediately regretted it and drank his water and remaining beer very quickly in an attempt to cool his mouth.

The waiter had apparently expected this and appeared at his side with a tray, asking, "Another beer?"

Tulzik nodded, unable to speak, and accepted a new mug.

"Believe it or not," the waiter said calmly, as Tulzik gulped beer, "one grows accustomed to it quickly, and many people develop quite a taste for it."

Tulzik gasped slightly as he put down the mug and said, "How did anyone ever learn to *make* it in the first place? Who decided that stuff was edible?"

The waiter shrugged. "The recipe is centuries old. It may have been milder once."

Tulzik finished the rest of his meal without incident, using the entire supply of soy sauce and perhaps half the mushroom sauce, but not touching the hot sauce again. *Drash*, he decided, was perfectly edible and reasonably filling, but unexciting – that it would be cheap was no surprise. He wondered what it was made from, but decided not to ask.

When he settled his bill, paying another three *jit* for his second beer, he did ask, "You're certain you haven't seen that man? Do you get much traffic coming across the crater?"

"No," the waiter said. "You're probably the first to come here from that direction in a year. There are a dozen other routes into the city, and hardly anyone comes overland from the west. We don't depend on travelers. People come up here for the view and the beer and the food."

Tulzik looked out across the terrace. The view was certainly spectacular, and the beer had been good, if not exceptional. "Thank you," he said.

His hunger and thirst assuaged, Tulzik left the beer garden, debating with himself whether to try to make his way down into the city immediately, or stay the night in the ruins and venture down in the morning. He looked at the unlit, deserted streets, remembered what the waiter had said about hotels down by the port, then took the measure of his own fatigue and reached a unanimous conclusion, choosing what appeared to have once been a modest home on a side–street. The ruin still had most of its roof – only a single man-sized hole stood open to the stars – and appeared relatively free of vermin and detritus. There were fragments of old *tek* here and there on the walls, but they all appeared to be utterly lifeless. Some of the plumbing was still intact, but dry; all that emerged when he managed to turn a corroded tap was a faint foul odor. It all seemed harmless, so he curled up in one corner of a back room, his pack serving as his pillow and his jacket as a blanket, and fell asleep.

When he awoke the next morning the uniform gloom of the ruin's interior had been transformed to a patchwork of sunlight and shadow, and Tulzik immediately realized he had slept later than he had intended – the sun was well up the eastern sky. He scrambled to his feet, brushed himself off, made what ablutions he could without

water, then gathered up his belongings and made his way back out to
the street. He hurried to the corner, where he could look down the
hill at the port.

The water of the bay shone painfully bright in the slanting sun,
the shadows of the half-sunken towers cutting dark paths across the
golden blaze; domes of gold and copper and silver shone brilliantly
in the city below. Here and there a gigantic dark ruin thrust up from
the city's colorful fabric – and very colorful it was.

Some roofs that in the previous night's darkness he had taken
from their uneven surface to be damaged he now saw were green
with growing crops – apparently the city's food did not all come from
elsewhere, even though the vast ring of ruins prevented the surrounding land from being effectively farmed. Many of these gardens
were bordered with bright colors that Tulzik guessed were flowers.
Other roofs were glassed over, glittering in the morning sun, but he
could see more greenery inside these hothouses, and here and there
other gardens grew on terraces and balconies.

The winged shapes he had glimpsed in the dark were still fluttering and where they had been mere shadows by night, in daylight
they shone with every color of the rainbow. Most of them were birds
of one sort or another, but there were others that gleamed like metal
and a few that looked more like flying lizards of one sort or another.

Many of the streets were hidden by buildings from this angle,
but where he could see people, they wore a gaudy rainbow of colors.

It all looked very different from what he had seen the night
before, but he was able to get his bearings after a moment and locate
the immense building that the waiter had said was the Imperial
Palace.

It was, he judged, the largest of the many palaces and one of
the most intact. Its central dome glittered gold, flanked by two lesser
domes sheathed in some silvery metal that appeared to have once had
red fancywork adorning them. Even without considering the domes,
the several turrets and towers, or the grand central mass, it rose at
least two or three floors above the surrounding buildings, which were
not themselves small. No crops grew anywhere on its many roofs.

That, Tulzik told himself, was his destination – at least, unless
he found some trace of his quarry before he reached it. He thought he
might well have given up the hunt as hopeless, now that he had seen
the extent of the city, had that bartender not given him the advice to
seek out the north arcade in the Imperial Palace – not that he was at

all certain what he would find in that arcade, or how it might assist him in locating Peval the murderer.

He hoisted his pack onto his shoulder and began walking down the slope.

As he descended, the city came to life around him. Within a few blocks the surrounding buildings were no longer ruins; within half a mile none were abandoned. The streets filled with people going about their daily business, and while the basic garb of shirts, trousers (or very occasionally skirts), hats, and shoes was similar to what he had seen back home, the additions and accessories varied greatly, and there was a certain stylishness, a flair, to most people's attire. Polychrome vests, brightly patterned jackets, jaunty hats worn at dashing angles, glittering jewelry, and flamboyant scarves and sashes gave the inhabitants an air of people who dressed as much to display themselves as for more practical purposes. Even the muddy, half-naked children whose games sent them shrieking in and out of the alleys were more likely than not to have a gold ornament hanging from one ear, or a gleaming strip of silk tied around one arm, or a green or blue stripe painted in curling hair.

Vika would have been fascinated, Tulzik thought; she had always liked bangles and gewgaws. He swallowed tears at a childhood memory of his sister smiling up at him as she played with bright jewels and ornaments.

There were far more machines than Tulzik was accustomed to seeing, though many of them did not appear to be working. Glass eyes peered down from hundreds of cornices, and wires crisscrossed above several streets. Screens adorned many walls – mostly dark, but a few displaying images of one sort or another. Here and there metal-shelled devices rolled or scurried in the alleys and byways, or occasionally buzzed overhead – or sat motionless, apparently defunct, in corners and gutters. The local people were even carrying a few glowing or talking devices that seemed to be functional magic; back home in Emniln no one would carry anything so rare and precious openly. What little *tek* they had was kept under lock and key and handled with reverence.

There were animals, as well, both the natural species – lizards, insects, birds, and rodents – and varieties, presumably artificial, that Tulzik had never seen before, with brightly colored fur, or iridescent scales, or leathery black hide. Some of these seemed to be observing the crowds; they clung to walls or lintels and stared out at the people passing below. Tulzik supposed they had been sent by some magician to perform a specific task, but what that task might be he could not guess. For all he knew, the magicians responsible for some of these marvels were long dead, their creations carrying on for decades because no one had told them to stop.

At first the street he was walking down was lined with houses; then a few peddlers' carts appeared here and there, selling copper trinkets or skewers of grilled meat, and before long the open shutters and colorful awnings of shop-fronts began to replace the narrow windows of private homes. He bought his breakfast from a smiling, gap-toothed woman who was frying strips of meat on a smoking griddle beneath a faded red awning and a flickering blue screen. She charged him seven *jit* for a chewy piece of scorched lizard and a mug of watered orange juice.

Tulzik was gnawing the last of the meat when he saw a stairway leading down at one side of the street. He could not see what lay at the bottom, but a handful of people were walking down into the gloom as he passed, below a screen that was displaying a brief text in a language Tulzik could not identify, let alone read. Apparently there were public cellars or tunnels of some sort beneath the streets.

He passed one of the High Piers and looked up at the domed temple that stood atop the ancient structure, and at the bronze panels that adorned its black stone walls, panels now green with a thick layer of verdigris that hid whatever scenes had once been cast into relief upon them. There was something about the size of a young child, with shiny red scales and red-gold wings, perched on the eaves just below the dome, staring out to sea.

Beneath the pier was a large and mostly empty cattle pen, where a dozen dusty brown steers watched him with dull eyes as he marched past. Two men were dickering by the gate, but even though Tulzik was fairly sure they were speaking Rogau, they were talking so fast and with such thick city accents that Tulzik could make out nothing of their conversation.

A few blocks later a shadow fell across the street, and he looked up to see a brightly painted airship cruising overhead, the scalloped trailing edges of its guidance vanes fluttering in the brisk morning breeze. Its great red propellers were spinning slowly, not yet up to full speed, as the pedalers or motors, whichever this particular vessel used, were only just beginning to warm up.

Not long after Tulzik passed through another shadow, but one that moved only with the sun, as he passed one of the great ruined towers. This structure stretched upward well over a hundred feet; he counted fifteen tiers of windows. It might once have been much taller, as the walls ended in a jagged break, with no cornice, no eaves, no sign that a roof had ever been there. A screen ran the length of the building between the second and third floor, but it was dark and blank.

And it was east of that first tower that he took a wrong turn at a six-way intersection and found himself following a curving street around to the south, when he knew he needed to go north. He took the next left, but that only made matters worse as this new street curved back on itself and descended into a tunnel beneath an ancient palace, where scattered white tiles still clung here and there to a crumbling brick–and–plaster facade, and a panel overhead flickered dimly blue. Tulzik realized he had left the crowds behind; he could hear voices in the distance, but he was alone in the unlit tunnel – except he felt that someone was watching him...

He doubled back, retraced his steps to the six-way intersection, and tried again.

This time he did better, but before long he realized he had lost his bearings again and could not recover them readily. He was no longer on a slope, but on a stretch of flat land between the ridge and the bay, and the buildings on all sides were now tall and intact enough to block any possibility of orienting himself on the High Piers or other distinctive structures. The sun was almost directly overhead, which did not help.

He stopped on a street corner, looking up helplessly as people hurried by on either side. He sighed and peered along each of the streets.

Then he blinked in surprise as he realized not all the people on one street were human.

He had heard all his life about trolls, dwarfs, and the like, but up until now he had never *seen* any intelligent beings other than humans and had not been entirely sure there were any left alive. Now, though, he saw two creatures hurrying along the street that he really couldn't believe were anything other than dwarfs.

They were short, of course, no taller than some of the playing children; Tulzik estimated that their heads would scarcely reach above his navel. They were not children, though; they were far too wide, with heavy bodies and short legs, and shoulders broader than his own. Their skin was dark brown, a shade not quite like any he had seen in humans, though he knew he had not seen every color that existed. Thick, unkempt black hair sprouted not just from atop their heads, but from their cheeks and upper arms. They wore simple sleeveless garments, midway between tunic and vest in design, that left this curious arm hair plainly visible. Despite the luxuriant tufts on their cheeks, their chins were beardless and their upper lips only slightly fuzzy. Their eyes were inhumanly large and dark, with almost no whites visible at all.

One carried a large sack slung over his shoulder, and together they were marching rapidly side-by-side, almost running, directly toward Tulzik, so that he was able to see more and more detail as they approached. The final thing he noticed about them as they rushed by was that their eyes had slit pupils, rather than round ones.

As they passed, though, Tulzik noticed that something in the sack was squirming. He started to call out, but then looked around and thought better of it – a hundred natives had seen the dwarfs pass, and no one else seemed to think there was anything untoward about their appearance or their writhing baggage.

If a pair of dwarfs had come rushing down the street back home in Emniln, or in Kalidar or Zaraquan, everyone would have been staring. If they were carrying a sack that size, as big as a woman, with something obviously alive in it, people would have been shouting. Here, though, the people of Ragbaan scarcely gave them a second glance and merely stepped politely out of their way.

Tulzik stared after them for a moment, then shrugged and headed down the street in the opposite direction from the one the dwarfs had taken. The city was large, but it wasn't infinite; if he continued in a single direction long enough he would reach the waterfront or the ridge or some other place where he could re-orient himself.

He wandered onward, trying to keep himself pointed northeast; it grew easier once the sun was clearly past its zenith and the shadows could guide him. The city's wonders began to lose their impact with repetition – the shadows of passing airships drew only his brief upward glance, hurrying dwarfs became just another part of the urban crowd, the glittering garments and jewelry became a colorful blur, the flickering panels and bright teklights were reduced to mere background, and the scents of spiced meat and exotic perfumes were so commonplace they barely registered. Palaces and towers and ruins that would have been landmarks and tourist attractions in any ordinary town stood unnoticed amid their equally ostentatious fellows.

Tulzik did still stop and stare at the horseless carts and carriages that sometimes clattered by, especially the ones with no visible driver. He had not known so many magical vehicles still existed in the entire world, and he marveled that none seemed to go out of control and veer into the shops or pedestrians, as he had seen happen in other towns.

He was not the only one who turned to watch as a jingling chain of laughing young women marched by, wearing little more than jewelry and scraps of silk. They seemed astonishingly cheerful, given that each of the dozen or so girls wore a golden collar joined by a golden chain to her companions on either side and was loosely chained at wrist and ankle as well. They were giggling and squealing even so, pointing and waving, and their various bangles were responsible for as much of the jingling as the chains. All of them were beautiful, with elaborately styled hair framing lovely, smiling faces and falling past shapely full breasts to narrow waists.

The stark contrast between their apparent captivity and their cheerful demeanor baffled Tulzik. Had they been weeping and calling for aid he would have leapt up and demanded an explanation from the surly mustachioed man who held the end of the neck–chain and led the party, but it seemed obvious that whatever was happening here, the women had no objection to it.

And whatever it was appeared to be sufficiently unusual and interesting that perhaps half the people in the street – largely the male half, unsurprisingly – had stopped their own activities to watch the chained women pass. Tulzik overheard a few exchanged remarks and questions, but little that hinted at any explanation. The only one that might have told him something, had he understood it, was one young man asking his older companion, "Is there a bell hunt tonight?"

"I don't know," the elder replied. "Seems like a lot for a bell hunt."

But then they shrugged and moved on, leaving Tulzik with no explanation of what a bell hunt might be. He watched as the women pranced through a wooden gate and vanished.

Then they were gone, and the watching crowd dissipated, and Tulzik almost tripped over a hurrying dwarf as he turned to continue his own search.

He wandered on as the sun crawled westward and the shadows stretched east; he was taking in as much of the city as he could, trying to comprehend it. He now understood very well why Uncle Urushak had despaired of finding Peval here; locating one person by ordinary means amid the thousands upon thousands living in this gigantic labyrinth would be impossible.

Tulzik, however, was not ready to despair of *extraordinary* means. Ragbaan was obviously home to a great many extraordinary things, and some of them might prove useful. At the very least, he wanted to see just what was in the north arcade of the Imperial Palace that the barman had thought might help. He owed it to Vika to do at least that much.

He came at last into a broad avenue, far wider than any other street he had ever seen in Ragbaan or anywhere else. Judging by the afternoon sun it ran due north and south, and it was as straight as an arrow, as broad as the Darambana River. Along either side ran stone pavement twice as wide as any normal street, and down the center was a strip of farms twice as wide as the pavements.

Tulzik guessed that in some ancient and glorious past that central strip had been parkland, but in these less grandiose times the city's people had decided that the land could be put to better use. He could see tidy rows of bean poles, of sprouting vines, of tied-off shrubs and carefully pruned fruit trees. Men, women, and children were at work in the fields, planting and cultivating. The pavements on either side were lined with stalls where the produce could be sold, in season; as it was still too early in the spring to harvest most crops, the stalls were mostly shut up tight.

Tulzik glanced to the south, where the avenue seemed to continue forever, and then to the north, where perhaps a dozen blocks led to a once-magnificent plaza now crowded with peddlers' stalls and dancers' stages wedged among the monuments and statuary.

Across the plaza, at an angle to the avenue, was an immense palace topped by three great domes, a gold one in the center and silver trimmed with faded red to either side.

Tulzik blinked, then slowly smiled as his tired mind registered what he saw. He was seeing it from below and to the southeast, at a distance of no more than a mile, instead of from above and to the southwest several miles away, but he recognized it all the same.

He had found the Imperial Palace.

CHAPTER 4

The red stone steps were broad and shallow, clearly not designed for hurrying, but Tulzik hurried up them all the same. He
scarcely glanced at the carvings on the great arched portico or at the
age–blackened statues in the several niches as he strode into the
palace.

He did notice, however, that the doors were gone; one corroded,
crooked fragment of hinge still hung from the cracked and spalling
stone frame, but there was no trace of the actual doors. The entry
hall was open to the elements.

He slowed as he passed through, registering that the doors,
when they had still hung here, had been about twenty feet high
and fifteen feet wide. He also noted that there were no teklights or
screens to be seen; presumably the Imperial Palace had been built
in a time when magic was not plentiful – or perhaps simply not displayed openly.

Then he turned his attention to the entry hall. This ante-
chamber was perhaps fifty feet from door to door and a hundred feet
wide, with the rotting remains of a coffered wooden ceiling some
twenty–five feet above the well–worn marble floor. Light came from
the open doorways and from a row of windows above and between
the doorways. There were wide paths clear from the outer doors to
the inner, but most of the rest of the floor space was taken up by
tables, shelves, boxes, and people – people who were selling things
from the tables, shelves, and boxes.

The single most common item offered for sale appeared to be
maps – maps of Ragbaan, maps of the entire Ragbaan Bay District,
maps of the Grand Avenue, maps of the Imperial Palace, maps of the
Old Continent, maps of the world.

Tulzik's pace slowed further. A map of the city...

But then he heard a man ask the price, and the woman behind that particular table replied, "Three *walu*."

Tulzik was not absolutely certain he had heard the exchange correctly, that the item in question was indeed a map of Ragbaan, but three whole *walu* for *anything* on that woman's table seemed outrageous. Clearly, these people preyed on foolish travelers, charging absurdly high prices, and he would not be cheated in such a fashion!

For one thing, he didn't have three *walu* left; he was down to one *walu* and a few *jit*. He would probably need to either find some honest work soon, or resort to theft or begging just to get home.

Some of the other peddlers might have maps priced more reasonably, but if there were any he could afford, one of the high-priced dealers would probably have bought them all up to re-sell. Either that, or they would be cheap because they were inaccurate or outdated or otherwise less than useful.

He wasn't going to buy a map. With a bit of a shrug, he walked on to the inner doors.

These doorways were partially blocked by moldering purple drapes, but only partially, and once again no actual doors were in evidence. He marched through and found himself in the Great Hall. Here even Tulzik, focused as he was on his quest and exposed as he had been to many of the city's wonders, had to stop for a moment to take the scene in.

His first impression was of height; the hall rose up and up and up above him, fifty or sixty feet at least. There were balconies along either side, supported by ornate pillars and lined with elaborately carved railings – three tiers of them, the first perhaps eighteen or twenty feet above the floor, and the others rising another dozen or so feet each. Above the highest balcony the walls drew in several feet, and tall windows lined them from there to the ceiling, windows that were somehow still clean and clear despite the centuries, giving the vast space a bright and airy feel.

The ceiling itself was intricately patterned in white and gold vaulting and was in surprisingly good repair. Tulzik was further surprised to realize there was no sign of the great golden dome. That must be farther in, or higher up, than any part of this immense hall.

The hall was not merely tall, but wide – at least a hundred feet from one balcony rail to its opposite – and long, so long that Tulzik could not really see its far end through the crowd, the smoke, and the haze.

For this hall was indeed crowded, not with the supplicants and courtiers for whom it had presumably been built, but with tradespeople and their customers. The red–white–and–gold patterned floors were hidden beneath carts and tables and boxes and bags; carpets and bolts of fabric were draped over the balcony rails. Trays of fresh fruit leaned against ancient carved pillars, and charcoal smoke from crude grills drifted up toward the gilded ceiling. Hawkers' cries echoed from the marble walls. Most of the crowd was human, but Tulzik saw a few dwarfs scattered about, as well, and for a moment thought he might have glimpsed a creature or two who was neither.

There was certainly plenty of room for more than one species. The hall was, in fact, the largest, busiest market Tulzik had ever seen.

He had had some idea that the Imperial Palace might still house all or part of the city's governance and that the north arcade might harbor a useful office or two, but now he reconsidered. Nothing about this throng looked very governed at all, and he suspected the north arcade, wherever and whatever it might be, housed businessmen, rather than bureaucrats.

The next step, then, was to *find* the north arcade.

The palace faced more or less east, and he had walked in the front door, so he was looking more or less west. North, then, would be to his right.

He turned, and wound his way through the maze of stalls and tables until he stood beneath the balconies on the north side, where he found himself surrounded by displays of ancient artifacts, undoubtedly salvaged from the miles upon miles of ruins that surrounded the still–living city. There were tools magical and mundane, knives with never–rusting blades, teklights and screens of various sorts, and a myriad of objects he could not identify.

He did not see how these could help him, so presumably this area was not the north arcade, or at least not the right part of the north arcade. He turned westward again, since he could see nothing of significance to the east.

He had made his way perhaps a hundred feet farther when he told himself, "This is stupid." He paused in front of a table displaying strange glowing jewelry and asked the proprietor, "Where's the north arcade?"

He had half–expected to be told he was standing in it, but instead the old man pointed. "Turn right just past that stair."

Tulzik looked in the direction indicated and saw that there was indeed a staircase forty or fifty feet farther along. He pressed his hands together and nodded. "Thank you," he said. Then he turned and hurried on.

The stair leading up to the first balcony was yellow marble and beautifully made and decorated, but Tulzik spared it only a brief glance as he rounded the corner. Then he stopped dead.

There before him was unmistakably the north arcade.

It was a passage perhaps thirty or forty feet across, extending into the distance for what seemed like a mile or so, with a single pillared balcony along either side and an arched ceiling rising to about thirty feet in height at the center. Where the dominant color scheme in the main part of the building was white, gold, and red, the walls here were patterned in black and white, and the pillars and trim were red; there was no gold in sight.

And unlike the entry hall and the central market, it had little natural light; there were no windows nor skylights to be seen. Some light leaked in from the great hall, but more came from teklights, dozens of them, arranged in rows along either side of the ceiling and scattered here and there beneath the balconies. Apparently the palace had not been built *completely* without magic.

The rows of teklights were not even; presumably they had been at one time, but many, perhaps most, of the fixtures had fallen, so that now there were bright stretches and dim stretches, and areas where one side was lit and the other shadowed. The black–and–white walls exaggerated the contrast of light and dark.

Like the great hall, the arcade was clearly an open market with tables and booths scattered along either side, but unlike the great hall there were no grand displays of merchandise, no piles of goods waiting to be sold; instead there were mostly signs describing the services being offered here.

Reading those signs, Tulzik understood why the barman had suggested he come here. "Residential Advisor" was not particularly promising, nor "Weather Prognostication" or "Travel Services," but "Seer & Medium" had potential, as did "Diviner." Reading on, he could see several businesses that offered to provide advice on any number of subjects by arcane means.

He strolled along the passage for several yards, reading the signs and studying the faces.

One sign caught his eye. In big letters it said, "Questions Answered & Things Found." Below that, smaller print read, "Any question answered for the right price. 'We Don't Know' is an answer, and that one's free – we go up from there."

A woman sat at the table beneath that sign, a tall, slender woman in a loose bottle–green blouse and matching pants, the golden drawstring at her waist tied in an absurdly elaborate knot. Gold jewelry gleamed on her wrists, ankles, fingers, toes, ears, and throat, and golden strands ornamented her waist–length hair. Her skin was a golden brown, and that long hair was dark, thick, and wavy. She was talking to a plump man at an adjoining table, where an oblong screen lay on a black velvet cushion, glowing softly blue, and a sign proclaimed, "Oracle and Summoner – Consult the Memories of the Ancients!" A second chair at the woman's table was vacant, and Tulzik pulled it forward and sat down, slipping his pack from his shoulder and letting it thump to the tiled floor – not so much because he thought this looked like the ideal place to continue his inquiries, but because it was the only empty chair in sight and he was tired, his feet aching after so much walking on hard streets and floors.

The conversation broke off abruptly as the woman turned to look appraisingly at him. Now that he saw her face, Tulzik thought she must be somewhat older than he had initially taken her to be; while she was still handsome, there were lines indicating that she had seen a good many more years than Tulzik had.

"Yes?" she said at last, breaking the silence as it began to grow uncomfortable.

"When you say you find things, does that include people?" Tulzik asked.

"Now, that's a question," the woman said. "We *charge* for the answers to questions, but I'll give you this one as a free sample. Sometimes it includes people. It depends just who you're looking for, and why, and how much you can pay."

"Fair enough," Tulzik said. He bent down for his pack. The woman and the man she had been speaking to watched with interest as he opened it and drew out the protective boards. He laid them on the table, untied the ribbons, and pulled out the portrait.

"This is the man I'm looking for," he said.

The woman took the picture and studied it intently; the man – a plump fellow in a glittering polychrome vest, black shirt, and striped pants – peered over her shoulder.

"Don't know him," the woman said. "Don't know if we could find him or not, and if we try the search could get expensive, with no guarantees of success. If you want us to try, we can talk."

Tulzik hesitated. "How expensive?" he asked.

"You get another free answer on that one – I don't know."

"Surely, Azl, you can give him a *hint*," the plump man said. His voice was surprisingly deep and rich.

She turned, still holding the portrait. "No, Hiji, I can't. I can tell him our standard rates, but I have no idea how long it might take to find this man, if we can do it at all, or what expenses might be involved."

"Then tell him your rates, my dear, and I'll tell him mine, and we can get on with business."

The woman glared at the plump man for a few seconds, then turned and handed the picture back to Tulzik.

"My partner and I charge three *walu* a day, plus expenses," she said. "If we feel we aren't putting in a full day's effort, we'll discount it." She grimaced. "If you hire us, all questions about the job are included at no additional charge."

"I'm not sure I understand," Tulzik said. "You and your partner – this man?"

"No, no, no!" the plump man exclaimed, waving his hands and sparing Tulzik any possibility of being charged for a reply. "I am merely a bystander here, my lad. I am Hiji the Oracle. Dear Azl's partner is her husband Hrus, and our businesses are *completely* separate, I assure you!"

Tulzik looked around, but saw no one else paying much attention to the conversation.

"Hrus isn't here at the moment," Azl said. "He'll be back later. You were saying you don't understand something?"

"Ah. Yes, what I don't understand is just what it is you do – how would you... I mean, how you would go about finding Peval."

"Is that his name?" She glanced at the portrait again.

"It's what he called himself. I don't know whether it's his real name."

"And you want to know whether we have some secret method of locating people, perhaps using some ancient, half-forgotten magic, or some mystic machine that still functions perfectly after centuries of neglect." She smiled. "No, we don't. What Hrus and I have is information, and the wit to use it. We both grew up in Ragbaan, and we know the city as well as anyone. We have contacts everywhere from the Peaks to the tunnels, and we're experienced in getting people to tell us things – and if we don't know something, or don't have the device we need, we know whom to ask and where to find it. If you want ghosts and magic and mystery, talk to Hiji here, or Bel the Churzkeeper, or any of a dozen people here who *do* have salvaged bits of the city's past in their possession – what Hrus and I know is the city's *present*."

"Indeed, they are both very knowledgeable about the byways and bargainers of Ragbaan," Hiji agreed. "You could do far worse than hiring Azl and Hrus – but as they say, they rely on the mundane, the commonplace, even though we live in a city of wonders." He put a hand on his chest. "Now *I*, as it happens, have access to the wisdom of the ancients. I am able to summon up certain memories from the distant past and consult with them. While I cannot guarantee results any more than my friends can, I can arrange for you to speak with these ghosts and ask them what *they* know."

"Ghosts?" Tulzik said, accepting the portrait back from Azl.

"Ragbaan is *full* of ghosts, my young friend," Hiji said, rising from his chair and sweeping one arm through the air. "How could so venerable a city avoid it? There are hundreds, perhaps thousands, of places in Ragbaan that are still undeniably haunted by the spirits of the past – some by the beings called *kaua* that our ancestors used as servants, some by the vestiges of long–dead men and women, some by essences not so readily catalogued. You can find them lurking in glowing screens or dark, speaking from walls and ceilings and empty air, or moving ancient devices in various ways that are subject to interpretation by those who know the codes. Azl will attest to this, won't you, my dear?"

"Of course," Azl said. "There are memories all over the city. We deal with some of them ourselves. You can call them ghosts if you like."

Tulzik had never seen any ghosts himself – at least, not close up and not definitely enough to be sure they were ghosts. His home town of Emniln was not known to have any ghostly memories – but Emniln was small and only a couple of centuries old, its only screens hand–held devices of no true intelligence. Tulzik had heard plenty of stories about memories and spirits lingering in ancient *tek*, though, and if they existed anywhere, Ragbaan certainly ought to have its share of them.

Whether they could tell him where to find Peval was another matter, but it didn't seem impossible. A glimmer of hope grew in

Tulzik's chest.

"As it happens, *I* know where, when, and how two of these eternal spirits may be contacted and questioned," Hiji said proudly, as he moved to Tulzik's side. "For the modest sum of five *walu* I will be happy to introduce you and set your question before them."

The flame of hope was instantly snuffed out. "I can't afford five *walu*," Tulzik said.

"How unfortunate," Hiji said, slumping visibly. "How very unfortunate. Why is it you are looking for this man, this Peval? Perhaps some arrangement could be made."

"He killed my sister," Tulzik said, looking down at the portrait he held. He felt his throat tighten as the words emerged, and he had to tighten his grip to ensure his hands would not tremble.

Azl had been growing visibly bored by the conversation, but she was suddenly alert and interested again.

Hiji was momentarily taken aback, but quickly recovered. "Ah, how terrible!" he said, throwing up his hands. "I grieve with you, my friend, and in the interests of justice I will see that you *may* speak with the ghosts – but I must have some recompense for my efforts, you understand. It takes a great deal out of me to summon the spirits and to translate their words to modern human tongues. Surely, you can spare *some* payment? You would not have come here, seeking to make a commercial transaction of this sort, if you did not have *some* funds at your discretion!"

Tulzik glanced from Hiji to Azl, hoping for some clue in her expression, but could see no indication of her thoughts. He hesitated, then said, "I can afford a *walu*. Just one."

Hiji spread his hands dramatically. "A pittance, no more than a token, but for you, my poor bereaved friend, in memory of your dear departed sister, for *you* I can do no less than accept your offer – though you must understand, if another customer should come along whose needs are equally urgent and who can spare the full amount, I may need to postpone our meeting; I can only summon the spirits once in a night, so exhausting an experience is it." He glanced around. "But as yet, no one has approached me with such a request, so let us make an appointment for this very night, my young traveler, let us speak with the dead *tonight*, and give this vile murderer no more time to make good his escape than we absolutely must. Perhaps the shades I will summon have spoken with your sister's ghost and will share in our outrage and see that justice is done, that this man will be delivered to you for the punishment he so richly deserves!" He clapped his hands on Tulzik's shoulders and smiled warmly.

"All right," Tulzik said, somewhat taken aback. He had not necessarily intended to spend most of his remaining money to consult with ghosts, but he had no better idea. Everyone knew the dead and their ancient *tek* knew secrets, even if they weren't necessarily the *right* secrets.

And the man *was* offering a generous discount.

"Then here is what you must do," Hiji said, leaning forward. "Late tonight you must come to my home, my workshop." He tapped the board in Tulzik's hand. "Bring this drawing with you and whatever information you have that would help me in convincing the ghosts to aid us." He chuckled. "Oh, and of course bring your money. You *must* be there well before midnight, for it is at midnight that the barriers between our mundane world and the higher realms are weakest, and at midnight that I will attempt to summon the dead to advise us. We will speak with them and see what they can tell us."

"What if you can't reach them, or they tell us nothing?" Tulzik asked, suddenly suspicious.

"Oh, I can reach them! Have no fear of that," Hiji said. "You will see, they will come. If they do not, then you owe me nothing – but if they come, then I am committed, and even if they can tell us nothing of use, I am afraid I must insist on payment. And lo, if they should tell us what we want and guide us to your sister's killer, then perhaps you will find another *walu* or two, or at least a few *fing*?"

"I'll try," Tulzik said, a trifle uncomfortably.

"Good! Then come to my home tonight, after supper." He pointed nowhere in particular. "From the plaza before this palace, you will count three streets between the two arms of the Grand Avenue – take the left-hand one of those three and follow it down toward the waterfront, but when you are just within sight of the docks, when you first glimpse a sail or a mast, you will be at a fork, where a smaller street angles off to the left. Follow *that*, and on the right-hand side, fifty yards along, you will find a red-painted door and a sign with my name, Hiji the Oracle. That is where I live, and on the third floor is the chamber where I conduct my summonings. Come tonight and knock loudly, and we will see if the spirits are kind, eh?"

"I'll be there," Tulzik said.

"Good lad!" Hiji clapped him on one shoulder again, then stepped back, and sank into his chair again.

Tulzik looked at Azl. She shrugged.

"See what Hiji can do for you, then," she said. "We'll still be here tomorrow if the ghosts don't help. You might want to see about scrounging up some more money, though – one *walu* won't last long in Ragbaan."

CHAPTER 5

Tulzik spent the remainder of the day wandering about the Imperial Palace, wondering just what he had gotten himself into. An oracle? Ghosts? And he was running out of money. He had left Emniln with what he had thought was enough for several days' travel, but he had not expected to be gone this long, or to be separated from his uncle, whose funds were more plentiful. They had assumed they would catch up with Peval in the next town or the one after, not chase him more than a hundred miles and wind up searching the streets of Ragbaan.

He was here now, though, and he had to make the best of it. He owed it to Vika.

Having committed his remaining money to Hiji, he saw little point in spending much more time in the north arcade. He did walk up and down its full length reading the signs, just in case one said, "Fugitives located free of charge, rapist–murderers a specialty," but of course he saw nothing of the sort. Instead he found various seers and oracles making outrageous claims of prophetic ability, importers, artifact hunters, airship ticket discounters, housing agents, romantic advisors, labor contractors, and a variety of other advertisements for services of every sort, many of which he had never heard of before.

He studied the faces, hoping that by some miracle Peval was here waiting for him, even though he knew how fantastically unlikely that was. He saw no one who looked like his dead sister's deceiver.

He decided not to venture into any of the side-passages or rooms opening off the arcade; he thought he might well get lost if he did. Instead, when he felt he had seen enough of that particular venue, he ambled back to the great hall and watched the crowds there, listening to the babble of voices, the jingle of the bells worn by many of the women, the pattering and shuffling of hundreds, perhaps thousands, of feet, the clicking and buzzing of gadgetry, and all the other pleasant little sounds of human beings (and others) conducting business, all compiled into a steady roar.

The crowd was at least nine-tenths human, but there were dwarfs scattered here and there. Tulzik noticed that they always seemed to be moving; he never saw any simply standing and talking, or looking over the goods on a merchant's display, as so many of the humans did. The humans came in a wide variety of sizes, shapes, and skin colors, from red-eyed, bone-white albinos to men and women so black they almost seemed to disappear when they stepped into shadow, but the dwarfs were all within a few inches of each other in height, all broadly muscular in build, and all within a narrow range of brown, from walnut to mahogany in hue.

There was something else, besides the humans and dwarfs – he only saw one, but it was hard to miss, as it towered above the crowd. He had to call it "it" because he could see no indication of the thing's sex, and although it had a head, two arms, and two legs, in more or less the traditional arrangement, there was no chance anyone would ever mistake it for a human. It was at least eight feet tall, its skin – if it was skin – a brilliant white, with vivid red diagonal stripes on either of its elongated cheeks. A crest of what appeared to be feathers rose roughly a foot from the top of its narrow head; its jaw was inhumanly long and narrow, its mouth set impossibly low. Its eyes were featureless disks of deep blue, its nose wide and flat, and it had no visible ears or hair at all. Its shoulders were narrow and something was odd about the way its arms were joined to them. It wore a simple white robe with wide sleeves that did not reach even its first set of elbows – it had two elbows in each arm, dividing them into three roughly equal sections. The robe, although it was clean bleached cotton, was not as white as the creature's flesh.

Whatever the thing was, it was standing at a jeweler's display, studying the merchandise with apparent interest, when Tulzik first saw it. He stared for a moment before he caught himself and remembered that staring was rude. He tore his gaze away, and, suddenly curious, scanned the hall for other such creatures. He saw none; there was just the one, now fingering a silver bracelet. It appeared to have too many fingers on the hand holding the trinket.

Tulzik leaned over and asked a woman selling peppers, "What is that?" He pointed at the white creature.

"What? Oh, you mean the Ilm? It's the Ilm."

"What's an Ilm? I've never heard of them."

"Not them, it. There's only the one, and that's it. That's the Ilm."

"But..." Tulzik tried to phrase a question that would express how unsatisfactory this answer was without being rude. He was not sure just why he cared, but something about the white creature fascinated him.

"Interested in some peppers, young man? These sweet red peppers here will enhance any dish, and they're just one *jit* apiece, or three *jit* for five."

"No, I don't..." He stopped and looked. The peppers actually looked quite good, amazingly so, and he was hungry – but what would he do with a pepper by itself?

"I'll take one," he said, "if you'll tell me more about the Ilm."

"Not much to tell," she said, reaching down. She held up a magnificent pepper, bright red with a streak of green on one side, and said, "Here's a nice one."

"Yes, it is," Tulzik admitted, reaching into his pocket. "About the Ilm? Where is it from?"

"Oh, it's been in Ragbaan for as long as anyone can remember," the woman said, as she set the pepper on a little shelf covered with brown paper. "My grandfather said he met it when he was a little boy, and even then, it had been here longer than anyone knew. No one knows where it came from – well, except the Ilm itself, I suppose." She rolled the brown paper up around the pepper.

"It won't say?"

"Oh, it will answer if you ask it, but it never gives the same answer twice. One day it'll say it was made by a mad magician, the next that it fell from the sky, a third that it's the last of a race that lost a war with us." She shrugged as she twisted the paper closed. "No one knows much of anything about it, really, except that it lives in a ruin over on Kyin Street, it likes shiny things, and it won't eat anything but *sithis*. At least, not where anyone can see it." She picked up the wrapped pepper. "One *jit*, please."

Tulzik handed over a little brown coin and accepted the parcel. "Thank you," he said, though he was still unsure what he would do with his purchase. He hesitated, then added, "I'm trying to find someone. Do you think the Ilm might be able to help me? Does it know things we humans do not?"

She shrugged. "Honestly, I have no idea. I've never spoken with it. I've never heard that it has any superhuman abilities, but it does know a great deal, after living in Ragbaan so long. Who are you trying to find?"

"A man. I have a picture. He arrived in Ragbaan yesterday, I believe." He started to open his pack.

"Don't bother showing me the picture," she said. "Even if I'd seen him, I wouldn't know what had become of him. And I'm terrible with faces in any case."

"Do you think the Ilm..."

"I don't *think* it has any sort of magical powers."

"What about the dwarfs, then?"

"The who?" She looked baffled.

"The...the little brown people." He pointed at one as he hurried past, carrying a pack twice his own size across his shoulders.

"The *baz*? You didn't call one of *them* a dwarf, did you? Not to his face?" The woman's expression was a study in shock and horror.

"Uh...no. But aren't they..."

"They're *baz*. They have several other names, too, but don't *ever* call one a dwarf. It's the only term I know that they consider insulting."

Tulzik scratched his head. "Why?"

"*I* don't know. They just do. Nobody really understands why the *baz* do anything. It's not as if they were human."

"But *aren't* they dwarfs? They look more or less like the descriptions, and I've never seen anything else that did."

"Maybe they are, I don't know, but you just don't *call* them that."

"I see," Tulzik said, baffled.

"I think you...oh, excuse me." She turned away to greet a young woman who was studying a tray of beans. The saleswoman was obviously relieved to have another customer to tend to, to get away from this inquisitive foreigner.

That left Tulzik standing there with his neatly wrapped pepper in one hand, his pack in the other, and a realization brought on by the smells in the great hall that he was ravenously hungry.

He found a baker under the south balconies and bought a small loaf of bread, which he cut open with his pocket-knife. A sausage vendor provided something to put in it, and the pepper was sliced up to garnish this sandwich, making an adequate supper – and one very different from the previous night's *drash*.

There were people selling *drash* in the palace, of course, and he discovered that it usually came in large blocks that could then be sliced or chopped up as the user chose. He still didn't know what it was, though – nor did he know where *sithis*, another local food of no obvious origin, came from. *Drash*, he discovered, varied from off-white to medium brown in hue, while *sithis* came in a variety of bright colors – pink, orange, and green were common – and hardly looked like food at all. Also, while *drash* always seemed to have that same crumbly, oily texture, *sithis* ranged from hard little bars to semi-liquid goo. *Sithis* also cost several times what *drash* did, and the state of Tulzik's purse therefore ensured that he was not going to find out what it tasted like.

A third unfamiliar food was a pasty reddish substance called krill that he judged from the smell to be some sort of seafood. It cost almost as much as *sithis*, so he did not investigate further.

But beyond those three strange comestibles, the foodstuffs offered for sale in the palace market were mostly familiar – breads and cakes and pastries, fruits both familiar and exotic, assorted grains, a hundred varieties of beans and peas, dozens of other vegetables, and a wide selection of meats and meat products.

Many of the vegetables were dried, or under-ripe, or otherwise undesirable, which was hardly surprising this early in the year. In fact, Tulzik was more surprised by the ones that seemed fresh and fully grown, like the pepper he had bought; he supposed they were grown in the rooftop hothouses he had glimpsed from the ridge top.

Some of the meats were unappetizing, as well – one fellow was proudly offering spit-roasted creatures that looked very much like giant rats. Tulzik hoped there was nothing in his sausage from that particular species.

The other, less edible merchandise in the market ranged from the utterly prosaic to the unrecognizably bizarre. Fabrics, jewelry, cutlery, shoes, boots, hats, carpets – but also machines and devices of unknown purpose, tools not quite like any he had seen before, and various strange little objects Tulzik could not identify at all.

He wandered through the market hall, sometimes marveling at the incongruity of a display of crude painted-wood icons below a niche holding a fine marble statue, or a cloth spread with vicious-looking daggers on a dais that had presumably once held an emperor's throne. No one seemed to think it strange to have a public market like this in an old palace, but Tulzik found the contrast of ancient glory and modern commerce slightly unsettling. He had seen ruins put to crass new uses before, but never such an extreme case – this place was hardly ruined at all. It looked as if a few days of cleaning and mending could have it worthy of an empire again.

As he walked he kept an eye out for a glimpse of Peval; after all, this was obviously a major gathering place, a center of trade in Ragbaan, and while the odds of a chance encounter were very low, this was as likely a place to see him as anywhere in the city – assuming he was still *in* the city and not already on a ship or airship bound elsewhere, or trudging down one of the highways leading out of the city to north, south, and east. Tulzik also kept his search in mind when studying merchandise, especially the ancient and magical machinery. If he could find a device that would locate a particular person...

But no such device came to his attention, and Tulzik saw no sign of Peval.

Finally, when his sandwich was gone, the windows above the balconies were dark, and many of the merchants had packed up and gone home for the night, Tulzik turned his steps back toward the entrance and made his way out to the plaza. The great hall was not fully dark when he left; lanterns and teklights still illuminated much of it. The plaza, too, was partially lit. That was a relief, since he had to find his way from here, but it was not a surprise; he had seen from the beer garden terrace that this area of the city remained active at night.

He found the two ends of the Grand Avenue easily enough; they were so broad as to be impossible to miss. He had come in by the southern leg; the one that led northeastward from the plaza was almost as wide. He noticed that it, too, had a strip of farms down the middle.

Just as Hiji had said, there were three streets leading eastward out of the plaza between those two oversized highways. As instructed, Tulzik ambled down the left–hand one.

And as Hiji had said, when he came within sight of one of the great ruined towers thrusting up from the bay, when he could unmistakably smell sea–salt and fish, a smaller street forked off to the left, and sure enough, fifty yards along it was a red door.

What Hiji had failed to mention, however, was that this red door was in the base of a gigantic ruined tower, one that rose up almost endlessly into the night sky. A few windows on the first two floors glowed with teklight, and a screen flickered blue on one corner, but above that the sheer stone sides were dark, the windows merely empty black holes. This tower extended from the fork to the next intersection, filling the entire block.

The red door was obviously a later addition; it was constructed of rough planks that did not accord well with the polished gray stone of the tower walls. It was set into a crude wooden wall that filled what Tulzik guessed might have once been a broad window.

There could be no doubt of his destination, however; the name "Hiji the Oracle" was neatly lettered on a sign just to the right of the door, gold-edged black letters on a white rectangle. Tulzik stepped up and knocked.

He was beginning to think there had been some misunder-standing and was debating whether he should knock again when the door was flung open and Hiji appeared, holding a lantern. He had changed his attire and now wore an ankle-length white robe embroi-dered with text in an alphabet Tulzik had sometimes seen in ruins, but could not read. A golden band encircled the oracle's brow.

"Ah, my friend from the arcade! Come in, come in!" he said, spreading his arms wide.

Tulzik stepped inside, but avoided the proffered embrace. There were no teklights here; the interior was dark. "Your ghosts?" he said.

"Upstairs. Come on, I'll show you." With that Hiji turned and led the way across a large room that Tulzik would have liked to have seen better – but the only light came from Hiji's lantern, and Tulzik hurried to follow his host across the dim chamber and up a broad stair at the back.

CHAPTER 6

On the third floor Hiji turned and led the way down a broad passage; the floor was dirty white tile, and the walls were covered in tapestries that had faded to blank gray. Dozens of identical doors opened off either side; Hiji chose one apparently at random and opened it, beckoning Tulzik inside.

The room was unlit and almost empty. Tattered remnants of rotting carpet clung to the floor here and there, but most of it was bare stone; the plaster walls were scuffed and stained, but mostly intact. The wall opposite the door was mostly window, overlooking the bay – Tulzik could see two of the rounded, half-sunken towers and a dozen ships riding at anchor beneath the stars.

Four chairs stood in a row to one side of the room. Hiji set his lantern on the floor and grabbed two of these. He positioned them on either side of the lantern at an angle to one another; then he seated himself and gestured to indicate that Tulzik should take the other.

Tulzik obeyed.

"Now," Hiji said, "before I summon the ghosts, you must tell me all about yourself and everything you can about the man you seek."

"You can't just sense that?" Tulzik asked.

"No, no," Hiji said, straightening and raising both hands. "I am disappointed in you, my lad – I am no festival trickster, no mere fortune-teller feigning supernatural knowledge through vague answers and knowing looks! I am a summoner of ancient spirits, using the great powers of the past that still linger in Ragbaan, the true magic, the true *tek*. I know nothing of you beyond what I have seen and heard, and if I am to ask the ghosts the questions you want answered, you must prepare me! Now, what is your name and where are you from and why do you seek this man whose portrait you carry?"

That was actually rather reassuring, and Tulzik replied, "I am Tulzik Ambroz, only son of Kiriz and Filrisi Ambroz of Emniln, and

I have lived all my life in the vicinity of Emniln, never before venturing farther from home than the airship station at Zaraquan." Without meaning to, he found himself slipping into the formal speech he had been trained to use on important occasions. "I was taught to read and write four languages and the uses of arithmetic and geometry, in hopes that I might find employment as a scholar or engineer, like my maternal uncle Urushak, but I have not found employment that suited me in those fields and have been working at whatever jobs might be offered – sometimes as a messenger, sometimes as an interpreter, but most often, especially at planting and harvest, as a simple laborer. Thus I had nothing to tie me down when the need arose to pursue my sister Vika."

Hiji nodded. "And how did that come about?"

"Last autumn this man Peval, as he called himself, the man in the portrait, came to Emniln." Tulzik resisted the urge to spit. "He did not say what his business was, or where he came from, but only that he traveled a great deal in making his living, and was between jobs for the moment and thought Emniln as good a place as any to stay the winter. He gave his last name one time as Lakaritar, another time as tik Dapas; I have no idea what it might truly be. He seemed to have plenty of money despite his unemployment and took the best room at the Sabbath Lodging. The landlord said that he paid by the month, in advance, in mixed coinage."

This was already the longest speech Tulzik had made in months, and his throat was going dry; he swallowed before he continued.

"My sister Vika was seventeen, an artist and musician and prone to fancies – when she was little she was fond of stories and poems about great romances and famous lovers, and would sometimes play in the ruins at Amabir and pretend she was a queen there in the old days, or that pirates had carried her off there as a prisoner. She thought this man Peval was very dashing and mysterious, and he was not blind – he noticed her interest and flirted with her. She flirted back, and one day she announced at the supper table that she was in love with Peval and that he loved her in return.

"My parents tried to talk some sense into her; the man was a stranger who could give no good account of himself, and we had observed that he sometimes displayed a foul temper. It was pointed out that his face was that of a man who had been in more than one serious fight. Vika would hear none of it, and said his rages were a sign of passion.

"Uncle Urushak had a quiet word with Peval, who assured him that the flirting was harmless, that he did not love Vika and had never told her he did, and that he meant no harm to my sister.

"Indeed, after that he stopped flirting and declined to respond to her advances, and in every way tried to gently discourage her attentions – at least in public, but we have no way of knowing what he might have told her in secret. Whatever may have passed between them we will never know, but it was obvious that she was not discouraged by his show of disinterest. She laughed it off as a sop to our parents, an attempt to keep them calm until his professional situation was such that he could honorably propose marriage.

"We asked what she meant, what his professional situation might be that would impede an honorable marriage – not that we wanted to encourage one, you understand, but merely to ascertain the nature of her fancies. She would not explain herself, but merely said we would all see in time.

"Then one day, as the spring thaw was upon us, a messenger brought Peval a letter, and he gathered his belongings, paid his bills, and departed.

"Vika was heartbroken at first, but then she developed an elaborate fantasy about how he had been called away by a mysterious employer, but would return soon and fetch her and carry her away from our tedious little village forever." He paused and cleared his throat. "You understand, I am using my sister's words; I never found Emniln particularly tedious. Oh, it's hardly the city Ragbaan is, or even a tiny fraction of it, but we have our virtues and entertainments."

"Of course," Hiji said. "Continue, please!"

"Yes. Well, the man was gone for some time – four or five weeks, all through the spring planting and the early rains – and we thought we had seen the last of him, but then one day he strolled back into town and took a room for the night at the Fortunate Traveler.

"The rest of the family did not hear of this immediately, since he had not used the Sabbath Lodging, but Vika did, somehow. We learned later that she had hurried to the inn and had spoken with him, though we can only guess at what was said. She came home that evening and acted very mysterious, after the fashion of foolish girls, but since we did not know Peval had returned we did not know what to make of it and did nothing to restrain her.

"And in the morning she packed a bag and hurried off to the inn, apparently intending to run off with Peval, only to find that he was already gone. The innkeeper later told us she had seemed shocked and distraught at first when he told her Peval was gone, that he had left for Kalidar without her earlier that morning, but then she decided that it was all just discretion on his part, so that they should not be seen leaving Emniln together. She swore the innkeeper to secrecy – an oath I am pleased to say he broke the moment she was out of sight – and then set out after Peval.

"The innkeeper promptly informed Uncle Urushak, who sent a letter to my parents, informing them of the situation, and then prepared to depart in pursuit. By chance I happened upon him just as he completed his preparations and I prevailed upon him to delay briefly so that I might accompany him. I gathered a few necessities of my own and fetched the portrait Vika had done of Peval – I thought we might need it to locate him, which Uncle Urushak agreed was a good idea. I was very concerned for Vika's safety; I had always thought Peval a dangerous man. That air of mystery that attracted Vika seemed to me to be an attempt to hide an unpleasant nature.

"Aside from anything else, my uncle said he was glad to have me along for the sake of a second strong arm, which might come in handy should Vika refuse to be parted from her lover.

"I said the early rains were over; well, for the most part they were, but a few storms still lingered, and one caught us on the road. Foul weather combined with our late departure made it impossible to reach Kalidar that night. We took shelter at a small roadside inn instead, hoping to find Vika, with or without Peval, still in Kalidar when we got there in the morning. We were dismayed by the knowledge that Vika might well be spending the night in Peval's bed, but there was little we could do about it." Tulzik sighed. "I am sorry to say that we did find Vika in Kalidar, and in Peval's bed, though not with Peval. The landlord of the inn let us in, and there she lay. Her corpse was already cold." Tulzik paused, swallowed, and blinked away tears. The painful memory of finding his sister's body made it impossible to speak for a few seconds.

"Dreadful, simply dreadful!" Hiji exclaimed.

Tulzik swallowed again, then continued. "A doctor was summoned, and the corpse examined, and while there was not enough evidence to be certain, every indication was that my sister was poisoned. Or perhaps strangled, though if so it was subtly done. There *was* enough evidence to be certain that she had been despoiled, though, by either rape or seduction. Given her age and innocence, I think it must be considered rape whether she cooperated or not. Someone in Kalidar suggested that she might have taken poison willingly when Peval abandoned her, but I consider it murder either way, whether by his hand or her own, for he must have provided the poison."

"I can hardly argue," Hiji agreed.

"Uncle Urushak sent a letter back to my parents, but then the two of us followed Peval – he had been seen leaving Kalidar and heading east. We were determined to find him and avenge Vika's death. We did the best we could, but we had to stop often to show the portrait and be sure we were still on his trail, so we followed him for days without catching him. When we reached the western wall of the crater, and it became plain that he was bound for Ragbaan, my uncle despaired of ever finding him and turned back, but I...well, here I am." Tulzik's dispassionate storyteller pose fell away, and his voice turned fierce, anger replacing grief, as he concluded, "And what I want, what I'm paying you my last *walu* for, is for your ghosts to tell me where I can find that lying, murderous pig, so I can make him pay for my sister's life."

"Of course," Hiji said. "I will do my very best – but the ancients were very different from us, and I cannot promise that they will tell you what you want to know."

"That man at the roadhouse said that the people in the north arcade of the Imperial Palace had some of the old magic – "

"I do! I told you, I *will* summon ghosts. I never fail. I merely warn you that I can't guarantee that the ghosts will give you the answers you seek."

Tulzik was beginning to regret his bargain – but he was here, and what else could he do?

"Summon them, then," he said.

Hiji glanced out the broad window, then seemed to be counting something to himself; then he said, "It will take perhaps half an hour, or a bit less. Let us begin. Your part is to sit here, but if I gesture like this, then repeat the next line I say." He demonstrated a sort of beckoning motion.

"All right," Tulzik said.

"Good. Then if you would pay me, we will begin."

"Pay you?"

"Yes, I'm afraid I must insist you pay me in advance; the strain is considerable, you understand, and I may be in no condition to collect my fee when all is done."

Tulzik hesitated.

Hiji sighed. "Young man, you can take your money back by force if you are not satisfied that I have upheld my end of the agreement. I will summon ghosts, you will see and hear them, but I cannot promise they will help you. Those are my terms. Now, if you pay me, we can begin. If you do not pay me, then you can leave, and our business is done."

Tulzik frowned, then fished out his last two half-*walu* coins and reluctantly handed them over.

"Thank you," Hiji said, bowing his head in polite acknowledgment. He pocketed his fee, then leaned down and turned the wick on the lantern down until the light died to the faintest possible glimmer. When that was suitably adjusted he bent forward, raised his hands, and began chanting, "O spirits of this place, ancient honored dead, ghosts of Ragbaan's past, hear me! Spirits of this place, ancient honored dead, hear me! Come to us! Heed my call!"

Tulzik listened silently as the invocation continued. After a few minutes Hiji abruptly switched to another language, one Tulzik not only did not understand, but did not even recognize. The oracle began to sway back and forth, his voice rising into a bellowing singsong, as he continued.

Nothing else happened, however. No ghosts appeared. Tulzik wondered whether something had gone wrong, or whether the man was simply a fraud.

Then he realized Hiji was beckoning. "Come to us, O spirits!" he said.

Tulzik cleared his throat and replied, "Come to us, O spirits."

"Come to us! Come! Come!"

"Come!" Tulzik said – and abruptly a man appeared before them, a figure that glowed brightly in the gloom. Tulzik jumped in his seat and stared up at the stranger, astonished; he was just *there*, with no transition, no gathering vapor or gradual arrival. He was tall and clad head to toe in a rumpled red garment unlike any clothing Tulzik had ever seen on a human frame – though he *had* seen similar garments in ancient images. His skin was light brown, his hair black and wavy, his nose long and straight, and he focused a pair of intense dark eyes on Tulzik's face. He raised an arm and pointed directly at Tulzik and spoke loudly and firmly.

Tulzik had no idea what the apparition said; the language was utterly unfamiliar. If it was the same tongue Hiji had been chanting, then Hiji and the ghost spoke with very different accents, or in different dialects.

A second figure appeared, just as suddenly – a blonde woman in a white gown, glowing as brightly and unnaturally as the man. The two of them looked as if they were standing in sunlight, rather than in a dim room at midnight. She spoke as well, in the same language as her companion.

The man lowered his pointing finger and made a speech, and Tulzik could not make out a word, could not spot a single clear cognate to any of the four languages he knew. The woman interrupted at one point; the man glanced over his shoulder and barked a command at her. She retorted angrily, then put her hands on her hips and delivered a speech of her own, directed equally at Tulzik and the male ghost. It began as a lecture, almost hostile in tone, but her manner softened, and by the end she was almost pleading.

Tulzik tried to interrupt, to ask them to speak in Rogau or some other intelligible tongue, but they ignored him. He began to rise from his chair, but Hiji leaned over and pushed him back in his chair. "Let me listen!" the oracle said. "If you don't understand, I'll translate for you later!"

Before Tulzik could reply the male ghost spoke again, declaiming dramatically about something, gesturing at the woman and the ceiling, and then pointing out the window at the bay. Then both ghosts turned to face Tulzik and spoke clearly and directly – and completely unintelligibly – to him, taking turns. They were clearly entreating him to do *something*, but he had no idea what.

And then the man turned to Hiji, waved a farewell, and vanished. The woman disappeared with him, and the room was dark again.

Tulzik stared at the empty gloom for a moment, trying to absorb what had just happened.

He had, it would seem, seen his first ghosts.

Then Hiji let his breath out in a great rush and almost fell from his chair as he slumped forward gasping.

"Hiji?" Tulzik asked, reaching out a steadying hand. He could not see the other man's face in the darkness. "Are you all right?"

The oracle held up a hand as he caught his breath. He shook his head. "It takes a lot out of me," he said. "I'll be fine."

Tulzik sat back, unsure. The oracle had summoned ghosts, just as he promised – Tulzik could hardly argue with that. He had called up two ghosts, and they had spoken – but what had they *said?* Hiji had not mentioned that the ghosts wouldn't speak Rogau. Had they said anything about Peval's whereabouts? Had they said anything about his situation at all?

"Ah!" Hiji said, sitting upright again and flinging his head back; the golden band on his brow came loose and almost fell off. He reached up and straightened it, then bent down and turned up the lantern. Then he shook himself and turned to Tulzik.

"He said you have no business demanding their aid," Hiji said. "He said that crimes committed in the hinterlands are not their concern. But his wife said they should help you anyway, since you had suffered so grievous a loss, and... well, then she reprimanded you and your family for not having done a better job of teaching your Vika how dangerous the world is, and told you that when you marry and sire the two daughters you will eventually have, you must be far more careful in training them. Then her husband said that he wanted to oblige his wife, but he explained that they could not say precisely where this Peval is, as he has been moving about and time is not to them as it is to us, but that he is still in Ragbaan, and on land, not above us in the towers, nor aboard an airship, nor on any of the ships in the bay. And then they both told you that you must seek out mortal aid – you must return to the Imperial Palace and talk to the heir of an ancient house."

Tulzik blinked, trying to absorb this barrage of information, but somewhat disappointed that it did not provide a specific address where he might find Peval. "Is that it?"

"Well, friend, they're both prone to histrionics; there was a great deal of flowery language, but I've given you the gist of it, I promise you."

"What language *was* that?"

"Old High Alomarkan. My invocation was in Middle High Alomarkan; I haven't mastered the elder dialect."

"How did they know what I wanted of them?"

"Oh, I told them, of course. During the summoning. In Middle High Alomarkan. They understand it well enough, even if they won't deign to speak it."

"And they said Peval is still in the city?"

"Well, they *said* so, but their understanding of time really is very strange, and of course he might be on his way down the highway, or boarding an airship even as we speak."

"Airships don't fly at night, do they? I mean, I know they *travel* overnight, but they don't load passengers at night, do they?"

"Well, none would be departing at this hour, I'll give you that, but I did not mean it so very *literally*, my friend; say rather, he may board one in the morning and be gone before we find him."

"They didn't say anything more?" He remembered that prophecy that he would marry and father two daughters, but that was of no immediate concern. "I mean, about where he is?"

"I'm afraid they did not."

"Can you bring them back, and ask them?"

Hiji threw up his hands. "Oh, no, lad! No, you've had your one summoning. I did my best, and for only one *walu*, at that. To ask them again would merely anger them, and I haven't the strength to summon them again for some time, in any case."

Tulzik frowned and looked at the empty air where the ghosts had stood. He *had* seen and heard them, certainly. "Do you have any idea who this heir of an ancient house might be?" he asked.

"Oh, certainly!" Hiji said. "Didn't I tell you? That would be Hrus Daundablo, the information merchant. You met his wife this afternoon – Azl, in the green?"

"Her?" Tulzik blinked.

"Well, her husband – though they work together, so yes, you need merely find her again tomorrow." He smiled. "I rather think she'll be expecting you." He rose.

Tulzik got to his feet, as well, as Hiji strode toward the door.

"I'll show you out, if I may," he said. "Have a pleasant night, dear lad, and in the morning may you find what you seek!"

Only after he was out on the street did Tulzik fully realize that he had just wasted the whole evening and paid Hiji an entire *walu* for little more than a referral. He turned to go back and protest, but the red door was firmly locked, and no one answered his knock.

At last he gave up and went to find somewhere to sleep.

CHAPTER 7

Finding an empty room to sleep in was more difficult in this thickly inhabited portion of the city than it had been up on the ridge, but Tulzik eventually managed to find an open door into a partially ruined tower, where he climbed up six flights. None of the permanent inhabitants made their homes that far up, but the building was largely intact to at least the twelfth story, so he had several acceptable rooms to choose from.

It was long after midnight by the time he finally fell asleep; not only had he had trouble finding a place to bed down, but his attempts to coax more useful information from the memory of his encounter with the ghosts kept him from dozing off immediately.

Vika would have enjoyed seeing them. She would have found their continued existence together after death romantic, Tulzik was sure. The way they had interacted had not needed an intelligible language to be understood; their devotion to one another had been obvious, and Vika would have appreciated that.

But Vika was gone, and he had not yet found her killer, and that, as much as trying to puzzle out what the ghosts had said, kept him awake deep into the dark hours of the morning.

At last, though, exhaustion caught up with him.

He awoke to the sound of rain blowing against glass; he rolled over to see gray sky and a steady downpour outside the window of his temporary lodging. He blinked and stretched and stared out, trying to estimate how late he had slept. With the sun completely hidden he could not judge by the slant of the light or the length of the shadows.

The time of day did not really matter, save that every moment wasted gave Peval that much more time to flee the city, or bury himself more deeply in whatever hiding place he had chosen. Tulzik knew there was probably no great urgency in going about his business, and if he had slept late, as he suspected he had, it was undoubtedly because his mind and body could use the rest.

His stomach was empty, and his purse nearly so – he discovered his entire remaining fortune came to nine *jit*, which would probably not buy a decent meal. He would need to find work.

Food, money, or vengeance – which, he asked himself, should he pursue first? He debated the question as he pulled out and unrolled his hat, then stuffed everything else back in the pack.

He decided upon a compromise. He would go to the Imperial Palace, spend some of his last few coins on something to break his fast, then see if this Hrus was in the north arcade – and then he would ask about employment. Perhaps Hrus and his green–clad wife could direct him to paying work, with the understanding that he would use a portion of his wages to pay their fees for helping him find Peval. That would make a start on all three concerns.

He slung his pack on his shoulder, clapped his hat on his head, and started down the stairs.

The streets were, unsurprisingly, far less crowded than they had been the day before; rain was coming down heavily, and uneven gusts of wind were swirling it about and slapping wetly against the buildings on every side. A screen on one wall showered sparks on the pavement every time rain spattered it, and here and there Tulzik could hear sizzling as water landed on exposed magic.

The rain and wind were oddly warm. When he reached the Grand Avenue and got a better view of the overcast sky and the movement of the clouds, Tulzik realized that this was a storm blowing up from the south, which explained the mild temperatures. He could also see, from the pattern of daylight behind the clouds, that it was past mid–morning; he had slept even later than he had thought. He picked up his pace.

The plaza before the Imperial Palace was almost empty. The monuments and statues were still there, but the peddlers' carts were gone, the remaining stalls mostly closed and locked, and the dancers' stages were bare and deserted. The palace's entry hall where maps were sold was less crowded than it had been the day before, with several empty spaces, but there were still more than a dozen merchants selling their wares. Rain blowing in the open doorways had pooled here and there on the marble floors, and muddy footprints surrounded the puddles.

Tulzik took off his hat and shook it out, adding to one of the puddles, then set it back on his head to dry before proceeding.

The great hall beyond was just as full as Tulzik remembered it, though the air was thick with moisture and the acoustics and smells were rather different in the sodden atmosphere. He paused long enough to buy a chewy yellow cake for three *jit*, dickered down from five, before heading for the north arcade. He gnawed on his purchase – tasty, but already starting to go stale – as he walked, ruefully aware that even at a bargain price, it had cost one-third of his fortune.

The north arcade seemed *more* crowded than before, but he thought that might just be from the profusion of coats and hats and the general humidity. He made his way up the passage to Hiji's table.

The oracle was seated there, his glowing screen glass still lying upon its velvet pillow; he wore the same polychrome vest as he had the previous day, but over a red shirt, and his pants were striped differently. He smiled and waved at Tulzik's approach.

The woman, Azl, was nowhere in sight. A dark-skinned man was sitting in the chair Tulzik had used the day before, apparently resting his feet. Tulzik took the opportunity to sit down and greet Hiji.

"My friend," Hiji said, with a nod.

Tulzik pointed at the screen. "You didn't use that last night," he said.

Hiji started, then smiled. "Indeed, I did not," he agreed. He leaned over and whispered, "Can I trust you, Tulzik Ambroz?"

"That would depend on what you ask of me," Tulzik said.

"Only that you do not give away a secret that's of no value to anyone but myself."

"Then you probably can."

"That glass?" Hiji gestured at it. "It's nothing. It doesn't work. Hasn't for centuries. All it does is glow. I keep it purely as an advertisement. Since I cannot set either of my helpful ghosts on display here, I use that to catch the eye of the passersby and to give them an indication of the nature of my talents."

"Oh," Tulzik said.

"You would be surprised, my friend, how few of my customers ever think to comment on it. You are among the observant few."

Tulzik had no idea what to say to that; he was staring at Hiji's conspiratorial smile, groping for a response, when a voice said, "You're in my seat."

He looked up to find Azl standing beside him. Her blouse and pants were now golden-brown rather than green, but she was otherwise just as Tulzik had seen her the day before. Tulzik glanced uncertainly at the man in the other chair, but that person was sitting motionless, one leg crossed over the other, head back and eyes closed. He looked asleep.

"Oh, have mine!" Hiji said, rising. He moved quickly for so heavy a man. "I have no more business with our young friend, and I'm sure you would both benefit from conversation."

"Would we?" Azl said.

"I'm *sure* of it, dear Azl – trust me!" Hiji smiled and waved, then ambled off toward the great hall.

Tulzik and Azl watched him go; then Azl sat down in the chair Hiji had vacated and said, "He told me the gist of your story this morning. He probably even got most of it right – he has a good memory, does our Hiji. He needs it, in his line of work."

"To remember the invocation he uses, you mean?"

"Among other things. Shall I tell you a secret?"

This was becoming a pattern, Tulzik thought – everyone was entrusting him with secrets. "If you like," he said.

Azl looked at him, then said, "Not yet. Later. Remind me, though, to explain why you can never hire Hiji's services again."

"He said it would anger the ghosts to ask them the same thing twice."

"I'm sure he did. And he told you to talk to us, and that's why you're here, yes?"

"Yes. Well – he said the ghosts told him I should seek the help of the heir of an ancient house, and Hiji said that meant your husband."

Azl smiled humorlessly. "It amuses Hiji to describe Hrus that way. Hrus' family can trace their line back to Ragbaan's prehistory, but I tend to think that calling someone an heir should indicate there's something more than a name and family tree to inherit."

"Oh."

"I assume you have no money, that you have not miraculously acquired more funds overnight."

"I can't pay you, if that's what you mean. I have all of six *jit* to my name, and if I intend to eat a decent meal tonight I'll need to find work. I was thinking I might ask you if you had any suggestions. If I can find steady work, then I can save a portion of my earnings to cover your fee."

Azl frowned at him. "I do have a suggestion. I'd have preferred the miraculous influx of cash, but we didn't expect it."

"I'm listening."

"Do you understand how Ragbaan is governed?"

Tulzik blinked, caught completely off guard by this apparent irrelevance. "No," he said.

"Neither do most of its inhabitants," Azl said. "Let me ask you this, though – you've seen this palace and the plaza out front and the Grand Avenue. You know this is the heart of the city. If there were a strong central government, do you think the great hall would be full of sausage vendors and rug merchants?"

Tulzik considered that for a moment and also thought back over everything he had seen since crossing the crater. He had seen no one in a recognizable uniform, no one acting as a guard or patrolman, no one treated as being of high rank.

"It could be," he said, "if there were other structures more suitable, more economical, or in better repair, but I take it you mean to tell me that there is no strong government."

Azl nodded. "Good," she said. "You're right. In point of fact, there is *no* effective government in Ragbaan at all. There is an old man who calls himself the Mayor and carries a gold seal around, stamping his official approval on things for a few *jit* apiece, but that's the extent of the formal government, and he's clearly more than a little mad."

"I see."

"There are various groups, factions, and organizations that take it upon themselves to carry out some of the functions of government – neighborhood councils, tradesmen's guilds, criminal gangs, and so on. It's sloppy, but it generally works – and some of us *like* it this way, so we want it to keep on working."

"Yes?"

"One thing that's necessary for it to keep working is to make sure that criminals are kept in check. Usually that's done by the friends, families, and factions of the victims, which works well enough."

"Much of the world is the same, whether there are governments or not. That's why I'm here, on Vika's behalf," Tulzik said.

"Exactly. And that's why Hrus and I are going to help you, on credit. We are going to see that you're fed and cared for, as well. Because we can't afford to let criminals from elsewhere think they can just come to Ragbaan and shelter here. We don't want them here, and we can't tolerate them. So we're going to find your sister's killer and make sure justice is done, and is *known* to be done, and we aren't going to worry about the cost until that's been accomplished."

"Thank you," Tulzik said, with heartfelt gratitude.

"But this is not a gift," Azl said warningly, raising a finger. "This is a *loan*. We expect you to pay our bill eventually."

"I will if I possibly can," Tulzik promised.

"Good. In that case, you are now working with us to find this man and determine the truth of what happened. You won't waste any more time or money on the likes of Hiji; you'll do what we tell you. If you have time when you aren't doing anything for us, then you can find other work to start paying your debt, but our needs come first. Agreed?"

"Yes."

"Good. Now, tell me what happened and how you came to Ragbaan. Hiji may have missed some important details, and we may have questions."

Tulzik hesitated. "Shouldn't we wait for your husband?"

"He's right behind you, hearing every word."

Tulzik turned, startled, to see the dark-skinned man open his eyes and wave a greeting.

"I'm Hrus," he said. "You just talk to Azl. Don't worry about me."

"Oh." Tulzik blinked at him and started to say some conventional pleasantry, but then Hrus had closed his eyes again and leaned back in his chair, and Tulzik decided to save his breath. He turned back to Azl.

"Tell me about your sister," she said.

"Vika is – was – five years younger than I am," Tulzik began. "She was talented as an artist and musician and given to romantic fancies..."

He went on to tell her the same tale he had told Hiji the night before, sometimes in the same words, but unlike Hiji, Azl interrupted often, asking for more details. She wanted to know when the portrait had been drawn, what Vika had been wearing when she ran off, what she had been wearing when her body was found, whether she had had any contact with ancient machines or other magic, whether Peval had ever mentioned Ragbaan, whether he had ever said anything about ships of any sort, whether there were any indications that Peval feared water or heights, all the surnames Peval had used, and on and on and on. Tulzik was astonished to discover how much he remembered and how little of it he had told Hiji and how many things he did *not* know, but he did not see how any of it helped.

The interview dragged on for hours. Tulzik took off his hat and stuffed it in his pack, brought out the portrait for further inspection, and answered more questions than he had thought possible.

Hrus sat silently, eyes closed, through the entire conversation. He never said a word.

Finally, though, Azl ran out of questions and leaned over, looking past Tulzik at her husband. "Did I miss anything?" she asked.

Hrus opened his eyes and sat up. "Nothing obvious," he said. "Courier, assassin, or something else, do you think?"

"Can't say for certain," Azl replied. "Definitely trying to slip into the city unnoticed, though."

"And not as smart as he thinks he is."

"What?" Tulzik looked from one to the other, confused.

Hrus looked at him pityingly. "Boy, if you were back home in Emniln, or in Kalidar, and you wanted to get to Ragbaan, how would you do it? Assume you have money and don't want to waste any time."

"I'd go to Zaraquan and catch the next airship, of course."

"How long would that take, all told, Kalidar to Ragbaan?"

"Um...a day to Zaraquan, two days from there to Ragbaan. Three in all."

"And what would it cost?"

"A night's lodging in Zaraquan and two *walu* for the ticket – less, if it's the off-season or they have too many unsold seats, or you're willing to pedal and they have a use for a pedaler. Say, three and a half, maybe four *walu*. Plus meals."

"And how *did* you come to Ragbaan?"

"By road, on foot. That took six days and cost about...well, my uncle was paying for most of it, but I started with three and a half *walu*, and it's all gone, and my uncle must have spent at least twice that."

"So you see?"

"No, I don't. You mean Peval was being stupid? What if he didn't know he was going to Ragbaan?"

"What route did he take?" Hrus demanded. "Did it wind about?"

"No, it was as straight as an arrow, Kalidar to Ragbaan," Tulzik admitted. "You're right. But I still don't see – "

"If he came by airship, people would know," Hrus interrupted.

"The crew would see him, recognize his face, know the name he used. There are people in Ragbaan who watch the ports to see who comes and goes. He took more time and paid more money so that wouldn't happen, so he wouldn't be seen. If you and your uncle hadn't been following him, the only one who would know he had come to Ragbaan would be the barman at that roadhouse who saw him head out across the crater, and who would ever think to ask him?"

"*That* means," Azl said, "that he's someone going about secret business here in the city. The most likely possibilities are a courier in some clandestine affair, or an assassin sent to kill someone here in Ragbaan."

"That would also fit his wait in Emniln and the letter," Hrus explained. "He was waiting until he was summoned – either the package he was to deliver was finally ready, or the timing was right to move against his assigned target."

"There might be a third explanation," Azl said, "but it isn't obvious."

"Especially when you consider your sister's death," Hrus added. "She was a nuisance, a delay, someone who would slow him down, make him more noticeable, perhaps serve as a witness. She may have seen or heard something he didn't want her to know."

"So he killed her," Azl concluded.

"The fact that he was able to do it on short notice without leaving a mark or alerting anyone else in the inn would make an assassin seem slightly more probable than a courier," Hrus said. "It would be very useful to know just what she did or didn't see or hear, but I don't have any way we can determine that. I don't see how there would be any memories or ghosts we could consult, for an ordinary girl in the inland towns."

"Wait," Tulzik said. "Wait a minute. You think..."

"Work it out for yourself," Hrus said. "Don't listen to us. If you can think of a better explanation, tell us."

Tulzik sat for a moment with his thoughts in turmoil, but after several minutes he could come up with no flaw in their reasoning.

"Oh," he said.

A courier or an assassin – that presumably meant someone had *sent* Peval. Avenging Vika might mean taking down an entire criminal conspiracy, rather than a lone killer.

That was more than Tulzik had been prepared for – but nonetheless, he would see his sister avenged, no matter what it took. He

frowned as he tried to think where he should start; he supposed
he would need to interrogate Peval before doing...well, whatever he
decided to do to the murderous fugitive.

"Now, quite aside from what Azl told you about not wanting
criminals to think they can hide in Ragbaan, we have a very good
reason to find this man," Hrus said.

"We do?" Tulzik asked, startled out of his reverie.

"Of course. Weren't you listening?"

Tulzik stared at him blankly.

"Tulzik, he's probably an assassin on a mission," Azl said gently.
"He's come to Ragbaan to kill someone – someone important. You
don't bring in an assassin from out of town to dispose of someone
who isn't important. He killed your sister because she got in the way,
which was stupid of him, since it resulted in someone following him,
but he may not even know that you're in pursuit. Whether he does or
not, he's almost certainly still after his original target, whoever it is."

"And we almost certainly want to stop him," Hrus said. "So do
you."

Azl added, "If it isn't already too late."

Tulzik turned from Hrus to Azl, then back to Hrus. They were
both looking at him as if they expected a response, but at first he
could think of nothing to say.

They were right, though – if Peval had killed Vika as an inci-
dental victim in a plot to kill some important figure in Ragbaan, then
Tulzik did indeed want the plot to fail, so that his sister's killer would
not profit from the crime.

"Oh," he said again.

CHAPTER 8

Tulzik followed Azl and Hrus up the stairs, his mind still awhirl.

"It may turn out to be a stroke of luck, your stubborn pursuit of this man," Azl said over her shoulder. "If you'd had your uncle's good sense, we wouldn't know an assassin is probably loose in the city."

"Not that we've done anything about it yet," Hrus said. "He may stick a knife in someone's belly while we eat our supper."

"But you said he may just be a courier," Tulzik said, trying to make sense of everything and avoid being caught up in unproven assumptions.

"He may be. A courier willing to kill a girl is still dangerous," Hrus said, as he stepped off the stairs on the fourth–floor landing.

"Assuming he did kill her," Azl said, following him. "Even that isn't proven."

"But...then I don't..." Tulzik almost tripped on the top step.

"We act on the most likely hypothesis," Azl said from the passage ahead. "That doesn't mean we're sworn to it. Just because we haven't thought of a better explanation doesn't mean there isn't one – or that some utterly stupid explanation isn't true. Remind me sometime to tell you about the sneezing airship captain."

"Sneezing...?" Tulzik found himself so overwhelmed with questions, about couriers and assassins and Hiji and ghosts and sneezing airship captains, that he could no longer assemble complete sentences. He followed in silence as the pair led him from the stairs along a broad red–papered corridor, then into a smaller side–passage done in dirty white and faded gold, and finally to a massive gilt–trimmed door that Hrus opened with a curiously twisted key.

"Welcome to our home," Hrus said, as he ushered Tulzik in.

Tulzik stumbled in and looked around in astonishment.

He had agreed to come upstairs for supper and a more private discussion, but had somehow not realized this meant he would be in his hosts' home – it had not occurred to him that they, or anyone else, *lived* in the Imperial Palace.

But then, why shouldn't they? There was no government using it, and portions of it had certainly been intended as residences originally. Why would it be any more immune to squatters than the rest of the city?

But even so, he would not have expected a home like this.

The rooms were spacious and airy, the ceilings about twelve feet high. A dozen windows along one side extended almost from floor to ceiling and despite the rainy gloom outside admitted more than enough light to see.

The other walls of the first room were mostly lined with books of every sort; Tulzik had never seen so many in one place. Bookshelves extended across the top of each doorway, as well as between them, all the way to that high ceiling; three wheeled ladders stood ready to provide access to the upper tiers. Most of the shelves held bound paper volumes, but one held a row of magical books, each a single thick page with a screen on one side. Tulzik knew each of those, if still functional, might hold thousands of texts.

Two gigantic oaken desks stood side-by-side in the center of the room, each half-covered in documents, oil lamps, teklights, screens of various sizes, and crystals of various kinds. A stack of still more books was piled on the floor beside the nearer desk. Behind the desks was a red leather sofa. Something furry that Tulzik did not recognize lay curled upon it. The floor was covered with rich patterned carpets of a sort Tulzik had only seen since arriving in Ragbaan, and then only draped over the balcony railings in the great hall; these were red and pale yellow and midnight blue in intricate swirls.

Double doors stood open between this room and the next, and what Tulzik could see of the second room seemed to be a sea of silken pillows surrounded by golden walls.

A third room beyond that one was too far away to see anything, even with the doors open, though he had a vague impression of blue. To his right were doors leading to other rooms, in addition to that straight line along the generously windowed outside wall.

This was nothing at all like the barren hallways and decaying rooms he had seen elsewhere; this was a comfortable home, obviously lived in.

But then, why shouldn't it be? The other places he had seen

had been ruins or refuges or places of business. He had been in Hiji's home, more or less, but he had only seen the room where the ghosts were summoned – clearly a workroom, rather than a residence – and a glimpse of that big room downstairs. Hiji probably had comfortably furnished rooms somewhere. Everything else he had seen in Ragbaan so far had been ruins or public places.

"This way," Azl said, indicating the second door on the right. Tulzik followed her into a modest dining salon; the walls were simple white-painted plaster, though the woodwork was elaborate. Light came from a row of clerestory windows high on the far wall, and the place was rather dim, due to the miserable weather; Azl did something to an ornament on the doorframe, and a teklight in the center of the ceiling, surrounded by ornately carved mahogany, blazed to life, brightening the room considerably. A round table stood in the center, with half a dozen chairs around it. Glass-fronted cabinets along one wall, displaying silver and china, were the only other furnishings.

"Sit down," Azl said, gesturing at the table. As Tulzik seated himself she took a chair two places over. "Now we can speak privately," she said.

"Where's Hrus?" Tulzik asked, suddenly realizing he had not accompanied them into the salon.

"In the kitchen, getting supper," Azl replied.

A rattle of pans from a doorway confirmed this, and Tulzik relaxed.

"What we're most interested in is who this man Peval is, and what his business in Ragbaan is, and whether we should stop it," Azl said. "I know you're more concerned with avenging your sister, and I sincerely hope our desires will coincide. I think it likely. Let me warn you, though, that if they do not, we'll abide by our own best interests. If that means throwing you out and aiding your sister's killer, we'll do that – though in that case we'll tear up your bill."

"My bill?"

"At the moment it's three *walu*. No interest; a year to pay – fair?"

Tulzik was not happy about owing anyone a debt, but he had agreed to their terms, and they were not particularly onerous. "I suppose," he said.

"The minute you take a bite of supper, it'll go up – feeding you is a billable expense."

"I understand."

"Lodging, though, is free – it's unrealistic to charge you for that, given how many empty places there are in the city."

"Lodging?"

"You'll be sleeping here, with us," Azl said, waving toward the other rooms. "We can't have you telling everyone in Ragbaan that there's an assassin on the loose."

"But I wouldn't!" Tulzik protested.

"Not intentionally – but you told *us* without realizing it, didn't you? Something might slip. So you'll sleep here. The bed's quite comfortable."

"I'm not your prisoner!"

"No, but you're our client, and you're supposed to take our advice. We *strongly* recommend you sleep here."

Tulzik thought for a moment, remembered sleeping on hard floors the last two nights, and nodded. A free bed would not, he had to admit, be a bad thing.

A thump and a sizzle sounded from the kitchen. Tulzik glanced toward the door.

"I don't want to get into anything really important before the food is ready," Azl said, "but would you like to know why Hiji's ghosts were useless to you?"

"They weren't *completely* useless," Tulzik replied. "They told me Peval is still in the city and that I should come to you two."

"No, they didn't. Hiji told you that. He told you that Peval is still in Ragbaan so you *would* come to us – he doesn't actually know."

"But he said the ghosts..." Tulzik, suddenly suspicious, did not finish the sentence.

"He lied," Azl replied. "He has no idea what the ghosts said. He's never been able to identify the language they speak, let alone translate it."

"He said it was Old High Alomarkan!" Tulzik exclaimed.

"He lied. He doesn't know."

"How do *you* know?"

"Because we have an agreement with Hiji, an understanding. We've seen his ghosts – the man in red and the woman in white, yes? The man pointed at you and gave a speech, then the woman interrupted him and gave a speech, and then the man again – that's what you saw, yes?"

"Yes," Tulzik admitted, uncomfortably.

Azl nodded. "It's the same every time. They appear every night at midnight, say and do exactly the same thing, then vanish. They've been doing it for as long as anyone can remember; Hiji inherited the business from his father, who got it from *his* father, who got it from his mother. She may have started it, for all we know, or it may go back thousands of years."

"I don't... I....Aren't they ghosts?"

Azl shrugged. "They may be. We don't know what they are. We just know they appear every night and say and do exactly the same things every time. Hiji's family business is showing them to people and 'interpreting' what the ghosts say. It's actually just his own advice, and he's not a stupid man, so the advice is often sound – but who would believe it from a fat man with a big grin? It seems so much more impressive coming from a pair of ancient ghosts. Of course, he can only take each customer to see them once, since you would recognize the words and actions a second time. That's why he charges so much – when you have no repeat business, you need to get every *jit* you can the first time."

"How do you know this?" Tulzik demanded, trying to hide his embarrassment at being so thoroughly fooled. "Did he tell you?"

"Oh, yes. Also, we've seen them half a dozen times. I told you, we have an understanding. Hrus and I have promised not to warn anyone away from Hiji's little show and to tell him if we ever find out who and what the ghosts are, or what language they speak, and in exchange he advises people to come to us if he thinks we can help them. He's a much better salesman, a much better showman, than I am, or Hrus, so we let him go first. He weeds out the ones we can't help – the people wanting to know where to invest their money, or who to marry, or that sort of thing – and sends the interesting ones, like you, back to us."

"So it's all a fraud?" Tulzik demanded angrily. "Then why am I here?" He started to rise.

Azl put a hand on his wrist. "You're here because you want us to help you find the man who killed your sister. Hiji is a fraud, yes, but *we* aren't – think about what we've already told you, about who and what Peval is."

"But I could have figured that out for myself! You didn't do anything!"

"But you *didn't* figure it out for yourself. We did. That's what we do. Now that we have, we're going to guide you in finding him, because we know more about this city than you could ever imagine."

Tulzik settled back in his chair, staring at her.

"You couldn't tell Hiji who his ghosts were."

Azl sighed. "We're fairly certain, from their appearance and the known history of that tower, that they're from the Third Imperial Era, but they aren't speaking either of the two languages from that period we have any real familiarity with. There were dozens of languages spoken in Ragbaan at that time, from all over the empire, and most have vanished without a trace."

"Third Imperial Era?"

"Thirty-eight hundred to thirty-four hundred years ago."

"Oh," Tulzik said. He had to admit to himself that being unable to identify a language that had probably been dead for three thousand years was not unreasonable.

At that point the kitchen door banged open, and Hrus appeared, both arms loaded down with plates and bowls. "Supper!" he called. He began distributing the crockery, with Azl's assistance, and a moment later Tulzik found himself looking at a generous plateful of *drash*. He swallowed, then looked at the bowls.

Hrus was already on his way back to the kitchen, so it was Azl who pointed her *drash* pick at a bowl of steaming black liquid. "Peppered soy sauce, with mushrooms," she said. "Hrus' family recipe." She pointed at another bowl. "*Karik* beans in honey – too sweet for me, but Hrus likes it, and maybe you will, too. He'd love an excuse to serve them more often." A third and final bowl was full of nuts and berries and needed no explanation.

"Here's the beer," Hrus said, re-emerging from the kitchen with three glass mugs and a gigantic pitcher.

A trifle reluctantly, Tulzik picked up his pick and stabbed a cube of *drash* as Hrus set a mug beside him and filled it with thick, dark liquid.

His reluctance vanished at his first taste of the peppered soy sauce, and he began devouring his *drash* hungrily. The beer, too, was surprisingly good, the thickest, darkest, and strongest he had ever tasted.

"Monkeyboy beer," Hrus said, noticing Tulzik staring at his mug. "They like it chewy. The way they work, they need all the fuel they can get."

"Monkeyboy?" Tulzik asked.

"The *baz*," Azl explained. "Those short brown people. We call them monkeyboys."

"The dwarfs?"

Azl and Hrus both winced. "Don't *ever* call them that," Hrus said, as he settled into a chair and stabbed a cube of *drash*.

"The *baz* live in the northeastern part of the city, along the curve of the bay," Azl said. "They mostly stay in their own neighborhoods except when they're working – but they work a *lot*, as you can get more hard labor out of a runt than out of any two humans, and at half the cost. They take pride in anything they do, no matter how nasty a job we might think it is. They're good people, honest and tough. They don't think much of most humans, though. And you *really* don't want to offend them."

"Calling one a dwarf is going to offend them," Hrus added.

"Why?" Tulzik asked.

Azl and Hrus looked at each other; then Azl shrugged. "It just will," she said.

"There is a reason," Hrus said, "but it's complicated and you probably wouldn't understand. You don't know how they think."

Tulzik decided not to pursue the matter further; instead he devoted himself to clearing his plate of *drash* and drinking his share of the beer. He also discovered that Azl was right about the honeyed beans; he thought they were disgusting and watched in amazement as Hrus wolfed most of them down.

Finally, when the *drash* and beans were gone, and the three of them were well into a second pitcher of beer, they sat picking at the nuts and fruit as they got back to the business of finding Vika's killer.

"Any chance he's just a smuggler, rather than an assassin?" Hrus asked. "He might already be on a boat headed east."

"What could he be smuggling?" Azl asked.

"*Tek*. Old magic. Maybe there's something out there in the inland towns that we don't know about."

"*I* don't know of anything like that," Tulzik said.

"That doesn't prove anything," Azl replied. "But if he's just a smuggler, he could still have taken an airship to come here. Nobody searches the luggage, after all. Who would care about one more smuggler arriving in Ragbaan?"

"Someone might – the Nine Families come to mind – but I take your point." Hrus cracked open a nut and tossed its meat into his mouth. "He didn't want to be seen entering the city. Then would he have been recognized? Is his face familiar to someone?"

"Perhaps not yet."

"Hmm."

"Who would he want to assassinate?" Tulzik asked. "You said there isn't any government here."

"There isn't," Hrus replied.

"But there are still important people," Azl said. "There are powerful groups and organizations."

"Why haven't they formed a new government, then?"

"The Guild won't allow it."

Tulzik blinked. "What Guild?" he asked.

"The Starfarers' Guild, they call themselves," Azl explained. "Whatever that really means. It's a secret society that's existed here for hundreds, perhaps thousands of years."

Hrus added, "Although my dear wife may disagree, it's mostly a pretty benign group. But it's part of their charter to prevent any new government from taking power in Ragbaan. They do whatever's necessary to play the various factions off against each other, so that no one group dominates."

"So – maybe the assassin was sent to kill the Guild's leaders, by someone who wants to rule the city?" Tulzik suggested.

"It's possible. It's also possible that the Guild *hired* the assassin, to remove someone they consider a threat but don't want to take on openly."

"Why would the Guild use an assassin from outside the city?" Hrus asked. "For that matter, they wouldn't ordinarily *hire* an assassin at all – they have their own already in place. It's not impossible that they're involved, but it seems unlikely. I think it's more likely that someone else entirely has hired an assassin to take out an enemy, and that the reason he came across the crater was specifically so the Guild wouldn't see him coming. They do watch the ports more carefully than anyone else, after all."

"They watch a great many places," Azl agreed. "But you're probably certainly right. In that case, maybe we should let them do our work for us – give them a good look at Tulzik's picture, tell them what we think, and let *them* deal with it. I don't think they'd like someone trying to slip assassins past them, no matter who the target is."

Hrus leaned back and stared at the ceiling. "Why would *anyone* use an assassin from outside the city?"

Azl blinked and looked at Tulzik, who stared back.

"You know, that's a very good question," Azl said.

"Maybe they just wanted someone the intended target wouldn't recognize..." Tulzik began.

Hrus snorted, and Azl said gently, "There are more than three million human beings in this city. It's not hard to find people no one knows who are willing to kill someone for the right price. That's not even mentioning machines or homunculi."

"Or the *baz*, I suppose," Tulzik said. "Or the Ilm."

Hrus lowered his gaze from the ceiling and looked at Tulzik with new interest. "Have you met the Ilm?"

"Saw it from a distance."

"I suppose the Ilm might kill someone if the whim struck it," Azl said, "but the *baz* don't kill for money, and I've never heard of the Ilm doing so, either. But there are other beings in Ragbaan who might."

"Except that the assassin we're after *is* human, so this is all moot," Hrus pointed out.

"He *appears* human," Azl corrected. "He could be a homunculus. I doubt Tulzik's poor sister would know how to tell."

"She wouldn't," Tulzik agreed. "*I* don't. There haven't been any homunculi in Emniln in centuries, so far as I know. I didn't know there were any left anywhere."

"Oh, there are hundreds, maybe thousands, of them here in the city, most of them kept as slaves," Hrus said. "They're definitely still around, and still being made. Most of them are harmless, of course, or people wouldn't pay the gene-cutters to make them, but there's no reason a good magician couldn't make one an expert killer."

"I didn't know there were still gene-cutters who could do that sort of thing," Tulzik said. "I thought the art had been lost."

Hrus shrugged. "Not in Ragbaan. Almost nothing ever *completely* dies out in Ragbaan. I wouldn't be terribly surprised if someone finds a *tsaughth* still hiding in a forgotten tunnel someday."

"*I* would be," Azl retorted.

Tulzik decided not to ask what a *tsaughth* might be – interesting as it might be, it wasn't advancing his cause. "So if there are plenty of potential assassins in Ragbaan already, why *would* someone go to so much trouble to sneak Peval in?"

Azl and Hrus exchanged glances.

"That's a very interesting question," Azl said. "You know, more than half of our business is just thinking of the right questions to ask, and I believe this is an example of that. I also believe my husband has thought of an answer – and now that I consider it, I may see it myself." Her gaze remained fixed on Hrus as she spoke.

"But I don't think we'll explain it tonight," Hrus said, pushing himself up out of his chair. "We'll continue this in the morning."

Tulzik started to protest, but to no avail; his two hosts quickly showed him to the guest room and left him there, still arguing, as they retreated into their own bedchamber and locked the door.

Tulzik stared after them for a moment, then sighed.

As promised, the bed was very comfortable, but it still took Tulzik some time to fall asleep.

CHAPTER 9

When Tulzik awoke and found himself staring up at the crimson velvet canopy over his bed in the dim morning light he remembered instantly where he was – on the fourth floor of the Imperial Palace in the center of Ragbaan, in the guest room of the so-called information merchants, Azl and Hrus.

What he could not remember was exactly how they had convinced him to stay, once Azl had revealed Hiji's trickery. He couldn't remember ever consciously deciding to hire them, yet here he was. He lay there for a moment, reviewing the situation, and then concluded that whether he had done it intentionally or not, hiring them had been a good thing to do. It provided him with food, shelter, and a great deal of local expertise, all on credit, even if the two of them should prove to be just as fraudulent as Hiji's ghosts – and really, they did appear to be clever and to know a great deal about Ragbaan. Their theory that Peval was an assassin involved in the city's complex internal politics made a great deal of sense. It still might turn out to be completely wrong, but it *did* make sense.

But why would someone smuggle an assassin in from outside? They had refused to explain that last night. Tulzik sighed and sat up.

"Good morning, honored guest," an unfamiliar voice said, speaking with an odd, archaic accent. Tulzik started and looked around, but saw no one; he was alone in the room.

The room was a modestly sized but luxurious bedchamber decorated in deep red, dark wood, and gold; a vanity table and a writing desk stood to either side of the one tall window, while the opposite wall held two wardrobes and an armoire. The lone door was opposite the foot of the immense canopied bed. That door was closed, so the voice had not come from there, but Tulzik wondered whether someone might be hiding in one of the wardrobes.

"Who spoke?" he asked, looking at the wardrobes.

"No one," the voice replied, but Tulzik still could not locate it. "Your hosts wish you to know that you are welcome to join them for breakfast."

Magic, Tulzik decided. He rose, found his pack, and undertook some basic morning ablutions before joining Azl and Hrus in the dining salon.

He was relieved to see no *drash* on the table – while he had to admit that the stuff was tasty with the proper sauce, its appearance was still thoroughly unappetizing. Instead breakfast appeared to consist of fluffy rolls, fried ham strips, assorted candied fruit, and tea. Azl gestured for him to join them, and he took a seat and filled a plate.

"Did you sleep well?" Hrus asked.

"Yes, thank you." The rolls had an odd texture, Tulzik noticed as he chose one, and he wondered what grain they were made of. "There was a voice that spoke to me in my room this morning."

Azl nodded. "The palace is haunted, of course," she said as she peeled a somewhat shriveled orange. "By dozens of ghosts and memories of every description – or perhaps hundreds, or even thousands. Anything this old and large that isn't completely dead to *tek* could hardly avoid being haunted. Our quarters are home to three *kaua* that we know of, among other things, and one of them is fond of relaying messages to the various sleeping quarters."

"I hope that doesn't bother you," Hrus said. "There wasn't any point in asking in advance whether you objected, since we don't have anywhere to put you that *isn't* haunted, but perhaps we should have mentioned it."

"No, it's fine," Tulzik said. "It was just startling." He glanced around. "Can they do anything special? Predict the future or help you find people?"

"If you're asking whether they can find your sister's killer, no, they can't," Hrus said. "One of them helps me with the cooking and claims to be able to foretell the weather, but most of the time it winds up making excuses rather than predictions and when it *does* manage a prediction it's usually wrong. But I never have to worry about burning dinner; it's very reliable on that and always turns down the heat at the perfect time."

"It doesn't like *me*, though," Azl said. "That's one reason Hrus does the cooking."

"The other reason being that I'm better at it to begin with."

"Exactly."

"Oh," Tulzik said.

"As for finding your sister's killer, we've done a little more thinking about that," Hrus said, brushing crumbs from his close-trimmed beard. "Tell us what you think of our conclusions."

"First off," Azl said, "we told you that there are many factions vying for power in Ragbaan. What we didn't mention is that every so often one will lose out in the ongoing power struggles, but rather than being destroyed or absorbed, its leaders will flee into exile. There are several of these exiles scattered around the world – most try to stay as close to Ragbaan as possible, in hopes of someday returning to their former positions of power, but a few abandon the area entirely. Some of them remain fiercely independent, while others form alliances with one another, or even with surviving factions still in the city. The interrelationships can get quite complex."

"We asked why anyone would want to smuggle an assassin into the city when there are already plenty of assassins here," Hrus continued. "Well, the exiles don't all have access to the assassins in the city. *They* might send outside assassins in."

"But there's another question," Azl said. "If the assassin is a stranger, why try to hide his arrival? Strangers wander into Ragbaan all the time – merchants, adventurers, young people out to make their fortunes. And another point – why did Peval wait in your town as he did, before being summoned and then heading for Ragbaan? He wasn't *from* Emniln. Why not stay in his native village, wherever it might be?"

"Do you see that one yet?" Hrus asked, smiling at Tulzik.

"I'm not sure," Tulzik said, frowning in reply.

"It's simple enough," Azl said. "At least, we think it is. We believe Peval is *from* Ragbaan and is known here. He slipped out of the city and went to Emniln to await further instructions from his exiled employer, and then when those instructions came he slipped back *into* the city, trying to remain undetected, because he did not want someone – his target, presumably – to know that he had ever been away. We believe he already had some connection with his intended victim, not close enough that his absence would necessarily be noticed, but close enough that he would be recognized if he tried re-entering Ragbaan by airship, and his trip outside the city would arouse suspicion and make his job more difficult. Hence, he tried to get in and out of the city unseen."

"But wait a minute," Tulzik said. "Why would he go anywhere? Even if he's working for one of these exiles, why not just have his instructions smuggled in somehow?"

"Ah!" Hrus pointed at him. "I believe you're getting the hang of this! That's *just* the right question to ask next!"

"Obviously, he got more than just instructions and payment from his employer," Azl said. "He was also equipped with whatever method of assassination he's meant to use – his weapon. Whatever it was that he used to kill your sister without leaving a mark. It was something that could not be done over a long distance; he had to go to the exile, whoever it might be, to have the spell cast upon him, or the device fitted to him, or to be equipped with whatever it was that made him deadly enough to be an effective assassin."

Tulzik stared at her.

"Most of the factions in Ragbaan draw at least part of their authority from ancient artifacts or magical power of one sort or another," Hrus said. "That's true of the exiles, as well."

"I don't know of any exiled magicians living near Emniln," Tulzik protested.

"I doubt the exile, whoever it might be, *advertises* the fact that he's a trouble-making sorcerer who got thrown out of Ragbaan when his intrigues failed," Hrus said. "He probably claims to be a retired merchant, or some such thing."

"So your theory is that the man who killed Vika is a professional assassin from Ragbaan in the employ of an exiled political leader, who's been equipped with some magical weapon that he used to kill Vika before returning to Ragbaan to use it against his assigned target," Tulzik said.

"Exactly!" Hrus beamed.

"And you're basing this entirely on the fact that he walked across the crater instead of taking the airship from Zaraquan."

Hrus opened his mouth, then closed it again and looked at Azl.

She considered the matter thoughtfully, then nodded. "Yes, that sums it up nicely," she said.

"That seems like a great deal to infer from a single odd detail," Tulzik said mildly.

"A philosopher once said that a sufficiently powerful and logical mind could infer the entire universe from a single grain of sand," Azl replied. "I think that's an overstatement, but sometimes not by much."

"However," Hrus said, "we did not really infer it entirely from a single odd detail. We inferred it from that detail *and* that he killed your sister. A courier or anyone else on a legal errand would almost certainly not have done that. Murder is serious business, not lightly undertaken by amateurs; thus, this man is probably not an amateur."

Tulzik could see the truth in that. "So what can we do about it?" he asked.

"We can test elements of our hypothesis," Azl said. "We can talk to the Guild, learn whatever there is to be learned about exiles in the vicinity of Emniln, show that portrait your sister did around, see whether anyone recognizes the fellow. The whole structure may collapse under the weight of new facts, or we may find the man we seek, or any of several possibilities between."

"I'm already fairly certain who hired Peval and why," Hrus said, "but we'll see what else we can learn before we try to put my theories to the test."

"You think you *know*?" Tulzik asked, startled. "How?"

"Timing. Location. Details. I do keep track of who sends whom into exile, you know, and what methods each faction prefers to use."

"He's showing off," Azl said. "Don't encourage him."

"What? You think he's wrong?"

"Oh, no, he's probably right, but there's no need to watch him strut and preen about it."

"But if he already knows..." Tulzik looked desperately from one of his hosts to the other.

Azl sighed, and Hrus smiled.

"Oh, go ahead and tell him, then," Azl said. "I'm not as certain of my guess as you are."

"Dardem Karianthis," Hrus said. "The Biologist. I believe that's who hired your sister's killer."

"The what?"

"Biologist," Hrus said. "That's what he called himself, the Biologist. It's an old word meaning a magician who uses only living things as his materials – herbalists and gene-cutters and animal trainers and the like. Dardem was one of the high-ranking sorcerers in the Cooperative, the organization that controls most of Ragbaan's food supply, but then he got into the slave trade, which the Cooperative won't touch, and he split off and formed his own organization. That worked for a few years, more or less, but he started accumulating enemies, and eventually it was decided mutually by everyone involved that he was no longer welcome in the city. A little over two years ago he boarded an airship to Zaraquan and hasn't been seen since. Rumor had it he greatly resented this turn of events."

"We don't know where he went from Zaraquan, though," Azl said. "But I'd say two years is about right for the timing of an attempt at revenge or reinstatement – a year to get reestablished, a year to prepare, and here we are. You do come from somewhere where Zaraquan is the nearest airship port, which fits nicely."

"Equipping an assassin with something that kills silently, without leaving a mark on the body, is very much his style," Hrus said.

"Agreed," Azl said. "He's probably hoping no one will even realize it's an assassination – assuming it *is* the Biologist behind this. Until Hrus suggested him I had thought it might be Verain Yu."

"Who's that?"

"He led a failed rebellion within the Antiquarians three or four years back. Then he disappeared. He's generally assumed to be dead, but I thought he might have changed his face and *become* this Peval. Or hired him."

"We haven't totally ruled that out," Hrus added. "But I think the Biologist is a better fit."

"I admit that he is."

That all made sense. If these guesses were right, then this "Biologist" was partially responsible for Vika's death and would need to be dealt with eventually, when Tulzik got back home. "Who's his target, then?" Tulzik asked. "Where can we find Peval?"

"I don't know," Hrus said. "Dardem had a *lot* of enemies."

"It was the Guild that convinced him to leave," Azl said. "The Guild doesn't intervene in power struggles lightly. For them to involve themselves, the Biologist must have angered so many people that the Guild was afraid the entire city was in danger."

"Should we start with the Guild, then? Was there anyone in particular in the Guild he would blame?" Hrus said. Then he answered his own question. "No, he'd probably blame one of the people who fought back when he tried to expand, on the grounds that their interference was what drew the Guild's interest."

"The Nine Families, or the Antiquarians, or the Vampire, perhaps."

Tulzik started. "There are *vampires* in Ragbaan?"

"What? Oh, no, not literally," Hrus said. "That's just what Azl calls the Sorceress."

"*What* sorceress?"

"Alsia ter Bithuni," Azl said.

"She's *the* Sorceress the way Dardem Karianthis is *the* Biologist," Hrus explained. "It's not that there aren't any others in the city, just that those two stand out, and each headed a faction rather than working for someone else. There's also the Ambassador, the Necromancer, the Astronomer, and so on. It's easier to keep them straight than memorizing everyone's personal names."

"They use the names to intimidate people," Azl said. "Sometimes it works, sometimes it doesn't. Sometimes people give them names other than the ones they choose for themselves. I think 'the Vampire' describes Alsia better than 'the Sorceress.'"

"She does tend to demand a lot of her underlings," Hrus said. "Though usually not literal blood, so far as I know."

"Do you think she's Peval's target?"

"She might be," Hrus replied.

"Or she might not," Azl said. "It could be someone in the Guild, or one of the Antiquarians, or the head of the Importers – that's old Parj, isn't it?"

"It could be Parj Importer, yes. Or it could be someone from Dardem's own organization, someone he feels betrayed him," Hrus suggested. "We don't know."

"I think we should have a word with the Guild," Azl said.

"I think *you* should have a word with the Guild," Hrus corrected her. "No need for both of us to go."

"They might still be annoyed with you about Filimon."

"Exactly."

Tulzik had the distinct feeling that the conversation was slipping out of his grasp. Who or what was Filimon? Who was Parj Importer? Who were the Antiquarians? What did the Guild have to do with this?

"I'll come with you," he said, hoping to grab back at least partial control of events.

Azl turned to him and raised one eyebrow. "You will?" she said.

"Yes. I'm more likely to recognize Peval if he's already infiltrated the Guild. You've only seen the portrait, whereas I knew him for months."

"Even if he has infiltrated the Guild – a very improbable proposition in itself – it's *very* unlikely he'd be in the particular bit of it I intend to visit," Azl said. "But if you want to come along, I have no objection."

"Bring the picture," Hrus said.

"Of course," Azl said. "Bring the picture. I'm sure you'd be more comfortable carrying it yourself than entrusting it to me."

"Yes," Tulzik said, relieved. "Yes, I would."

"Then get yourself ready. We leave in five minutes." She rose and strode away.

Startled, Tulzik stared after her; then Hrus remarked, "She meant it, you know."

"Oh." Tulzik scrambled to his feet.

Five minutes later Azl was striding down the palace stairs, Tulzik stumbling after her, his pack on his shoulder – rather than sort out what he might need, or carry the portrait separately, he had simply brought the whole thing. They descended to the ground floor, marched down the north arcade, through the crowded and bustling great hall, and out onto the plaza.

CHAPTER 10

Tulzik looked up at the tunnel's tiled ceiling with misgivings. "Are you sure this is safe?" he asked.

"No," Azl said. She did not elaborate as she marched on.

"Oh," Tulzik said, following her into the gloom.

They were a hundred yards into a round tunnel lined with yellow tile – or rather, that had once been lined with yellow tile; perhaps a third of the tiles were now cracked, broken, or missing entirely, the gaps revealing a gray surface spider-webbed with tiny cracks. The floor beneath was littered with bits of yellow ceramics. The stairs up to the street were still visible behind them, since the tunnel was almost perfectly straight, but little daylight reached this far; a few faint, dying yellow teklights still shone overhead here and there and dimly illuminated their way.

Once they were a few feet past the last functioning teklight, though, the darkness ahead looked total.

At least it was dry, Tulzik thought. A cool, wet wind had been blowing off the bay as they had made their way through the streets, and his shirt felt unpleasantly damp, clinging to his upper arms as they walked.

Azl did not seem to have noticed the dampness above, nor the darkness here; she was walking on as if they were still in full daylight. But then something clicked ahead, and Azl stopped so suddenly that Tulzik almost ran into her – and although he had never seen Azl do anything threatening, he suspected that running into her was not a good idea.

"It's Azl apek Tiriyilin," Azl said, apparently addressing empty air. "I'd like to talk to a Guild member."

A section of tunnel wall to their left suddenly slid silently upward, revealing a well-lit room; light spilled out into the tunnel, revealing just how dusty the floor was and how decrepit the tile walls

were. Azl promptly turned and stepped into the room, and Tulzik
hastily followed.

When both of them were inside the curving door descended,
closing them into the hidden chamber. Tulzik blinked, his eyes
adjusting to the light as he looked around. The room was perhaps
fifteen feet on a side, with bare stone walls and floor. Benches stood
against either wall, and four bright white teklights hung from the
ceiling. There were two doors – the curving one they had entered
through, and a more ordinary one in the opposite wall.

"What is this place?" Tulzik asked.

"A contact point," Azl replied.

"No, I mean, why was it ever built? What are all these tunnels?"

Azl glanced at him. "Who knows? Tulzik, the city is thousands
of years old, and at its peak it held more than twenty–five million
people and had more magic than we can even imagine in these decadent latter days. There are a million things in it that nobody understands anymore, but we use them when it's convenient, and one of
those things is a ridiculously elaborate system of tunnels and underground passages weaving around one another, most of which haven't
fallen in yet. There are entire communities living below the city, you
know – some human, some not, and some of them have been there
for centuries. At some point someone built *this* tunnel and *this* room,
and I doubt anyone knows why, but it isn't being used regularly by
anyone, so it makes a good meeting place when you don't want to be
interrupted."

Before Tulzik could say anything more the other door slid
open, and a man stepped in. He was of medium height and rather
thin and wearing the most outlandish outfit Tulzik had ever seen – a
suit of shiny black fabric that covered his entire body and most of his
head, tight in some places and baggy in others, apparently at random.
A pair of oversized goggles covered his eyes, and dozens of brightly
colored devices were attached to the black garment in various places;
Tulzik had no idea which ones might be actual magic and which were
merely decorations.

Tulzik was too startled to say anything when this apparition
entered – and after the initial shock, too busy trying not to laugh.

"Guildsman," Azl said, bowing – not deeply, but it was definitely a bow – as the door slid shut behind the new arrival.

"Azl apek Tiriyilin." The goggles bobbed, but it was barely a
nod, let alone a bow.

"My husband and I believe we have discovered something that may be of interest to the Guild."

"This man is not your husband." The man's voice was flat, with an odd buzzing quality.

"No," Azl agreed. "This is our guest, Tulzik Ambroz. It was he who brought certain things to our attention."

"Indeed. What payment would you expect?"

"Information. A modest amount, and nothing forbidden."

"You do not know what is forbidden and what is not." Something about the Guildsman's phrasing made this sound like an accusation.

"True," Azl acknowledged, "but I am fairly certain the information we ask is not."

"Then proceed."

Azl nodded at Tulzik. "The portrait?" Then she turned back to the Guildsman as Tulzik hastily lowered his pack and fumbled with the drawstring.

"Hrus and I believe that an exile, probably Dardem Karianthis, has sent an assassin to Ragbaan. The assassin used the name Peval in the wilds; Tulzik has a picture of him, drawn by a young woman in Emniln. We do not know his identity beyond this, nor do we know his intended target, though it would presumably be one of Dardem's plentiful enemies. The information we seek is the identity and location of this man, or any other knowledge of him the Guild might be willing to provide."

"An assassin?"

"We think so."

"A serious accusation."

"Yes."

"The Guild does not allow exiles to interfere in urban affairs."

"So I understood. This is why I am here."

"I see."

Tulzik finally managed to free the boards from his pack; he knelt and carefully untied the black ribbons. Azl and the Guildsman stopped speaking and watched silently as he separated the boards and revealed the portrait Vika had drawn of her love.

"This is the assassin," Tulzik said, displaying the drawing. "This is the man who killed my sister."

The Guildsman looked at it closely, then reached up and fiddled with his goggles. Tulzik and Azl waited silently for a long moment; then Azl said, "Although we think he has lived in Ragbaan, he was out of the city for some time and returned surreptitiously just three days ago. We believe that during his absence he met with his employer, whoever it is, and may have acquired a weapon of some sort to use in a planned assassination."

"We will contact you in the north arcade," the Guildsman said, straightening up. "You may leave now."

"Thank you," Azl said, bowing again. The inner door slid open with a slight hissing, and the Guildsman backed through it. Azl remained bent over as Tulzik carefully re-packed Vika's drawing.

Then the inner door closed, and the outer one opened, and Azl took Tulzik by the elbow and hurried him out of the room, back into the darkness of the tunnel.

"He didn't tell us anything!" Tulzik protested, as he stuffed the bound boards back into his pack.

"Later," Azl said, pointing him toward the stairs at the end of the tunnel.

"Why does he wear that bizarre outfit?"

"That's a Guild uniform," Azl said. "They're carefully made to traditional designs dating back centuries. Each of those little devices has some sort of symbolic meaning, or some magical purpose, or sometimes both. Another Guildsman would know his rank and lineage instantly from the markings, but to outsiders they all look alike."

"They look absurd!"

"Would you know him again if you saw him in ordinary clothing?"

Tulzik considered that, as he stumbled and crunched a bit of tile beneath his boot. "No, I suppose not," he said. "The goggles and the way the hood wrapped around his head and covered his jaw hid most of his face, and the baggy places distorted his shape..."

"That's the intent," Azl said. "The Guild is a *secret* society, remember – those uniforms are disguises, as well as demonstrating their place within the Guild."

"If it's so secret, how do you know all this? How did you know where to find him?"

"It's my job to know things," Azl said. "Believe me, plenty of people in Ragbaan don't even know the Guild still exists, let alone where any of their meeting points are."

Tulzik was not entirely sure he believed this, but he did not argue further. For one thing, Azl was moving so fast that conversation was difficult. He hastened to keep up as she strode up the passage.

A moment later they trotted up the steps to the street, and as they emerged into the wet wind and the crowd of pedestrians passing the tunnel mouth, Tulzik found himself looking up at the strange red-striped white face of the creature he had seen in the great hall of the Imperial Palace, the thing the pepper vendor had called the Ilm. It was looking down at the two of them with interest.

"Azl," it said, in a voice that was clear and pleasant, but definitely not human.

"Ilm," she replied. "Excuse me." She brushed past and strode on.

Tulzik, however, did not. He had no idea why Azl should be in such a hurry, and he did not appreciate being rushed, and he was curious about the tall being. Instead of following Azl he stopped and looked up at the Ilm, then nodded politely.

"I am Tulzik Ambroz, newly arrived in Ragbaan," he said. "I understand you are called the Ilm?"

The creature tilted its head and stared down at him with those immense blue eyes. "I am probably called a great many things when I am not present," it replied, speaking Rogau with precisely the same accent as Azl and Hrus. "I am the Ilm, however."

"Is that your name, or your species?"

"Yes."

Tulzik suppressed a frown; that answer was obviously deliberately unhelpful, but to demand an explanation would be rude. "I see you know Azl."

"I know the names of a great many people. I would not say I know many of them in the sense of understanding them. I know Azl's name and occupation and a few other facts about her, but I would not say I know her."

Tulzik smiled crookedly. "I wonder whether anyone does."

"I would say her husband knows her quite well, actually," the Ilm said mildly.

That observation was so obviously correct that Tulzik felt slightly ashamed of himself for his own attempt at a clever remark – he had seen Azl and Hrus talking and had observed the way their

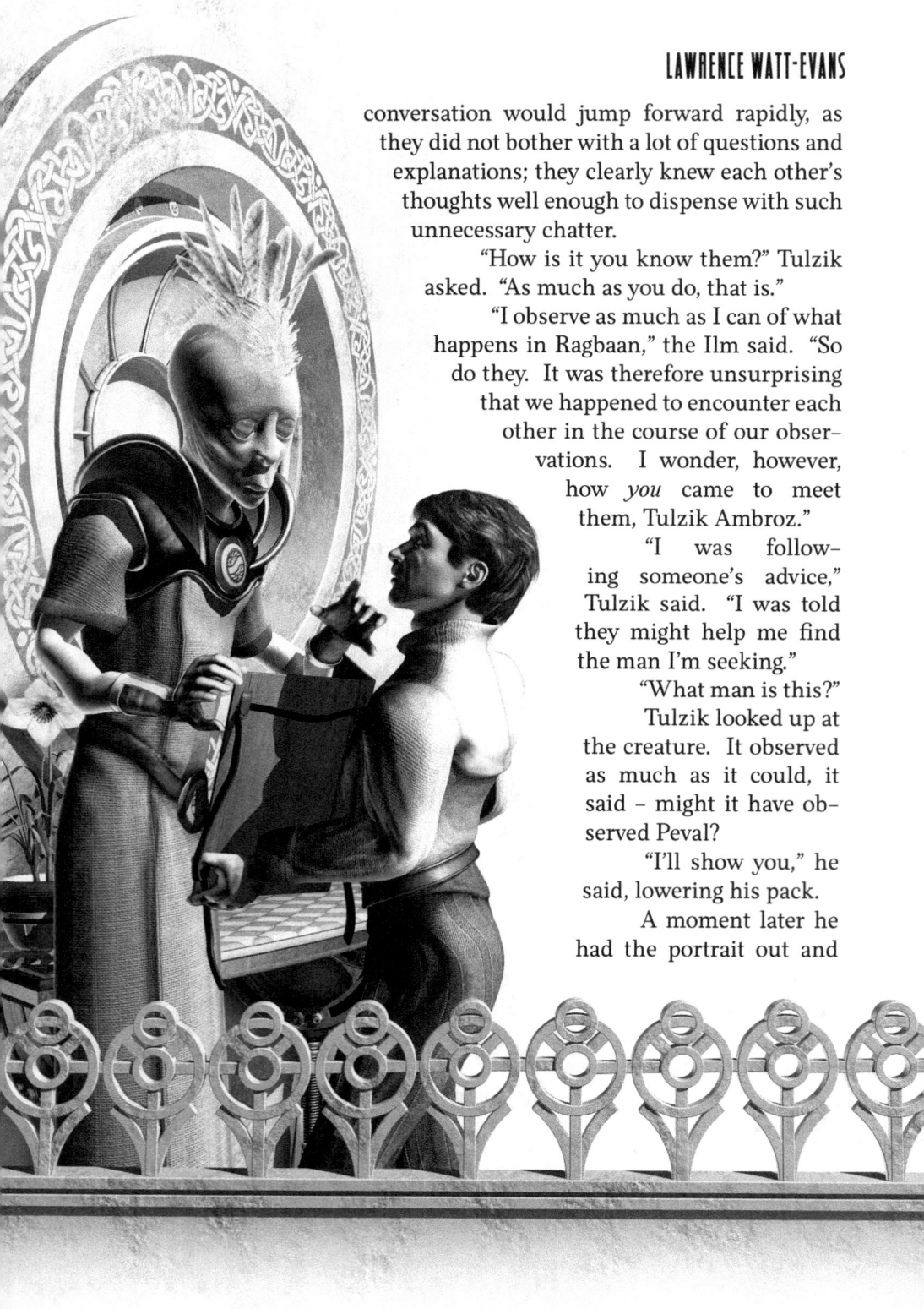

conversation would jump forward rapidly, as they did not bother with a lot of questions and explanations; they clearly knew each other's thoughts well enough to dispense with such unnecessary chatter.

"How is it you know them?" Tulzik asked. "As much as you do, that is."

"I observe as much as I can of what happens in Ragbaan," the Ilm said. "So do they. It was therefore unsurprising that we happened to encounter each other in the course of our observations. I wonder, however, how *you* came to meet them, Tulzik Ambroz."

"I was following someone's advice," Tulzik said. "I was told they might help me find the man I'm seeking."

"What man is this?"

Tulzik looked up at the creature. It observed as much as it could, it said – might it have observed Peval?

"I'll show you," he said, lowering his pack.

A moment later he had the portrait out and

held it up. The Ilm reached down with one of its multi-jointed arms and took the drawing carefully in one hand – a hand that had too many fingers; Tulzik was unsure whether he saw seven or eight.

"Peval Salinzi, if I am not mistaken," the Ilm said. "An excellent likeness. Your own work?"

"My sister's," Tulzik said, struggling to hide his excitement. "You know Peval?"

"As I know Azl, or slightly less," the Ilm answered, handing the picture back.

"Name and occupation?"

"Perhaps not his present occupation. I have not seen him in some time."

That was a disappointment. The Ilm had provided a surname, which might be useful – assuming Peval was using it, and it wasn't just an alias he had abandoned – but for a moment Tulzik had hoped the creature knew where to find Vika's killer.

"Why are you seeking him? Did you want a homunculus made?"

Tulzik had been placing the picture back between the boards; now he stopped and blinked. "What?"

"Did you want a homunculus? I believe the so-called Sorceress controls the supply at present."

"Wait. What does Peval have to do with homunculi?"

It was the Ilm's turn to blink – a disturbing process in which its eyes sank back into its head, thick white membranes slid across them from the sides, and the membranes then folded back as the eyes returned to their former prominence.

"My understanding was that he worked for a maker of homunculi," it said.

Tulzik assembled a few facts his hosts had mentioned and asked, "Dardem Karianthis?"

"I believe that was the name, yes."

"Peval worked for him?"

"Well, so he claimed. I confess I never troubled to confirm this with Dardem Karianthis."

That fit the known facts and existing theories very well; the Biologist apparently hadn't recruited an assassin, he had simply turned one of his employees *into* an assassin. But did homunculi fit in somewhere?

"So Peval was a supplier of homunculi? That was his occupation when you met him?"

"So I supposed, but I may have been mistaken. He did not actually attempt to sell me any." The Ilm eyed Tulzik with an inscrutable expression – which was hardly surprising, given how inhuman its face was. "I take it this was not the occupation you thought him to pursue?"

"I really didn't know what his former occupation was," Tulzik said, pulling the black ribbons into place.

"And what is his *present* occupation, then?"

He tied the first ribbon. "When I met him he was working as a messenger."

"Ah, perhaps not so different, then – he was acting as a messenger when I met him, as well. Perhaps the nature of his message fooled me."

Tulzik finished securing the boards and slid the bundle back into his pack. "I don't understand."

"He tried to hire me, on behalf of his master, to instruct them in better methods of producing homunculi. I had therefore assumed that this meant Peval Salinzi and Dardem Karianthis both worked in the manufacture of homunculi – I *know* that Dardem Karianthis did, but perhaps Peval Salinzi was merely his messenger and not involved in production or sales."

"He tried to hire you?" Tulzik looked up at the Ilm. "Are you known to be expert in that sort of magic, then?"

The Ilm's feathery crest rose, and its face twisted into a new, if equally unreadable expression. "There are those who believe me to be expert in everything," it said.

"*Are* you?"

The crest rose further, and the expression looked something like a smile. "No."

"A shame," Tulzik said. "It would be useful to be expert in everything. Right now, though, I'd settle for expertise in finding this man."

"Why do you seek him?"

Tulzik hesitated. He had no way of knowing the Ilm's opinions on anything, or what faction, if any, it might be allied with. It admitted Dardem Karianthis had tried to hire it; perhaps the relationship had gone farther than that.

Trusting something so inhuman was perhaps too large a risk to take just now. There was no reason to think the Ilm would share human ideas of morality or justice; it might warn Peval that Tulzik was after him.

"Personal business," he said.

"Ah," the Ilm said. Then it stepped back. "May you succeed admirably, Tulzik Ambroz." With that, it turned away.

Tulzik hoisted his pack to his shoulder and watched it go, wondering if he should call after it.

In the end he decided not to; if the Ilm had truly wanted to help him, surely it would have stayed. He had no idea whether he could believe the creature, in any case; every word it had said might be false. He shrugged, hitched up his pack, and trudged back toward the Imperial Palace to see whether Azl and Hrus had learned anything more.

CHAPTER 11

The north arcade was relatively crowded, and Tulzik could not see Azl or Hrus until he was almost at their usual post. At last, though, he slipped between two black-robed men wearing strange, tall hats and saw the two of them seated side-by-side. Hrus was slumped in his chair, eyes closed, hands folded on his belly, while Azl was erect and alert.

"There you are," she said before Tulzik could speak. "What kept you?"

"I was speaking to the Ilm," Tulzik replied. "I didn't see any need to hurry."

"That's because you've never dealt with the Guild before," Azl said. "If they say they'll contact us in the north arcade, we had damned well better be here when they arrive."

"They couldn't have sent anyone here that fast!"

"Yes, they could," Hrus said, without changing position or opening his eyes. "But they didn't."

"How could they have?"

"Magic."

Before Tulzik could reply, Azl asked, "You spoke to the Ilm?"

"Yes. I thought it might have seen Peval. It said it had, but not recently – and it said his full name is Peval Salinzi and he once tried to hire the Ilm to work for the Biologist."

Azl glanced at Hrus, who opened his eyes and looked at Tulzik.

"Interesting," Hrus said.

"I thought so. It confirms your theory. Peval has been working for the Biologist all along; he wasn't just hired as an assassin."

"That's if the Ilm is telling the truth. Do you believe it?"

Tulzik blinked and rather than admit his doubts said, "Why wouldn't I? The Ilm has no reason to lie to me!"

"The Ilm lies for fun," Azl said. "Not always, but sometimes."

"I can't see what would be fun about lying to me about this."

"The Ilm isn't human," Hrus said. "Neither is its idea of fun."

"You don't think it's a little too convenient that out of three million people, the Ilm just happened to know the one you're looking for and to have had business dealings with him?" Azl asked.

"The Biologist thought the Ilm knew old magic he could use!" Tulzik protested. "So he sent his errand boy to recruit the Ilm. A couple of years later he sent the same errand boy to kill one of his enemies – it makes perfect sense! How could the Ilm have known we thought there was a connection between Peval and the Biologist? Coming up with that particular lie would be even more of a coincidence!"

"It does sound reasonable," Hrus said, "but this is the Ilm. We don't know what it can do; it may have ways to have spied on us. What it said might be true, or it might be an Ilmish game."

"Ilmish?" Azl asked her husband.

"Do you have a better word?"

Azl shook her head. "It might be true," she told Tulzik. "But you can't be sure. As an outsider, you can't trust *anyone* in Ragbaan – not the Ilm, not Hiji, not us, not the Guild, not anyone. You don't know enough of the situation; anyone could be lying to you. *I* could be lying, telling you this. Don't take anything for granted."

"That's ridiculous," Tulzik said. "Why would anyone who isn't working with Peval or his employer *bother* to lie to me?"

"To get your money, as Hiji did, or as a cruel sort of amusement, or simply because he *can*."

Tulzik shook his head. He knew that people would lie if it suited their needs, but Azl's attitude seemed far too cynical to him. *Usually*, in his experience, people told the truth, if only because it was easier than thinking up a lie.

Whether the Ilm qualified as "people" was another question, of course. Azl and Hrus might be right about not believing what it said, but Tulzik still thought it had probably told the truth – its claims were consistent with everything else Tulzik knew, after all.

He was about to say something else, to ask a question about the Guild, when one of those short brown people, the ones he had been told *not* to call dwarfs, came striding up.

"Are you Azl apek Tiriyilin?" the creature asked Azl in a musical, high-pitched voice.

Tulzik noticed that Azl did not seem the least bit startled by this sudden approach. "I am," she said.

"Then this is for you," he said, holding out a white envelope tied with a blue ribbon.

Azl accepted it.

Hrus opened his eyes. "Anything else, runt?" he asked. "Something for Hrus Daundablo Hangalef Tir-Dondarai, perhaps?"

"Not today, friend," the *baz* replied with a toothy smile. "I was just told to deliver that one envelope. I've done my job."

"Thank you," Azl said, as she untied the ribbon. "Was there a fee?"

"Paid in advance." The creature made a sort of salute with one hand, then turned and hurried away through the crowd.

Hrus watched him go, then asked Azl, "From the Guild?"

"I assume so," she said, as she pulled out a single sheet of paper.

"What does it say?" Tulzik asked, resisting the impulse to crane his neck and try to read it over Azl's shoulder.

Azl did not reply immediately; she read the message carefully, flipped it over to be sure there was nothing on the back, then turned it back and read it again. Then she handed paper and envelope to Hrus and stared at Tulzik.

"What does it say?" Tulzik asked again.

"I think we will forgo our fee," she said. "Our relationship is ended."

"Hmm," Hrus said, reading the message.

"What?" Tulzik said. He stared at Azl's expressionless face, and then at Hrus, who was rereading the paper. "What relationship?"

"Your relationship with my husband and myself," Azl said. "We are refusing to continue with your case."

"*What?* But why?"

"When I told you a moment ago never to trust anyone in Ragbaan, I should have listened to myself," Azl said bitterly. "We believed every word you told us – you played the naive outlander perfectly. I congratulate you on that."

Hrus was stroking his beard and staring at the letter. Now he glanced up. "Let us not be too hasty, Azl," he said. "Things may not be as they appear. But I am afraid, Tulzik, that we must indeed decline any further role in your investigations, at least for the moment, and ask that you leave."

"But why? What did the Guild tell you?"

Hrus wordlessly handed him the paper.

"The man in your picture is Peval Salinzi," Tulzik read. "He is a journeyman gene-cutter, formerly employed by Dardem Karianthis and now working for Alsia ter Bithuni. As a potentially dangerous associate of an exile he has been under moderate surveillance, and he has not left the city at any time, so far as we can determine. He has definitely not been gone long enough to have visited Emniln or to have received a weapon from Dardem Karianthis. The person calling himself Tulzik Ambroz, whose identity we have been unable to determine, has misinformed you."

The name and background was just as the Ilm had said – but what was this about being under surveillance and not having left the city? That wasn't possible. Tulzik had seen him in Emniln, talked to him! Vika had drawn his portrait, and he had killed her!

"Let me venture a guess," Azl said, breaking into his thoughts, her voice even colder than usual. "The Biologist sent you to kill Peval Salinzi for betraying him by taking a position with the Sorceress, and you came up with this story about a murdered sister to convince us to help you find him."

"No!" Tulzik protested, staring at the paper. "Everything I told you was true – he *was* in Emniln, and we *did* find Vika's body in his room in Kalidar, and my uncle and I *did* pursue him to Ragbaan!"

"The Guild says otherwise," Azl said. "I have more faith in the Guild than I should in some stranger I just met the day before yesterday."

"His story has been superbly consistent," Hrus remarked. "And why place his supposed encounters with Peval so far from the city?"

"So we would conclude Peval was an assassin!" Azl said. "There had to be an airship route that fit."

"You assume remarkable subtlety, dearest."

"What if I do?" Azl turned to Tulzik. "Go away! Get out of here!"

"Did you leave anything upstairs?" Hrus asked.

"I don't think so," Tulzik said. "But I don't understand – I'm telling the truth, I swear it!"

"It's possible you believe it yourself," Hrus said. "The Biologist was good with false memories. If we find anything of yours in our rooms, we'll bring it down here. Stop by in a day or two."

"In a day or two?" Azl protested. "But he's probably going to kill Peval Salinzi!"

"We know he's here, though," Hrus said. "So does the Guild. I'd be surprised if the plan continues as originally proposed."

"He's still the Biologist's errand boy."

"He may be. And we may do something about it."

"I'm *not* his errand boy," Tulzik said. "I know I'm not – he can't be *that* good with false memories!"

"You'd be surprised," Hrus said.

"But – "

"Just go away," Azl said bitterly. "We can't make plans with you listening."

"But I – "

"Go!"

Frustrated and confused, Tulzik went, marching back down the north arcade, shouldering aside anyone in his path, then continuing across the great hall and out into the plaza. There he stopped, blinking in the sun, trying to think what he should do next, where he should go. He had no money beyond the six *jit* in his pocket, no friends, no place to stay – though that last was not a real issue in Ragbaan. Powerful people believed him to be untrustworthy and perhaps dangerous, and he still did not know where to find Peval Salinzi.

He didn't know where to find work, either, but that was easier – a willing and able-bodied young man could always find a way to earn a few *jit*. But finding Peval...

Well, he could always just head westward across the ridge and the crater and go home, but he was not about to admit defeat. Vika had *died* at that man's hands! The image of his sister's body, stretched across that bed in Kalidar, filled his thoughts. Peval Salinzi was responsible for that.

He knew Peval's surname now, and the Guild had said he was working for that woman, the Sorceress. It *should* be possible to find him.

It would be easier if he could just ask Azl and Hrus where to find her; they undoubtedly knew, just as they had known how to contact the Guild. He couldn't, though; they no longer trusted him. Hrus seemed to be staying neutral, but Azl clearly thought he was in the Biologist's pay.

Odd, how certain she was that the Guild wasn't mistaken. She hadn't trusted the Ilm for a second, but despite her own advice, she apparently had absolute faith in the Guild. She undoubtedly had her reasons, but still, it seemed odd.

The thought of the Ilm reminded him that the creature knew a great deal of what went on in Ragbaan. *It* could tell him where to find the Sorceress, he was sure.

Of course, first he would have to find the Ilm, but that shouldn't be so very difficult, since it seemed to like wandering through crowds, watching and listening. Finding a particular human in the crowds might be tricky, but an eight-foot-tall *thing*?

He would want to do it quickly, before it had time to wander off into some distant part of the city. That decided the question of whether to look for Peval or work – he needed to find the Ilm *now* and ask it where the Sorceress was. Then, once he knew that, he could worry about a source of income.

For that matter, the Sorceress might just provide an income, too. She obviously employed people; why shouldn't Tulzik be one of them?

He turned his steps to the north, up the slope toward the tunnel mouth; that was where he had last seen the Ilm, after all, and it had been in no hurry.

The scents of perfume, smoke, and sweat drifted by him, and the shadow of an airship slid across the street ahead; he heard a hundred voices and the delicate jingle of bells as he wove through the crowds. A *baz* trotted past with a bundle on one shoulder, something fluttered overhead, and a woman laughed.

For a city of anarchy deep in a centuries–long decline, half ruined and seven–eighths abandoned, Ragbaan certainly seemed crowded and vigorous. It was somewhat overwhelming. Tulzik hated to think of himself as an ignorant farmboy, but that was really almost what he was here. The skills and knowledge that had equipped him to live in Emniln did not begin to cover what he needed to succeed in Ragbaan.

He squeezed past a horseless wagon that was blocking half the street, dodged a party of priests in red robes, and stopped to reorient himself. The stairs down to the abandoned tunnel were three blocks farther on, if he remembered correctly, and if the Ilm were in the area it ought to be visible by now; he grabbed a sign bracket and hoisted himself up, bracing one foot on the side of a building, as he peered over the heads of the pedestrians.

There was no sign of a white head and feathery crest. Disappointed, he dropped back to the pavement, narrowly missing a boy who was running past.

Another boy saw this and stepped up. "You looking for something?"

Tulzik looked down; the child looked about nine or ten and wore a red tunic with golden rosettes – clearly a native of Ragbaan, as no one would dress a boy like that anywhere else Tulzik had ever seen.

"The Ilm," he said. "You know what that is?"

The boy snorted. "*Nobody* knows what the Ilm is – but I know what it looks like, and I saw it headed that way a couple of minutes ago." He pointed to the southeast, toward the waterfront.

"Thanks," Tulzik said – and then he noticed the boy's outstretched hand. With a sigh, he fished out a two-*jit* piece and dropped it in the waiting palm.

That left him all of four *jit*; the boy probably had more cash than Tulzik did.

"It was headed down Emperor Vishak Street, right there," the boy said, pointing with his other hand as his fist closed around the coin. "You might try the Old Fisher's Gallery, on the right. I've seen it in there sometimes."

"Thank you," Tulzik said, tipping his hat – the boy tried to give good value for the money, at any rate. Then he straightened his hat and hurried across the avenue and down Emperor Vishak Street.

The Old Fisher's Gallery had no sign or other marker, but the smell identified it well enough for Tulzik. It was a fish market, open to the streets on two sides, and jammed with buyers and sellers. Tulzik pushed his way in, past browsing customers, and made his way between the tables and tanks of goods and fish deep into the interior, where he almost immediately spotted his quarry. The tall creature had to stoop slightly to clear the web of wires overhead and had its crest folded down, but it still stood up well out of the human crowd.

Tulzik shouldered his way through the horde of customers, debating whether to say anything, and if so, what. He had not yet decided when he found his way blocked by an amazingly fat woman who was carefully inspecting a tray of iced cassamon, prodding at their bellies and lifting the fins to see whether the rainbow flesh beneath was bright or dull. There was no graceful way past her, nor even a marginally polite one; he had no choice but to wait impatiently until she moved on to a wider space, or to retrace his steps to a cross-aisle twenty feet back.

He waited, staring over her shoulder at the Ilm. It was not looking at fish, but at a display of pictures made by gluing fish scales of assorted sizes, shapes, and colors to velvet. Its expression was un-readable, as usual, but Tulzik did not think it was impressed by these artifacts.

Then it glanced around and spotted him. It abandoned the fish-scale art and took two long strides toward him, the crowd parting uneasily before it until it stood on the other side of the fat woman.

"Tulzik Ambroz," it said.

"Ilm," he replied, trying to match the creature's speech. "It is a pleasure to see you again."

"It is a curiosity to see *you* again," it replied. "I had thought you would be busily conferring with Azl and Hrus at the Imperial Palace."

The woman glanced up at the conversation going on over her head and suddenly decided she didn't need to buy cassamon after all. "Excuse me," she said.

Tulzik stepped aside as best he could, and she squeezed past, leaving a small open space between Tulzik and the Ilm.

"There has been an unfortunate misunderstanding," Tulzik said. "Azl refuses to help me further."

"Oh? How peculiar."

"She has been led to believe I lied to her about my reasons for wishing to find Peval Salinzi," Tulzik explained.

"So you have come to me in hopes I might assist you in her stead, as one liar to another?"

Tulzik opened his mouth, and then closed it again. He looked up at the Ilm's calm, inhuman face and tried to decide whether he saw the ghost of a smile there. "Say rather," he said, "as one person Azl falsely accuses of lying to another."

"Ah! Has Azl falsely accused us both?"

"Well, she certainly falsely accused *me*, and she warned me not to trust *you* and said you lie for fun. You would know better than I whether that constitutes a false accusation."

The Ilm cocked its head to one side so that it could partially raise its crest without tangling in the wires. "On the contrary, it is an accurate, if unflattering, statement. I *do* lie for fun. I had not realized that Azl understood this. But I often tell the truth, as well; it can sometimes be far more amusing."

"I didn't think you lied when we spoke earlier," Tulzik said.

"Neither did I."

"I was hoping you could tell me a few things. That's why I came looking for you."

"I could tell you a great many things, many of them true – but is it not odd that you have come to me, when one of your own people has told you I am not to be trusted?"

"I don't think so. Why should I rely on Azl's opinion of you, when I *know* she's wrong about me?"

"Ah. I see."

Tulzik waited a moment, expecting the creature to continue, but it did not; instead it stared down at him for a moment, then lowered its crest and started to turn away.

"Wait!" Tulzik said. "I wanted to ask you something!"

The Ilm did not turn back, but said without looking at him, "You may ask me something. I may answer."

"I'm still trying to find Peval Salinzi, and Azl and Hrus say he's working for the Sorceress – for Alisa ter... Alsia..."

"I know who is called the Sorceress," the Ilm replied, fingering a fish–scale picture of an airship gleaming in the sunset. "Alsia ter Bithuni."

"I want to contact her, to find Peval."

"Contacting her organization is not difficult. Speaking to *her,* on the other hand, is said to be *surprisingly* difficult."

"Well, her organization, then. I just want to find Peval. I don't need to talk to her directly."

The Ilm turned back and stared down at him again. "So your goals remain unchanged since last we spoke?"

"Yes, of course!"

"Yet your relationship with Azl has changed."

"Yes. She thinks I lied to her. I didn't."

"How does this disagreement come to exist?"

"Because someone *else* lied to her. One of her informants assured her that Peval Salinzi never left Ragbaan for any length of time, but I *saw* him spend months in Emniln. So she thinks I made up my whole story. But I *didn't*. It's all true."

"How intriguing! Why would this informant, who Azl obviously trusts more than she trusted you, lie about this man's whereabouts?"

"I don't know," Tulzik admitted unhappily. "I think it must be a mistake – why *would* they lie?"

"A mistake is semantically distinct from a lie, though the effect and factual content may be the same," the Ilm said.

"I know. Maybe it was a lie; maybe it was a mistake – but either way, I don't see why it happened. And it doesn't matter; I just want to find Peval." Tulzik hoped that the Ilm would not recognize the touch of desperation that had crept into his voice.

"Who is said to be working for the Sorceress," the Ilm calmly replied. "Does this news come from the same source that was mistaken or lying about Peval's whereabouts when you believe him to have been in Emniln? If one datum is false, can the other be trusted?"

Tulzik closed his eyes wearily. "I hope so," he said. "I can *ask*, anyway."

"Is Peval a messenger, then, or a maker of homunculi? Should I direct you to Alsia'a laboratories, or her offices?"

Tulzik's eyes opened again. "A maker of homunculi..." he said thoughtfully.

"Then I – "

"No, I mean I don't know which he is," Tulzik interrupted. "He might be both. But I had a thought."

"Ah. Was it painful or disorienting, then, that you display rudeness in consequence and interrupt me?"

"Disorienting," Tulzik said, realizing that he had indeed been rude. "My apologies, Ilm."

The creature lifted its head slightly. "Interesting," it said. "I might find this thought amusing, then."

"Yes, you might," Tulzik said. "Suppose Peval didn't want anyone to know he was leaving the city – could he have made a homunculus in his own image and left it here in his place?"

The Ilm's mouth changed shape dramatically, and its crest sprang up, brushing against wires and triggering a small shower of sparks and rust.

"Indeed he could," it said, as it quickly retracted its crest again. "Creating a near-duplicate of oneself is quite easy, as these things go. However, it would be far younger than him. It could be made to grow to adult size in a matter of a few months, but it would not show the normal signs of aging, and it would be quite stupid and inexperienced. Even with intensive training it could not function as an independent adult until years after its creation, if ever. The Peval you saw in Emniln could not have been such a homunculus."

"But the one they saw *here*, in Ragbaan, might have been."

"Yes. *Might*."

"That would explain it."

"Then will you return to the Imperial Palace and present this theory to Azl?"

Tulzik shrugged. "No," he said. "Why should I? Let her figure it out for herself. No, just tell me where I can find the Sorceress and her organization."

"Any number of people could tell you this, you realize. There was no need to seek *me* out."

"I *know* you," Tulzik said.

The Ilm once again went through the complex and unsettling process of blinking at him. It did not correct him by pointing out that he did not, in fact, know it, in any meaningful sense.

Then it told him, "You must go to the Red Museum on Broken Idol Street, between the Boulevard of the Third Dynasty and the Avenue of Silver Leaves. Bow when the door is opened for you; don't wait to be instructed. If anyone asks, you do not want to be a slave – do not even *consider* attempting that role as a deception. If offered a choice of ways, take the left. And now I wish to stand straight." With that, it turned away, ducked its head, and strode toward the nearest exit, moving through the crowded aisles as if they were empty but somehow never quite colliding with anyone. Its speed made plain that it did not wish to be followed or to continue the conversation.

Tulzik watched it go, then turned to the nearest fish merchant and asked, "Can you direct me to Broken Idol Street?"

CHAPTER 12

The Red Museum was housed in an ornate structure that had once fit the name, but much of the gilt and red enamel on the facade was now peeling, revealing ancient gray wood and brown stone. The three screens that adorned the walls were shattered and dark, the gilded trim that had once surrounded them splintered and mostly gone; a gap indicated where a fourth might once have been. There were three doors into the building, but two of them had obviously not been used in years; only the central one still appeared functional.

Something large was moving around on the Museum's roof; Tulzik glimpsed a large, batlike green wing for an instant and heard something heavy scraping across tile. He watched for a moment, but the wing did not reappear, so with a shrug he strode up the broad stone steps to the door and knocked on it, on a spot that had clearly been rapped on many, many times – not only was the red enamel gone, but the wood itself was deeply indented from the impact of thousands of knuckles.

He glanced up at the chipped carvings overhead and at the immense pillars on either side, wondering what was on the roof, but then the door swung open, and he redirected his gaze. Remembering what the Ilm had told him, he bowed immediately.

The black-haired woman in the gold brocade robe who had opened the door bowed in return and stepped aside to allow him past. Tulzik hurried in, saying, "Thank you."

Once inside he stopped, unsure what he should do next. He was in a fair-sized chamber, standing on a floor of heavily shel-lacked blond wood, looking at an array of pillars, niches, panels, and a great deal of peculiar statuary. Daylight from the single big fanlight window above the door was augmented by half a dozen oil lamps, but none of the teklights suspended from the ceiling were lit, and the back corners were still dim. He could see several doors and two stairways leading off in various directions.

He turned to the woman as she closed the door.

"I've come to... I'm looking for work," he said.

She answered in a tongue he did not quite recognize at first; then he realized it was Buwa.

He spoke no Buwa, but knew it was closely related to Daur, so he replied in Daur, "I'm sorry, I don't understand."

"You do not speak Buwa?" she asked in Rogau, clearly startled.

"No," he said, switching back as she had.

"My apologies. From your clothing I assumed you must be from Bagud. I thought to use your own tongue to put you at ease."

Tulzik looked down at himself; he knew he was not dressed in Ragbaan's style, but he had not thought he looked *that* bad. "I've been traveling," he said, a bit defensively.

"Of course."

"I need work. I understand the Sorceress is hiring."

She looked at him appraisingly. "You know she sells slaves? You want to be a slave?"

"No, of course not! She hires free people. I know she does."

"Yes, she does. I'm just the doorkeeper, though, and this is not my concern. Go upstairs, then and talk to the manager." She gestured toward the stairs at the back of the room.

"Thank you," he said, bowing again.

"Don't open any doors," she said.

"I won't." He turned and headed toward the back. Once again remembering the Ilm's words, he directed his steps toward the stairs on the left.

The doorkeeper remained where she was, watching him go; he glanced back at her, wondering whether she was entirely human, or perhaps a homunculus or changeling. Her eyes and behavior both seemed a bit odd – but then, he scarcely knew what was normal in Ragbaan.

As his gaze turned forward again he noticed one of the figures that he had earlier taken for statuary, and he stopped in his tracks to look at it.

That was not a strangely painted statue, he realized; that was a man who had been skinned and then sealed in some sort of clear coating, with layers of fat and muscle neatly preserved and displayed. One eyeball had been removed from its socket; the other was still there, and Tulzik could see that the dead man's eyes had been green. One hand had been flayed down to the bone; the other was, except for the missing skin, intact.

Tulzik remembered that this building was called a museum and was home to an organization that sold intelligent living creatures; perhaps this gruesome exhibit was somehow considered appropriate. He shuddered.

Then he turned his gaze forward and marched on, aware now that *most* of the "statuary" was anatomical displays of one sort or another. He wondered how long these things had been here and who these people had been – if they really were people and not just artificial creations grown specifically for the museum. Had they been human beings who lived normal lives centuries ago and their bodies then been rendered into what he now saw, or had these things been made for this, grown in vats or assembled piece by piece? Or perhaps the truth lay in between, and they were discarded homunculi.

He strode up the stairs, ignoring the creaking of the ancient steps, and found himself in a short passageway leading past two closed doors to a large room. He obeyed instructions and left the doors closed and walked into the large room.

Half a dozen men were sprawled about on couches and chairs, watching a nude woman dance to faint, tinkling music; she was astonishingly beautiful but very small, less than five feet tall, with golden-red hair that, when not sent flying by a spin or leap, reached to her ankles. Her skin was almost golden, as well, so that it took Tulzik a moment to notice that she had golden bells on her wrists and ankles that were providing part of the music. She was manipulating the wrist bells with her fingers as she danced, controlling which ones jingled – apparently they produced several different notes. Tulzik could not tell where the rest of the music came from; it sounded like a tambour and a small flute, but he saw no musicians.

One of the men looked up as Tulzik entered. "Yes?" he asked.

"I've come to find a job," Tulzik said, removing his hat and trying not to stare too blatantly at the dancing woman.

The man turned and cocked his head, taking in Tulzik's drab, travel-worn attire. "You're a gene-cutter?"

"No," Tulzik admitted. "I'm not a magician at all. I'm just someone who needs some paying work, and I'd heard that the Sorceress was a good person to work for."

The man glanced at the dancer. "She is," he said, "but unless you have some hidden talents, I think you're out of luck. I admire your courage, walking in here like this, but we don't need a farmboy."

"I'm not a farmboy," Tulzik replied. "I can read, write, and speak four languages, and I'm a quick learner – what does she need done?"

"Farmboy, if the Sorceress needs an errand boy, she'll hire a few runts from Monkeytown or make her own, just as she made Umi over there." He pointed at the dancer.

Tulzik considered for a moment as he looked at the dancer – the homunculus, apparently. It did make sense that someone who made, bought, and sold slaves for a living would not have any need to hire unskilled human labor, but he was not about to give up so easily. For one thing, he had not really come here seeking a job. He was after something else entirely.

"She hired my friend Peval," he said.

"Who?" the man asked; one of the other men glanced up at the name.

"Peval Salinzi. He'll vouch for me."

"Peval Salinzi?"

"I know him," the other man said. "He's the new gene–cutter in the laborer section; he used to work for the Biologist. He just signed up yesterday. If he's already trying to bring in his friends he works fast."

"*I* don't know him. Go fetch him and see if he really does know the farmboy."

The man who knew Peval rolled off his couch and got to his feet. "I'll be right back," he said. He vanished through a door at one side of the room.

"Have a seat, then," another man said, gesturing at an empty chair. "Watch the show until he gets back."

Tulzik looked at the man who had questioned him, who shrugged. "Why not?" he said.

"Thank you," Tulzik said, as he settled gingerly onto the chair.

He tried hard to keep his expression neutral, but in his heart he was rejoicing. In just a few minutes these people would bring Peval Salinzi right to him, and he would be able to confront his sister's murderer. He would prove Uncle Urushak wrong; he had found Peval, even in the teeming maze of Ragbaan.

Of course, what he would do about it he wasn't entirely certain yet. He couldn't just kill Peval on the spot, not with all these others present. A lesser confrontation would probably not serve him well, with his word against Peval's, when he had already lied to these people about how he came to be there. He needed some way to get

Peval alone, but it was not likely that Peval would risk that.

If he did get him alone, just what would he do? Kill him? Tulzik had a good knife in his pack – it would hardly be sensible to travel any distance without such a basic tool – but he had never killed a man, and Peval, a killer himself, would not just stand there while Tulzik got up his nerve.

Not to mention that if he *did* kill Peval, Azl and Hrus and the Starfarers' Guild would see it as proof that Tulzik *was* an assassin working for the Biologist, and his own life expectancy might be significantly reduced. Azl had never actually said how the people of Ragbaan dealt with murderers, but Tulzik was quite sure that it wasn't pleasant.

Then on top of *that*, there was the little matter of finding out more about the Biologist himself – he had presumably sent Peval on his murderous mission and might well have told him to remove witnesses and obstructions along the way, which amounted to ordering Vika's death. Tulzik did not want to kill Peval without finding out just how much responsibility Dardem Karianthis had for his sister's murder. Just finding Peval wasn't the end of the matter at all.

But it would be a very satisfactory start.

Of course, this also meant that *Peval* had found *him*. Peval really would recognize him, since they had known each other back in Emniln. It would be interesting to see how he reacted, and it might say something about whether he really had deliberately murdered Vika. Peval might simply deny knowing anything about it, might deny knowing Tulzik at all...

"My name is Tulzik Ambroz, by the way," Tulzik said, reaching out to shake hands with the spokesman.

"Kiv Talyin," the other said, waving the hand away. "Watch the dance – her buyer's picking her up tomorrow, so this is our last chance."

"We're making sure she meets his specifications," another man said.

Tulzik focused his attention on the dancer. She was very beautiful and very graceful, perhaps inhumanly so; her features were delicate, her figure slim but very feminine. Her movements were almost hypnotic.

Tulzik realized he had been staring, and that his body was responding, and he straightened on his chair and glanced around. It was obvious that the other men had been equally appreciative of the dancer's performance; all were staring, perhaps half had their mouths slightly open, and one was actually drooling slightly. He had been so focused on her that he had forgotten about why he was there. He still hadn't decided what he would do...

"Hey, farmboy," someone called from the door. Tulzik turned. "Peval says he isn't expecting..."

"*You?*" Peval said, as Tulzik rose, and Peval got a good look at his face.

Tulzik got a good look at the new arrival, as well. It was Peval, just as Tulzik remembered him, though his customary crooked smile had been replaced with gaping astonishment. Peval, the rough but pleasant fellow who had promised to keep his hands off Vika, the man Vika had run off to follow, the man who had left her dead in the inn in Kalidar.

The man Tulzik had come to Ragbaan to kill.

There was no more time to plan, only to react.

"Peval! I'm glad I found you!" Tulzik said quickly, holding out a hand. "I promised Vika I would. She was very angry with you, you know, leaving her there like that!"

"She... What?" The expression of baffled confusion on his face was oddly gratifying. He ignored Tulzik's outstretched hand.

"You didn't even tell the landlord she was ill!"

Tulzik watched Peval's expression; he was clearly trying to gather his thoughts and deal with the implication that Vika was still alive. "I... Was she ill? I thought she was just sleeping soundly." It was a good lie for such short notice, but his tone was not very convincing.

"It was a little more than *that*," Tulzik said. "We were afraid at first it might be serious, but after a day or two – well, it's all over with now."

"I take it you *do* know him?" the man who had fetched Peval said dryly.

"What?" Peval's head jerked around. His gaze had been locked onto Tulzik's face, and he had clearly forgotten everything and everyone else. "Oh – oh, yes. This is Tulzik. His sister Vika – uh..."

"She fancied him," Tulzik said. "Ran off after him, in fact, but he managed to slip away."

"Yes," Peval said, and it was Tulzik's turn to be astonished – the man was *blushing*. The man who had callously murdered an innocent girl was turning red at the mention of her foolish infatuation.

"So you were looking for him and not a job?" Kiv asked Tulzik.

"No, no," Tulzik said. "I really *do* need a job, and I came here because Peval had said he was coming to work for the Sorceress, and I thought that if she was hiring..."

"He's a gene–cutter," Kiv interrupted.

"And I'm not. I know. But I don't know many people in Ragbaan, so I thought it was worth trying. Peval, you couldn't use an assistant, perhaps? You know I'm not stupid; I'm good with my hands..."

Peval shook his head. "I'm just starting here myself," he said. "I'm not in a position to hire anyone!"

One of the others snorted. "That's certain," he said.

"Oh," Tulzik said. He sighed and glanced at the dancer, who was still gyrating, bells jingling. "Then do you know anywhere else that needs workers? I'm down to my last few *jit*."

Peval glanced helplessly at the other men. "I don't... I can't think of any. Anyone have any suggestions?"

No one spoke for a moment, then Tulzik sighed again and said, "Could you stand me to a meal, then, for Vika's sake? I'm really – well, I'd like a chance to talk and just to see a familiar face across the table."

The play of emotions on Peval's face was fascinating; he was obviously trying not to show any reaction at all, but Tulzik could see some of what he felt all the same. He was confused and frightened and angry and frustrated, and Tulzik took grim pleasure in seeing that discomfiture. Pretending that Vika was still alive had thrown Peval completely off–balance – which was just what Tulzik had wanted.

"I guess I could manage that," Peval said.

"Well, take your family reunion somewhere else," Kiv said. "We're still assessing this slave–girl."

"Of course, of course," Peval said. "Listen, Tulzik, I need to finish up a few things, but I can meet you out front in, say, half an hour, and we'll get supper out of my purse, and you can tell me how Vika is doing."

"Excellent! Thank you, Peval!" Once again, Tulzik held out his hand, and this time Peval clasped it briefly.

His palm was slick with sweat, and Tulzik smiled in response.

It took superhuman effort to keep that smile unthreatening.

Then Peval was hurrying out, and a man called Sirimar was escorting Tulzik back down through the lobby, past the anatomical

displays and the brocade–garbed doorkeeper, and out to the crumbling pavement of Broken Idol Street.

There Tulzik turned and looked up at the weathered facade of
the Red Museum. Once he was alone, he smiled again.

Now that he had no need to deceive anyone, it was not at all a
pleasant smile.

He had found his sister's killer – and he was about to have
dinner at the murderer's expense. What would happen at that meal
and afterward, what he would say, what he would do, he did not know
yet, but all the same, he was satisfied with his progress.

"He'll pay, Vika," Tulzik murmured. "He'll pay for what he did."

CHAPTER 13

Peval appeared in significantly less than half an hour; Tulzik doubted it had been more than twenty minutes. He came hurrying out of the Red Museum wrapped in a billowing green coat and trotted down the steps to where Tulzik was leaning casually against a light pole. He wore no hat, and his hair was in spectacular disarray, with tangled curls spilling over his forehead into his eyes, or sticking up like strange black weeds.

Tulzik took careful note of where the killer held his hands as he approached and where the coat bulged; he was fairly sure Peval had at least one weapon hidden away. He surely wouldn't try to kill Tulzik immediately, though – not until he had heard an account of what had happened in Kalidar after his departure and what Tulzik was doing in Ragbaan. He must want to know why Vika had survived, and what she had told her family.

"Tulzik," Peval said. "Good to see you. You said you wanted supper?" Tulzik could hear tension in his voice.

"If you would be so kind, yes," he said, pushing off from the lamppost. "Perhaps one of the fish dinners Ragbaan is famous for?"

Actually, he had never heard anyone say a word about fish dinners in Ragbaan, unless you counted the fishmongers at the Old Fisher's Gallery hawking their wares, but it seemed logical that the world's greatest seaport would offer a variety of fish, and he did not want to eat another plate of *drash*. Furthermore, he did not care to accompany Peval to the sort of place where a knife in the ribs might go unnoticed and a corpse unreported, and he didn't think of such places as serving fish, though he belatedly realized that might be merely because he had always lived inland, where fish was something of a delicacy.

"If you like," Peval said, pausing to get his bearings. "There's a decent restaurant over that way, on Kelzi Street, just past the Thousand Star Tower." He pointed.

Tulzik straightened his hat. "Lead the way."

Five minutes later they were at the door of what appeared to be a rather luxurious establishment, not at all the sort of dive Tulzik had feared; when Peval opened that door a scent of lamp oil, fresh bread, and frying meat spilled out, rather than the usual smell of spilled beer and stale sweat.

A pretty hostess showed them to a table, and Tulzik was relieved to see that it was in sight of several other diners, but far enough away from any occupied tables to allow for private conversation. He settled carefully onto one chair, while Peval took the one opposite.

The hostess hesitated, holding a large green card Tulzik supposed must be a menu; Peval held out a hand. "I can read," he said.

"I can read, but I don't need to," Tulzik said. "I'll have your best fish, with whatever vegetables your cook deems appropriate, and a pint of the best dark beer."

"Fine," Peval said, handing back the menu. "I'll have the same."

The hostess bowed and hurried away.

For a moment the two men stared at each other; then Peval said, "How *is* Vika? You said she was ill?"

Tulzik had spent his time waiting in the street in concocting details for his lies, so he was ready for this. "Oh, only for half a day. She had mostly slept it off by the time we found her."

Peval glanced nervously at the other tables, then looked back at Tulzik. "'We'?"

"Uncle Urushak and I. He stayed behind to see her safely home, and I came to Ragbaan to find you."

"How did you know I was in Ragbaan?"

"You told Vika, of course. At least, you said you were bound for Ragbaan."

"I did?" Peval's eyes narrowed. "I don't remember that."

"Well, *she* said you did, and here you are, so you must have said *something*."

"Hmph."

Tulzik shrugged. "She's a clever girl, when she's not busy being foolish. If you didn't say it straight out she may have figured it out from some little hint."

It felt very odd to be speaking of Vika in this fashion, knowing that she was really dead and that this man was responsible. It seemed somehow disrespectful, but Tulzik knew the pretense was

his best chance of finding out what had really happened and properly avenging her death. Maintaining a cheerful demeanor made his
heart hurt, but he forced himself to smile.

"I might have," Peval admitted, "but it's a big city, Tulzik; how
did you *find* me? How did you *get* here?"

Tulzik had expected this question and had worked out what he
would have done if Vika *had* lived. "I took an airship from Zaraquan,
of course. How *else* would I get to Ragbaan?"

"You could have just walked, I suppose."

Tulzik snorted derisively. "Why would I do that, when the
airship is there? We could afford a few *walu*. I went straight from
Kalidar to Zaraquan – I was hoping to catch you before you boarded,
but I couldn't find you, so you must have already gone. I think I must
have gotten the airship next after yours."

"Of course." Peval eyed him warily. "But how did you find me,
once you got *here*, to Ragbaan? Unless I talked in my sleep, I'm *sure* I
didn't tell your sister who I'd be working for – after all, I didn't even
know I'd get the job!"

"I asked the Ilm," Tulzik said. "It seems to know a great deal of
what goes on in the city. It suggested I try the Red Museum."

"The *Ilm?*"

"Yes, the Ilm. You know it – it said you'd spoken to it when you
lived here years ago. Very tall and thin, white skin..."

"I know what the Ilm is!" Peval snapped. He was clearly struggling to keep his temper in check.

"*Fine*," Tulzik said, feigning offense. "Then why sound so surprised?"

Peval took a deep calming breath, then asked, "How did you
ever happen to ask the *Ilm*?"

"One of the stewards on the airship suggested it."

"The Ilm remembered me? It knew I was working for the Sorceress?"

"Well, it knew you were a gene–cutter – that's a magician who
works with living things, yes? I hadn't realized you were a magician,
Peval." Tulzik knew perfectly well what a gene–cutter was, but was
playing the role of a country bumpkin to allay any suspicions. "It
recognized you from a picture I brought."

"A picture? Of me?"

"A drawing. Vika made it."

"Oh."

"At any rate, the Ilm knew that the Sorceress was the best employer for gene-cutters here and told me how to find her workshop."

Peval grimaced. "That's it? That's all it took?"

"Well, yes. Why would it take more?" Tulzik did his best to look puzzled.

Peval considered that for a moment, then said, "And you came after me because...?"

Tulzik straightened in his chair and exclaimed, "Because you debauched my sister and left her lying sick in your bed!" He glanced around to see if anyone had overheard this outburst, then relaxed again and looked Peval in the eye. "Look, I know she threw herself at you, and I don't suppose you had anything to do with her illness, but surely you don't expect us to consider your behavior admirable! No, we want an apology and some assurances as to just what your intentions are and some pretty words I can take back to Vika to let her know you got here safely and didn't die of whatever illness it was. She was worried you might have caught it and wound up lying dead in a ruin somewhere."

"Well, I obviously didn't," Peval said, straightening in his chair in turn. "I'm sorry if I hurt your sister, Tulzik, but she really *did* follow me to Kalidar and climb into my bed uninvited. I'm no ascetic, to refuse a girl in that situation, but I didn't seduce her. I left her asleep because I was in a hurry to get to Ragbaan – I'd gotten word that the Sorceress was hiring, and I wanted to get here before someone else got the job. I didn't know Vika was sick."

Tulzik nodded. "I think your haste was unseemly, but understandable." He sighed. "Are you planning to come back to Emniln? Vika would like to see you, even if it's just to say goodbye properly."

Tulzik could see Peval tense at the suggestion and wondered just what had happened between the two of them in Kalidar.

Peval shook his head. "No, I'm not coming back. I intend no offense, Tulzik, I'm sure you're proud of your home town, but I prefer the city, when there's work to be had for someone with my skills, and right now I have a fine job and I'm expected to be there every day. I can't take the time for a trip to Emniln."

"Then would Vika be welcome, if she came here?"

Peval hesitated. "Tulzik, you're a smart young man, and you know your sister. She's a sweet girl, but...no, I can't say I'd welcome her. If you want to tell her I already have a wife hidden away here, I won't deny it – that might be the easiest way to discourage her even if it *does* make me out a scoundrel."

"*Do* you have a wife here?"

Peval smiled crookedly. "No. I live alone. I've never married."

Something about the tone of his voice made Tulzik doubt that he was speaking the exact truth. He asked, "Where *do* you live? In case Vika wants to see it."

Peval seemed startled by the question, but answered it. "I have a place on the west side of Grand Avenue a little over a mile south of here. But really, Tulzik, think about it – wouldn't it be better for everyone if Vika and I never saw each other again? Because I do *not* intend to marry her, I never did, and anything less is sure to end badly, wouldn't you say? So you tell her whatever lies you like, and I'll agree to them if anyone asks. Tell her I consulted an oracle and was told we mustn't see one another, if you want. We have some excellent oracles here in Ragbaan."

Tulzik remembered Hiji's ghosts. "I'd heard that," he said.

"Tell her...oh, tell her that night was wonderful, but I'm not worthy of her, or that I've joined the Genealogists, and they say our bloodlines mustn't mix. Or that I've joined one of the Star Cults and need to spend a year meditating, or that the Sorceress wants me for her harem – whatever you choose." He smiled his unpleasant lop-sided smile again. "The truth is, Alsia really *might* want me for her harem, and I can't say I'd mind."

"She has a harem?"

Peval smirked most unbecomingly. "Oh, yes. She's famous for it."

Tulzik gazed thoughtfully at Peval for a moment.

He had hoped Peval's nerve would break, and he would say or do something incriminating. He had thought perhaps the assassin – if he truly was one – would agree to come back to Emniln to see whether Vika really *was* still alive, or to learn how his mysterious murder weapon, whatever it might be, had failed. If he could once get Peval to admit that he had thought Vika was dead, he might be able to coax out *why* she had been killed, and who, if anyone, had told Peval to kill her.

Unfortunately, Peval wasn't cooperating. He had not even lost his temper. Tulzik knew he might just be asking the wrong questions, but he could not think of better ones that would not raise suspicions. He needed a new plan, and he needed it quickly.

"Tell you what, Peval," Tulzik said. "Why don't you write Vika a letter full of explanations and apologies? I can take it back with me. Can you do that?" A letter to the dead girl might give a few clues about how she died.

Peval considered that for a moment. "I could, I suppose," he said.

"I think you owe her that much."

Peval frowned.

"I can carry other letters to Zaraquan or Emniln, if there's anyone else you want to send a message to," Tulzik added.

He hoped he wasn't being too obvious. What he really wanted, he had realized while suggesting a letter, was for Peval to send a letter to his superior in the assassination scheme – the Biologist, or whoever it was who had sent him. Then Tulzik could follow that letter and find Dardem Karianthis, and perhaps find out whether he had ordered Vika's death as a test of some kind, or to remove a witness to some crime, or whether perhaps Peval had acted on his own initiative.

"No, thank you," Peval said. "I don't believe I have any more business back west. But all right, I'll write to Vika, if you want."

"I'd appreciate it," Tulzik said, hiding his disappointment. "I think we all would."

"Then I'll do that – tonight or tomorrow. Do you want to carry it, or should I use the regular post?"

"I'll carry the letter for you. That would be faster, wouldn't it?"

Peval shrugged. "The post uses the same airship you would, I think; it *might* be faster than you, if you were planning to stay in the city for a few days."

"No, now that we've had this conversation I'm planning to leave as soon as I can. I don't want to keep Vika or our parents in suspense." He did not want Peval to know he was staying in Ragbaan until he could bring his sister's killer to justice; it wouldn't fit his story. Besides, the sooner a letter got written, the better. Even if it didn't name anyone else in the assassination plot, that letter might give Tulzik a little more information about what had really happened. And if Peval thought Tulzik had left Ragbaan, he would let down his guard. Tulzik might be able to learn something by spying on him.

"You have a ticket?" Peval asked. "You said you have no money."

Tulzik silently cursed himself for letting his lies get too complicated. "I thought I'd pedal for my fare," he said.

"Then you'll have to wait until they need a pair of legs. Perhaps I should use the post after all."

"No, give me the letter, and if I can't get a place on the drive-shaft I'll post it myself. I'll be able to find Vika better than any mail carrier could."

Peval nodded. "I suppose that makes sense," he said. He eyed Tulzik – a little warily, Tulzik thought.

Just then the hostess arrived bearing a tray, and they turned their attention to a splendid meal of batter-fried tazzelfish, buttered brullies and potato slices, and black beer.

At first the meal was largely eaten in awkward silence; there were few things they could safely discuss. Tulzik, in particular, was being very careful to say as little as possible about his trip to Ragbaan, lest he become further entangled in his own lies. About halfway through, though, Tulzik asked Peval about what it was like to work for the Sorceress, hoping to find out whether she was indeed his intended assassination target. After a little coaxing – and another beer – Tulzik got him talking freely.

Peval didn't really *know* yet what it was like to work for the Sorceress; he had only just started and was still learning his job. He had yet to meet his new employer; she was notoriously wary about meeting strangers, for fear of attack of one sort or another. She controlled the supply of slaves in Ragbaan and the surrounding area by virtue of certain trade secrets – her products were more reliably obedient and happy in their servitude than anyone else's, so buyers could be sure that their purchases wouldn't suddenly announce that they wanted to be free. That annoyed some of her would-be competitors; she had been accused of deliberately sabotaging other manufacturers by using viral infections to make their homunculi ask for their freedom.

"I understand Ragbaan doesn't have much of a government," Tulzik said. "Would it really be so terrible if they *did* ask for their freedom?"

Peval looked shocked, though Tulzik thought it might be feigned. "We may not have any official police here, Tulzik, but we aren't *barbarians*. If someone says it's free, then it's free. Holding a slave against his or her will, either human or homunculus – that's a capital offense here, just as much as it is anywhere, and there are plenty of people who will see to it that no one does it."

Tulzik nodded. "I hope I haven't offended," he said. "One does hear stories about how decadent Ragbaan is."

"Lies, in this case. No one here is *that* vile."

Tulzik had to fight down the urge to argue that he was sitting face to face with someone just as vile as a slaver. "Did she really sabotage her competitors, do you suppose?" he asked.

Peval shrugged. "Who knows?" he said. "Many people believed it, certainly, and it *could* be true. If she did, what could anyone do about it? Once a slave asks to be free, it's free – removing the virus won't change that, and besides, who's got the right to remove the virus in the first place, assuming there really *is* a virus? The former slave would have to agree, and the virus itself makes *that* unlikely."

"So there really were slaves that asked for their freedom?"

Peval gulped beer and glared bitterly at Tulzik. "Oh, yes," he said. "Hundreds of them. There was a man called the Biologist a few years back who tried to get into the slave business – not the same way the Sorceress is, making dancers and personal servants and sex toys and the like, but turning out cheap workers, hundreds of them. He wanted to use them to clear and farm land and raise food, to give ordinary people something better than *drash* for the price, but he was just getting started when his homunculi began saying they didn't want to be slaves. He had to let them all go – almost three hundred of them! It ruined him. Then when he tried to start over, he couldn't get the money he needed, because he still owed the Nine Families thousands of *walu*, and the Cooperative objected to the project and got the Antiquarians worried about the whole idea of clearing away ruins, and...well, a good many people made it clear to him that he was no longer welcome in Ragbaan. So he left."

This accorded with what Azl and Hrus had told him about the Biologist, though it was slanted differently and they had not mentioned exactly what went wrong with the Biologist's plans. "You knew this person?"

Peval nodded.

"He left Ragbaan? Where did he go?"

"I don't know *that*," Peval said, but Tulzik noticed he looked away slightly as he spoke, not meeting Tulzik's eyes.

"You think the Sorceress was responsible? That she sabotaged his workers?" If she had, that would certainly explain why the Biologist might have sent an assassin after her. Tulzik still couldn't be sure that the Sorceress was the intended target, or even that Peval really was an assassin and not just a monster, but it did fit the available evidence.

"I don't know," Peval said, stabbing a fork angrily into his half-eaten tazzelfish. "The *Biologist* certainly thought she had, but maybe he just messed it up himself. Building obedience into the genes is tricky, tricky stuff. *I* can't do it." He thrust a forkful of fish into his mouth.

"But the Sorceress can?"

"Apparently. Not one of her creations has asked for its freedom in over a hundred years."

"A hundred years? Is she that old?"

"*Oh*, yes. That's one advantage to learning biological magic, rather than any of the other kinds. She's about three hundred, I hear, and looks as if she's no more than thirty." His tone was undisguisedly bitter. "That's *another* thing she keeps secret. So does the Biologist. I don't know how they do it."

"The Biologist knows how to stay young, too?"

"So they say. He's not as old as the Sorceress, but he's been around since before I was born. He doesn't show it off the way she does, though."

"You said you might wind up in her harem, but it doesn't sound as if you *like* her much," Tulzik ventured.

"I don't... I mean, I've never met her."

"But you took a job with her?"

"I'm a gene-cutter. There are only so many places for someone like me to work."

"Couldn't you work on food crops or livestock?"

"I want to make homunculi," Peval said, in a tone that brooked no argument. "It's challenging work. And the Sorceress pays well – since most of her products are one of a kind, she needs a lot of gene-cutters, and she needs the best, so she *pays* the best. Which is why slaves are so expensive in Ragbaan." He took another bite of fish. "You might think that she wouldn't see someone making cheap, stupid, ugly workers as competition, mightn't you? But the theory is that her slaves are *so* expensive, she was afraid people who wanted playthings would try to use the Biologist's workers instead, because even if they killed a few trying to make them prettier or better behaved, it would still be cheaper than buying from the Sorceress."

"The theory, you call it? Then you don't think it's true?"

"Oh, who knows?" He flung his fork across the table; it rattled to the floor. "Maybe she sabotaged them, maybe she didn't – I used to think she did, that the Biologist couldn't have botched his work that badly, but now I'm not sure." He picked up a napkin to wipe his mouth. "It doesn't matter whether she did or not."

That was interesting, in a way, Tulzik thought as he stooped to retrieve the fork. If Peval had been sent to kill the Sorceress to retaliate for her sabotage of the Biologist's plans, didn't it matter whether she had, in fact, sabotaged them? Didn't he want some moral justification for the killing?

Perhaps the only justification that mattered to him was whatever reward Dardem Karianthis had promised him – or perhaps he no longer intended to kill Alsia. Perhaps he no longer thought he *could* kill her – what if he had tested his intended murder weapon on Vika and now believed it hadn't worked? Maybe that was why he now thought the Biologist *might* have botched the obedience spells – because he had apparently botched whatever had killed Vika.

Vika had not had a mark on her. Tulzik and Urushak had known she was murdered because a healthy teenager does not simply die, and there was no evidence of suicide, but if a woman three hundred years old, one who had magically tampered with her own lifespan, were to turn up similarly deceased, it might well be attributed to natural causes. Such a weapon would be ideal for the Biologist's revenge – and now, because Tulzik had lied, Peval thought it hadn't worked.

But surely there was some other way to kill the Sorceress, even without this mysterious weapon; after all, even if she had modified herself and lived three centuries, she was still mortal. Could he not merely change his plans slightly and carry out his attack by some other method?

"You said the Sorceress is wary of strangers," he said as he set the fork back on the table. "She lives in fear of assassins?"

"So I've heard. I told you, I've never met her." Peval slumped forward, his elbows on the table.

"Perhaps her fear is justified, if she has been sabotaging her competitors," Tulzik said.

"It may well be, yes. If she *is* sabotaging them, and they aren't blaming her for their own failures."

"If they blame her, then as you say, the truth may not matter."

Peval finished his beer with one long swig, then set down the mug. "Indeed," he said.

"I'm surprised she hasn't been assassinated, then."

Peval eyed him for a moment. "You think Ragbaan is full of assassins, do you? To accompany our slave-holding barbarians?"

Tulzik realized he might have gone too far. "No, no! That's not what I meant. But surely, if this woman has been taking extreme measures to undercut her competition, the competition would take extreme measures in return. Not assassination, perhaps – I spoke hastily – but something? As I said, I have heard that Ragbaan is a place where...well, where things are not tightly controlled."

Peval snorted. "Oh, *some* things are tightly controlled, but it's the likes of Alsia ter Bithuni doing the controlling. Haven't I just said how completely she controls slave production? I've scarcely worked a day in her employ, but already I feel as if she controls *me*. Her workers go where she tells them when she tells them, wear what she tells them, carry what she tells them – what she tells *us*, I should say. You ask why she hasn't been assassinated – well, some have tried, believe me. No, the streets of Ragbaan aren't awash in assassins, but there are a few in the city – but fewer than there would be if some hadn't tried to remove our dear Sorceress. None has ever survived the attempt, so far as we know. She has old, old magic protecting her. I don't know what all of it is, but I've heard stories. And not just *tek*, but other precautions. It's common knowledge that no one is permitted into her presence bearing anything but his own flesh – her guests, even her paying customers, must strip naked before approaching her and speak with her as bare as the day they were born, lest they carry concealed weapons. Her doctors cleanse all visitors of disease, lest she be infected or contaminated – an audience with her at least ensures one's own health, as well as hers! Her famous harem also serves as her guards; if anyone tried to harm her with bare hands, all weapons having been removed, half a dozen strong handsome men would defend her. There are said to be other, hidden defenses, as well. Naturally, she does not trumpet the details abroad; why tell enemies what they must defeat? But in my lifetime four attempts on her life have been reported, and in each case the perpetrator perished in the attempt."

"Do you think they *really* tried to assassinate her?" Tulzik asked. "What sort of fool would do that, if she's as crafty as you say? Maybe those four were just people she wanted dead for other reasons, and she *said* they were assassins to justify murdering them."

Peval stared at him for a moment.

"Maybe," he said at last. Then he sat back and beckoned to the hostess. "I've eaten my fill, Tulzik. I'm going home to write that letter to Vika and perhaps an apology to your parents. Shall we meet outside the Red Museum tomorrow evening at sunset, and I'll give them to you?"

"If it's not too much trouble, could we meet at the airship port, instead?" He still had hopes of intercepting a letter to the Biologist, even though Peval denied any plans to write one. If he could get Peval to the port the man might post that theoretical letter there at the same time, to save himself a trip. Then it would just be a matter of getting it away from the mail carriers.

Not that that would necessarily be easy; mail carriers did not readily yield up their charges. Still, it should be possible.

"Then you're leaving Ragbaan?"

"As soon as I have the letter, yes. I don't want my family to worry."

"Of course." He nodded. "We'll meet at the pier – you're taking the four o'clock airship to Zaraquan?"

Tulzik had no idea what the airship schedules were like, or even where the airship to Zaraquan docked, but he could scarcely admit that. "That's my intention, yes."

"I'll need to take a little time off work, but I think I can manage it. If I don't make it, well, then I couldn't manage it, and I'll send the letters by post. Good enough?"

"Good enough," Tulzik said, though he had no intention of leaving the city without those letters. If Peval did not meet him at the dock he would instead be waiting outside the Red Museum after work, with a story about missing his flight.

He had no intention of leaving Ragbaan even *with* the letters – not while Peval was here and alive. Not unless there was something in the letters that made it more urgent to go after Peval's exiled employer. After all, it was Peval who had actually killed Vika, and who most definitely had to pay for it.

The hostess arrived, and Tulzik watched as Peval settled the bill. He remained seated at the table as Peval rose, said farewell, and left the restaurant.

Then he set about eating every bit of the remaining food on both plates; after all, Tulzik had no idea when or where he would eat again.

CHAPTER 14

Tulzik knocked firmly on the gilded door, determined not to show how nervous he was about his position. Then he stood and waited, glancing idly along the dim corridor, back toward the stairs. His last four *jit* were clutched in one hand.

It was late enough in the evening that it seemed reasonable to find Azl and Hrus at home, but early enough that he didn't expect to wake them. They hadn't been at their customary place in the north arcade at this hour; the arcade had been almost deserted, with only a handful of rather desperate-looking tradespeople still manning tables, calling out their services to Tulzik as he passed through.

The Great Hall had been largely empty of life, as well, though the sounds of music and laughter and clinking glass had come from the far end, where Tulzik had glimpsed dancing women under colored teklights. Whether it was an impromptu party or a permanent nightclub he could not tell, and he made no effort to investigate further, as he had more urgent business.

He turned his attention back to the door at the sound of the latch and got ready to thrust his foot in, to prevent anyone from slamming it in his face.

The door opened, and Azl stood there in a maroon robe, holding something that gleamed silver in one hand – a weapon, probably. She was pointing it at his belly. Tulzik raised his hands – but he also shoved his foot forward.

"I'd like to buy an answer," he said. "A very simple one. I can pay four *jit*." He waved the fist that held his last few coins.

"We're closed for the night," she said. "Come back in the morning, downstairs."

"I'd also like to tell you a few things, if I might, and I'd rather do it privately."

Azl considered this for a moment.

"Oh, let the boy in," Hrus called from somewhere behind her.

Grudgingly, Azl stepped aside – though she kept the weapon, if that was what it was, trained on Tulzik's belly. "You heard him," she said.

Tulzik stepped in, keeping his hands up.

The suite was just as he remembered it, awash in books and papers and *tek* paraphernalia. Hrus was looking at Tulzik from one of the big desks in the center, a fabric-bound book in his hand and that mysterious furry creature curled up on his lap.

"What's the question?" Hrus asked, as Azl closed the door behind Tulzik.

"Where does the four o'clock airship to Zaraquan board passengers?" Tulzik said, hands still raised.

Hrus stared at him silently for a moment as Azl locked the door and turned to keep her weapon trained on Tulzik.

"Azl?" Hrus said at last.

"You could have asked any stranger on the street that," she said. "You don't need to pay four *jit* for it."

"I came here to buy that answer," Tulzik said. He lowered his fist. "Here's the money." He opened his hand to reveal the four tiny coins.

"That's absurd," Azl said. "What do you *really* want here?"

Tulzik threw her a glance, then looked back to Hrus.

"Eighth Street Pier, above the candy factory," Hrus said. "Turn right as you come out of the Imperial Palace, then right again at the statue of Emperor Kazur the Third, and up the hill past the Temple of Forgotten Glory – that's the one with the dark blue dome and the big stone feet on either side of the steps. Then take one last right up the Cauldron Steps, go straight for a block at the top, and at the fork bear left. You'll be looking right at the pier and can find your way from there by eye."

"Thank you," Tulzik said. "If you could write that down for me, I'd be grateful."

"Azl, take his four *jit* – it'll pay for the paper." He thumped his book down on the desk and reached for a scrap of paper.

Azl held out her free hand, keeping the weapon trained, and Tulzik gave her the coins. She glowered at him, but said nothing while her husband scribbled his note.

Then Hrus pushed the furry thing off his lap and stood up, note in hand. "You aren't flying to Zaraquan," he said.

"Of course not," Tulzik said. "Not while my sister's killer is walking free here in Ragbaan."

"And not when you've just handed my wife your last *jit*. Which is, I assume, why you did it." He handed Tulzik the paper; Tulzik tucked it away.

"Yes."

"As for Peval Salinzi, the Guild says he's been in Ragbaan all along," Hrus said.

"Peval is a gene–cutter. The Ilm says he could easily have made a doppelganger of himself. The doppelganger would be childlike, unable to do anything as complex as an assassination, but it would be good enough to convince the Guild that Peval never left the city."

"Very good." Hrus nodded. "Do you have any evidence that Peval *did* create such a thing?"

"No," Tulzik admitted. "Not yet. I know that Peval says he lives on the west side of the Grand Avenue about a mile and a half south of here, but I don't have an exact description and haven't had time to see whether he has a homunculus of himself living there."

Hrus nodded. "Nicely done, learning that."

"He's just recently been hired by the Sorceress, who Dardem Karianthis wants dead because he believes that Alsia ter Bithuni sabotaged three hundred of his cheap slaves intended for agricultural work. Peval spoke of joining the Sorceress's harem – I assume so that he can get close enough to kill her."

"Good. How did you manage to speak to him?"

"I told him Vika was still alive, but angry that he had abandoned her, and that I was here to speak to him on her behalf. He took me to dinner to discuss his intentions toward her."

"Hrus, this is absurd!" Azl said angrily.

Hrus smiled at his wife. "Actually, I think that's rather clever, saying his sister is still alive. Assuming that anything he says is true."

"The Guild says it isn't!"

"The Guild has been wrong before."

"Not often."

"Admittedly, not often," Hrus said, "but I think this may be one of those rare occasions. If we assume, for the sake of argument, that it is, and Tulzik is telling the truth, then it does all fit together."

"But why is he *here*, in our apartment, then? That part doesn't make any sense! And what's this about the airship to Zaraquan?"

"Ask him," Hrus said, his eyes once again fixed on Tulzik.

Azl had been glaring at her husband; now her gaze, suddenly uncertain, turned to Tulzik. The weapon was no longer aimed at his belly, but had been allowed to droop.

"*I* don't charge for answers," Tulzik said, smiling. He was fairly sure he had Hrus convinced.

Azl hesitated, then said, "No, I see – you want Peval to *think* you're taking the airship and going home. But you aren't."

"That's right."

"You told him you had come here by airship? That's why you couldn't ask *him* for directions. Why? Why not admit you followed him across the crater?"

"You can see that one," Hrus said.

Azl threw him a glance, then looked back at Tulzik. "Oh – yes. Because then you'd know *he* came across the crater, and that would be suspicious. Assuming, of course, that your original story is true. But you could have asked a stranger in the street, or perhaps the Ilm."

"The Ilm might find it amusing to misdirect me," Tulzik said, "and a stranger might not know – how many people travel between Ragbaan and Zaraquan? I might need to ask several, and the odds of word getting back to Peval increase with each one."

"But they stay very small," Azl said thoughtfully. "That's not the real reason. No, you wanted to talk to us and tell us what you claim you'd found out, and the airship was an excuse."

"Well, both," Tulzik said.

"But it could still all be lies."

"I suppose it could be. It isn't. I had hoped I could convince you of that."

"We don't want to disturb the Guild," Hrus said.

"Of course," Tulzik said. "But I assume you don't want the Biologist's agent to assassinate anyone, either."

"That implies that Dardem really *did* send an assassin. That's not proven," Hrus said.

"If he did," Azl added, "we don't know whether it's you or Peval or someone else entirely. Nor who the intended target is."

"Well, I have my own opinion, of course," Tulzik said, "but I'm well aware that you might think I'm lying or that my memory has been revised."

"You think that Peval Salinzi has remained loyal to the Biologist and followed him into exile after creating a doppelganger so his absence wouldn't be noticed. You think that Dardem Karianthis then equipped him with a weapon that he can somehow get past all her defenses and use to kill the Sorceress," Azl said. "He tested that weapon out on your sister, slipped back into Ragbaan on foot so no one would realize he'd been gone and got a job working for the Sorceress with the intention of being invited into her harem, which would give him the chance to use the weapon on her. If it works, I suppose he and Dardem plan to take over the slave trade here."

"Yes," Tulzik said. "Except that...you're quick. Had anyone mentioned the idea that he tested it out on Vika? I only thought of that tonight."

Hrus did not answer the question directly, but said, "If he thinks your sister is still alive, then he must think the weapon didn't work, that the test was a failure."

"If it *was* a test and not just removing a witness," Tulzik said.

"What could she have been a witness to?" Azl asked.

"He might have told her where he was going. But he said he didn't; he asked how I knew he had come to Ragbaan."

"A test," Hrus said. "If any of this is true that seems the most likely explanation for her murder."

"Or simple sadism," Azl suggested.

"Or possibly even an accident, if the weapon were used inadvertently," Tulzik said. "But a test seems most likely." He hated speaking so coldly of his sister's death, but he knew cool logic would be more effective on these two than any show of emotion.

"Assuming any of this is true," Hrus said. "Perhaps this is all an elaborate cover story, and you're desperately trying to convince us so that we will believe it was all an accident, or legitimate revenge, when you kill Peval tomorrow at the airship dock."

Tulzik started to reply, then stopped.

His hosts waited politely while he gathered his wits; at last he said, "I am not going to kill Peval Salinzi tomorrow, unless something goes very wrong, and I'm forced to act in self-defense. Right now, I don't think there's *any* way I can kill him without convincing you and the Guild that it means I was the assassin all along. Even if we found his doppelganger, it might not satisfy you."

"Oh, I might give you the benefit of the doubt," Hrus said. "The Guild wouldn't."

"And they don't like outsiders meddling in Ragbaan's affairs," Tulzik said.

"No, they don't," Hrus agreed.

"Besides," Tulzik said, letting just a little of his rage show, "if it *was* a test of this weapon the Biologist gave him, then Dardem Karianthis probably ordered it, and in that case I want *him* dead, as well." His hands clenched into fists as he spoke.

"I don't think the Guild would have any objection, should you manage to kill the Biologist," Azl said. "Are you hoping Peval will go back to Dardem to tell him the weapon failed, and you can follow along?" She answered herself before Tulzik could. "No, that's not it – you don't have the fare. Peval would have to give up his job if he left the city, which would ruin any chance of getting at the Sorceress. A letter, then? There are no magical links outside the city, but the mail system works fine. You think he's going to send Dardem a letter?"

"I suggested he write Vika a letter, to give him the idea," Tulzik said. "I'm supposed to be meeting him so that I can take the letter to her."

"So you plan to intercept the letter to Dardem?" Azl asked. "How?"

"That's part of why he's *here*, Azl," Hrus said. "He wanted us to consider the doppelganger theory, but more than that, he wants us to intercept the letter, to show us who the real assassin is. Not to mention that we're more likely to be able to do it, since Peval doesn't know us."

"It won't be enough to convince the Guild," Azl said. "They'll say it's a forgery. Once they decide on a position they don't like to change their minds."

"I wasn't just concerned with *convincing* you," Tulzik said.

"Oh?" Hrus said.

"I was hoping you could help me forge a substitute letter and lure the Biologist to Ragbaan."

"He's forbidden to come here," Azl said, in the slightly bored tone of a teacher repeating an oft-cited rule.

"Exactly," Tulzik said.

"Oh, *very* nice," Hrus said.

Azl took a moment to consider before saying slowly, "You want the Guild to kill him *for* you."

"If he ordered Peval to kill Vika, then yes. I do."

"You don't insist on delivering the fatal blow yourself?" Hrus asked.

"Dead is dead," Tulzik replied.

"Well, no, it isn't always," Azl said. "You saw Hiji's ghosts. We have a lot of things like that in Ragbaan."

"It will be *this* time," Tulzik said, "if I have anything to say about it."

"He may not write a letter," Hrus said.

"And the Biologist may not come, and the Guild may not co-operate by killing him, and any number of other things might go wrong," Tulzik acknowledged. "Or I might be lying about everything and have some other scheme in mind that you can't begin to guess."

"Killing the Biologist is all very well," Azl said, "but that would leave Peval alive."

"I know," Tulzik said. "I'm still working on that. But at least I'm doing *something* to avenge Vika."

"There's another problem with your plan," Hrus said.

"Oh?"

"You want us to intercept Peval's letter to Dardem. I have no intention of doing that."

Tulzik stared at him for a moment, then turned to Azl, who shrugged. "To be honest," she said, "I don't quite know how we would go *about* intercepting such a letter. The postal system is *designed* to make it difficult to tamper – an airship purser or stationmaster who doesn't keep a close eye on the mail is risking his job."

Tulzik frowned.

"All right," he said, "but if *I* get the letter, will you help me forge a replacement?"

"I think we could attempt that," Azl said, with a glance at her husband.

"Also, would you know of any way I could get aboard the airship briefly without paying the fare? I don't want to *stay* on board."

"You're asking too many questions without paying us for the answers," Azl complained.

"I think we might arrange something, though," Hrus said.

"Maybe we could trade our answers for yours," Azl said. "For example, do you have any idea just how Peval plans to get past the Sorceress's defenses? Assuming, for the sake of argument, that everything you've said is true, and he really does intend to assassinate her."

"No," Tulzik admitted, "but he works for someone called the Biologist, so I would assume there's gene-cutting involved somewhere."

"Azl, you should have this one figured out," Hrus said.

Azl turned to glare at her husband. "She has everyone she sees cleaned of bacteria and viruses, and she's made herself immune to every disease ever invented!"

"Then it's not a virus or any sort of disease."

"Well, he can't carry *anything* foreign on his skin or inside his body through her defenses! She scans and irradiates everyone."

"Azl..."

"Oh," Azl said, before Hrus could say anything more. She blinked.

"He doesn't just want to *talk* to her," Hrus said.

"He wants to join her harem," Azl said. "Of course. Yes, he *would* want to test that, wouldn't he? He probably seduced Tulzik's sister deliberately, precisely to test it." She frowned. "Do you really think that will get past her protections?"

It was at that point that Tulzik's own thoughts caught up with his hosts. "His semen?"

"Where else can he hide his weapon?" Azl said. "Foreign genes that Alsia will permit directly into her body – what else could it be? I wonder how the poison works."

"It's clearly something subtle enough that the Biologist thinks it will get past her defenses," Hrus said.

"We could just warn her," Tulzik said.

"Why would we want to do that?" Azl asked. "*I* wouldn't mind if someone got to her." Then she looked at Tulzik. "Of course, the Guild might object, and they might blame you. The poison probably doesn't work immediately – Peval would want to get away alive. Another reason to have tested it on your sister."

"We *should* warn her," Tulzik said.

"It would be the humane thing to do," Hrus agreed.

"She probably won't believe us," Azl said.

"She'll kill Peval, though," Hrus said. "Just to be sure. And she might well kill the messenger, too."

Tulzik frowned. "She might?"

"Think about it, Tulzik," Azl said. "This is a woman so cautious that she won't allow anyone into her presence until he's been stripped naked, searched, scanned, and irradiated. If she finds out that two sides are accusing each other of trying to kill her, she'll just exterminate them both, to save herself the trouble of figuring out who's telling the truth."

"So if I warn her, she'll kill me? What sort of gratitude is that?"

"Gratitude is not an attribute Alsia is known to possess," Hrus said dryly.

"But if I don't warn her, and Peval does kill her, the *Guild* will kill me in retaliation."

"Possibly, yes. If he covers his tracks well enough."

"If I kill *Peval*, the Guild will kill me."

"Possibly. Or the Sorceress might – after all, Peval is one of her employees."

Tulzik shook his head in disgust. "Maybe I should just go home after all – but I *can't*. He killed my sister!"

Hrus spread empty hands. "No one said vengeance was easy."

"You might get the Guild to kill Dardem Karianthis for you," Azl said. "That's a start."

"Maybe I can get them to kill Peval, too," Tulzik said.

"Or get someone to, at any rate," Hrus said. "It wouldn't need to be the Guild, so long as it demonstrably wasn't *you*."

"That's true," Tulzik said thoughtfully.

For a moment no one spoke; then Azl said, "It's late, and we still don't trust you." She glanced at Hrus. "At least, *I* don't. You can't afford any more questions, and I don't have anything else to tell you for free. I'd say it's time for you to go and find a place to sleep, so you can meet Peval tomorrow and steal his letter, if that's really what you're planning."

Tulzik had hoped that he would be invited to stay, that he had convinced Azl and Hrus to trust him again, but he was not surprised that Azl was turning him away. He was disappointed by it, but not surprised.

What surprised him was *how* disappointed he was. He had really hoped they would accept him back, and that they had not was like a blow. "Yes," he said, trying to hide his hurt. "All right."

He turned and allowed Azl to herd him out the door.

CHAPTER 15

Tulzik waited on the dock, in the shadow of the looming airship, for over an hour. He talked to various people, passengers and crew and groundlings alike, and did everything he thought he would have done, had he really been booking passage, that did not involve boarding the craft, signing any contracts, or paying anyone. He kept his pack on his shoulder or close by at all times. He told several people he intended to work his way to Zaraquan and chatted idly about the trip, while always keeping a careful eye out, watching every arrival. Finally, he glimpsed Peval coming up the street past the candy factory, whereupon he stepped out of the shade into the sun and waved.

Peval waved in return, and a moment later he stepped up on the dock with a letter in his hand and made his way through the crowd.

Tulzik had been standing by a rail; now he pushed his own way through the throng, back toward the stairs. His eyes were fixed on the letter. It was folded, rather than in an envelope, and not sealed. Peval held it out to Tulzik when the two were a few feet apart.

"I thought you might want to read it," he said.

"No," Tulzik answered. "It's none of my business. It's for Vika."

"Of course," Peval said. "I just thought you might want to reassure yourself that I'm not trying to lure her to Ragbaan with promises of undying love."

"Ah," Tulzik said. "I might, at that." He accepted the paper and glanced at it.

VIKA AMBROZ was written on it, but no address. The sight of his sister's name made Tulzik's throat tighten. "I'll read it later," he said.

"As you please," Peval said. "I don't know how well you can read while you're pedaling, though. You *are* pedaling? They have a space on the shaft?"

"That's *my* problem," Tulzik snapped. "Don't worry about it."

"You want the letter to get there quickly, don't you? On this run? If you're waiting for another airship – "

"I'll manage," Tulzik interrupted.

"I'm posting another letter anyway," Peval said. Tulzik's heart jumped. "To an old friend. If you give me Vika's address I can seal this one up and send them both."

"I'll take care of it," Tulzik insisted, trying not to grin. "I want to be able to tell Vika that I found you and got you to write and not have any doubt I'm telling the truth. Posted letters go astray sometimes."

Peval eyed him uncertainly. "You'll give it to her unaltered? No editing, to make me look like a scoundrel?"

"I don't think I need to make you look like any more of a scoundrel than you really are," Tulzik retorted. "If I did, it would only hurt her, and why would I do that? Besides, forgery is not a skill I've mastered. I'm sure she can tell my handwriting from yours."

Peval hesitated, then nodded. "As you please. I do wish her well."

"If your other letter is going to Emniln, I could take that for you, as well, and save you the postage fee."

"It's not," Peval said. "I'll give it to the purser."

"Whatever suits you," Tulzik said with a shrug. "She's over there."

He had not wasted the long wait before Peval's arrival; he had met a few of the airship's crew and had others pointed out to him. The woman he indicated was indeed the ship's purser. Peval gave Tulzik a glance, then began making his way through the crowd to the purser's station by the lift, where passengers and their luggage were being hoisted aboard. Tulzik followed.

A moment later Peval was handing the letter and two *fing* to the purser; Tulzik leaned forward and said, "Peval, you're sure your friend is still there? That he hasn't changed address?"

Startled and annoyed, Peval turned and said, "Of course he is!"

Tulzik threw up his hands. "All right, all right, I merely asked! It has been some time since you spoke to him, hasn't it?"

"What if it has? It's none of your business! You have the letter for your sister. This other doesn't concern you."

"Yes, I do have the letter for Vika," Tulzik said, glancing down at the folded paper he still held. "Thank you, again. This really will help to smooth matters at home."

Peval calmed. "Well... I did treat her poorly, I admit."

The purser listened politely, then said, "You're sure of the address?"

"Yes, I am," Peval told her. "Don't pay any attention to Tulzik." He glanced again at the letter the purser held, though, before turning away.

Tulzik followed him to the edge of the dock, but when Peval began descending the stairs to the street Tulzik stopped.

"Goodbye, Peval," he said.

Peval waved a farewell, but did not bother to speak again.

Tulzik watched him go, then turned and waited a moment longer, watching the thinning crowd.

Most of the passengers and crew were aboard now, and the ground crew was starting to adjust the moorings, while those who had come to see friends or family off were scattering. The purser was starting to tidy up.

Tulzik took a deep breath, then ran across the dock panting and grabbed at the purser's sleeve as she folded up her table and turned toward the lift.

"Wait!" he said.

"What?" She turned, startled.

"That letter – you haven't put it in the sealed box yet, have you? The address *is* wrong!"

She glanced down at the folio that held many of the airship's papers and half a dozen outgoing letters.

"Well, *look* at it!"

Annoyed, the purser set down her folded table and opened the portfolio. She fished out three of the letters, then pulled out one. "Is this it?" she asked, holding it out for Tulzik to inspect.

"Yes, that's it," he said, reading the address. Dillum Kardris, Room Four, Orrister's Lodgings, Old Potter Street, Berez – he quickly committed it to memory, in case he could not get her to give him the letter and he found reason to visit Dardem Karianthis, for he was quite sure that that was who was using the name "Dillum Kardris."

"It looks fine to me," she said.

"But it's nonsense," Tulzik insisted. "They tore down Orrister's Lodgings over a year ago!"

"Did they?"

"Of course! It was something of a scandal; Selder's brother Russun hadn't agreed to it, and the money to build the new inn went missing – you hadn't heard? I don't know what Peval was thinking, he *must* have been told."

"I'm not familiar with Berez," the purser said. "It's not on our route."

"Well, if you'd been there, you'd have heard about it. Selder's widow was furious with Russun and threatened to have him exiled if he didn't give back the construction money, but he insisted he hadn't taken it..."

She silenced him with an upraised hand, which was just as well, as Tulzik was unsure how much longer he could elaborate this hasty fiction without losing the thread of the story or contradicting himself. "Fine," she said. "I'll take your word for it. I told you, I don't know Berez, and I never heard of any of these people, or this Orrister's Lodging. So the address is wrong; what do you want me to do about it?"

"I'm not sure," Tulzik said. "I doubt anyone there would know where Dillum's gone to; he doesn't like to stay in one place. He's probably not anywhere near Berez anymore; he could be anywhere from Kalidar to Kanguen. We'll need to ask his niece. Do you know Sherreh ak–Tobin, in Emniln?"

"No."

Tulzik frowned. "Well, I don't know what to do, then. You can't deliver it."

"I wasn't going to deliver it personally in any case," she said. "That's not my route. I was going to turn it over to the stationmaster in Zaraquan and let *him* deal with it."

"But then it'll just sit there – I'm sure *he* knows that Orrister's is gone!"

She shrugged, as a bell chimed overhead. "I need to get aboard."

"Oh, but...oh, just give me the letter, and we'll figure out what to do and send it on the next airship."

"I don't..."

"You can keep one *fing* for your trouble, of course."

She hesitated, then looked down at the letter. She frowned. She had seen Peval and Tulzik talking like old friends and had no reason to distrust either of them. "Of course," she said. "That seems fair." She handed him the letter and dug out a coin.

Five minutes later the lift and the purser were aboard the airship, which began to rise as the ground crew cast off the dozen lines that had held it down. The propellers were starting to turn.

Tulzik was watching from the ground, with both Peval's letters in one hand, and a fat silver *fing* in the other. He felt quite pleased with himself; not only had he managed to filch the letter, but he had a little money again.

He waited until the airship had turned west and vanished over the ridge, then climbed down from the dock and headed toward the Imperial Palace, humming quietly to himself.

CHAPTER 16

Hrus read the letter with interest. "It would seem that we guessed right," he said.

"Oh?" Tulzik said. "It appeared to me that while it doesn't contradict anything we had theorized, it's distressingly vague."

"Well, of course," Hrus said, handing the paper back. "You can hardly expect him to confess to murder in a letter that might be intercepted. It fits very neatly, though, and I accept it as significant corroboration."

Tulzik glanced down at it again.

"Dillum – " it read, in Rogau, "I conducted an experiment on the way here, as we discussed, and it seems the results were not what we anticipated. I am reliably informed that there was no permanent effect. As I'm sure you'll understand, I am not about to carry out your wishes unless I know that the device provided will perform as intended. For now, I am employed as you suggested and awaiting further counsel."

It was signed "P.S."

"*I* already *knew* he was a murderer," Tulzik said, "but I can't see that this will convince the Guild of anything. There are too many innocent explanations. I'm just glad it seems to convince *you*."

"Oh, I'm still keeping an open mind," Hrus assured him. "You might well have written this yourself. After all, I don't know Peval Salinzi's handwriting, and even if I did, you might well be a master forger. But that seems less likely than the idea that you're telling the truth as you know it."

"There's no point in reassuring you again that I am indeed telling the truth," Tulzik said. "Nonetheless, it's becoming a habit, so I'll say it. I'm telling the truth. Peval Salinzi killed my sister to test some abominable weapon the Biologist provided for him, a weapon intended to kill the Sorceress. This letter sets *my* doubts to rest, but

I know my circumstances are rather special, since I believe my own memory."

"Memories can be forged almost as easily as letters," Azl grumbled.

"But they usually aren't," Tulzik said, smiling at her. "If mine *are* forged, someone did an extraordinarily good job. I've been thinking back, ever since the notion was first suggested, and I haven't found any gaps or other oddities at all."

"So you are convinced of your own veracity," Hrus said. "Most of us are, I think. And now you have this letter. What are you planning to do about it?"

"I have the Biologist's address and the name he's using," Tulzik said, looking at the letter. "I could just go find him and try to kill him for what he did. He may be a magician, but I'd have the element of surprise." He looked up. "But that wouldn't help me get Peval, or convince the Guild of anything. I think I'll stick with my original plan and send the Biologist a somewhat different note."

"You can simply alter this one," Hrus suggested. "There's room for another line between the text and the signature."

Tulzik looked down at the paper. "You'd need to match the handwriting exactly."

"That isn't impossible."

"'Awaiting further counsel,'" he read. "Maybe add, 'Please meet me at slaughterhouse on the first of the month to confer.'"

"That would seem reasonable."

"What slaughterhouse?" Azl asked. "What makes you think Dardem Karianthis would know which slaughterhouse you mean?"

"There isn't room to fit directions," Tulzik said, rather irked. "I wanted someplace where there wouldn't ordinarily be any people around. There was a slaughterhouse out by the crater – I passed it on the way into the city, so I'm fairly sure Peval must have seen it. I don't know the city very well; do you have some better place to suggest?"

"Several," Azl said.

"That would be a reasonable place for a secret meeting with an exile?"

Azl considered that for a long moment, as Hrus watched in amusement. "Perhaps not," she grudgingly admitted. "Getting to most of them unseen might be difficult. But I still don't know this slaughterhouse you mention. You may know that Peval is familiar with it, but does that mean the Biologist is?"

"I certainly hope so," Tulzik said. "It's the first thing anyone who comes across the crater will see. Anyone who's come into Ragbaan by that route would know it."

"But the Biologist *hasn't* come into Ragbaan from across the crater," Azl said.

"But surely, he's researched the available routes," Hrus said. "I think, my dear, that Tulzik has a point on this. And if not, if he's wrong, what has he lost?"

"The element of surprise," Azl pointed out. "Dardem will know it wasn't Peval who sent the letter."

"Oh, not at all," Hrus said. "Not if the forgery is good. More likely he'll simply write back to ask which slaughterhouse Peval has in mind."

"Are there many slaughterhouses in Ragbaan?" Tulzik asked.

"Several, I'm sure," Hrus said.

"The one I had in mind wasn't built by humans."

"Oh?" Hrus smiled. "Then by whom? Monkeyboys?"

"The Ilm?" Azl suggested, mockingly.

"*I* don't know," Tulzik said. "Whatever built that whole area near the crater."

Hrus' smile vanished. "The *tsaughth*?"

"What?"

"The *tsaughth*. They conquered and ruled the city a couple of millennia back. They built themselves an enclave on the west side of the ridge."

"That might be the ones," Tulzik said. "They ruled the city? What happened to them?"

"What do you mean?" Azl asked.

"Well, they aren't here now, are they? Was there an uprising that overthrew them?"

"No," Hrus said. "They simply died out. I'm not sure anyone knows why."

"Well, if they're the ones I mean, they built a slaughterhouse, in a place called Slaughterhouse Pass, right at the crater's edge," Tulzik said.

"Then perhaps we should specify," Hrus suggested. "'Please meet me on the first of the month at the *tsaughth* slaughterhouse beside the crater to confer.'"

"If you think so," Tulzik replied.

"I will certainly concede that a *tsaughth* slaughterhouse would be distinctive."

"So this will get the Biologist to the slaughterhouse on the first of the month," Azl said. "What about Peval?"

Hrus and Tulzik exchanged glances.

"He won't know he's supposed to be there," Tulzik said. "We'll have to deal with him later, after we've shown the Guild that the Biologist is behind it all."

"Dardem may send a reply confirming the meeting," Hrus pointed out.

Tulzik blinked. "Could we intercept that?"

"Unless you want to spend the next several days trying to catch every letter coming in from the west and have some way of doing that without being noticed by the mail carriers, I don't think so," Hrus said. "I don't quite know how you intercepted *this* letter."

Tulzik did not explain. He considered and decided that no, he could not reasonably hope to intercept a letter to Peval. But he didn't need to. Getting the Biologist to the slaughterhouse, inside the city limits, would be enough. He could send messages to the Guild and the Sorceress, telling them that Dardem would be there.

But what if he didn't come? What if he instead asked Peval to meet him somewhere outside the city, where he would not be violating the terms of his exile?

"How much space is there on that letter?" he asked.

Hrus cocked his head. "Why?"

"Could we fit something about being unable to go any farther than the slaughterhouse? Perhaps that his employer has forbidden him to leave the city, that as a new employee he's being watched?"

Hrus stroked his chin and studied the unfolded piece of paper. "Perhaps a postscript?" He frowned. "I'm sure something can be arranged."

"You might also specify a time of day for this imaginary meeting," Azl said.

"Afternoon should be specific enough, I would think," Hrus said, without looking up.

"We don't want to be *too* specific," Tulzik said. "Not when he was so carefully vague with the rest of the letter."

"Hmm." Hrus stared at the letter.

Silence fell over the room. Tulzik had thought Hrus was going to speak, but he said nothing, he simply continued to stare at the missive he held.

After a moment Azl said, "Well, that's it, then. You've gotten him interested."

"What?" Tulzik turned to her.

"He's gotten interested. You've set him a challenge, and he won't be satisfied until he's met it. He probably won't hear a word we say until he's worked out the exact phrasing and just where on the page each letter will fit."

"Oh, I'll hear you," Hrus said, without lifting his gaze from the letter. "I just won't pay any attention."

"There, you see?" Azl said. "He'll work it out, he'll talk to the *kaua*, he'll skip dinner and stay up all night matching the ink and handwriting, and some time tomorrow you'll have a letter you would swear was all written by a single hand, ready to be mailed. And I'll sleep alone tonight, which was not what I had planned."

"Oh," Tulzik said.

"So with any luck, Dardem Karianthis will be at this famous slaughterhouse on the first of the month, in violation of his exile," Azl said. "What of it? Will you meet him there and kill him?"

"Me? No," Tulzik said. "*Could* I kill him? I'm just an ordinary young man, and he's a great magician, a scientist. He probably has a hundred devices protecting him and could give me a fast-killing plague with the touch of a finger."

Azl grimaced. "Let it not be said you are a *stupid* young man. Then what *do* you plan?"

"I intend to tell the Guild and the Sorceress that he'll be there and let *them* kill him – though I hope they will first question him enough to establish that it's Peval, and not I, who was sent to Ragbaan as an assassin."

"Ah. And how do you intend to convey this information to the Guild?"

"I was hoping *you* might do that."

"Indeed." Azl sighed and looked at Hrus, who was measuring something on the letter against the middle joint of his left index finger. "I suppose I might as well," she said.

"Excellent! Thank you, Azl."

"And the Sorceress?"

"Oh, I'll get word to her myself," Tulzik said. "I know where to find her people, after all."

"You think you can get to her without Peval finding out?"

"I think so, yes. He believes I've left the city, after all."

"Not a *completely* stupid young man, but perhaps a shade over-confident."

"Perhaps," Tulzik agreed. "Perhaps I am. But I might as well try."

"If you get yourself killed, I trust you won't haunt me claiming I didn't warn you sufficiently."

"I can make no promises, since I know no more of how haunt-ings work than does anyone else, but I assure you, at present I do not in any way hold you at fault for insufficient warnings. I know you think I may be killed, and you may be right. If I am, I would appre-ciate it if you could do whatever you can to ensure that Peval Salinzi and Dardem Karianthis follow my example by dying expeditiously."

Azl smiled crookedly. "I'll do my best," she said. "But may I say, Tulzik Ambroz, that you are getting a great deal of our services for your money?"

"Indeed, I most fervently appreciate it, Azl apek Tiriyilin." Tulzik looked at Hrus, who had produced a small gleaming tool of unknown purpose from somewhere, which he was pointing at the letter; then he looked back at Azl. "I think it's too late to approach the Sorceress today," he said. "I'll try the Red Museum first thing in the morning. Do you have any suggestions for what I might do to make myself useful this evening?"

Azl also looked at Hrus, then back at Tulzik.

"Can you cook?" she asked.

"I can try," he answered.

She studied him for a long moment, then shook her head. "That would be 'no,' then," she said. "Come on, we'll find something to eat out on the street somewhere, and I can show you a little of the city."

"Bring me back a sausage, if you can," Hrus said, without looking up from his work.

"You'd get grease–spots on the letter," Azl protested.

Hrus blinked at the paper, then frowned. "You're right," he said. "Never mind."

Azl sighed. "Come on," she said to Tulzik.

He came. Together, the two of them left the apartment and headed for the stairs.

CHAPTER 17

"We'll head north," Azl said, as they emerged from the Imperial Palace through a door Tulzik had not previously known to exist. "You did say Peval lives on Grand Avenue south of the square, didn't you?"

"Yes," Tulzik said, looking around at the street. He didn't recognize it, but that was no surprise. There were no streetlights here, either natural or magical – or if there were, they were hidden and were not yet lit, though twilight was well advanced. The palace filled one entire side of the street, while the other was lined with large houses that had been elegant a few centuries ago, but were now in varying states of disrepair, though most had lights in the windows demonstrating that they were not entirely abandoned. "You're worried he might see us? But it's such a big city!"

"You'd be surprised at who you run into, all the same. We'll go north." She started walking in a direction Tulzik would have guessed was west.

Tulzik didn't argue with Azl's choice of direction, but at the same time he found himself wondering just where Peval did live and whether he really lived alone. Had he lied about living on Grand Avenue? But that had seemed so specific and unhesitating a response – he could have just waved in a general direction and said, "That way," rather than naming a street and distance. Tulzik thought he had probably been sufficiently flustered to tell the truth without thinking about it.

But alone? Had he really made a doppelganger of himself? If so, did it still live with him? Might it know something useful? Or might it be useful in some other way? That might be worth investigating.

Azl led Tulzik around a corner and through an arch, and then they were in a small square lined with shops. A gigantic tower loomed over the far side, soaring upward at least fifty stories. Flick-

ering red teklights a few floors up on the side of the tower spelled out
a few words in a language that wasn't quite anything Tulzik recognized, though it was related to Rogau; he thought the message might
be something about financial services, but there were missing letters
and archaic spellings that made it hard to be sure.

The rest of the square was mostly lit with candles and oil
lamps and smelled of smoke, fish, and grilling meat. A chatter of
voices filled the air; bells jingled somewhere. The weather was mild,
and the breeze had swung around, blowing the worst of the dampness back out to sea, so a good many people were out enjoying the
evening air. A few small animals were prowling the square, as well,
staying clear of the humans while foraging for dropped food or edible
vermin. Some of them resembled the pet Hrus and Azl kept in their
apartment; others looked much less natural.

"Resurrection Square," Azl said. "There are at least three separate legends about why it's called that."

"Is one of them true?"

Azl shrugged. "There's no way to be sure. The name dates to
at least the fall of the Fifth Empire, a little over eight hundred years
ago."

Tulzik remembered that Hiji's "ghosts" dated from the Third
Imperial Era. "How many empires have there *been*, anyway?" he
asked.

"Five. Five that the historians count, anyway – if Ragbaan
wasn't the capital or the Emperors weren't human, then those don't
qualify." She sniffed the air. "Pork, fish, lizard, or sausage?"

"As you please," Tulzik said, then immediately regretted saying.
He had already eaten fish and lizard and sausage since arriving in
Ragbaan, and he liked to vary his diet. Pork was probably too expen-
sive. Rather than retract his response, though, he pointed and said,
"That fellow has poultry of some sort."

The vendor in question had three birds on a spit, and Tulzik
thought they looked appetizing enough, but Azl shook her head.
"Not for me," she said. "This way."

Tulzik followed as she led the way across the square to a cluster
of tables set out on the pavement and joined her in taking seats at one
of them. A young woman with gleaming orange hair sat at another,
slowly stirring a cup of steaming liquid as she watched them appraisingly; Tulzik steadfastly ignored her.

"Hrus believes you," Azl said, leaning across the table.

"I had hoped you did, too," Tulzik said, startled.

"I don't believe anyone entirely," Azl said. "Not even Hrus. Not without good evidence."

"I have the letter from Peval," Tulzik protested.

"You could have written it yourself. We don't know Peval's handwriting."

Tulzik could not deny this, but asked, "*Why* would I do that?"

"We don't know what you really want," Azl said. "This whole business with the Biologist and the Sorceress could be a feint, a ruse – you might be here to get something from *us*."

"But what would I want from you?"

"I don't know yet. Something to do with the Guild, perhaps?"

"I don't know anything *about* the Guild, except what you've told me!"

"So you say." She cocked her head and stared at him for a moment, then leaned forward further and whispered, "Are you an Initiate? *Iterum ad astrem?*"

"What?" Tulzik blinked. The words weren't anything he understood; they sounded as if they might be Nilni, but he could not make sense of them.

Azl straightened in her seat, and just then a young woman appeared beside the table. "Can I – " the waitress began.

"Pork," Azl said. "Both of us. And *tsir*."

Tulzik hadn't drunk *tsir* since he was a child, but he was not going to argue with Azl in her present mood, especially since she was presumably paying. He nodded.

The waitress clicked her recorder and flounced away, and for a moment Tulzik and Azl stared uncomfortably at one another – or at least, Tulzik was uncomfortable. He assumed Azl was, as well.

At last he broke the silence. "Azl," he said, "I don't understand why you're so determined not to believe I'm exactly what I appear to be."

"The Guild says you aren't."

"The Guild bases that entirely on believing that Peval Salinzi was in Ragbaan when I say he was in Emniln. *I* say they're mistaken, that he somehow managed to appear to be in both places at once. Maybe he made a doppelganger; after all, he's a gene–cutter, he could do that. Maybe he made a recording somehow, like Hiji's ghosts; you told me yourself that Ragbaan is full of mysterious old *tek*. The Guild was fooled, that's all."

Azl glared at him. "You think it's that easy to fool the Guild?"

"Are you so sure it's not?"

"*I* never managed to fool them."

The obvious bitterness in Azl's voice caught Tulzik off guard. "What?" Then he recovered. "Did you ever try?"

Azl didn't answer the question. Instead she leaned forward again and said, "Do you think I don't trust the Guild?"

"*I* don't trust the Guild!" Tulzik exclaimed. "You told me not to trust anyone in Ragbaan, including yourself!"

"Do *they* think I'm doing something I shouldn't? Other than staying with Hrus, I mean?"

"Who are *they?*"

She stared at him. He stared back.

"*Iterum ad astrem,*" she said again.

"I have no idea what that means," Tulzik said, annoyed.

Azl did not respond immediately, and again, the two stared at each other.

"You're not an Initiate," she said at last. "But that doesn't mean the Guild didn't send you."

"What?" Tulzik stared at her, baffled. "They said they couldn't determine my identity! Do you think they lied to you about that?"

"They might have," Azl said grudgingly.

"Then why are you so sure they didn't lie about *Peval?*"

Azl didn't answer that. Instead she looked up. Tulzik's gaze followed hers and found the waitress returning with a tray.

Azl and Tulzik sat silently as the waitress set down two plates and two mugs, and glanced from one unwelcoming face to the other before tucking the tray under her arm and departing.

The food was not quite what Tulzik had been expecting; while the reddish-brown strips were presumably pork, they made up less than a fourth of what lay on the plate. The rest was strips and slices of assorted vegetables, mushrooms, and substances Tulzik could not immediately identify. He took a sip of the steaming golden liquid in his mug and almost gagged. It wasn't that the beverage was *bad*; it was simply not what he had been expecting. The *tsir* served here bore the same resemblance to what he had drunk as a child that lightning bore to a flickering teklight. He remembered the waiter at the beer garden on the ridge saying that Penzerene hot sauce might have been milder once and evolved to its present inedible-to-foreigners state and wondered whether Ragbaan's version of *tsir* had done something similar.

Azl glared at him and began eating her pork.

Tulzik took another sip of *tsir*, appreciating it properly this time, then looked at Azl. "You know, the Guild didn't say I was evil incarnate. They just said I was wrong about Peval and that they didn't know who I was."

"You made us look like fools," Azl said, putting down her fork. "You put us in the Guild's debt."

"I did?"

"We were trading information about an assassination plot for Peval's identity – except according to the Guild, there *is* no assassination plot, and they were already watching Peval Salinzi. So they identified him for us in exchange for *nothing*, and what's more, they warned us about *you*, for nothing. That puts us doubly in their debt."

Tulzik had not really considered that aspect of the situation and did not really see why it was significant. "Is that so very terrible?" he asked.

"It is for *me*, yes," Azl said.

Tulzik frowned and stabbed a piece of pork with his fork. "Why?" he asked, as he lifted the meat to his mouth.

"My relationship with the Guild is...difficult," Azl said. "I am forbidden to explain exactly why, but it's a family matter. That's why I was able to contact them so easily. Hrus's relationship is simpler – it's open hostility. He's done several things that the Guild did not appreciate, so the Guild doesn't like him, but they haven't yet found an excuse to remove him entirely, and doing so without sufficient reason would further complicate its relationship with *me* and with other people the Guild prefers not to antagonize."

Tulzik had been chewing as she spoke; the food was good, if a little spicier than he liked. Now he swallowed and said, "You mentioned someone named Filimon."

"That was one of the things the Guild didn't appreciate, yes. Hrus told the Antiquarians that Filimon was a Guild spy."

"Was he?"

"Oh, yes. Otherwise the Guild wouldn't have minded."

"But *you* were the one who suggested consulting the Guild about my situation in the first place!"

"Because it all seemed so simple," Azl said angrily. "We would prevent an assassination, and the Guild would have that much less excuse to treat us as outcasts and troublemakers, but we would not be *giving* them anything, merely catering to a paying client. But it *wasn't* simple, and now I'm in debt to them, and I can't afford to be, not while I'm...while Hrus..." She didn't finish the sentence, but jabbed her fork into her food.

"You think the Guild set this up deliberately?"

"I wouldn't be surprised."

Tulzik shook his head. "You're over-complicating it. The Guild was fooled, that's all. Peval and the Biologist knew they'd be watching, and tricked them, probably with a doppelganger. Everything is just as I told you."

"That's what you want me to believe, yes – but I *don't* believe it."

"Hrus does."

"Hrus is too trusting sometimes."

"Or you're too suspicious. Sometimes things really *are* what they seem."

Azl looked at him. "Sometimes," she said. "And sometimes there really *are* subtle conspiracies at work."

"Well, there's almost certainly a conspiracy at work here, but the question is whether it's the Guild trying to get a hold over you, or the Biologist trying to kill his rival. Which seems more likely?"

"That's the problem. They're both entirely possible."

Tulzik stared at her. She *really* thought it was just as likely that the Starfarers' Guild had arranged all this just to create some sort of ill-defined moral debt Azl owed them?

But then, she hadn't seen Vika lying dead on Peval's bed. She hadn't seen that letter come from Peval's own hand. She and her husband had reconstructed an entire conspiracy from a dead girl and her killer walking across a crater instead of taking an airship, and everything Tulzik had found since had confirmed their theory, but because one easily explained detail didn't fit, she was ready to discard the whole thing in favor of some bizarre scheme in which Tulzik was either a mind-altered dupe or a lying scoundrel, and quite possibly an assassin.

He wondered whether such things were commonplace in Ragbaan. He knew he just a simple country boy, but he found it hard to believe. And he *certainly* didn't believe he was a mind-altered dupe or a lying scoundrel.

"If we find out that Peval really did make himself a doppelganger or a ghost, *then* would you believe my story and help me avenge Vika?" he asked.

She shook her head. "He wouldn't have kept it."

"Why not? He doesn't know anyone suspects anything, and he might need to leave the city without being missed again sometime. And killing a doppelganger might not be that easy for him."

Azl considered that. She looked down at her plate and ate a few more forkfuls of the pork as she thought it over.

Tulzik ate, too, but watched Azl.

"If he really has a doppelganger, then yes, I'll believe your story," Azl said at last.

"Even though it means the Guild was wrong about something?"

Azl grimaced. "They've been wrong about Hrus for years, so yes."

Tulzik grinned. "Good! Then as soon as we've eaten, we'll go find it."

"Tonight?" For the first time, Tulzik saw Azl look genuinely startled.

"Why not? The sooner the better, and you said Hrus will be busy all night with that letter."

"You think you can just walk into Peval Salinzi's home and find the doppelganger? He'll have hidden it away somewhere, and you don't even know where he lives!"

"Well, we may not find it, but if we don't *look* for it, we *certainly* won't find it."

Azl eyed him suspiciously. "This could all just be a scheme to lead me into a trap of some sort."

"I suppose it could," Tulzik acknowledged, "but it isn't."

"I thought you didn't want to let Peval know you're still in Ragbaan."

"I don't – but you know, now that we have that letter, now that I've had time to think about it, I'm willing to risk it. I can always say that the airship wouldn't let me work for my passage after all."

"You're flexible," Azl said. "That can be useful in Ragbaan."

"Eat," Tulzik said, pointing his fork at the food on Azl's plate, then plunging it into his own.

CHAPTER 18

"A little over a mile south, on the west side of Grand Avenue," Tulzik said, as they stood in front of the restaurant. "That's what he told me over dinner."

"That doesn't necessarily narrow it down much," Azl said. She pulled a small silvery device from her pocket and glanced at it, then looked back at Tulzik. "Let's go, then."

They turned and began walking south.

"How do you intend to find this supposed doppelganger?" Azl asked.

"I don't know," Tulzik admitted. "I'm planning to improvise."

"You seem to do that a lot."

"I know," Tulzik said. He shrugged. "So far, it's worked out for me."

"You've been lucky." Tulzik thought Azl sounded slightly disgusted.

"I know that, too."

"That never lasts."

"I know *that*, too. My sister found that out."

"Hmm."

They walked in silence for several minutes, threading their way through the crowds. Azl pointed the way whenever there was any question of which way to turn. Fifteen minutes later they emerged onto Grand Avenue, with its strip of farmland down the center and broad pavements on either side.

There were no crowds here; the farmers and gardeners had gone home once the sun was down, and the produce stalls and grain merchants had closed up for the night. Here and there a bored guard sat atop a small watchtower to ensure that the crops were not looted or vandalized. Elsewhere red teklights flickered a warning that some sort of protective magic was in use. Most of the avenue and its median, however, was dark.

On either side of the avenue stood a variety of buildings, some dark, some lit by flame, others illuminated by teklights.

"How far have we come?" Tulzik asked.

Azl consulted her device. "About half a mile," she said. She pointed. "We'll want to cross over up ahead."

Tulzik nodded. They were on the east side of the avenue, and Peval had said he lived on the west. Cutting through any of those gardens or farms in the dark seemed unwise, but there was a cross street where Azl was pointing. They ambled toward it.

"You aren't worried about being seen?" Azl asked.

"By Peval?" Tulzik shook his head. "Not particularly."

"I was thinking of the Guild."

That brought Tulzik up short. "They have Peval under surveillance, don't they?"

"In theory," Azl said.

"They think I lied to you."

"And to them, when you showed the Guildsman that picture."

Tulzik frowned. "What would they do, if they did see me and recognize me?"

"Oh, there's no question about it. They'd recognize you. Their *tek* is very good at that."

"What would they *do* about it?"

"That I don't know."

"I haven't done anything to *them*," Tulzik said.

"You lied to them. You may be here to assassinate the Sorceress."

Tulzik considered that for a moment, then said, "I got the impression they wouldn't particularly mind if someone killed her."

"They probably wouldn't," Azl agreed. "They generally don't interfere with these things – they try to stay neutral and just observe and only intervene if it looks as if the city as a whole might be damaged, or as if one faction might become too powerful. That doesn't happen often. But they don't know who you are, or who you're working for, and that's likely to make them more cautious than usual. If you really *are* an outsider, that's a problem, too – they don't like outsiders meddling in Ragbaan. Anyone they've exiled is defined as an outsider, so if you're working for the Biologist, that would be bad."

"I'm not working for anybody."

Azl shrugged.

Tulzik let that go. "So what would they do about it? Kill me?" he asked.

"Probably not right away," Azl said thoughtfully. "They'd probably give you a warning first. They don't want to provoke your employer if they don't need to."

"I don't *have* an employer."

Azl did not reply to that. They walked on silently, crossing over to the western side of the avenue.

"I'm not stupid," Tulzik said. "If I'm warned off, I'll...well, I won't just give up, but I won't be stupid about it. I'd try to talk to them."

Again, Azl didn't bother to answer. Instead she pulled out her device again. "Nine-tenths of a mile," she said.

Tulzik looked at her, then at the buildings ahead, trying to judge just where they would reach the end of the mile. They were passing a row of four-story structures, their windows gleaming with bright teklights. Might Peval live in one of them, perhaps?

Or just beyond them...

"Oh, no," Tulzik said.

Azl's gaze followed his. "This could be interesting," she said.

A little over a mile from the restaurant, on the west side of Grand Avenue, one of the city's tallest surviving towers stood alone, looming black against the starry sky. Tulzik could not begin to estimate its height – hundreds of feet, certainly, perhaps thousands. Fifty, sixty stories, perhaps much more. If he was misjudging in the dark, it might be a hundred. Hiding a doppelganger, or anything else, would be easy in a tower that size, where most of it was empty. The four-story structures just to its north, on the other hand, were probably entirely in use, and to the south was a crumbled ruin that appeared completely uninhabitable.

If Peval lived in the tower and had hidden his doppelganger somewhere in those dozens of darkened upper stories, finding it would not be easy. In particular, finding it without alerting Peval would not be easy.

Still, what else could Tulzik do but try? He marched on.

Lights flickered in several of the tower's lowermost windows – for the most part natural lights, not teklights. That meant it was inhabited. There were no signs indicating businesses, or at any rate none in living languages; something had once been carved into a lintel in an alphabet Tulzik didn't recognize, but that was all. This implied that the building was a residence, but was by no means conclusive.

Tulzik took this in while walking; he did not want to stop and study the structure for fear of drawing unwanted attention. Peval might not notice him or might not recognize him if he was just another evening stroller, but if Tulzik stopped to stare at the tower he was far more likely to be spotted.

He turned and walked into the central entrance to the tower, just as if he had been heading there all along and had every right to be there. He was startled by the sudden tingling sensation he felt as he marched through what he had thought was an empty archway, and the change in temperature from the warm humidity of the city street to the cool, dry air of the interior. Given the dearth of teklights he hadn't expected the building to still have a functioning invisible door.

Azl followed close on his heels. "I hate those things," Tulzik said with a shudder once they were through the intangible barrier.

"You're familiar with them?"

"Oh, yes," Tulzik said. "There's one at the Emniln library. We aren't *that* backward out where I come from. We still have a little *tek*."

Azl made no reply to that, and Tulzik quickly regretted saying it. While it was true that Azl seemed not to think much of anyone from outside Ragbaan, there was no point in being rude about it.

Once through the arch they were in a broad, dark corridor leading deep into the tower's interior, where the only light came from the outside world behind them, a faint glow on one wall ahead, and a little red teklight moving along the floor far beyond that. There were faint whirrings somewhere in the gloom, but no voices or footsteps, and Tulzik could see no movement other than the one red light.

"Not exactly crowded," Tulzik remarked, as he strode forward toward that glowing section of wall.

"One thing Ragbaan is never short of is space," Azl replied.

Tulzik could hardly argue with that, but he still found it a bit puzzling that the tower seemed so empty, yet was apparently in good repair, with significant working *tek*. The floor was clean and smooth, the invisible door was working, and the tower was in a convenient location.

Well, perhaps the occupants were either homebodies and already settled behind closed doors for the evening, or still going about their business elsewhere. Or perhaps nobody liked the combination of an invisible door and no lights.

The glow, he discovered, came from an illuminated screen set in the wall. As Tulzik neared it the image it had displayed, of a gleaming tower surrounded by green trees and blue sky, vanished, and words appeared, in archaic lettering glowing gold on a blue background.

"Welcome to the Rusbik Tower on Grand Avenue," Tulzik read. "Are you expected, dear guest?" He turned to Azl. "Are we?"

"No," she said. "We're prospective tenants," she said to the wall. "We'd like to look around."

The panel flickered, and then a new message appeared.

This time Tulzik could not read half of it, but Azl translated. "The management apologizes," she read, "but this *tek* cannot understand you. Can you repeat your response in Rogau?" She snorted. "It doesn't like my accent."

"It's probably too old," Tulzik said.

"Of course," Azl said. "This is hardly the first time." She paused, studying the panel, then said something that sounded almost, but not quite, intelligible. Tulzik was fairly certain he heard "tenant" and "look," and guessed Azl was, indeed, repeating her response in an older dialect of Rogau.

Tulzik was impressed; he didn't think he could have done anything like that. How did she know which variant to use?

"Thank you," the image said. Tulzik had to guess at a couple of words, but was fairly sure the next sentence meant, "The rental office is ahead on your left; please follow the..." The last word he couldn't guess at all.

Something hissed ahead and to the left, and light spilled out into the corridor from a now-open door. "That would be the rental office," he said, starting toward it.

Azl grabbed his arm. "Where do you think you're going?" she demanded.

He blinked at her. "The rental office," he said.

"What do you plan to do there?" she said. "You don't really think there's anyone in there, do you?"

"No, of course not," Tulzik said, annoyed, "but if we *don't* go there, the building will realize we lied, and it might be able to do something about it. If we go in, *then* go poking around the building, we'll still look like we might really be prospective tenants. It's a good thing it can't understand modern Rogau, because otherwise it would hear me telling you this."

Azl released his arm. "Oh," she said. "Well, I said you weren't completely stupid, didn't I? That's not bad thinking, but it's probably unnecessary. Almost none of these old buildings still have working guardian *tek*."

"*Almost* none?"

Azl hesitated.

"What about buildings with functioning invisible doors that are home to gene–cutters who may be involved in assassination conspiracies?"

Azl smiled crookedly. "Shall we take a look in the office, then? I was going to look for stairs, but after all, we aren't in any hurry."

Tulzik led the way into the teklit room.

It might have been a rental office once, but it was a large empty room now, without any furnishings at all; the ceiling glowed softly, providing light, and the door obviously still worked, but that was all. Disappointed, Tulzik stepped in, while Azl waited in the doorway.

Tulzik looked around at bare green walls and smooth black floor, then turned to leave. That was when he saw the map. It was on the wall beside the door – a perfectly reasonable place for it, really, but one that was not visible from the corridor. He smiled and began studying it. Seeing him stare at the wall, Azl leaned in to see what he had discovered.

"There are the stairs," he said, pointing. "And the lifts – do you think any of them might still work?"

"I wouldn't trust them even if they did," Azl replied.

Tulzik nodded, looking at the map.

"Don't put too much faith in that. The residents may have re-arranged things," Azl warned him.

Tulzik nodded. "Shall we go?" he said.

A moment later they were in an unlit stairway, slowly making their way upward by feel.

"You'd think the residents would keep this lit," Tulzik said, as his foot groped for the next step.

"They probably bring lights with them," Azl said.

Then they both froze at a chittering noise from somewhere in the darkness ahead.

"You heard that?" Tulzik said.

"Of course I heard that," Azl snapped.

"Then it wasn't my imagination," Tulzik said.

"Shut up!"

Tulzik obeyed; he, too, wanted to hear as much as he could, as the chittering was followed by a scrabbling noise and various other sounds.

That was not any sort of machinery or magic Tulzik had ever heard before, nor was it anything human. There was some sort of animal on the stairs above them. He remembered the ratlike things he had seen on spits in the great hall of the Imperial Palace and hoped he hadn't just walked into a nest of them. Some of the other creatures he had seen in the streets wouldn't be much better. At least the sounds seemed to come from *small* animals, so far as he could tell.

Then a light appeared high ahead of them, a dim greenish-yellow glow, and Tulzik found himself staring at what seemed to be a small teklight with teeth.

Another light appeared beside it, the same size and color, and another, and another, in a diagonal line, and as the stairwell grew lighter Tulzik was able to make out more of his surroundings and more of the source of the glow.

There were animals on the stairs above them – not the flight they were on, but the next one up. They were no species Tulzik recognized, but they were golden-furred, green-eyed creatures, each about the size of a woman's head, with four feet and a long, fluffy tail. The animals were arranged in a line, one on every other step, looking out through the railings and holding their mouths wide open, showing distressingly sharp fangs. The glow came from their open mouths.

Tulzik stared. "I've never seen anything like *that* before," he whispered.

"Neither have I," Azl admitted.

"They aren't for sale in the local markets, or something we'd find lurking in alleys?"

"Not that I ever saw."

"So it's likely a magician made them right here, then."

"Yes."

"If Peval made those, he's a pretty good gene-cutter," Tulzik murmured.

"No argument. Or he might have gotten them from the Biologist before he was exiled. We don't really know we're in the right building at all, for that matter. They might be someone else's doing entirely."

"How many gene-cutters *are* there in Ragbaan?"

"Several," Azl said. "But I admit these are probably either Peval Salinzi's work, or a leftover made by Dardem Karianthis."

"They're lighting the way up the stairs for us, aren't they?" Tulzik asked.

"So it appears."

"Should we follow them?"

"Your guess is as good as mine."

"Let's see where they lead," Tulzik declared. He began marching up the stairs. Azl seemed less certain than Tulzik of the wisdom of this decision, but followed without protest.

As they climbed, the little creatures ahead of them sat motionless, glowing mouths open, lighting the stairs above, while those they had passed closed their mouths and scurried up the steps past them to take up new positions further on. At the third floor, however, the creatures stopped climbing and instead lined up on either side of a doorway.

"Clearly where they expect us to go," Azl said, as Tulzik stepped onto the third floor landing and stopped.

"Clearly," Tulzik agreed. "So let's see what happens when we don't."

Azl hesitated. "I don't like the look of those teeth."

"Then don't look at them," Tulzik said, as he started up the stairs toward the fourth floor.

There was a fresh outburst of chittering, and several of the creatures closed their mouths, plunging the stairwell into semi-darkness. By the time Tulzik and Azl were half a dozen steps above the third floor only one of the animals, standing by the third-floor door, was still emitting light.

When Tulzik rounded the next corner the last mouth closed, and total darkness descended. He felt his way forward blindly, across the next landing, and groped for the door. His fingers found a latch, and the door slid open, revealing only darkness beyond.

"We should have brought a light," Tulzik said.

"We shouldn't need one, if what we're looking for exists. I doubt this theoretical doppelganger we seek is able to see in the dark."

"You don't think he's in there, then?"

Tulzik could not see whether Azl shrugged, but her tone suggested it. "Who knows?" she said.

Tulzik frowned, then said, "Let's try farther up, then."

"Oh, why not?" Azl's tone was resigned, rather than enthusiastic, but she did not argue. Tulzik turned and brushed past her, feeling his way to the next set of steps.

The fifth floor was just as dark as the fourth. It was between the fifth and sixth that something growled at them out of the darkness ahead.

Tulzik stopped dead, and Azl's groping hand slapped into his back.

"Something growled," he said.

"Yes, I know," she replied. A light flared. Tulzik blinked in the sudden brightness and looked around at a bare stairwell.

Then he turned and stared at the device in Azl's hand; it was about the size of his thumb and glowing brightly. "Why didn't you use that sooner?" he demanded.

"Why should I?" Azl retorted. "Why draw attention?"

Tulzik started to say something about their chances of stepping onto a broken stair or hostile creature in the dark, then changed his mind. "You're using it now," he pointed out.

"We've already *drawn* attention." She pointed up the stairs.

Tulzik looked where she indicated and saw something wide and furry on the landing ahead. It did not seem to be threatening; it simply lay there, blocking their way. Its fur was soft gray, and he could see no claws or teeth. In fact, he could see no limbs. It was simply a soft gray blob, perhaps two feet in diameter and half a foot high, with a pair of orange eyes that were blinking furiously in the bright light. Tulzik could not even see a mouth.

"What *is* it?" he asked.

"I don't know," Azl said.

Tulzik hesitated only a second, then climbed up to the landing, watching the blob carefully. The orange eyes watched him, but the thing didn't move. No claws or fangs revealed themselves.

Tulzik reached down and touched it gingerly.

Nothing jumped out; nothing stung him. He felt only fur.

"It's soft!" he said.

The eyes looked up at him. He stroked the fur cautiously, and the thing began making a peculiar humming noise.

"It's purring," Azl said from behind Tulzik's shoulder. She held her light up.

"It's what?"

"Purring. It's a sound cats make."

Tulzik glanced at her. "Cats?"

"A variety of small animals kept as pets. You must have seen ours. And there were feral cats in Resurrection Square."

Tulzik remembered the creature that had sat on Hrus' lap and the ones prowling the square. They had distinct heads, and he was fairly sure they all had four legs apiece, while the thing in the stairwell had neither a head nor legs. "This doesn't look like yours."

"No, it doesn't," Azl agreed, "but it's purring, and the fur looks like cat fur. I think some gene-cutter made this out of a cat."

"Peval?"

"Maybe."

"Are cats dangerous?" Tulzik felt stupid almost as soon as he had asked the question; after all, if they were dangerous, would Azl and Hrus keep one as a pet and give it the run of their apartment?

"They can be," Azl said. "This thing isn't really a cat, in any case. It might be poisonous."

Tulzik stared at the immobile, toothless, clawless thing. "How?" he asked.

"Maybe it exudes venom through its fur. *I* don't know. But whatever it is, it's not Peval Salinzi's doppelganger. Shall we proceed, or just call this off?"

"We proceed," Tulzik said. "Come on." He stepped carefully past the cat-thing and continued up the stairs.

CHAPTER 19

They found him on the eleventh floor.

Tulzik was not really sure why he kept going that far. When they hadn't found anything but a dozen bizarre and obviously artificial varieties of animal for half a dozen floors he had begun to doubt his own theory. When they passed three more floors without even seeing any animals, he had to admit that the rest of the tower was probably empty. If Peval had told the truth about where he lived at all, he had probably meant some other nearby building. Tulzik had admitted this to himself, not to Azl, and had kept going out of sheer stubbornness.

But on the eleventh floor, when Tulzik opened the door from the stairwell to the hallway, he saw immediately that one of the inner doors was open and brightly lit.

"Well, *someone* is here," Azl said, grudgingly, as she doused her own light and slipped it out of sight.

"Come on," Tulzik said, leading the way down the corridor. He fought down an urge to creep along the wall, or tiptoe up and peer around the doorframe; if anyone saw him here, he wanted to look like a legitimate visitor, not some skulking intruder. He walked down the center of the corridor, his steps loud on the bare concrete, until he reached the open door and looked in.

The room was large and comfortably furnished; a bed with a thick green coverlet stood against the far wall, while two big green armchairs flanked a table in the center. Two *tek* floor–lamps glowed softly yellow behind the chairs. Three round rugs, patterned in blue and green, covered most of the floor. Peval Salinzi, or his double, was sitting cross–legged on the central rug, in front of the table, drawing on a pad of paper. An empty plate lay on the floor nearby; presumably he had recently finished eating.

For a moment Tulzik wanted to turn and flee before he was recognized – Peval wasn't supposed to find out he was still in Ragbaan.

But he remembered that he was looking for, and had apparently found, Peval's double, so he held his ground.

Then the man on the floor looked up and smiled at Tulzik with no sign of recognition at all, a guileless smile nothing like the bitter expression Tulzik had seen on Peval's face over their fish dinner.

His face was like Peval's except for one detail – his nose was unmarked. Peval's distinctive scar was missing. Tulzik thought he might also look slightly younger, that his features might be a trifle less worn, but that could have been a trick of the light or his memory playing tricks.

"Hello," the black-haired man said. "Who are you? Did my brother send you?"

"I'm not sure," Tulzik said. "Who's your brother?"

"Peval Salinzi," the cross-legged man said. He put down the pad and pencil and got to his feet. "That's my name, too," he added.

"I'm pleased to meet you," Tulzik said, holding out a hand. "I'm Tulzik Ambroz."

"I'm Lizi Tamial," Azl said over his shoulder.

Tulzik resisted the impulse to turn and look at her when she gave this false name – assuming it actually was false, and that Azl apek Tiriyilin wasn't the fiction. She was probably being wise, and he wished he had thought of it, rather than giving his real identity.

Peval smiled and nodded. "Did my brother send you?" he asked again.

There was no question at all in Tulzik's mind – this was not the Peval Salinzi who had seduced his sister, not the Peval Salinzi he had dined with the previous night. The body was outwardly the same, but the mind was clearly not.

"No, he didn't," Tulzik said.

The man's smile vanished. "Oh," he said. He looked worriedly from Tulzik to Azl, then back. "Then what are you doing here? No one ever comes up here except the two of us."

"We were looking for you," Azl said.

Peval's eyes flicked from one face to the other. "I don't think you should be here," he said. "My brother said no one ever comes up here but us."

"But we'd heard so much about you!" Azl said. "We'd heard that Peval had a brother who looked just like him, so we came to see for ourselves." She smiled.

Peval stared at her. "Who told you he had a brother? That's

supposed to be a secret. Only the two of us and his boss are allowed to know. No one is supposed to say anything about it anywhere but here. This is where *we* come to talk about things in private. You aren't supposed to be here!"

"But we wanted to meet you!" Azl insisted.

"Why? How'd you know I was here?"

In a sudden burst of inspiration, Tulzik said, "The Ilm told us."

Peval turned to stare at him, instead of Azl. "It did? How did *it* know?"

Tulzik shrugged, relieved that the doppelganger was familiar with the Ilm. "How does the Ilm know anything?" he said. "It just does."

Peval suddenly looked seriously worried. "Did it know – can it tell us apart?"

"I don't know," Tulzik admitted. "I didn't ask." He didn't mention the missing scar.

"I don't want the Ilm to know about me!" the doppelganger protested.

"Why not?" Azl asked.

"Because it's a secret! No one below the tenth floor is ever supposed to know there are two of us, except for my brother's boss."

"Why not?" Azl asked again.

"I... I don't know," he replied, puzzled. "They just aren't. My brother keeps telling me that."

"But isn't your brother below the tenth floor right now?" Tulzik asked.

The doppelganger glared at him. "That's different," he said. "We don't count. It didn't count when I was downstairs, either. It's *our* secret."

"Well, maybe the *Ilm* doesn't count," Tulzik suggested. "After all, it isn't human."

Peval considered that. "Maybe you're right," he conceded. "But it shouldn't be telling anyone. It shouldn't have told *you*."

"But we're up here; we aren't below the tenth floor."

"Well, you aren't going to stay up here forever, are you?"

"No," Azl said. "We aren't."

"In fact, I think we should go now," Tulzik said.

"You probably don't want to tell your brother we were here," Azl said, as if the idea had just occurred to her. "He might get mad that you talked to us."

"Instead of hiding when you heard us coming," Tulzik said.

"I thought it was him!" the doppelganger protested.

"Well, of course," Azl said. "Besides, we already knew you were here, because the Ilm told us, so there's no harm done, but your brother might not see it that way."

Peval looked from one to the other uncertainly.

"Maybe you thought we were your brother's boss," Azl suggested.

"He can't come here," the doppelganger immediately replied.

"He can't?" Tulzik asked.

Peval shook his head. "He would *die* if he came to Ragbaan!" he said. "That's why he's paying my brother to do everything for him. He's promised to make us both stay young forever. He was the one who taught my brother how to make me. He knows *lots* of magic! And he's going to teach my brother as much as he can."

"Really?" Azl asked. "What's his name?"

The doppelganger's face fell. "That's another secret. I can't tell you. I don't even know it myself."

Tulzik had hoped to confirm that it was the Biologist who had been giving Peval orders, but apparently they would have to go on relying on inference. The description certainly seemed to fit what he knew of Dardem Karianthis.

"You're good at keeping secrets!" Azl said. "So you can keep it a secret that we were here."

That seemed to puzzle the doppelganger. "But why should I do that?"

"So your brother won't be mad at you for talking to us."

"But...I should tell him."

"But he'd be mad," Tulzik said. "You know how angry he can get." He hoped the doppelganger really *had* seen the original Peval's nasty temper.

"Yes..."

Tulzik shrugged. "You know better than we do, of course, but I just wouldn't mention that we were here."

Peval still looked uncertain, but he did not protest further.

"It's been a pleasure meeting you," Azl said, with a small bow.

"He doesn't come up here very often, since he came back," Peval said, his expression suddenly sad. "I wish he would. I liked living downstairs better, but I had to move up here when he came home, so no one would know there are two of us, and it gets lonely."

"I'm sure it does," Tulzik said. The poor man clearly wanted them to stay, just for company, but that wasn't safe. "So you really don't want to make him angry with you, do you? He might stay away even more."

"No, I don't," the doppelganger agreed.

"Well, then, thank you for seeing us." Tulzik held out his hand again. The doppelganger hesitated, then grasped it briefly and released it. Tulzik and Azl turned to go.

"How did you find your way up here, anyway?" the doppelganger asked. "Did the lamp-hogs show you?"

"The lamp-hogs?" Tulzik glanced at Azl, who turned back to the doppelganger.

"We had our own light," she said, holding up her little gadget.

"Well, that's good, because the lamp-hogs aren't supposed to obey anyone but me and my brother, and we told them to stay on the lower floors, down where the other people live. If they had helped you, they'd be in big trouble."

"I see."

"You didn't step on the lumpcat, did you?"

"No, we were careful."

"Well, that's good, then." He hesitated, then waved. "Goodbye."

"Goodbye, Peval," Tulzik said.

Then the two of them were out of the room, walking briskly back toward the stairs. Tulzik glanced at Azl, but said nothing; they were still too close to Peval's duplicate.

They passed the lumpcat carefully; Tulzik paused to pet it, but only very briefly.

When they reached the third floor the little glowing creatures began opening their mouths again, lighting the way. Azl turned off her device and tucked it out of sight.

"You think these are the lamp-hogs?" Tulzik asked.

"I would assume so," Azl replied.

"It seems as if they could be useful. I wonder why he hasn't been selling them?"

Azl shrugged. "I'd rather have teklights. You don't need to feed teklights."

"For all we know, these things feed themselves. Maybe they eat rats."

Azl gave a brief snort of laughter. "I take it you haven't seen the rats here in Ragbaan."

Annoyed, Tulzik said, "Not live ones, but I've seen them cooked. I didn't mean *one* lamp-hog would make a meal of a rat; from their behavior I'd guess they hunt in packs."

"You could be right," Azl conceded, looking around at the gaping little animals. "They do seem to coordinate their actions." She glanced up into the darkness of the stairwell above.

Tulzik's gaze followed hers. "I think we're out of earshot now," he said.

"Of *that* one," Azl replied.

"Right."

They did not speak again until they were out on Grand Avenue, striding north. Then Azl said, "Why did you give your real name?"

"Because I'm a fool," Tulzik snapped. "Do you believe me now about who's the assassin?"

"I see two possibilities," she replied. "Either you've been telling the exact truth as you knew it all along, and matters are very much as you said, or you and Peval Salinzi are both part of some complicated scheme I don't yet understand, and you set up that little encounter as a bit of theater intended to fool me."

"I didn't set up anything!" Tulzik protested. "And that couldn't be the real Peval; his nose wasn't scarred."

"He could have repaired it. He *is* a gene-cutter, after all."

"He never bothered to fix it before," Tulzik said. "If he was trying to fool anyone, why would he fix it *now?*"

"To make us think we'd found his doppelganger."

"And how would he explain not having the scar when he goes back to work?"

Azl considered that, then changed tack. "We found that double pretty easily."

"Well, there weren't many places Peval could hide him! He needed somewhere close at hand, and somewhere he could go without being noticed; what would be better than the upper stories of the tower he lives in? So far as he knew, no one suspected anything, and no one would have any reason to be *looking* for his copy."

"True enough." She sighed. "I am inclined to believe you, as it happens. While conspiracies intricate enough to explain everything without accepting your version have been known to happen, they aren't common. For the Starfarers' Guild to make a mistake, or to be successfully fooled, isn't common, either, but in this case it seems the more likely alternative."

"I'm glad to hear you say that," Tulzik said. "What now, then?"

"Back to the palace, I suppose, to see how Hrus is doing with that letter."

Tulzik nodded, and they walked on in silence for a time.

Then Tulzik asked, "Just how stupid was it for me to give my real name?"

Azl glanced at him, then looked ahead again. "Stupid," she said. "Stupidity isn't easy to quantify, but that was definitely stupid."

Tulzik shook his head. "I'm not used to this sort of skullduggery. I've never done anything like this before."

"No?" She favored him with an appraising glance. "You seem to have a knack for it. Telling Peval your sister had survived and stealing that letter – those were clever."

"Getting taken in by Hiji wasn't," Tulzik said.

Azl shrugged. "Everyone falls for that."

"Giving my real name wasn't clever, either."

"No, that one was, as we agreed, quite stupid. But everyone makes mistakes sometimes."

"Do you think he'll tell the real Peval Salinzi that we were there?"

"I hope not."

"If he does, will he remember my name?"

"Yes."

Azl's flat, one-word reply startled Tulzik; he looked at her in surprise.

She saw the look and sighed. "He's not stupid," she said. "The original is a gene–cutter, and from the look of the lamp–hogs, and the fact that both the Biologist and the Sorceress took him on, he's a good one. He thought of making a duplicate of himself to cover his absence from the city; that wasn't stupid, either. And if the original isn't stupid, then the copy shouldn't be, either – naive and ignorant, yes, and childlike, since after all he's probably only a few years old, but not stupid. He'll remember the names we gave. I just hope he goes on believing the Ilm exposed him; that will make a good false trail to confuse matters."

"So not *everything* I said was stupid."

"No. Just your name."

Tulzik nodded.

A horseless carriage whirred past, and the conversation faded.

A few blocks further north Tulzik heard applause and laughter from one of the side-streets; he peered in that direction and saw a crowd and bright teklights.

"Any idea what's happening there?" he asked.

Azl listened briefly, then said, "It sounds like a bell hunt."

"What *is* a bell hunt?"

"They don't have them in your village?"

"Not by that name, at any rate."

Azl sighed. "There's a roped-off area. Inside there's a woman wearing nothing but bells, and a blindfolded man who tries to catch her. If he catches her, he gets to keep her – at least, that's what he's told. There's a time limit, and he's disqualified if he steps outside the ropes."

"You say that's what he's told – it isn't true?"

"Oh, sometimes it is, if she's really a slave. Often, though, she's a real woman, and it's a set-up – he catches her, and then once the crowd has scattered and her partner has hidden the money, she demands her freedom, in front of witnesses."

"What money?"

"Oh, the man in the blindfold puts up a bet that he can catch her. Usually it's a hundred *walu*; after all, slaves aren't cheap. Sometimes someone will take up a collection from the audience to get the entry fee. Sometimes the person staging the hunt will make it so much per minute. And there's usually audience wagering involved, too. There are a lot of variations."

"I see."

"Some men think it'll be easy, with such a limited space and the bells jingling every time she moves," Azl continued. "They're fools. The audience makes so much noise it's hard to hear the bells, and usually the quarry is jumping around constantly. Some women are athletic enough to put on quite a show."

Tulzik looked at the cheering crowd.

"I suppose you want to go watch," Azl said.

Tulzik hesitated. He was curious – but he was also eager to get back to the Imperial Palace and see what Hrus had accomplished, and perhaps discuss the situation further with both his hosts, now that he had more or less convinced Azl that his story was the truth.

Then he glimpsed a face in the crowd, a familiar face beneath black curls, much like one they had seen just moments earlier. He turned north and started walking again, carefully not breaking into a run. "Peval is there," he said.

"Ah," Azl replied. "That would explain why he wasn't home to welcome us."

"Yes."

A moment later, Tulzik said, "I suppose you've seen a few bell hunts."

Azl grimaced. "Yes," she said.

Something in her tone puzzled him; Tulzik threw her a glance.

"I was *in* a few," she said. "When I was younger."

"You mean you were the quarry?"

"Yes."

The image of Azl wearing nothing but bells was interesting and slightly disturbing. "Were you ever caught?"

"Twice," she said. "The first time and the last. The first because I didn't yet know what I was doing, though of course I thought I did, and the last – well, that was why it was the last. It didn't end well."

"You said the quarry has a partner who handles the money?"

"Yes, of course."

"Was Hrus your partner?"

"No. I hadn't yet met him when I started." She sighed. "Before you ask who my partner was and what became of him, I told you it ended badly."

"Oh." Tulzik decided not to pry further.

They walked silently for a moment; then Azl asked, "What would you have done if the original Peval Salinzi had been home?"

"I don't know," Tulzik said. "Improvised, I suppose."

"You had no idea whether he was there or not?"

"Not really, no."

Azl absorbed that, then said, "You take needless risks."

"Perhaps," Tulzik conceded.

"You do seem to improvise well, but I would not recommend relying on improvisation too often."

"I cannot argue," Tulzik said. "I have already agreed that I was stupid at least once tonight."

"Do you have a plan to get one Peval or the other to the *tsaughth* slaughterhouse to meet the Biologist, or were you planning to improvise that, as well?"

"Do you think he needs to be there?" Tulzik looked at her. "I had thought it would be enough to have members of the Guild there, ready to mete out punishment for returning from exile."

"That might be enough to dispose of the Biologist," Azl agreed, "but didn't you want to get Peval, as well? If he's at the rendezvous, that will go far to convince the Guild of your veracity and his guilt."

"A good point," Tulzik said. "A very good point." He was thoughtful for the remainder of the walk back to the Imperial Palace.

CHAPTER 20

When Tulzik and Azl entered the apartment Hrus was still bent over the letter – or rather, the letters; there were now two copies.

"What's the other one for?" Tulzik asked.

Hrus looked up, startled. "I didn't hear you come in," he said.

"You wouldn't have heard a dozen monkeyboys," Azl said.

"I suppose not." Hrus smiled at her, then turned his attention to Tulzik. "The copy is for test runs. I'm matching the ink, and I don't want to make a mistake that might permanently damage the original."

"You know," Azl said, "I doubt the Biologist is going to subject every individual word in that letter to close scrutiny."

Hrus grinned crookedly at her. "You can't be sure." He glanced down at the two letters.

"Wait," Azl said. "Before you go back to work, you should know that we met Peval Salinzi's doppelganger."

"Good." Hrus' gaze settled on the letters. "If he was that easy to find we aren't outmatched."

"I wouldn't be too sure of that. Tulzik gave his real name."

Hrus' head snapped up. He stared at Tulzik. "Why?" he asked.

"Failure to think quickly," Tulzik said. "I have no better excuse."

"Do you make that sort of mistake often?"

"I can't really say," Tulzik said, trying to give an honest answer. "I'm not aware of having been in many comparable situations."

Hrus' mouth twitched. "You don't regularly encounter doppelgangers created to provide alibis for criminal conspirators? What a very dull life you must lead!"

"Why, yes, my existence is so tedious it's a wonder I bother to keep breathing," Tulzik said.

Hrus smiled and looked at Azl. "I like him," he said. "Do you think his little slip did much damage?"

"There's no way to know," Azl said. "We don't know how often the original Peval talks with his duplicate, or what they might discuss, or how good the copy is at keeping secrets. We advised him not to say we had been there, but I have no idea if he'll take that advice."

"True. You're sure it was a doppelganger and not Salinzi being clever?"

"The scar on his nose wasn't there."

"Ah. Then either he's playing a *very* deep game, or it really was a copy and we aren't outmatched at all." His smile dimmed and he said, "If you want to convince the Guild of Tulzik's honesty, you should talk to them as soon as possible."

"We could go now."

"Or you could leave Tulzik here. I might find him useful."

Azl glanced from her husband to Tulzik, then back. "Suit yourself," she said. She turned and left without another word.

When she had gone, Hrus stared at Tulzik for a moment. Tulzik looked back calmly.

At last, Tulzik said, "I would suggest you either ask me for whatever it is you want me to tell you before Azl returns, or go back to work on the letter. This little mutual assessment isn't accomplishing much."

Hrus grinned again. "I *do* like you," he said. "Are you sure you aren't from Ragbaan? Most of the country folk I meet aren't very quick."

"I'm sure. Emniln isn't exactly a rural wasteland, though."

"It isn't like Ragbaan."

"No." Tulzik could hardly argue with that.

"Still, you're bright enough, so you saw that Azl was being even less trustful of you than was appropriate."

"Yes."

"Did she tell you why?"

Tulzik hesitated. "Her relationship with the Guild appears to be complicated," he said.

"But she didn't say that."

"She said it was a family matter."

Hrus nodded. "Her father was an Initiate in the Starfarers' Guild. She should have been one, as well. There was a falling out, an ultimatum, and she chose me over the Guild."

"I see."

"There's emotional residue. She's a very sensible person as long as the Guild isn't involved, but anywhere the Guild is concerned, she can be completely irrational. It's as if every stupid misjudgment she avoids elsewhere all crops up there, instead. She'll start out as she did with you, treating the Guild as just another part of Ragbaan's community, but then something will touch on an unresolved issue of some sort deep in her brain, and it becomes personal."

Tulzik considered this – not just what Hrus was saying, but why he had thought it necessary to say anything. "This is a warning, then?"

"Exactly."

"She seemed to think that she had incurred a debt to the Guild by giving them apparently false information in exchange for the apparent truth of Peval's innocence. She also seemed to think the Guild might have *arranged* this."

"Oh, dear. I was afraid of that." All trace of his earlier smile vanished. "We're going to do this one again." He sighed. "When we can prove that your story is true the Guild will be in *our* debt, and everything will be fine. That won't be a problem, but until it's done Azl is going to be difficult."

"If the Guild sees the doppelganger...?"

"It may be that simple. It *should* be, especially with the scar. With Azl and the Guild, though, I'm never certain." He grimaced. "It makes my life interesting."

"I would think Azl would do that by herself."

The grin reappeared. "Oh, she does. Now, would you prefer to tell me everything about your visit to the doppelganger, or should we go over the letter first? You know Peval better than I do, so I want you to go over my word choices."

"The letter," Tulzik said.

"Very good. Come here, then, and see which of these you think is closer to how Peval would phrase it."

With that, the two men began going over the dozens of alternate versions Hrus had created, trying to choose the one most likely to bring the Biologist to Ragbaan and least likely to be seen as a trap. They had scarcely made a good beginning on the project when Azl returned with word that the Guild was going to take a look at the doppelganger.

"They'll know what to do," she said.

Hrus did not bother to reply; Tulzik said, "I hope so," then turned back to Version 6 of the letter.

An hour later they finally reached agreement on Version 8 as the best choice, and Hrus sat back in his chair.

"*Now*," he said, "I want to hear about this doppelganger."

Tulzik glanced at Azl.

"Your version first," Hrus said. "I can hear Azl's any time."

Tulzik nodded, then began.

The description took considerably longer than the actual visit had; the first glimmerings of dawn were beginning to lighten the windows when Hrus was finally satisfied. He had been working on the forged letter as he listened, and when he finally told Tulzik he had heard enough, the job was almost finished.

"Go to bed," Hrus told Tulzik. "When you wake up I'll have this ready to go out on the four o'clock airship."

Tulzik nodded sleepily and found his way to his room. He barely remembered to remove his boots before he fell into the bed.

When he next opened his eyes the room was bright with full daylight.

"Good afternoon, honored guest," the *kaua* voice said.

"It's afternoon?"

"Yes. The time is two hours, fourteen minutes, and some seconds after noon."

"That late?"

"Azl wanted to wake you some time ago, but Hrus said you should be allowed to sleep. They gave instructions to inform you, though, that your hosts are eager to speak with you."

"About what?"

"They wish to inform you of a message they received earlier today."

"What message?"

"A message they received earlier today."

"Yes, but what *was* the message?"

The *kaua* seemed to hesitate ever so slightly before saying, "They wish to inform you of its content."

"So *you* can't tell me?"

"They wish to inform you of its content," it repeated.

Tulzik nodded and looked around for his clothes.

Five minutes later he presented himself in the front room, where Hrus and Azl were leaning over the desk, studying something.

"The *kaua* says you got a message," he said.

Azl looked up. "Yes. From the Guild."

"They saw the doppelganger?"

"No," Hrus said. "They found the eleventh floor deserted. They acknowledge that there were signs of recent habitation and that the place is full of signs that *someone* with Peval Salinzi's genes was there, but they prefer to think it was Peval Salinzi and not his illegal duplicate."

"So they don't believe me?" Tulzik asked.

"They do not," Hrus replied.

"They're wrong," Azl said. "I know that."

Tulzik was slightly surprised she felt any need to say so, but nodded politely.

"The letter is ready," Hrus said, gesturing at the document he and Azl had been studying.

"Ah!" Tulzik hurried over and took a look.

"Dillum – " he read, "I conducted an experiment on the way here, as we discussed, and it seems the results were not what we anticipated. I am reliably informed that there was no permanent effect. As I'm sure you'll understand, I am not about to carry out your wishes unless I know that the device provided will perform as intended. For now, I am employed as you suggested and awaiting further counsel, which I trust you will provide. Please meet me at the *tsaughth* slaughterhouse near the crater rim at three in the afternoon on the first of next month, so that we may confer."

The added sentence blended in perfectly, and the signature initials did not seem crowded at all. Hrus had done a fine job.

"Excellent," Tulzik said.

"Adequate," Hrus replied. "Now, to get it delivered."

"I can send it on the four o'clock airship," Tulzik said.

"You have the postage?"

"No," Tulzik admitted.

"Then I'll accompany you and see that it's sent," Hrus said.

Tulzik glanced at Azl. He had become accustomed to roaming the city with her, rather than Hrus, but he was forced to concede to himself that he had no reason to object to a change in companions. "As you please," he said.

"We'll eat first, then go," Hrus said. "No reason to leave it any later than necessary."

Tulzik nodded.

Forty minutes later the two men descended the staircase to the north arcade, dressed casually and carrying nothing but the letter. They emerged from the stairwell to find the Ilm standing there, its crest raised. The normal afternoon crowd was giving the creature a wide berth, so that it was impossible to avoid seeing it immediately.

Tulzik blinked in surprise. Hrus' face gave no sign of his reaction.

The Ilm noticed them as soon as they noticed it. "Ah, Tulzik Ambroz," it said. "And Hrus Daundablo Hangalef Tir-Dondarai. I take pleasure in the sight of you on this occasion."

"Ilm," Hrus said. "What brings you here?"

"I sought Tulzik Ambroz."

"You seem to have found him."

"Yes." The Ilm blinked in its slow and disturbing fashion. "I have learned a fact I think it would be amusing to convey."

"What fact?" Tulzik asked.

"Let me first say that I have learned several facts, some of which amuse *me*. It would seem I have been falsely accused of delivering information that I did not actually possess, and that I now possess only because the accusation was made."

It took Tulzik a second to interpret that. "Was it the Starfarers' Guild or Peval Salinzi who told you?" he asked, when he had figured it out.

"Ah, is the Guild involved? Still more information I did not previously have!" The Ilm's expression distorted into something that Tulzik hoped was its equivalent of a smile.

"Then it was Peval?"

"Indeed it was. He is looking for you, Tulzik, and I do not think he means you well. He found me and spoke to me this morning, inquiring whether I knew your whereabouts."

Tulzik was not happy to hear that. "What did you tell him?" he asked.

"I said I did not."

That answer seemed too simple and unadorned; Tulzik did not trust it. He knew he did not understand the Ilm, and that the flat statement might be nothing more or less than the truth, but he did not care to rely on it. "Yet here you are," he said.

"Indeed."

"Did you tell Peval anything else, then?"

"Ah. I suppose I did. In the course of any normal conversation, does one not tell one's fellows any number of things? The angle of an elbow, the tilt of a head, may convey far more information than the speaker might realize."

The Ilm's features had distorted oddly as it spoke, and Tulzik had the distinct impression it was doing its equivalent of laughing at him. "I am sure that's true," he said. "And I'm happy that I seem to amuse you so. However, this is a matter of some urgency to me. Peval Salinzi killed my sister, and I suspect he would like to kill me, as well. I would prefer not to leave my parents mourning another lost child. Did you say anything to Peval that could lead him to me?"

The Ilm's expression changed abruptly, though it was still alien and virtually unreadable. "Your concern is valid, and I regret my mockery. No, I did not volunteer any information. I neither denied nor confirmed telling you where you might find his doppelganger. I offered Peval Salinzi no counsel. When he was well out of sight I came to warn you, and I have now accomplished that goal."

"Thank you, Ilm."

"I admit to curiosity regarding further details of your situation. You implied that the Starfarers' Guild is involved."

"It is after a fashion, yes..." Tulzik began.

"Listen, Ilm," Hrus interrupted, "this is not a good time. We have an errand to run, an urgent one."

Thus reminded, Tulzik said, "Yes, we do."

"Perhaps I shall accompany you."

Hrus and Tulzik exchanged glances.

"Could we stop it, even if we wanted to?" Tulzik asked.

"Probably not," Hrus admitted.

"Will it attract attention?"

"A little. But it's not as if it hasn't always been here." Hrus gestured at the other people in the passageway. Every so often one or two of them would glance curiously at the Ilm, but no one was actually staring.

"I see," Tulzik said. He shrugged. "We're just posting a letter."

"It may get bored or distracted," Hrus said.

The Ilm replied, "You know me well, Hrus Daundablo."

Hrus snorted. "I don't know you at all, Ilm. I don't even know what you are."

The Ilm did something with its shoulders. "I am the Ilm," it said.

"But what's an Ilm?"

"I am."

It was doing that thing with its face again – laughing at them, Tulzik was sure. "Come on," he said to Hrus.

The two men marched southward down the arcade, paying no further attention to the Ilm. When they reached the great hall Tulzik glanced back over his shoulder and saw that the Ilm was only halfway along the passage, apparently talking to one of the trades-people seated along the arcade wall.

Distracted, just as Hrus had suggested.

Relieved, Tulzik followed Hrus as he wove his way through the crowds, and shortly thereafter they emerged from the Imperial Palace onto the plaza. They made their way around to the south, then turned west at the statue of Kazur the Third and headed up the slope toward the Eighth Street Pier.

Tulzik did not notice that a moment later the Ilm, too, turned west at the statue and ambled toward the Temple of Forgotten Glory, walking about a hundred yards behind them.

CHAPTER 21

The airship to Zaraquan was loading right on schedule, and Hrus gave the letter and postage to the purser without incident. Then he stood back and leaned against a rail, watching as the half–dozen passengers made their way up into the cabin. The corporate sigils on the airship's great hull gleamed brightly in the afternoon sun, while the airship itself cast a long shadow over the streets below the pier.

Tulzik hesitated, then decided there was no harm in being casual and settled against the rail beside Hrus.

They rested in companionable silence for only a moment before Hrus spoke. "I would suggest you not look around when I tell you what I am about to tell you," he said in a conversational tone, not moving from his position.

Tulzik shot him a quick glance, then said, "I'll try not to."

"The Ilm is watching us from the west end of the pier."

Tulzik absorbed that, but managed not to look. "It followed us after all?"

"So it would appear."

"Did it see you post the letter?"

"I really don't know. I don't have a clear idea how its vision compares with ours."

"I think it sees quite well," Tulzik said.

"All aboard!" the purser called, taking a final look around the platform. Then she heaved her table onto the lift and rose out of sight into the airship's belly. The three men of the ground crew released the half–dozen lines, waving as each one came free, and the ropes retracted into the ship as the propellers hummed to life. Hatches clanged and bolts thumped as the vessel was properly secured for its flight; then it began to rise and turn its nose to the west.

"The letter's safely on its way," Tulzik said, risking a quick glance to the west – now that the airship was moving, it didn't seem unreasonable to look where it was headed.

As Hrus had said, the Ilm was standing at the uphill end of the pier. It was not even pretending to watch the departing airship, though; its gaze was fixed on the handful of people still in the launching area.

The ground crew had clearly finished for the day; they were chatting with one another as they gathered their belongings from a locker in a corner of the staging area. A few friends or family members were still standing around, waving to the airship, which was now at least a hundred feet up and starting to pick up speed. The propellers were just a blur now, their bright red and yellow stripes transformed into concentric rings of color.

"It's on its way," Hrus said. "Whether it's safe or not isn't proven."

Tulzik threw him a startled glance. "What could happen to it?"

"It's been at least thirty years since anyone shot down an airship, but it's not impossible it could happen again, and even if nothing external attacks it, we don't know who's aboard that thing, or what motives they might have for stealing or destroying the mail."

Tulzik stared at him. "You have a strange way of thinking," he said. "You're worrying about something that hasn't happened for thirty years?"

"I'm not worrying," Hrus said. "I am merely pointing out possibilities. In my line of work it's a good idea to consider every possibility I can."

"Even incredibly unlikely ones?"

"Sometimes *especially* the unlikely ones. Those are the ones most people ignore, after all."

"They ignore them *because* they're unlikely!"

"Unlikely things do happen, though, and if you haven't considered them they can really hurt you."

Tulzik snorted. "Most of the time, though, you've wasted your effort."

"Yes."

"Most of the time that airship is completely safe."

"Never *completely*."

"But all in all, it's about as safe as anything can be. Safety is a relative thing."

"I will agree the letter is safer on the airship than it would be in your possession."

"It's also not any *use* in my possession."

"Well, *that's* true."

"So getting it aboard the airship has rendered it safer *and* more useful. I'd say that's a gain all around."

"*Closer* to being useful," Hrus amended. "It won't actually *be* useful until the Biologist reads it."

"Fine! Fine!" Tulzik threw up his hands. "It's *on its way* to being useful!"

Hrus clearly considered a possible objection to this statement, but decided not to make it.

"At any rate, the Ilm can't interfere with it," Tulzik said.

"I hope not," Hrus said. "I don't *know* what the Ilm can do."

"You're just *full* of encouragement and good cheer, aren't you?"

"So Azl tells me."

Somehow Tulzik did not believe that, but he was not inclined to argue. "Any idea why the Ilm followed us?" he asked.

"Probably just curious," Hrus said. "That's one trait it definitely shares with humans."

"You don't think it intends to play some nasty trick on us?"

"It might," Hrus acknowledged. "A sense of humor is something else it has, but its idea of a joke doesn't always match mine." He shrugged. "But then, there are plenty of members of our *own* species who don't share my idea of what constitutes a good joke."

Tulzik sighed. "I don't think it's going away," he said. "We might as well head back to the Imperial Palace."

"There's no reason to stay here, certainly," Hrus agreed. He stood up straight. "And perhaps we might have a few words with our white-skinned friend."

"I don't think it means us any harm," Tulzik said, as the two of them began ambling along the pier.

"I suppose not," Hrus agreed, "but that doesn't mean it won't harm us anyway."

"I know."

They were nearing the Ilm now, and it was looking around, rather than at them. Its crest was erect, even more so than usual. Then it turned as they approached and fixed its gaze on them.

"I apologize, Tulzik Ambroz," it said.

Tulzik blinked up at it. "For what?"

"For leading your enemy to you. It was not intentional." It pointed.

Tulzik looked where the Ilm pointed and saw Peval Salinzi standing in the shadows of a temple entry, watching them.

"I thought I had eluded him. I was in error," the Ilm said.

Tulzik's belly tightened. "He knows I'm here," he said.

"He already knew it," Hrus said. "From his conversation with the doppelganger."

"He assumed it," Tulzik said. "Now he *knows* it."

Peval stepped out of the shadows, the older and scarred Peval. Something metal glinted in his hand.

"I believe he's armed," Hrus said.

"I believe you're right," Tulzik replied.

Peval raised his hand, aiming an object that very definitely looked like a weapon.

"Run," Hrus said.

Tulzik ran, cutting sideways and diving over the side of the pier, then catching himself on a section of fence before dropping to the street below.

"Tulzik!" Peval's voice called after him. "Wait!"

Tulzik did not wait. He could not see how anything good could possibly come of waiting. Instead he charged headlong down the street, through sunlight and shadow, past startled pedestrians, gleaming machines, and a furry scavenger that was prowling along the fence below the pier.

The forged letter had been sent, and with any luck at all the Biologist would be at the slaughterhouse at three o'clock on the afternoon of the first. If Tulzik could arrange for representatives of the Starfarers' Guild to be there as well, then the entire plot might be exposed and Vika's murder avenged – but he could not do that if he was dead, and he had little doubt that Peval intended to kill him, so he ran.

He headed down the slope partly because it was easier to run downhill, but also because he thought it would be easier to lose a pursuer in the crowded streets of Ragbaan's surviving core than in the largely deserted ruins that ran along the ridge top. Up there the sound of his footsteps would be audible; down on Grand Avenue it would be drowned out by the city's traffic. Among the ruins any movement would stand out; on the waterfront it would blend in.

He did not merely run in a straight line, though; that would give Peval a clear shot with that weapon of his, whatever it was. Instead

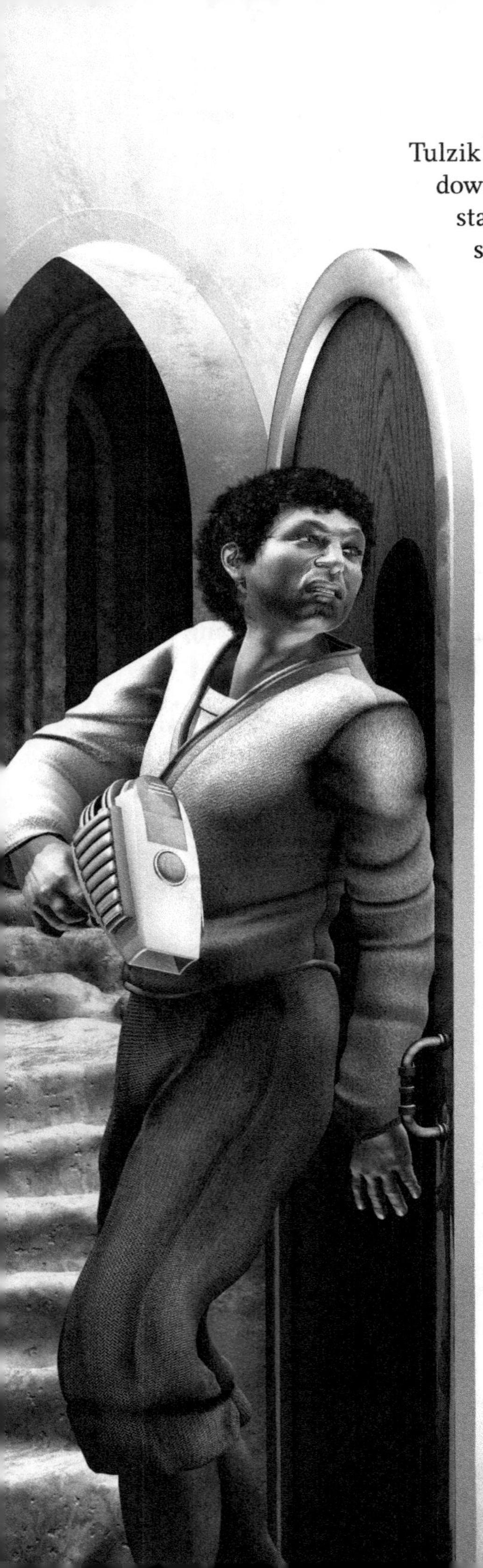

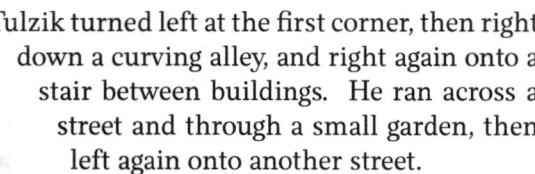

Tulzik turned left at the first corner, then right down a curving alley, and right again onto a stair between buildings. He ran across a street and through a small garden, then left again onto another street.

He was now lost, on a street he was fairly certain he had never seen before, but he did not let that trouble him. He was sure he could find his way back to familiar territory once he knew he was safe. He slowed and looked back to make sure he had eluded his foe.

As he did Peval came around the corner, weapon raised.

Tulzik immediately ducked through the nearest opening, which turned out to be the open door of a temple. He found himself in a large, dim chamber full of sweet-smelling smoke; colored light spilled through stained glass windows high in the western wall. He saw no worshipers, but somewhere ahead he could hear bells and chanting. Rather than follow the sound he looked for an exit nearer at hand and found another door. He dashed to it and hurried through.

That led him into a narrow corridor that ended in a stair heading up; Tulzik hesitated, but then heard a door flung open against a wall somewhere behind him, and hastily began trotting up the steps. A moment later he emerged into a gallery overlooking a garden; several doors opened off the side away from the garden. He chose one at random and tried the latch.

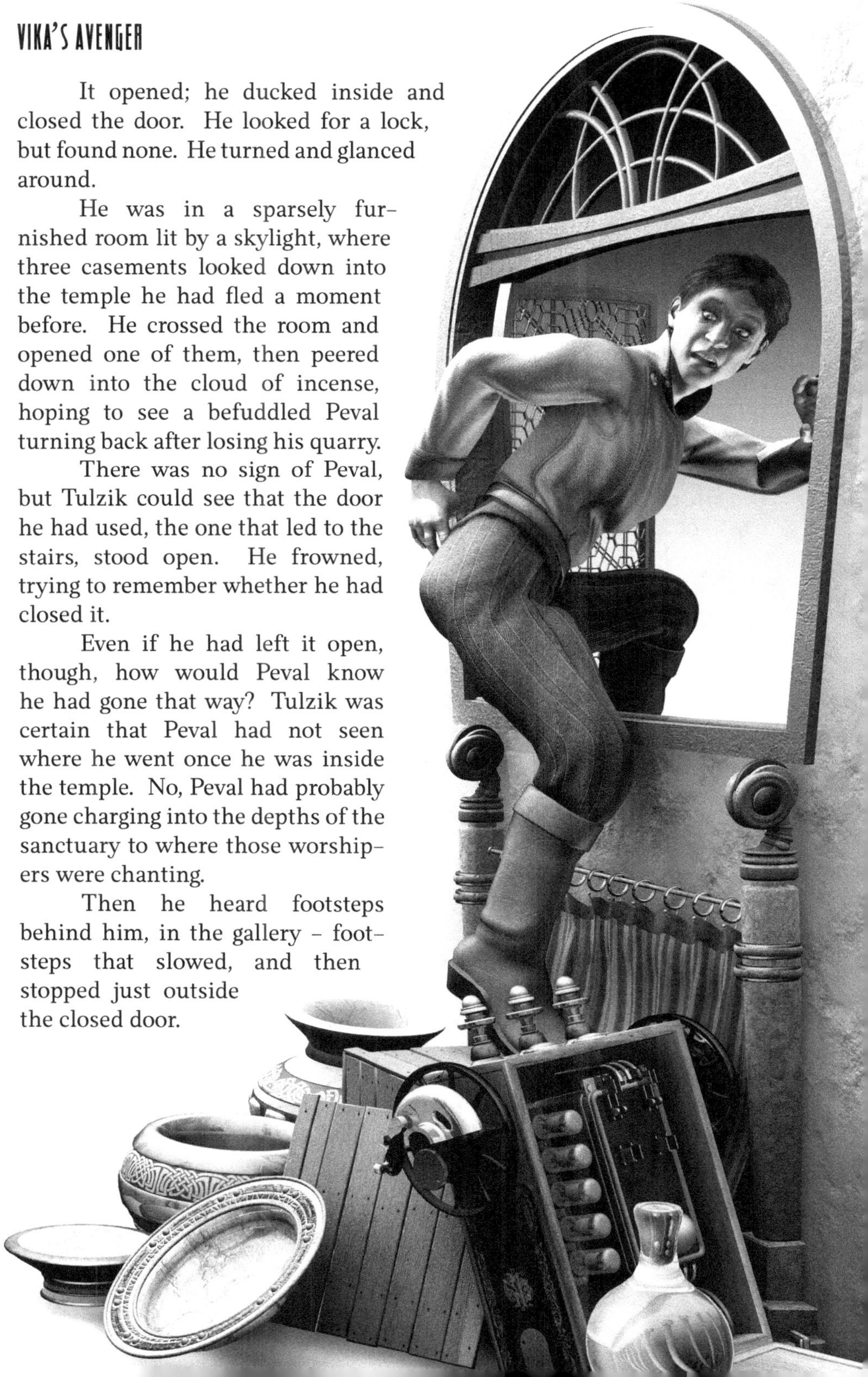

It opened; he ducked inside and closed the door. He looked for a lock, but found none. He turned and glanced around.

He was in a sparsely fur-nished room lit by a skylight, where three casements looked down into the temple he had fled a moment before. He crossed the room and opened one of them, then peered down into the cloud of incense, hoping to see a befuddled Peval turning back after losing his quarry.

There was no sign of Peval, but Tulzik could see that the door he had used, the one that led to the stairs, stood open. He frowned, trying to remember whether he had closed it.

Even if he had left it open, though, how would Peval know he had gone that way? Tulzik was certain that Peval had not seen where he went once he was inside the temple. No, Peval had probably gone charging into the depths of the sanctuary to where those worship-ers were chanting.

Then he heard footsteps behind him, in the gallery – foot-steps that slowed, and then stopped just outside the closed door.

If that was Peval, Tulzik realized, then the man was tracking him somehow. He must have some magic, some *tek*, that told him which way Tulzik had gone.

But was it really Peval outside the door, or merely some priest who had coincidentally arrived at this particular time? Tulzik tried to work out which was more likely as the doorknob started to turn.

He decided it didn't matter which was more likely; *any* chance that it was Peval was too much. If it was Peval, then Tulzik was trapped – or was he? He looked around and spotted a way out – not a very comfortable one, but a possibility. He hastily climbed up into the open casement; it was a tight squeeze, but he could fit through the opening.

The door opened, but only a foot or so. Peval's head appeared in the opening, followed immediately by the hand holding the weapon. Tulzik pushed himself through the casement and jumped, hoping he would not break a leg or turn an ankle when he hit the temple floor.

His knee buckled when he landed, and he sprawled sideways, slamming his elbow against the stone. He ignored the pain and got quickly to his feet, then ran for the door to the street. As he exited the temple he looked back up at the casement.

Peval was there, pointing the weapon at him.

How, Tulzik wondered as he ran blinking down the sunlit street, had Peval followed him? It had to be magic.

There were several varieties of magic that would allow someone to track a person, but the most common ones required some sort of tag on the quarry, and Tulzik could not see how Peval could have placed such a tag on him. Furthermore, if he had, why would he have troubled the Ilm with his questions?

No, it was probably one of the more sophisticated forms of tracking *tek*, one that did not require a tag. It could not be anything dependent on any sort of vision, since Tulzik's dodge into the temple had not allowed him to escape. Sound, perhaps? Something that listened for the distinctive sound of his heart, or his breath?

Once again, though, ducking into the temple and turning to run up the stairs should have been enough to elude such a device.

Tulzik dashed around a corner, glancing back to see whether Peval was on his trail, and thought he saw someone emerging from the temple and looking about. He did not pause to be *sure* it was Peval, but he did not really doubt it.

Could Peval be following his scent, perhaps?

That could be it. Indeed, the more Tulzik thought about it, the more certain he became that Peval must have a sniffer. Tulzik had heard of such things, but had never seen one and was unsure what one would look like. Perhaps that thing Peval held was not a weapon at all, but a sniffer.

Or more likely, it was both – a weapon with a sniffer built into it.

That was bad. A fully functional sniffer, according to the stories, could identify the faintest trace of a person, and indicate the direction he had taken. Eluding one was very difficult indeed.

It was not *impossible*, though.

Sniffers could identify the tiniest bit of a person, in the air or on the ground. A particle of hair or skin too small to be seen, or a particular pattern of odors from sweat and breath, was as good as a teklit signboard. But these traces faded rapidly. If Tulzik could get far enough ahead of Peval, he could escape the sniffer.

In particular, airborne traces faded rapidly. The trail he left on the ground, on anything he touched, lingered much longer – especially indoors, out of the sun and wind, so his detour through the temple had been a mistake, despite the incense. A sniffer would not be confused by other smells.

If he could get *off* the ground, his trail would be that much harder to follow. Boarding an airship was too slow and too obvious, but if he were to cross water...

He turned again at the next corner, but now he had a specific goal in mind – he was heading for the harbor. In fact, there was no particular reason to be subtle about it, no need to dodge about; if he was right, if Peval did have a properly working sniffer, dodging would not help and would just mean he needed that much longer to get to the water.

Speed, though, *was* important – he needed to stay far enough ahead so that Peval could not shoot him. He ran flat out, dodging around startled pedestrians, whirring machines, and the occasional cart. A *baz* glared at him as they almost collided, and Tulzik called a quick, "Sorry!" as he ran on.

Crossing Grand Avenue he glanced back over his shoulder and thought he saw Peval, with the silver device, whether weapon, sniffer, or both, raised high. Peval, if it was he, was several blocks behind.

That was good. Tulzik did not slow, though; he maintained his pace as he ran down toward the harbor, praying he would not make a wrong turn and find himself in a dead end.

He did not; a few minutes later he staggered out onto the waterfront and came to a stop, looking around and gasping.

Tulzik was from an inland area and did not know the fine distinctions between the various sorts of docks, piers, and wharfs, but he could see several structures protruding out into the sea, with boats of various kinds on or around them. He knew what he wanted – a boat heading away from shore, big enough that he could duck down out of sight. Beyond that he really wasn't concerned with the details. It was late enough in the day that fishing boats all seemed to be coming in, or already docked and unloading the day's catch, rather than heading out. He assumed most of the delicate, brightly colored vessels with elaborate sails were pleasure craft, which would not welcome intruders. Big freighters – he saw two ships he would put in that category – were not quick enough.

That still left an assortment of boats to choose from, and rather than try to figure out any more details, he simply pointed himself at the nearest, a boxy thing apparently propelled by magic that had pulled away from a pier a block or so to the south and was now moving across the harbor. He ran out the closest dock, his feet pounding on the planks, and dove off the end into the harbor.

The water was somewhat chilly, but not as cold as he had expected, and he did not think he was in any danger of hypothermia, but there were other problems. He had never tried swimming while fully dressed before. Fortunately, it wasn't as difficult as he feared; his wet clothes did seem to drag at his arms as he paddled, and his shoes definitely didn't help, but air trapped in his garments seemed to be helping him stay afloat. He was very glad he had left his pack back at Hrus and Azl's rooms in the Imperial Palace.

He was able to catch up to the boat without too much difficulty, but getting a hold on it was another matter; the sides were smooth and wet, with no obvious places to grasp. He thumped at it, hoping to find a finger hold.

He was too focused on staying afloat and grabbing the boat to notice the attention he was receiving from the boat's passengers until a hand reached down and closed around his wrist. He allowed himself to be heaved up out of the water and hauled aboard, but immediately twisted around, shivering, to look back at the shore, to see if Peval had seen him. He did not see the gene-cutter right away, which was promising.

"Who are *you*, and what are you doing here?" someone demanded in a strange, high voice.

On the shore, a figure appeared from the street where Tulzik had reached the waterfront. Tulzik quickly dropped down, still shivering, trying to get out of sight before Peval spotted him. "My name is Tulzik," he said, his attention still focused on Peval, "and I'm trying to get away from someone who wants me dead."

For a moment no one responded to that, and Tulzik, satisfied that Peval had not seen him, looked up from his crouch at his rescuers.

He did not need to look up very far; they were *baz*. Two of them were glaring down at him with huge dark slit-pupiled eyes. Their hairy arms were crossed over their chests.

"How does that involve *us*?" one of them asked.

That did not sound to Tulzik as if these two were going to be friendly or cooperative. They weren't human, so he could not rely on human responses; he decided his best course of action was to be as literal as possible. "You pulled me into your boat," he said.

"You *ran into* our boat," the *baz* said.

"Yes, and then you pulled me into it."

"To make you stop hammering on it before you damaged it."

Tulzik smiled and nodded, which triggered another shiver; he could feel his neck tense. "That's right," he said.

"Why were you hammering on our boat?" the *baz* asked.

Tulzik risked a quick glance over the side. The boat was still moving briskly through the water, pushed along by whatever magic it had, and Peval was still standing on the waterfront, holding that silvery thing out. It was impossible to see his features from this distance, but Tulzik was fairly certain he was not happy. There was no sign he had any idea where his quarry had gone.

"Does it matter?" he asked. His shivering had mostly stopped, but it still took an effort to keep his teeth from chattering.

The *baz* exchanged glances. "It might," said the one who had not previously spoken.

"I was fleeing for my life," Tulzik said. "Your boat was in my path."

"You had no business with us?" the first *baz* asked.

"No."

"You did not intend to pay for passage?"

"No. I have no money."

"The boat was in your path, nothing more?"

"That's right."

The *baz* exchanged glances again, and one of them said something that sounded midway between a cough and a squeak that Tulzik supposed was in their native language.

Then two hands reached down and clamped onto his arms, and he was heaved up into the air so quickly he had no time to react, beyond noticing that these monkeyboys were *strong*. The sky flashed past, and then he was flying through the air, and then he landed back in the harbor with a tremendous splash – they had thrown him out of their boat.

They had, however, thrown him out the *other side* of their boat; after all, he had said it was in his way, so they had sent him on past it.

He managed to hold his breath before he went under, and the air trapped under his shirt during his brief flight served to pop him back up to the surface like a cork, so a moment later he was swimming again, trying to blink his eyes clear and keep from shivering uncontrollably in the cool water.

He was not a strong swimmer, and he had no idea how far the boat had carried him, so for a moment he feared he might be in real danger of drowning, but then he managed to clear his vision to see where he was.

One of the ancient, misshapen, half-drowned towers that dotted Ragbaan's harbor shone like crystal in the setting sun no more than fifty feet away. Tulzik turned and swam toward it.

CHAPTER 22

Tulzik heaved himself up the two feet or so from the harbor onto the fragmentary balcony and sprawled onto the hard surface, water pouring from his clothes. For a few seconds he did nothing but lie there, breathing and trembling; the long run and the swim had left him exhausted. Then he risked a look back at the shore.

He saw no sign of Peval, which was good, nor did he see any boats heading in his direction, which was even better. It appeared that he had successfully escaped his pursuer.

On the other hand, he was on a balcony of a half-sunken tower in Ragbaan's harbor and had no idea who else, if anyone, might be in the building. He had no boat to take him back to the mainland and had serious doubts about whether he could swim the entire distance even after he had rested. He was alive, but this detour didn't get him any closer to avenging Vika.

He grimaced and turned to look at the tower wall.

The original surface had been weathered until it was as rough and pockmarked as natural stone. The several surviving windows Tulzik could see had presumably been as clear as any other window glass originally, but had been scoured to opaque white by centuries of dust and wind, so he could see nothing of the interior. That any of the windows were still there at all testified to the tower's magical origins; only powerful *tek* could have created glass that would survive so long under such circumstances.

The balcony, or what was left of it, was perhaps fifteen feet long and three feet deep at its widest point. A metal and glass door had once provided access to it, flanked by two large windows; the door and both windows were more or less intact, but Tulzik could see nothing through the whitened glass. The door's frame *looked* undamaged and functional, but Tulzik knew it might well be corroded inside, holding the door more tightly than any vault.

Or it might be fine. After all, Tulzik had seen lights in some of these towers.

To either side of the balcony were more windows, spaced along the tower's facade. To the right at least one, halfway to the corner, had been smashed out, leaving a gaping hole.

Tulzik considered that. He could swim *that* far, he thought, and climb in the hole – but that would mean getting soaked again, and his clothes had just begun to feel as if they might someday be dry again. Besides, there might be sharp edges in the bottom of the empty frame, and in that case pulling himself up through the opening would not be pleasant. He might resort to that, if necessary, but there was no harm in trying easier methods first. Soaked and shivering, he pulled himself to his feet, stumbled across the weathered balcony, and tried the door.

To his pleased surprise it opened easily, so easily he almost fell. The hinges squealed and metal scraped somewhere, but it moved so freely that there could be no doubt that it was still in regular use. Clearly, this tower was not abandoned. Swinging the door wide, Tulzik stepped inside.

The room beyond was dim. The only light came from the late afternoon sun, pouring through the open door or filtered through the etched glass of the two windows. The floor and walls were bare and rough, but the room was not empty; two mismatched couches in the style of the last century stood on either side, and a desk and chair stood opposite the balcony door.

A woman was sitting in the chair. She was dressed in some-thing blue and shimmering and had been looking through a stack of papers. She had apparently turned at the sound of the door and was staring at Tulzik. Her eyes narrowed. "Who are *you?*" she demanded.

"I could ask the same thing," Tulzik replied.

"I'm not the one who's trespassing," she said.

"You aren't the one who fell out of a boat and swam for the nearest dry surface, either," Tulzik retorted.

"What do you want here?"

"A ride back to the mainland."

For a moment the two of them glared at each other across the room; then the woman asked, "That's all?"

"That's all."

"Can you pay for it?"

Tulzik blinked, and shivered slightly. "I don't have any money," he said.

"None?"

"Not a *jit*." He had left his pitiful supply of money, the *fing* refund he had gotten from the airship's purser, in his pack in the Imperial Palace.

"The fare's a *fing*."

"I don't have it."

She nodded toward the balcony door behind him. "Then I think you had better get out there and start swimming, before Dazzer Pilot gets back."

"Oh, but surely we can work something out!" Tulzik spread his hands and smiled, trying to look charming.

"I doubt it."

It seemed charm was not going to be sufficient. "But why? I mean no harm; I'm here entirely by accident."

"You can tell Dazzer that, but I doubt it will help. The Pilots don't believe in accidents. None of the Nine Families do."

Tulzik blinked, and his contrived smile widened and turned real as a possibility occurred to him. "The Nine Families?"

"You're in Ragbaan Harbor, aren't you? Of course, the Nine Families. Who did you *think* owned this tower?"

"I didn't have any idea. I'm not from Ragbaan."

She glared at him. "I could tell that from your accent. You still haven't told me who you are, or what you're doing here."

"So I haven't. My name is...is Agros Talarik." He did not want to repeat the mistake he had made with the doppelganger. "I was fleeing an assassin and came here hoping he couldn't track me across water."

Her eyes narrowed further. "Fleeing an... Whose assassin? Do you know?"

"Shouldn't we wait until this Dazzer Pilot you mentioned arrives?"

Her eyes could not narrow any more without closing, but her brows rose. "You *want* to meet Dazzer?"

"Well, it occurs to me that the Nine Families might want to know about who's chasing me, and why."

"No one's chasing you *here* that the Families would need to know about, Agros Talarik, if that's really your name. This is the Harbor, and nobody comes or goes here without the approval of the Nine Families. If there's an assassin after you here, one of the Families sent him."

Tulzik shook his head, sending trickles of cold water down the back of his neck. "No, I don't think so. He was after me on shore, and I came here to get away from him. I'm just afraid he might have followed me."

"If this assassin of yours really exists and followed you here without permission from the Families..."

"...he'll need to pay a *fing* for a ride back?"

She looked annoyed. "If he tries to kill you here, and he's not working for one of the Nine Families, he's dead. He may not know it right away, and he may kill you first, but he's dead."

Tulzik's smile broadened even further. "Isn't it worth a *fing* if I can tell Dazzer who's after me and who hired him and where the Nine Families can find them both?"

"That depends who these people are and who *you* are," a voice said from somewhere to the side, out of sight.

Startled, Tulzik turned and peered into the gloom – the already-dim room was darkening further. The sun was apparently dropping below the western ridge. There was still enough light to see that the new arrival was a man of formidable build and indeterminate age, dressed in slick gray leather. He was standing in a door that Tulzik hadn't noticed before. "Dazzer Pilot, I presume?"

"Kinl has been talking, I take it," the newcomer said. "At least, I don't remember ever meeting you before." He stepped into the room.

He was holding a weapon – an arcgun, by the look of it, though Tulzik was too far away to be certain of it. That was almost reassuring, since arcguns were intended to incapacitate, not kill.

It was certainly *possible* to kill a man with one, of course, if nothing more effective came to hand. Tulzik did not intend to take the device *too* lightly. Whatever it was, it was pointed directly at him, and he had heard that an arcgun charge was very unpleasant indeed, even when it wasn't lethal.

"I have not had that pleasure, no." Tulzik nodded politely. He decided he had reached a point where honesty was advisable after all – he did not know very much about the Nine Families, but he knew they were a major power in the city, and they might compare notes with the Starfarers' Guild. It would be better to stick to the truth as far as possible. "Ignore the name I gave a moment ago. I am Tulzik Ambroz, late of Emniln, and I came to Ragbaan in pursuit of the man who killed my sister."

Dazzer cocked his head to one side. "You're looking for him here, in Hanil Tower?"

"No, no. I fled here when he caught me off guard. He's trying to kill me."

"He dislikes your entire family? A blood feud, is it?"

"No, nothing like that. I found out – well, I know things he doesn't want me to know."

Dazzer frowned. "That brought you here? Why? You do know you're trespassing?"

"So this woman told me." Tulzik nodded toward the desk. "I apologize for the intrusion, but I hope I can pay my fine, and the fee for passage back to the mainland, with information I think the Nine Families would want to know."

"Oh, so you came here looking to sell information?"

"No, I came here to avoid being killed, but as long as I'm here and have nothing else of value to offer – well, honestly, I think what I know ought to be worth at least a *fing*, probably half a *walu*."

"If you're looking to dicker – "

The Nine Families might be absolute masters of the local water traffic, but this particular member of the clan did not seem terribly bright. "No, no, no," Tulzik said. "I'm not dickering. I'm trespassing here, I know that, and I need a ride back to shore, but I don't have any money, so I'm offering to tell you what I know in exchange for being delivered safely back to dry land. That's all. I think it works out better all around than if you kill me."

"What's this information, then?"

"The man trying to kill me, the man who killed my sister, is working for the Biologist, Dardem Karianthis. I believe Dardem owes the Nine Families a large sum of money and that this debt was a part of why he was exiled from the city?"

"I don't – " Dazzer looked uncertain. He kept the arcgun pointed at Tulzik, but looked from him to the woman.

"He's right," the woman said. "I remember that. It was mostly the Importers who were involved."

"Yes, well," Tulzik said. "Dardem is planning to return secretly from exile, and he sent one of his people, a gene–cutter named Peval Salinzi – "

Dazzer held up a hand. "Stop," he said. "This isn't anything I know about."

"But *someone* in the Nine Families would like to know, I'm

sure," Tulzik said.

"Maybe," Dazzer admitted. He lowered the arcgun. "All right, come on, then." He beckoned.

"Come on where?" Tulzik asked.

"You're going to talk to someone who knows more of this than I do. Kinl, you, too. You're coming with us to see Grandma."

Kinl suddenly went pale. "Me?"

"Yes. If he's right about this information being worth something, I don't know who else should hear it, and it would probably need to get to her sooner or later, so we might as well skip the preliminaries and go straight to her. Come on."

"Why me?" Kinl whined. "Why not just you? You don't need me, and I have all this work to do!"

"You were here when he got here." He gestured with the arcgun. "You talked to him first. You're coming to see Grandma with us."

"But I – "

"Confound it, woman, move! *I* am responsible for this tower, and I am telling you we're both taking him to Grandma!" He pointed the arcgun at her. "I'm not taking him alone. I don't want to handle a boat and a gun and keeping an eye on him all at once."

She froze. Then she said, "Whatever you say, Dazzer." She looked at her unwelcome visitor with a look of ill-concealed loathing. "Tulzik, was it?"

"Yes."

"Not Agros?"

"No. Tulzik. My apologies for that initial lie."

She did not look mollified. She clearly did not appreciate his presence, or being forced to see this mysterious Grandma. "Come on," she said. "You're about to have the privilege of meeting the head of the Pilot family." She rose. "That way." She pointed.

The three of them left the room. At first Dazzer was in the lead, followed by Tulzik and Kinl, but this made it difficult to keep the arcgun trained on Tulzik, so once they were through the first door Dazzer stepped aside. Kinl took the lead, Tulzik followed, and Dazzer brought up the rear with the arcgun trained on the small of Tulzik's back.

"If you don't mind my saying so," Tulzik said as they made their way down an ancient corridor, lit only by open doors on either side, "this seems like a rather harsh way to treat someone who happened to wander in by accident."

"We're in a tower in the harbor, in sixty feet of water," Kinl said. "You can't wander in here by accident."

"But I did! I fell out of a boat, and this was the closest thing to swim to."

Tulzik was momentarily distracted by the sight of a stairwell where dark water lapped gently against the second step of the flight leading down, swirling across the next step down. He almost missed Dazzer's reply.

"No one is stupid enough to come close to this tower without permission," Dazzer said, as Kinl turned a corner ahead and led the way into a large room.

"I'm from out of town," Tulzik said. "I didn't know."

"What sort of boat?" Kinl asked, as Tulzik stepped into the room after her.

Tulzik didn't answer at first; he was taking in his surroundings. Kinl had led them into an immense room that had once been at least two stories in height; they were standing on what had once been a balcony along the back. The walls and ceiling were mottled gray; any other colors had long since been erased by centuries of mold and neglect.

The lower half was flooded, of course, and what's more, the huge windows on the far side had been broken out, leaving three gaping holes in the side of the tower that let in the sea and the remaining daylight. Three small boats were tied to what remained of the balcony's railing. All three were painted dark blue, but so grotesquely ornamented with large and elaborate gold figures that the blue was almost invisible beneath the gilded wings and claws. Each of these boats was unique in its decoration.

An immense unlit crystal chandelier hung from the ceiling, its lowest point a glittering inverted teardrop that dotted the surface of the water with a tiny splash of white every so often as the movement of the waves closed the minuscule gap between ornament and sea.

"What sort of boat?" Kinl repeated.

"*I* don't know," Tulzik said. "I'm no sailor."

"Let Grandma question him," Dazzer said. "Get in the boat." He gestured toward the nearest of the three craft.

Kinl was already clambering into it, steadying herself with one hand on the wing of a golden swan as she climbed down steps that represented the ribs of a skeletal monstrosity. Once in the bottom of the boat she headed for the bow.

Tulzik might have hesitated if not for the arcgun at his back; as it was, he climbed down the ribcage on Kinl's heels, then looked around.

"Over there," Dazzer said, pointing to a bench formed of the monster's lower jaw.

Tulzik sat as instructed, then watched as golden serpents' mouths released their hold on the balcony, and Dazzer cast off a far more ordinary rope that had been secured to the rail. The swans' wings lowered – there was a bird on either side of the boat – and the craft glided forward toward the nearest of the broken windows, then through the gap and out into the twilight.

The trip across the harbor was uneventful. Tulzik made no attempt to escape or to question his captors; he would know soon enough where they were going. He did enjoy the opportunity to see Ragbaan from the water, a thousand teklights gleaming from its shadowed towers and palaces as the sunset blazed golden behind the western ridge. The tower they were leaving was the closest to the shore; glancing back, Tulzik could see it rising perhaps two or three hundred feet above the water, a humped and broken peak of silvery metal and dark stone, patterned with white–etched glass that gleamed in the fading daylight.

Turning his attention back to the shoreline he could see the towers along Grand Avenue and thought he could identify the one where Peval Salinzi and his magical creations lived. Further north a golden dome was visible between two towers, and Tulzik was fairly sure that was the Imperial Palace.

He wondered what Hrus was doing. Was he safely home again? What had he said to the Ilm? Had the Ilm really not known it was leading Peval to Tulzik?

What was Peval doing, now that his quarry had escaped? Was he still prowling the streets with his sniffer, looking for some trace of Tulzik? Now that he knew some scheme was afoot, that Tulzik had not been entirely truthful, might he contact the Biologist by some method faster than airmail? Perhaps the gene–cutters had designed fast-flying birds or insects to help them communicate in such an emergency.

How much did Peval really know about Tulzik's activities in Ragbaan? Did he have any idea that Tulzik and Hrus were trying to lure Dardem into a trap?

Who or what was Grandma? Why was Kinl so reluctant to visit her?

There were far too many unanswered questions. Tulzik frowned as he leaned back on the padded golden teeth that formed the bench's back.

The journey lasted about fifteen minutes, giving Tulzik's clothes and hair time to dry, and ended when Kinl guided the boat into an immense hangar that held a veritable menagerie of water craft – a dozen or so of the blue-and-gold beast-boats, assorted sleek little sailboats, a hulking boxy white freighter, and others Tulzik did not get a good look at.

He was not certain whether this boathouse was on an island or a headland; he didn't suppose it mattered. He did know it was north and east of where he had started, around the curve of the coast from Ragbaan's heart, but he had not been able to see details as they approached. He could tell from the architecture that it was very old, probably older than the Imperial Palace, perhaps of roughly the same vintage as the Red Museum; there were inexplicable bits of orna-mentation along the walls and ceiling, along with blank and broken screens, and teklights gleamed and flickered here and there, scatter-ing the shadows. The entire place smelled of age, decay, seawater, and machinery.

The boat pulled up to a dock, the golden serpents uncoiled from the sides and bit into the timbers, and Dazzer raised the arcgun. "Out," he said.

Tulzik stood, a trifle unsteadily – the boat was still swaying – and climbed up the ribs and onto the worn black surface of the dock. Several people were going about their business; some turned to look at him.

"Dazzer, who's *that*?" someone called.

"A trespasser I'm taking to see Grandma," Dazzer replied.

The audible intake of breath that followed that worried Tulzik. He had thought that Kinl's reluctance to visit Grandma might just be a personal quirk of hers, but apparently it wasn't. It seemed Grandma frightened everyone here.

"This way," Kinl said, climbing past Tulzik and pointing the way.

The threesome left the dock and found their way into teklit corridors, then up three flights of stairs, past people wearing workers' jumpsuits, iridescent glamour dress, and every sort of attire in between.

As they walked, Kinl said, "Don't bother trying to lie to Grandma, *Agros*. She can tell when you're lying."

"I wouldn't think of lying," Tulzik replied. "I have no reason to lie."

Kinl did not respond.

At last they marched down a long corridor where Tulzik noticed a humming, a sound he recognized as serious *tek* at work. Grandma apparently used powerful magic of some kind.

The door at the end of the corridor slid open, and Kinl and Dazzer escorted Tulzik into Grandma Pilot's presence.

The hum had given him a chance to prepare mentally, but Grandma's appearance was still something of a shock. From her skin and the occasional clumps of hair, and the two eyes that peered out of her bloated, misshapen face, he guessed she had been human originally, or at least some similar species, but that had been a long time ago. Now she was an immense shapeless mass of flesh and machinery, filling half of a good-sized room. Except for the face, Tulzik could not identify any specific parts of her anatomy; he saw no human arms or legs, just lumps of brown-skinned meat tangled with metal and glass and plastic. Several metal arms, as well as other tools and devices, were built into the assemblage, but no trace remained of the limbs Grandma had presumably been born with. The hum he had heard from the corridor came from Grandma herself, along with various faint hisses and wheezes, and the room reeked of oil and blood and sweat. The air was thick with the smell.

It was hard to tell which parts of the room's contents were furniture and which were Grandma. The only things Tulzik was *sure* weren't parts of the grotesque creature were half a dozen metal chairs pushed up against the back wall. Most of the walls and even part of the ceiling were lined with gleaming *tek* that was incorporated into the once-human monstrosity. Screens were displaying text, graphs, and images of living organs that Tulzik could not interpret, but which he assumed were providing constant information about Grandma's state of health.

He had heard of people kept alive by machinery, but this was not how he had pictured them. The sight was horrifying. Tulzik swallowed. He knew that showing just how unpleasant he found

Grandma's appearance would not serve him well, but he could not keep his disgust entirely hidden. He hoped that either no one would notice, or they would tolerate this involuntary reaction.

It was now completely obvious why Kinl had not wanted to come. Visiting this thing would not be an appealing prospect for anyone.

The face rippled, and the two eyes peered at the new arrivals. "Who's this, Dazzer?" a voice asked, but it did not come from anything like a mouth. It seemed to come from a black disc that was mounted on a tangle of wires and rods embedded in one of the protruding lumps of flesh. It sounded very much like the voice of a querulous old woman, though.

"He turned up in Hanil Tower, trespassing," Dazzer said. "Kinl found him."

"He swam up and climbed on the balcony outside my office," Kinl said. "I didn't see where he came from."

"And he's here because...?"

Kinl and Dazzer looked at one another, and Dazzer gestured for Kinl to answer. "He didn't have the boat fare to shore, so we were going to just throw him back in the water..." she began.

"Alive or dead?" Grandma interrupted.

"That wasn't settled yet. Anyway, he said he had information that ought to be worth boat fare, but we couldn't tell whether it was anything important, so we brought him here."

The pale blue eyes in the bulging flesh turned slightly, from the Pilots to Tulzik. "What's your version?" Grandma asked.

"The same as theirs," Tulzik said. The exchange with Kinl and Dazzer had given him time to recover his composure. "I got there because I was fleeing from an assassin who was using a sniffer to track me, so I wanted to get across some water to cut my trail. I fell out of the boat and swam for the nearest place I could get dry, which was the tower where I met these two."

"Oh, I like that," Grandma said, her tone sardonic. "Assassins are always good. And falling out of a boat? You couldn't climb back in?"

"No, I couldn't," Tulzik snapped back. "I'm from inland. I don't know much about boats."

Grandma seemed to accept that without offense, at least provisionally. "All right, then," she said. "You wanted to trade information for being set loose on the mainland, right? What's the information?"

"When and where Dardem Karianthis will be sneaking back into Ragbaan."

For a moment the only sound was the hum of machinery and a faint hiss of air. Grandma's eyes remained fixed on Tulzik's face, but she did not speak.

"Ah," Grandma said at last. "And your name is...?"

"Tulzik Ambroz. I'm from Emniln."

The sagging, oversized face sank slightly in what might have been a nod. "That's who I thought you must be. I suppose you know the Starfarers' Guild says *you're* the assassin."

"The Starfarers' Guild is wrong," Tulzik answered immediately. He hoped that the Nine Families weren't as convinced of the Guild's infallibility as Azl had been.

"They say your story's impossible."

"They're wrong. They think I'm lying because they never saw Peval Salinzi leave the city, but I know he made himself a doppelganger to cover his absence."

There was a very brief pause this time before Grandma answered, "This is interesting. You're either a very good liar, young man, or you don't know you're lying, or you're telling the truth. Your pulse and pupils didn't change at all."

It seemed Grandma did indeed have ways to tell truth from falsehood, as Kinl had warned him, though Tulzik was not certain how reliable they were. "I have no reason to lie," he said.

"You've been staying with Hrus Daundablo Hangalef Tir-Dondarai."

Grandma obviously had good sources of information, which was hardly a surprise. "Is that his full name?" Tulzik said. "I've been staying with the information brokers called Azl and Hrus, yes."

"The Guild doesn't like him."

Tulzik shrugged. "I do."

"The Importers don't much like him, either."

"I'm sure they have their reasons."

"The Guild has reasons. The Importers just don't like people who think they're smart. Especially if they really *are* smart."

Tulzik smiled. "That would be Hrus, yes."

"Your claim, as I understand it, is that Dardem Karianthis has armed one of his former associates as an assassin and sent him to kill someone here in Ragbaan."

"Yes. A gene-cutter named Peval Salinzi has been sent to kill the Sorceress."

"The Sorceress? Not Parj Importer? Or me?"

"To the best of my knowledge, his only target is the Sorceress. But I don't claim to know everything."

Grandma's eyes shifted. "Dazzer, why don't you go fetch our guest a cup of *tsir*? Kinl, find yourself a chair, won't you?"

Dazzer turned and hurried out, the corridor doors sliding shut behind him, while Kinl dragged two chairs, one for herself and one for Tulzik, from the back wall to the middle of the room. She and Tulzik settled onto them.

"Now, my dear boy," Grandma said, swinging several metal tubes and both her eyes to point at Tulzik, "suppose you tell me *all* about it."

CHAPTER 23

Tulzik told Grandma about Vika's infatuation and death and how he and Uncle Urushak had pursued her killer. He explained how he had gone to the Imperial Palace seeking information and had found Azl and Hrus there – he skipped any mention of his evening with Hiji the Oracle. He described his meeting with Peval Salinzi, and how he had stolen the letter, and how Hrus had forged a replacement. He swore that he had indeed met Peval's doppelganger in the half–empty tower on Grand Avenue, and explained about the missing scar as proof that it had not just been Peval himself playing a role. Finally, he told Grandma how the Ilm had led Peval to him, and how he had fled through the streets to the harbor and wound up in Kinl's office.

"...and here I am," he concluded.

"Here you are," Grandma agreed. "Why do you think your information is worth anything to us?"

Tulzik had been expecting that. "Hrus said that the Nine Families were one of the factions that exiled the Biologist, and Peval said Dardem owed the Nine Families a lot of money. That would imply that the Biologist is of some interest to the Nine Families, so I thought you would find it valuable to know that he plans to return from exile without your permission."

Machinery hissed; then Grandma said, "That assumes the information is accurate."

"Of course."

"That brings up the issue of whether we should believe anything you say."

"Well, yes, I suppose it does."

"There are ways of lying to me undetected."

"I'm sure there are, Grandma, but to the best of my knowledge I'm not using any of them." He smiled.

"You wouldn't necessarily know."

The smile dimmed. "I'm aware of that."

"Hrus Daundablo seems to trust you."

Tulzik bowed his head. "I hope I'm worthy of his trust."

"Do you know why Parj Importer doesn't like your friend Hrus?"

"No," Tulzik said. "I've never met Parj Importer."

"You probably don't want to. He doesn't like Hrus because Hrus figured out a few Importer family secrets and was tactless enough to let Parj *know* he had figured them out."

"That sounds like Hrus."

"Do you know why the Guild doesn't like Hrus?"

"Azl told me he had uncovered a spy in the Guild..."

"Filimon? Pfah!" Several metal arms waved in a dismissive gesture. "That was just the final tap of the hammer. He wasn't much of a spy; he was just making sure the Guild lived up to their agreement with the Antiquarians. No, the Guild hates Hrus because Azl turned down an invitation to Guild membership so she would be free to marry him. Not that the Guild would ever admit it. Her father was a high-level initiate and had trained her as his heir, and she threw that away to marry Hrus, who did not have the right bloodlines."

Tulzik frowned. "I thought Hrus came from a very old family."

"Ah, now, who told you *that*? I'm sure *Hrus* didn't mention it."

"Hiji told me, and Azl agreed."

"Well, I don't know who this Hiji is, but it's true – Hrus is from one of the oldest and proudest families in the city. His ancestors lived in the Imperial Palace *before* the Empire fell; his hereditary rank is too *high* for the Guild. They don't allow ancient nobility to join. Not that he has the right sort of temperament for the Guild, in any case."

Tulzik found that easy to believe. Somehow he didn't think Azl had the right temperament, either, and he wondered whether she had deliberately chosen an unsuitable spouse to avoid being pressured to join.

But then, she and Hrus seemed to be a very fine match for each other, Guild concerns aside. She probably hadn't considered his unsuitability a drawback, but Tulzik doubted it had really been a significant factor either way.

"Oh," he said.

"My *point*, young man, is that the people who don't like Hrus Daundablo don't like him for what are essentially stupid reasons – clashing personalities, or personal differences, not any moral or intellectual failings on his part. I have never met him, but I am familiar with his reputation. Everything I know of him indicates he is an intelligent and honest man, if a bit whimsical. You made a very fortunate choice of friends."

"*I* thought so," Tulzik said.

"That is, assuming your story is true."

"Well, yes. *I* think it's true, but I'm no magician. I suppose I might have been fooled, or had my memories altered."

"The simplest explanation is that it is true, and the Guild is being stupid because of their resentment of Hrus, and their idiotic rock-headed pride, and just because they're human beings and humans are stupid sometimes. Simple explanations are usually best. I haven't lived eight hundred years by ignoring unlikely possibilities, though."

"Eight hundred years?"

"About that. You don't think anyone could do this *now*, do you?" A steel bar swept across the center of Grandma's mass.

"It seems improbable, but one never knows."

"One never knows!" A machine made a stuttering noise that vaguely resembled laughter. "Exactly my point. So I think your story is true, but I can't be certain."

"Very sensible," Tulzik replied.

"Again, I didn't survive eight hundred years by being foolish."

"Of course."

"When and where, then, is this supposed meeting between Peval Salinzi and Dardem Karianthis to occur?"

Tulzik hesitated, then said, "What am I offered for the information?"

"What I propose, lad, is to release you on the mainland and forgive you your trespasses, but to keep an eye on you and kill you instantly should it be proven that you have lied to me."

"Oh." Tulzik swallowed. He could not really see an alternative to accepting this, and he hoped very much that the Biologist did not detect the forgery, or refuse to oblige Peval. "Fair enough. The meeting is to be at three in the afternoon on the first of next month, at the *tsaughth* slaughterhouse by the rim of the crater west of the city."

A map of the city appeared on one of Grandma's screens, then zoomed in on a spot that Tulzik assumed was the slaughterhouse; it matched his memory of the ruin's location, at any rate.

"A place we would not ordinarily have any reason to watch," Grandma said.

"Yes."

"It's well inland, outside our territory."

"I did not have the Nine Families in mind when I chose it, I'm afraid," Tulzik said. "That part of the city is all deserted ruins, though. I don't think anyone could object to your presence there." He quickly added, "Not necessarily *your* presence, Grandma, but some members of your family."

That mechanical stutter sounded again. "Good enough," the monstrosity said. "The Nine Families will have representatives at the *tsaughth* slaughterhouse on the first of the month – hidden, of course – to see whether the Biologist does indeed try to enter the city."

Tulzik nodded. "I would be happy with such an arrangement."

"Those representatives will have orders to kill you if he fails to appear."

"I hope you will make some provision for unforeseen circumstances – he has not yet replied to the letter. He could be dead, or delayed."

"Oh, I think we will listen to reason."

Tulzik would have preferred something a little more encouraging, but he nodded. "All right."

"Our agents will also guard you against this Peval between now and the meeting at the slaughterhouse," Grandma said.

Tulzik rose from his chair and bowed. "Thank you, Grandma."

"Don't thank me yet. You aren't going to have much privacy for the next few days."

"Oh."

"Kinl, you heard all this, I trust?"

Tulzik had almost forgotten the woman was there.

"Yes, Grandma," she said, rising from her chair.

"I want the Gada Clan to watch him until this proposed meeting takes place – or fails to occur."

"I'll see if I can get them, Grandma."

"You might also talk to the rats. They could be useful at the slaughterhouse."

Kinl grimaced. "I can send an emissary."

"Do."

That puzzled Tulzik, with the implication that there were rats intelligent enough to talk to. He remembered the roasted rat-things he had seen for sale at the Imperial Palace. This did not seem an appropriate time to ask questions, though, so he simply said, "Thank you, Grandma," again.

"Off with you, then!" The door slid open.

Tulzik hesitated, then gave Grandma a final friendly wave and followed Kinl out into the corridor.

Dazzer was leaning against one wall, arms folded across his chest, with a tray on the floor by his feet. "The *tsir* is getting cold," he said.

Tulzik glanced back at Grandma just as the door slid shut again.

"She doesn't drink *tsir*," Kinl said. "She gets everything she needs through hidden tubes."

"She could just tell me the conversation is too much for my delicate ears," Dazzer said, as he stooped to retrieve the tray. "I know she thinks I'm a blabbermouth who can't keep secrets. I'd be happy to wait out here without going down to the kitchens for *tsir* no one's going to drink."

"I'd like to drink mine," Tulzik protested. "I'm parched."

"Really?" Dazzer turned, startled. Then he glanced at Kinl.

"He gets to live," Kinl said. "Grandma thinks he really does know where to find an exile sneaking back into Ragbaan, one who owes the Nine Families money."

"I assumed he got to live, since he's still standing," Dazzer retorted. "Grandma's never minded doing her own killing as long as there's someone around to clean up the blood."

"He gets a bodyguard, too," Kinl said. "The Gada."

"Oh, for..."

Tulzik decided he had waited long enough and reached out to snatch a cup off the tray. Dazzer's statement notwithstanding, the *tsir* was still pleasantly warm and was almost as strong as the one Azl had bought him in Resurrection Square.

Kinl shrugged. "Grandma said to use the Gada to guard him, so we ask the Gada. Do you know where I can find one?"

"There's usually at least one on the docks somewhere," Dazzer said.

Tulzik wondered idly who and what the Gada Clan was – another of the Nine Families, perhaps? Some other faction in Ragbaan's complex society? A cult? He did not bother asking, though. He would find out soon enough.

He followed along, sipping his *tsir*, as Kinl and Dazzer led the way back along the corridor and down the stairs. The two Pilots argued mildly the entire way, more or less ignoring Tulzik – though he had no doubt that if he tried to flee, they would react quickly enough.

Back in the boathouse Kinl pointed at a *baz* who was tugging at a rope; Tulzik could not see what the rope was attached to. "There's one," she said.

Dazzer shook his head. "Wrong markings. That's Sibok Clan. You said Gada."

"What's a Sibok doing here?" Kinl asked. Tulzik thought she sounded offended by the very idea, though he had no idea why one clan would be welcome and not another. He had not realized *baz* belonged to different clans – but then, he knew almost nothing about the *baz*.

"I have no idea. Is that a Gada, over there?" Dazzer pointed.

"The Gada Clan are *baz*?" Tulzik asked.

Dazzer glanced at him. "What did you *think* they were? Yes, they're monkeyboys."

"I'd assumed they were human," Tulzik admitted. "I'm a country boy, remember?"

"Human?" Dazzer snorted. "No, the Gada Clan are monkey-boys, all right. You can *trust* the runts – contracts are sacred to them so you don't need to worry that they'll sell you out to a higher bidder. Grandma has a service contract with the Gada Clan, binding on all of them. Come on, I see one over there."

The *baz* in question was cleaning the hull of a capsized boat, scrubbing vigorously with a black rag, and Tulzik could smell old varnish. It looked just like any other monkeyboy to Tulzik, and he had no idea how the Pilots could tell Sibok from Gada. It did not look up as the three humans approached.

"Hey," Dazzer said. "We need to talk to you."

"You can," the *baz* said, still scrubbing.

Dazzer looked at Kinl, who said, "Grandma wants the Gada Clan to do something for her."

The *baz* still did not look up as it said, "Busy. Not authorized."

"Who do we talk to, then?"

"Gada Jingarn can negotiate." It pointed.

It took several minutes to locate Gada Jingarn, and when they did Tulzik still could not see any way to tell it from any other *baz*.

Dazzer and Kinl seemed to have no such difficulty. This *baz* was bent over a tiny hand-held desk, writing something. Tulzik wondered whether Jingarn was a name, or a title.

"You talk to it," Dazzer whispered loudly, nudging Kinl. She cast him an angry look, then turned to the *baz*.

"Grandma wants the Gada Clan to do something for her," Kinl said.

The *baz* looked up, then put down its pen. "The Gada Clan signed a service contract with Grandma Pilot. What service does she request?"

"Two things. First, keep this man alive until the afternoon of the...let me see...until six days from now. Someone may be trying to kill him, and we don't want him to die until then."

The *baz* glanced at Tulzik, then turned its attention back to Kinl. "No guarantees, but we can guard him."

"He needs to be at the old *tsaughth* slaughterhouse out by the crater at three in the afternoon, six days from now."

"I do?" Tulzik said. While he had more or less intended to be present at the rendezvous, nothing had been said to that effect until now.

"You do," Kinl said. She told the *baz*, "Your people need to be out of sight at the slaughterhouse."

"Understood."

"We'd also like you to send an emissary to the rats. We think they could be useful at the meeting at the slaughterhouse, too."

"We can send an emissary. Can't promise how the rats will respond."

"Of course. Excellent. Thank you."

"We bill at the usual rates?"

"Grandma didn't say anything about a bonus, one way or the other."

The *baz* nodded. "Where shall we find him?" It pointed at Tulzik.

"We'll wait here until you have a crew to take him ashore."

"Half an hour."

"We'll wait."

The *baz* nodded, picked up its desk and pen, and hurried away in the brisk not-quite-running pace that the *baz* seemed to prefer. Tulzik watched it go, then glanced at Kinl and Dazzer.

He looked restless. She looked bored.

"At least I know it won't be my guards who are supposed to kill me," Tulzik remarked, trying to strike up a conversation.

"You do?" Dazzer asked.

"The *baz* won't kill for money, I'm told."

Dazzer glanced at Kinl. "Is that true?"

Kinl shrugged. "I don't know," she said.

That seemed to end the discussion, and for a moment no one spoke. Then Tulzik asked, "Why did you ask *them* to send the emissary to the rats?"

Kinl gave him a disgusted look. "Have you ever talked to a rat?"

"No," Tulzik said. He decided not to mention that he hadn't known *anyone* could talk to rats and get answers. "Country boy, remember?"

"They have squeaky little voices that are almost impossible to understand," she explained. "Not to mention their language has sounds in it humans can't make, so it's hard to learn it at all. The monkeyboys hear better than we do in that range and are better at making those sounds, so we use them to interpret."

Dazzer added, "Rats can't hear us any better than we hear them. Our voices are too low." He glanced at Kinl. "At least, they can't hear men; they do better with women."

"I didn't know. I don't think we have any rats in Emniln." This was not strictly true, as Emniln did have rodents that the natives called "rats," but Tulzik was fairly certain they were not the same species that Kinl and Dazzer were discussing. He had certainly never heard of any rats in Emniln having a language of their own. They could be trained to do certain jobs and to understand simple instructions, but none of them spoke, so far as he knew. "You know, I saw someone selling cooked animals at the Imperial Palace that looked like rats."

"Wild tunnel rat, probably," Dazzer said. "It's not bad."

"So it's not the same kind of rat?"

"Eww! I *hope* not!"

Kinl gave Dazzer a disdainful glance. "The tunnel rats are just animals," she said.

"Oh," Tulzik said. "But they look alike?"

"Pretty much," Kinl acknowledged.

"How do you tell them apart?"

She turned her disdain upon Tulzik. "If it's wearing a shirt and carrying a knife, I'd suggest you don't try to eat it."

"Oh."

"You *really* shouldn't try anything," Dazzer said. "If you see one rat, there are probably a hundred more you *don't* see, watching you."

"If you see one rat, it probably *wanted* you to see it," Kinl said.

"But ordinarily, you won't see any," Dazzer said. "We have an agreement. They stay in their district, and we don't bother them."

"Where's their district?"

Dazzer and Kinl exchanged glances. "Under the city," Kinl said. "Not all of it, but a lot."

"Mostly the northern part, east of the ridge and west of the runts."

Tulzik nodded.

"They mark their tunnels, though," Dazzer said. "So you'll know when you're in their territory."

"Mark them how?" Tulzik knew how garfs and other animals marked their territory; was he supposed to *smell* the rats' markings?

"With warning signs, of course," Kinl said. "They usually say something like, Keep Out, Rats."

"I wish they'd write them larger, though," Dazzer said. "Once when I was a kid I walked right past one without seeing it. My mother had to come get me. It was embarrassing, and she took the interpreter's fee out of the money I'd saved up running errands."

Tulzik was considering what to say next when four *baz* appeared around the corner and came charging toward the three humans at their usual brisk pace.

"Which one?" one of them asked as they drew near.

Kinl and Dazzer promptly pointed at Tulzik.

"Keep him alive for six days, then get him to the old slaughter-house by the crater – that's our job?"

"That's it," Dazzer said.

"Good. Agreed." With that, the four *baz* marched forward and formed a square around Tulzik, crowding Kinl and Dazzer aside. Tulzik found himself looking out over a head of brown hair, no matter which way he turned, and for the first time he noticed a distinctive odor that he realized must be the *baz*. It wasn't quite like anything he had ever smelled before; it reminded him of cinnamon, but with a certain rankness to it, as if cinnamon had somehow gone bad.

"Well, I think we're done here," Dazzer said. He turned to leave.

"Wait a minute!" Tulzik called, over the heads of the *baz*. "Grandma said she would release me on the mainland!"

The *baz* who had spoken before looked up at Tulzik, then at the two Pilots. "She did?"

"She did," Kinl said.

"We'll take care of it," the *baz* said.

"Good enough," Dazzer said.

"Thank you," Kinl added.

Then they turned and hurried away, not looking back. Tulzik watched them leave, unsure whether he was relieved to see them go.

CHAPTER 24

The boat the *baz* provided had no motor or other visible *tek*; Tulzik's four guards propelled it by rowing. That was still sufficient to get him to a dock on the mainland in a matter of minutes.

He was not permitted ashore immediately, though. Two of the *baz* scouted the area first. "We were easy to see out on the water," one of the two who remained aboard explained. "If someone *is* trying to kill you, this is when they would have their best shot."

Tulzik looked at his surroundings. The boat was riding low in the water beside a pier that held a large windowless warehouse. An overhang blocked out much of the rapidly darkening sky. They had approached along a long, crooked, unlit channel. There were no lights nearby; the glimmer of distant teklights reflected off the clouds and the water, but the area immediately around the boat was dark. He could hear water slapping against pilings, and the whole area smelled of rotting wood. He did not see anywhere someone trying to shoot him could get a decent shot at all. Clearly, the *baz* had their own standards about these things.

He doubted very much that Peval had any idea where he was, in any case, and so far as he knew no one else in Ragbaan had any reason to want him dead. He had tried to tell his guards that on the way here, but they had ignored him.

The two scouts reappeared. "All clear," one of them reported.

"Good!" The *baz* who appeared to be the leader of the foursome turned to Tulzik. "Here we are. Climb ashore, and you're released on the mainland."

"Thank you," Tulzik said, clambering up the ladder onto the pier, where the two scouts waited. They immediately took up positions on either side of him, watching in opposite directions.

One of the other guards followed him, while the last secured the boat. Tulzik began walking up the pier. He was not sure just where in the city he was, but the Imperial Palace would not be hard to find. He had learned a little of his way around.

"Where are you going?" the lead *baz* asked.

"I'm staying with friends in the Imperial Palace," Tulzik answered.

The *baz* exchanged glances, then one shook his head. "Crowds," he said. "*Kaua*. Secrets."

"Crowds," another agreed.

Tulzik shrugged and kept walking. "I'll be fine," he said.

"Not there," the lead *baz* said.

"Yes, there."

"No."

Before Tulzik could react, four inhumanly strong arms reached out, four hands locked onto his arms, and he was lifted into the air, his feet still moving comically.

He had seen enough of *baz* in action to know better than to struggle; he stopped moving. "What are you doing?" he demanded.

"We agreed to do our best to keep you alive for the next six days, so that's what we're going to do. We didn't say anything about free or happy – just alive. The Imperial Palace is too dangerous. You aren't going there."

"You can't hold me against my will!" Tulzik protested.

"Yes, we can."

"By what right? By what authority?"

"By our contract with the Nine Families."

"I'm not part of the Nine Families!"

"You were in the Pilot House. The Nine Families have authority over everything there."

"I'm not there now!"

"No, but you're only here because we brought you here. You're still our responsibility, and we will do what our contract requires. If you have a problem with how we do our job, talk to Grandma."

It was obvious to Tulzik that he wasn't going to get anywhere with this line of argument, but at least now he had a clearer idea of his situation. "Are you going to stuff me in a sack, then? I've seen you monkeyboys carrying people that way."

"Not Gada Clan, you haven't. Besides, six days in a sack would be unhealthy. No, we're going to let you do whatever you want, as long as it isn't dangerous. Anywhere crowded is dangerous."

"So where am I supposed to sleep?"

"Anywhere you want. We'll stand guard."

"My *bed* is in the Imperial Palace."

"Find another. Or sleep on the floor."

"What am I supposed to eat?"

"Whatever you want, though we may want to check for poison."

"I don't have any food, and I don't have any money."

"No money?" For the first time, the lead *baz* looked disconcerted.

"Not a *jit*. That's why I had to talk to Grandma in the first place. My hosts at the Imperial Palace have been feeding me on credit."

The *baz* frowned. "Then we'll feed you as part of keeping you alive and add it to Grandma's bill. I hope you like *drash*."

"Why?"

"Because it's all we're going to feed you. Grandma doesn't mind legitimate expenses, but she doesn't tolerate padding the bill. *Drash* is cheap."

Tulzik considered this for a moment. He was not going to accomplish much as a Gada Clan captive, but it didn't appear he was going to be able to talk his way out of it, and he *certainly* wasn't going fight his way free of four *baz*. They were superhumanly strong, and he was hardly a trained warrior. He might be able to outwit them eventually, but for now, he really didn't have much choice. It wasn't forever, just until the afternoon of the first of the month, and while he might not be able to do much about Peval while under Gada supervision, at least he would be safe and would be able to observe whatever happened at the *tsaughth* slaughterhouse.

As for an all-*drash* diet...

"With sauce?" he asked.

"We don't – "

"I won't cause trouble if you get a good sauce with it. Think of it as an investment in peace."

The *baz* exchanged looks; then the leader shrugged. "With sauce."

"Fine. You probably know the city better than I do, and you definitely know what you consider safe better than I do – *you* find us a place to stay and something to eat."

That prompted a hurried conference in a language Tulzik had never heard before; then he was lowered to the ground, and his arms released. He rubbed them to help restore the circulation; they were a little sore from the squeezing.

"This way," one of the *baz* said.

They led him through a tangle of narrow streets and up a flight of stairs to a large room on the second floor of a mostly empty building. Three of the *baz* stood guard over him while the fourth went to fetch food and supplies. There were three ancient chairs, one of them reasonably comfortable, and a pile of matting that would serve as a bed. Most of the windows were boarded up, but one was still clear and gave a view down a sloping street toward the harbor. The only light in the room was provided by a few candles one of the *baz* had had in a shoulder-pouch and by the glow from outside; there were no teklights anywhere in the building. The place smelled of dust and neglect, but nothing particularly noxious; the worst odor came from the *baz* accompanying him.

It was far from luxurious, but it could certainly have been worse.

The *drash*, when it arrived, was plentiful and a bit sweeter than the varieties Tulzik had eaten before. The *baz* had only brought a single sauce, a distressingly bland green one of uncertain origin, but Tulzik was hungry enough that he didn't care very much and quickly ate the entire serving.

The *baz* had supplied water as the only beverage. "Alcohol is dangerous," one of them explained. That was annoying, but tolerable.

He was just finishing the meal when a fifth *baz* arrived. At first Tulzik thought this implied some sort of emergency or important message, but his protectors quickly disabused him of the notion. One of them explained, "I'm done for today. My cousin is taking the next shift."

In fact, every three hours one of the guards was replaced – at least, Tulzik assumed the pattern continued while he was asleep, but he had considerable difficulty in telling one *baz* from another in the dim candlelight, so he could not be entirely certain. None of them were interested in polite conversation; they were there to protect him, not to talk to him.

He slept well, largely because he was exhausted, and he awoke refreshed. Things seemed to be going reasonably well, really. He was alive, well fed, well guarded, and in just a few days Dardem Karian-this should come to Ragbaan and find the Nine Families waiting for him.

Tulzik did not know whether the Nine Families would kill the

Biologist, but he hoped so. The man who had casually ordered Vika's death merely to test a weapon, if that was indeed what had happened, deserved to die.

The man who had wielded that weapon, Peval Salinzi, deserved death as well. Tulzik frowned at the thought; he had not had a chance to arrange for Peval to be at the slaughterhouse so the Nine Families would see that he was Dardem's accomplice.

Well, once the Biologist had been brought down, Peval could be handled somehow. The Nine Families would surely inform the Starfarers' Guild that the Biologist had violated his exile, and the Guild would see that Tulzik had told the truth.

At least, he hoped they would.

"If I'm not allowed to go to the Imperial Palace," Tulzik asked the head *baz*, "may I at least send my friend a message?"

"No."

"Why not?"

"It's not safe for anyone to know where you are."

"Then I won't tell him that! I don't even *know* where I am. I just want him to know I'm alive."

"We get paid to carry messages. You don't have any money."

"Charge it to Grandma!"

"She hasn't agreed."

"Then ask her!"

"We don't solicit work that way. Besides, that would be carrying your message to *her*."

"This is ridiculous. I just want Hrus to know I'm safe. Last he saw Peval was chasing me, trying to kill me."

The *baz* didn't answer.

"Look, if you don't take a message for me, I'll have to try to find some other means of communication. That could be dangerous."

The *baz* glared at him, then yielded. "Nothing written," it said. "Only a few words."

"Just tell him I'm alive and well and will be at the slaughterhouse."

Grudgingly, the *baz* said, "At the next shift change. The *baz* going off duty will take your friend your message."

"Thank you!"

It was two changes later that the newly arrived *baz* looked at Tulzik and said, "You're the man we threw out of our boat."

Tulzik looked at the *baz* and thought he saw something familiar about the face, but he could not be entirely sure. "Oh, was that you?" he said. "Quite a coincidence, meeting you here!"

"We were in a boat. That means we were there with the knowledge and approval of the Nine Families. The Nine Families employ the Gada Clan for many of their errands. You're being guarded by the Gada Clan. This is not a great coincidence at all."

Tulzik threw up his hands. He was getting very tired of the humorless, literal-minded *baz* attitude. "Fine. It's not a coincidence. Yes, I'm the one you threw out of the boat."

"I knew that. I just told you that."

"Yes, I noticed."

That seemed to satisfy the *baz*. It nodded and turned away.

As the second day dawned, Tulzik began to think he might go mad with boredom if his guards kept him confined here. There was no sign of Peval or any other dangers, and what little amusement could be had from his guards had been exhausted. He was getting very tired of the rotting-cinnamon smell of *baz*. A breakfast of *drash* with an insipid mushroom sauce did not help.

He told himself it would only be a few days, but that was not a great comfort.

He watched out the window for a time, but the view did not include anything of great interest, so he turned to exploring his temporary home.

The building's original purpose was not obvious. There were no distinguishing features. The walls showed signs of several repairs, but nothing stood out as indicating a particular intent. He spent several minutes calling every invocation he knew – admittedly, not many – without getting a response from any *kaua* or other ghosts; the place did not appear to be haunted. Given the lack of teklights, that wasn't particularly surprising. Everyone knew hauntings and teklights generally seemed to go together.

He was lying on the floor, staring up at the cracks in the ceiling and trying to decide whether they meant anything or were purely random, when a familiar voice called, "Tulzik?"

He sat up quickly, then got to his feet as Azl stepped into the room. Two *baz* promptly placed themselves between Tulzik and his visitor.

"Azl! It's good to see you!" he called. It would have been good to see *anyone* other than the *baz*, but Azl was an especially welcome sight. Tulzik's entire day suddenly seemed brighter.

She stopped about ten feet away, rather than defy Tulzik's guardians. "I'm pleased you're alive," she said. "The Ilm didn't think you would be."

That was mildly disappointing; Tulzik had thought he had made a good impression on the white-skinned creature, but apparently not *that* good. "It doesn't know me very well," he said. "What did *you* think?"

"I didn't have enough data," Azl said. "Hrus was unsure just what Peval had in the way of armament, or whether he was acting alone. We weren't as pessimistic as the Ilm, but when you didn't come back to the Palace we did worry a little. We didn't think you were cautious enough to stay away intentionally."

"I'm not, but it seems my guards are." He gestured at the *baz*.

"So I see. Who are the monkeyboys working for?"

"Grandma Pilot."

"I thought their clan markings looked like the Nine Families gang."

"You were right. They belong to the Gada Clan, and they're under contract to Grandma Pilot."

Azl eyed the *baz* blocking her path, neither of whom seemed inclined to say anything. She looked past them at Tulzik again. "Are you a prisoner, then? Did you annoy Grandma?"

Tulzik smiled grimly. "Actually, I got the impression she rather liked me. These fellows have been ordered to keep me alive until the meeting at the slaughterhouse and to make sure I attend. They find it easier to keep me alive if they don't let me go out in public, where there might be assassins waiting for me."

Azl grimaced. "That's typical runt thinking."

"How did you find me?"

Azl cocked a reproving finger at him. "You know I'm not going to answer that with the runts listening."

"No, I didn't know that," Tulzik replied, "because I thought they might have told you where I was. I take it they didn't."

"They didn't."

"Then of course you won't say here and now. I hope you'll have a chance to tell me later." He glanced at the nearest *baz*, who seemed to be paying no attention at all to the conversation going on above his head.

"We'll see."

"About that meeting," Tulzik asked. "Do we know whether it will happen?"

Azl shook her head. "Not really. The letter should have reached Zaraquan by now, and we hope it will work, but Peval may have other means of communicating with the Biologist in an emergency and may warn him off."

"So far as we know, though, Dardem Karianthis should be there?"

"Yes."

"It would be useful if Peval is there, too."

"I can see how you would think so. You want them both dead, don't you?"

"Oh, yes. They conspired to kill Vika," Tulzik said, surprised at how bitter his own tone was. "At least, I think they did. If they did, then yes, I want them both dead. Very much so."

"I'll see if we can arrange something."

"The Nine Families will have representatives there, with orders to kill me if the Biologist doesn't show and I don't have a good enough explanation," Tulzik said. "That might complicate matters, though I suppose they'll try to stay out of sight."

Azl frowned. "That's unfortunate, but we aren't going to do anything to prevent it. We can't operate in Ragbaan effectively if we make an enemy of the Nine Families."

"I assumed as much. You know, Azl, one reason I like you is that you don't pretend. You admit right out loud that you value your own life more than mine."

She shrugged. "We're in the business of selling truth. It gets to be a habit, being honest."

"I wouldn't know."

Azl smiled at that.

"Didn't Hrus already make an enemy of Parj Importer, though?" Tulzik asked.

"Hrus mildly irritated Parj Importer. That's not the same thing. Besides, that was only the Importers. The Divers were pleased with a job we did last year, and the others don't care about us one way or the other."

"Grandma does."

"Oh?"

"She thinks Hrus is a man of good judgment."

"I had no idea Grandma was so easily fooled," Azl said dryly.

Tulzik glanced at his guards again. They had stood silent and impassive throughout this conversation. "Do the...do monkeyboys understand sarcasm?"

"Sometimes. I don't think it matters in this case."

"Maybe not. At any rate, the Nine Families will have someone there. They may have rats observing, as well."

"This is turning into quite a gathering," Azl said.

Tulzik nodded. "I think Peval's doppelganger might enjoy it, too."

"He might, at that, but finding him could be challenging. Even if he's back in his tower, getting him out could be difficult."

"I suppose so."

"The Guild may be interested, as well."

"I hope so, yes."

"I'll ask if they'd like to observe."

"Not too visibly, of course."

"What about the Sorceress?"

Tulzik frowned. This was the first question he had not expected. "What about her?"

"Do you think she should be informed and offered the opportunity to attend?"

"I really don't know," Tulzik said. "She's involved, certainly, but if the Biologist detects her presence – "

" – he'll turn back. Good point."

"She might be able to send someone, though."

"Shall we defer to my husband's famous good judgment on that one?"

"I think so, yes. I don't know the people involved well enough to have a useful opinion."

"And that, Tulzik, is one reason *I* like *you*. You know your limitations."

Tulzik smiled wryly. "My uncle Urushak doesn't think so."

"Perhaps he misjudged your limits."

Thinking back to his uncle's absolute certainty that Tulzik would never find Peval in a city the size of Ragbaan, and the fact that he had found his man in just a few days, Tulzik smiled. "Perhaps he did."

"So Peval, his doppelganger, the Guild, perhaps the Sorceress." She ticked them off on her fingers. "Anyone else we should invite?"

"I'll trust your discretion."

"Wise of you, I'm sure. Anything else?"

Tulzik glanced at his captors. "Perhaps you could bring me something to read, or something to do, while I'm being so vigorously protected? A better sauce for the *drash* these monkeyboys feed me would also be welcome."

"Penzerene hot sauce?" Azl smiled innocently.

"By the thousand gods, no! I'm just a country bumpkin. I can't handle your spicy city foods. That stuff Hrus makes is delicious, though."

"I'll see what I can do. Assuming, of course, that your guardians don't whisk you off to some other hidden lair now that your secrecy has been compromised."

"You aren't going to do that, are you?" Tulzik demanded, addressing the leader of the *baz*. "She'll just find us there the same way she found me here."

The *baz* exchanged glances. "Don't tell anyone where we are," the leader told Azl.

"I wasn't planning to," she replied.

"Then..." The *baz* looked around at his companions before finishing, "...then we'll stay, at least for now."

"Good!" Azl said. "I'll be back later, then. Take good care of Tulzik, monkeyboys. We find him amusing."

With that, she turned and marched back out the door.

The five occupants of the room watched her go; then one of the *baz* turned to Tulzik and said, "That one's dangerous."

"Not to me," he said. He smiled. "Not to me."

CHAPTER 25

The last night before the scheduled meeting, Tulzik's guardians relocated him. They wanted him somewhere closer to the slaughter-house, to ensure he would be there on time.

Tulzik put up no resistance beyond insisting that they bring the books and papers Azl had delivered and the little jug that still held a few ounces of Hrus' peppered soy sauce, as well as the change of clothing he had convinced them to provide a few days before. He trudged along happily as they made their way through tunnels and deserted back streets, up the ridge and beyond, into the ruinous western reaches of the city.

The *baz* were not quite as happy – they were matching their own pace to Tulzik's, and he walked far more slowly than they usually did. They made no protest, though, and only rarely tried to hurry him.

Around sunset they selected a reasonably intact ruin along the Old West Road, perhaps half a mile from the slaughterhouse, as their lodging; it was right at the end of the human architecture, just before the *tsaughth* area began. Tulzik lit a few candles and settled down to read while the *baz* set about doing everything they could to make the ancient roofless structure once more fit for human habitation.

Supper was *drash* again, of course, and after so many repetitions even Hrus' sauce was not enough to make it interesting. Tulzik slept on bare ground that might once have been a concrete floor, after as-suring the monkeyboys that one night without any sort of bed would not kill him. He awoke the next morning with a bruised shin and a stiff back but otherwise intact and found the *baz* repairing the ruin.

"Why are you doing that?" he asked curiously, as two of them wedged a beam back into place.

"Because we're here," one of them answered.

Tulzik considered that for a moment, then shrugged. After several days in their presence he knew that the runts didn't think quite like human beings; sometimes he had no choice but to just accept that their actions wouldn't make sense to him. They might be perfectly normal and sensible by *baz* standards, but to humans they sometimes seemed crazy.

After a breakfast of *drash* – a substance Tulzik hoped never to eat again after this little adventure – the *baz* cleaned up every trace of their brief residence other than the repairs, then escorted Tulzik out of the ruin and turned him westward.

"We think you should arrive early, so that you can conceal yourself before Dardem Karianthis arrives," his lead guard explained.

Until then, Tulzik had not been entirely sure the *baz* even knew the nature of the planned meeting. Obviously, though, they did. They probably didn't *care*, but they did understand something of what was going on.

"He's not due until mid–afternoon," Tulzik pointed out. "The sun's barely over the ridge."

"He might be early," the *baz* said. "He might want to scout the terrain, or set traps."

Tulzik started to say something deriding this idea, then stopped. The runt was right. That sounded like exactly the sort of thing a former member of Ragbaan's intrigue–ridden elite might do. Still, staying hidden for half a day was not an appealing idea.

"Someone should watch the Pass and let us know when he's coming, so we can all hide," he said.

"It's being done," the *baz* replied.

"By whom?"

The *baz* frowned. "I think the commander's name would translate as Gnaws Wood Vigorously, born in the First Litter of the Matriarch of the Fourth Tunnel to the Southeast Storage Area. That's only approximate; there's a part about the shape of the fourth tunnel that's untranslatable. In her own language, it's..." He made a weird prolonged squeaking sound.

"A rat," Tulzik said.

"Of course."

"Then we don't need to hide until Gnaws Wood Vigorously says we do."

The *baz* did not actually deny this, but there was a reproving tone to his reply. "It would be wise to have a place chosen and prepared."

"I suppose so," Tulzik admitted. That settled, he accompanied his guards without further protest.

Finding a suitable hiding place was actually fairly difficult, as the *tsaughth* slaughterhouse did not lend itself readily to any human purpose, including concealment. Tulzik had forgotten, during his stay in Ragbaan, just how strange the slaughterhouse was. The vivid blue of the exterior, streaked with unpleasant reddish-brown, did not stay in his memory easily, nor did the unsettling dimensions.

Eventually, though, he clambered into what he supposed had been an upstairs room of some sort. The slaughterhouse had no intact stairs or ramps, and the surviving upper levels were not connected or related to one another in any obvious way, but a pile of broken machinery let Tulzik climb into what he thought had once been something like an office. The ceiling was too low for him to stand upright, though the *baz* had no such difficulty, but he could sit comfortably by the door and look down into the heart of the slaughterhouse. The inhuman proportions made it difficult to judge distances, but other than that he thought he would have a fine view of the proceedings.

Assuming, of course, that the Biologist took the bait and appeared on schedule.

He leaned back against a wall and was startled by a sudden squeaking. He turned to see a huge brown rat looking at him from atop a pile of debris in one corner of the room. It was wearing a yellow garment around its middle. It wasn't exactly a shirt, but it was close enough that he assumed this was what Kinl had meant. It also wore a black strap, somewhere between a belt and a sling, that held several tiny tools. One of them was presumably a knife. The rat was walking on all fours, but Tulzik had no doubt it could sit up and draw that knife easily enough.

One of the *baz* squeaked back at it.

"Is this Gnaws Wood Vigorously?" Tulzik asked, when the squeaking seemed to have paused.

"No, this is Scampers Too Fast to Be Seen," the *baz* answered. "A messenger."

"Is Dardem Karianthis arriving?"

"No."

Since the *baz* did not seem inclined to translate, and Tulzik did not know where to begin with questions, he said, "Please give Scampers Too Fast to Be Seen my regards, and my thanks for helping out." It could not hurt to be polite, even to a rat.

"She's being paid," the *baz* said.

"Nonetheless, I appreciate her participation. Please tell her so."

"It's not easy to say that in [squeak]," the *baz* grumbled. He proceeded to say something to the rat, however.

The rat listened intently, then looked past the *baz* at Tulzik and bobbed its head. Then it turned and scurried away.

"Thank you," Tulzik said.

The *baz* didn't answer.

"What did she say?" Tulzik asked.

The *baz* shrugged. "Mostly she wanted to be sure we would stay out of sight."

"Ah."

"Stay out of sight."

"Of course." With that, Tulzik reached for a book and settled down to read. Since most of the roof was gone, he had plenty of light.

He looked up when something whirred past. His nearest guard pointed to a small black object clinging to a nearby wall, an object Tulzik was fairly sure had not been there before. "*Tek*," the *baz* said. "Someone's watching."

Tulzik thought that might have been sent by the Starfarers' Guild, or the Nine Families, or some other faction that had heard of the expected meeting. He very much hoped it wasn't the Biologist's doing.

But the Biologist was a gene-cutter; if he wanted to scout ahead, he would probably have sent a bird or a small animal. At that, Tulzik looked out, through the hole that had once been a window and up through the shattered remnants of the roof, to see if any birds were nearby.

He saw none, but that was hardly conclusive. In any case, there was little he could do about it. He went back to his book.

Later he was vaguely aware of distant voices and the crunch of footsteps, but he was involved in his reading and did not look up.

Finally, though, he heard squeaking. He closed the book and turned to find a rat in a yellow shirt talking to his guards. He supposed this was Scampers Too Fast To Be Seen again, but he was not certain enough of the identification to say so. It certainly looked like her to his eyes, but he knew he could easily mistake one rat for another.

"Dardem Karianthis is climbing up the crater toward Slaughterhouse Pass," one of the *baz* told Tulzik, before he could ask. "You must take shelter, stay quiet, and stay out of sight."

Tulzik nodded and ducked down into the darkest corner of his refuge. His guards seemed to melt away into the shadows around him; Tulzik was startled at how well they concealed themselves. The rat watched this, then dashed away, vanishing through a hole in the floor.

Once positioned, Tulzik peered out through the door–hole into the main room of the slaughterhouse and waited.

A few minutes later he heard footsteps and wondered whether the alien acoustics of the ruined building were confusing him – the sound seemed to be coming from the east. Had Dardem circled around, perhaps?

Then a figure stepped into view in the slaughterhouse below, not from the west, but from the east, and Tulzik sucked in his breath.

It was Peval Salinzi, the original with the scarred nose, and he held the same device he had held when Tulzik last saw him, the thing that Tulzik thought was a sniffer, or a weapon, or both.

"Tulzik?" he called.

Tulzik had no intention of responding, but he was not given the chance; hard brown hands clamped over his mouth and pressed his arms and legs to the floor as three of the four *baz* leapt silently forward to ensure his silence.

He did not resist. Instead he stared down at Peval, trying to figure out how he came to be there and what he thought he was doing.

"Tulzik? Are you here? I only want to talk."

Tulzik had asked Azl to get Peval here, and here he was – and it seemed that Azl and Hrus had accomplished this by telling Peval that Tulzik would be here. That was moderately clever, Tulzik thought. He would have liked the idea better if Peval had not brought the sniffer.

Indeed, upon receiving no response, Peval was now fiddling with his device.

"I *know* you're here," he said. "Or at least you were, and it wasn't long ago." He looked up from his equipment and scanned his surroundings, but did not look up at the office where Tulzik lay – not yet, at any rate. Tulzik thought it could not be long before he would think to raise his gaze.

But Peval was staring at something, something Tulzik could not see from his perch.

He realized he could *hear* something, though. Something was buzzing.

"Oh, damn," Peval said. He froze, and as Tulzik watched a cloud of insects flew toward the gene-cutter, then began circling his head.

That explained the buzzing, but why these insects should appear so suddenly and focus entirely on Peval...

Well, really, there was only one likely explanation. These were not natural insects. They were the Biologist's emissaries, come to see whether Peval Salinzi had come to the meeting.

"Hello, sir," Peval said. "You shouldn't have come."

For a moment nothing happened; then there was a rustling, and more footsteps, and then Tulzik got his first look at Dardem Karianthis, the Biologist, the man who had apparently instructed Peval Salinzi to test his weapon on some gullible young woman. The Biologist had his back to Tulzik, so Tulzik could not see his face, but even so, the view was interesting.

Dardem Karianthis was tall, broad-shouldered, wearing a loose black leather coat and carrying a large leather pouch on a strap slung over one shoulder. His hair was black streaked with white and green, with what appeared to be feathers in it, as well; a pair of antennae swept back behind his ears. Tulzik guessed he had not limited his magical meddling to others, as those antennae appeared to be growing from his skull. Dozens of insects of various sizes buzzed around him; he had obviously come prepared.

"Peval," the Biologist said, in a deep, carrying voice. "I got your letter. What's this about the weapon not working?"

"It *didn't* work," Peval said. He held up a hand. "But sir, what are you doing here?"

Tulzik could not see the Biologist's face, but he saw the man hunch his shoulders and thrust his head forward. "You *asked* me to come! Your letter said you wanted to meet me here, and here you are."

Peval frowned and stepped back, looking from side to side. "I didn't ask you to come, sir," he said. "It must be a trick."

"A trick? What kind of trick? Didn't you send me a letter?"

"I sent...sir, we need to be careful what we say. Very careful." Peval continued to look around, obviously on alert for observers. Tulzik hoped the various observers were all well hidden.

"What? Why?" Now Dardem was looking around, as well. Tulzik caught a quick glimpse of a large and impressive mustache.

"You remember I told you about a girl I bedded at the inn in Kalidar?"

"You mean the..."

Peval opened his mouth to protest, and Dardem concluded, "Fine, yes, I remember."

"Her brother followed me to Ragbaan," Peval said. He lifted his hand-held device and scanned the area, apparently without result. "I think he's nearby, and I don't know whether he's alone."

Tulzik smiled behind the monkeyboy's hand. While Peval had not confessed to Vika's murder, or the assassination plot against the Sorceress, he was making it clear that he and the Biologist were old friends who had been in communication after the Biologist's exile. The Starfarers' Guild was presumably listening – Tulzik thought the black *tek* that hung on the wall nearby was one of their devices – and this should make it clear that Peval was the assassin, not Tulzik.

"Her *brother*? She had a brother?"

"Yes, sir. His name is Tulzik Ambroz." Peval raised his gaze and his voice. "Tulzik? Come out, please, so we can talk."

The grip on his limbs tightened needlessly. Tulzik did not move. But he heard footsteps.

The two men on the ground level turned at the sound – and then kept turning, as more footsteps joined the first pair. Tulzik also heard, close at hand, the scrabbling of tiny claws, but he was being held too tightly to turn his head to make sure it was a rat.

He could see the new figures appearing below, though – half a dozen of them, all pointing weapons toward Dardem and Peval.

"Dardem Karianthis?" a woman said.

"No, my name is Dillum Kardris," the Biologist responded mildly. "Who are you?"

"My name is Zara Fisher," the woman said. "I believe you *are* Dardem Karianthis, who owes the Nine Families a great deal of money."

"And who was sentenced to exile," one of the other newcomers added.

"That's a serious charge," Dardem replied. "Fortunately, I'm not this person you're looking for. Let me show you my identification." He reached for his leather pouch.

The *baz* snatched Tulzik up and began hauling him away from the scene as quickly as possible. Two of them jumped out the nearest window, then the next thing Tulzik knew he was being heaved out after them, only to find them waiting to catch him. A moment later he was being carried off, away from the slaughterhouse, northward into the surrounding ruins.

"Wait!" Tulzik said. "What are you doing?" He wanted to watch the confrontation – all the more so because he heard the snap and whine of weapons fire. This was what he had come to Ragbaan for, and now he was being dragged away!

"Keeping you safe," one *baz* said.

"But your job is done!" he protested. "You delivered me to the slaughterhouse, I was there at three o'clock – you don't need to protect me anymore!"

The *baz* exchanged glances, but did not slow their pace.

Tulzik was about to protest further when the screaming began.

CHAPTER 26

The screams had faded in the distance when the *baz* finally set Tulzik on his feet and released him. He immediately turned back toward the slaughterhouse.

"Don't," one of the *baz* said.

"You're done," Tulzik said. "You did your job."

"Good business to do a little extra, beyond what's in the contract," another *baz* replied.

"You know what a biologist is?" the first asked. "Why this person is called the Biologist?"

"I saw those bugs," Tulzik said, but he hesitated, and did not start walking.

"He's good with diseases, too."

Tulzik frowned. He had not thought about that. He had assumed that the screaming was a response to highly-toxic insect stings, but perhaps that wasn't the cause at all.

Still, Dardem Karianthis had armed Peval Salinzi with his sexual weapon and told him to test it. He had murdered Vika. He could not be permitted to escape. Tulzik began trotting back toward the slaughterhouse.

The *baz* exchanged looks, then followed him.

The screaming had stopped, but now Tulzik heard another sound – the hum of badly maintained motors and the crunching of wheels on dirt. Vehicles were approaching, magical ones.

A movement made him look up, and he saw an airship approaching, as well – a small one, not more than two hundred feet long, not one of the regular passenger craft. Brass fittings gleamed in the afternoon sun, and four big propellers were turning steadily at the tail as the vessel churned over the ruins toward the slaughterhouse. Several elaborately worked metal shafts protruded from the gondola, shafts that Tulzik thought were weapons of some kind.

Clearly, someone was coming in force. The Nine Families

appeared to have underestimated the Biologist; Tulzik hoped that whoever was manning these vehicles was not making the same mistake.

He turned a corner, bringing himself back in sight of the slaughterhouse, and saw a horseless wagon stopped in the street ahead. People were getting out of it. They all wore the shiny black uniforms and big goggles of the Starfarers' Guild, and their faces were further hidden by thick masks over mouth and nose – protective gear, presumably.

Tulzik slowed. The Guild had not seemed very fond of him at last report.

But he could not hang back; he had to see that justice was done, see that his voice was heard on Vika's behalf. He marched onward.

He was still fifty yards away when one of the Guildsmen started toward him. The temptation to stop and wait, or turn and flee, was strong, but Tulzik marched on as if the uniformed man had nothing to do with him.

The two approached one another and were about twenty feet apart when the Guildsman called, "You who call yourself Tulzik Ambroz!"

"What can I do for you, Guildsman?" Tulzik replied, still walking.

"Put this on," the Guildsman said, holding something out.

Tulzik stopped and looked and saw that it was a mask, a hard black thing that incorporated a large pair of goggles. That was not at all what he had expected.

"For your own protection," the Guildsman added.

Tulzik accepted the mask, but said, "I had not realized the Guild had any interest in protecting me."

"The Guild is interested in learning the truth," was the reply. "It will be easier to question you about your role in this situation while you are still alive."

The possibility that the mask was some sort of control device that would take over command of his body had not eluded Tulzik, but he decided to risk it. After all, the Guild was supposed to be a relatively benign group. He accepted the mask, untangled the straps, then fitted it over his own face and slid the bindings into place.

So far as he could tell, the mask did nothing but make it slightly harder to breathe and limit his peripheral vision. It had an odd, slightly damp smell, but he felt no alteration in his mood or memories or intentions. It did indeed seem to be merely a protective device – or at any rate, if it was doing anything more to him, it was doing it subtly.

The *baz* watched him put on the mask, but said nothing. He turned to look at them.

They did not react. They made no move to avail themselves of masks or other equipment. Presumably they felt no need for such protection. He shrugged, then turned his attention southward once again. Mask securely in place, he resumed his steady march toward the slaughterhouse.

A moment later he ducked through one of the low doorways and found himself back inside the alien structure, where Peval Salinzi and Dardem Karianthis faced each other, and where half a dozen hideous corpses lay around them, faces frozen in gaping, wide-eyed expressions of terror, streams of rapidly drying blood trailing from every mouth and nostril. Their weapons were scattered on the ground; some of them were clicking and buzzing.

So much for the effectiveness of the Nine Families, Tulzik thought.

Peval, facing away from Tulzik, was holding his now-familiar sniffer-equipped weapon and pointing it at the Biologist. The Biologist, for his part, clutched several small gleaming tubes. A few insects, though not as many as before, buzzed around his head.

One of the tubes lay open at his feet, and Tulzik guessed that it had held whatever had killed those six people.

"...a trap?" Dardem was saying, as Tulzik came within earshot.

"I didn't lure you here at all!" Peval protested. "I came here looking for Tulzik Ambroz – Vika's brother. The Ilm told me he was here." He lifted his weapon slightly higher and glanced at an indicator of some kind. "The sniffer says he was here."

"You sent me a letter telling me to meet you here today," Dardem insisted. "To discuss why this Vika didn't die."

"I sent you a letter, but I didn't tell you to come here," Peval replied. "Why would I do something stupid like that?"

"I assumed you wanted me to fix..."

The Biologist stopped in mid-sentence as he finally noticed that the two of them were no longer alone. He turned his head without moving the hand that held the tubes.

A Guildsman stepped forward out of the shadows, pointing a weapon of his own at the Biologist. "Dardem Karianthis," he said,

"you are under sentence of exile from the holy city of Ragbaan, yet here you are. Do you have anything to say in your defense?"

Tulzik saw the Biologist studying the Guildsman's mask, as if assessing how effective it would be against whatever plague he had unleashed against Zara Fisher and her companions. Then he called back, "I was tricked! I received a letter begging me to return and meet with this man, to treat a disease the doctors of Ragbaan could not cure. He assured me that I would be safe if I came no further than this *tsaughth* ruin, despite my exile."

"Do you have this letter with you?" the Guildsman asked, his tone mild.

"No, I don't," Dardem answered. "I left it in Berez, where I live now."

"Do you say you believed this assurance of safety?"

"No, of course not! But I thought it was worth the risk to help my old friend and former employee. I assumed he would have the sense to keep the meeting secret and come alone."

"I didn't send any such letter!" Peval protested to the Guildsman. "I wrote to him, yes, but I never suggested a meeting, or said I needed any medical treatment. I'm a gene-cutter myself, even if I'm not in his class. I can cure my own ailments."

"It *was* in your handwriting," Dardem said, looking thoughtfully at Peval. "I recognized it."

"It must have been forged!" Peval retorted.

"Who could forge your handwriting?"

"*I* don't know," Peval said. "Anyone who has a sample of it, I suppose. I've been working for the Sorceress, and I've written down a few things. Maybe it was her, or one of her people."

"How could she have my address in Berez?" Dardem asked. "You didn't give her *that* as part of your duties!"

"Of course not. Maybe she bribed someone in the Brotherhood. Or maybe..." His voice trailed off.

"Maybe *what?*" the Biologist demanded.

"Tulzik," Peval said. "He saw a letter I sent you. I didn't think he got a close enough look at it to read the address, but he was at the dock when the four o'clock to Zaraquan took off a few days ago."

The Guildsman who had been questioning the two turned to Tulzik and demanded, "Did you forge a letter from Peval Salinzi to Dardem Karianthis?"

Peval whirled, astonished by this interruption. He had not seen Tulzik until now.

"No," Tulzik said. "I wouldn't know *how* to forge one."

"Tulzik!" Peval exclaimed. "You *are* here!"

"Hello, Peval, you murdering filth," Tulzik said.

"What?" Peval stepped back, shocked.

"You killed my sister." Tulzik took a step forward.

Peval looked absolutely flabbergasted; apparently Tulzik's ruse had fooled him completely. "Vika's *dead*? But you said – "

"I lied. I wanted to know why you killed her and who you were working for."

"I didn't kill anyone!" Peval cried.

"Now who's lying?" Tulzik called.

"Someone is," the Guildsman replied. "Perhaps you *all* are." He turned to the Biologist. "Dardem Karianthis, you are in violation of your terms of exile, and you have killed six members of the Nine Families."

"That was self–defense!" Dardem protested. "They were armed and threatening me! Are you even sure they're dead? I violated my exile to save a life – isn't that an allowed exception? I'm only here because someone tricked me!"

"Is that your defense?"

"Yes! Someone lured me here. I was abiding by the terms I agreed to – I would stay out of the city *unless I was asked to return*. Well, someone asked me!"

"The Guild did not."

"The Guild didn't exile me."

For a moment, no one spoke; the Guildsman had no ready answer for that. Tulzik looked from one face or mask to another, looking for a reaction.

"You didn't," the Biologist insisted. "Not unless the Ambassador lied, and we all know she would never do that."

Tulzik hadn't known it. He had heard the Ambassador mentioned in passing once, but knew nothing about her.

"The Ambassador said she was speaking for the Sorceress and the Cooperative and the Nine Families and the Genealogists," Dardem continued. "The Guild wasn't included."

"We preferred not to be involved in the negotiations," the Guildsman said. "Nonetheless, the Guild may enforce any sentence of exile."

"But *someone* invited me back!" Dardem insisted. "I thought it was Peval, who works for the Sorceress, but he says the letter was forged."

"Why should we believe this letter ever existed?"

"Ask the Brotherhood of the Air! One of their couriers delivered it."

"Why would someone forge such an invitation?"

"Oh, do you *really* need to ask that? It's some scheme to grab power, it must be. Think about it! Yes, I'm here – but so are you, and so were those idiots from the Nine Families. How did they know I would be here? How did *you* know? Someone's making a move – I don't know who, or how it's supposed to work, but it *must* be part of some intrigue."

"You do not know who?"

"How could I? But whoever it is, six members of the Nine Families are dead – maybe that was deliberate. Whoever is responsible must have known I would defend myself."

"An interesting point."

For a second everyone was silent, and Tulzik was afraid the Biologist might actually talk his way out of his crimes. It seemed the right moment to stir up more trouble, true or not. "Peval works for the Sorceress now," Tulzik called. "What if the letter wasn't forged at all?"

"I didn't write it!" Peval angrily replied. He had stepped to one side and had been partly focused on Tulzik, but now he turned his attention back to the Biologist and pointed his weapon at his former employer.

"Who could forge it?" Dardem retorted, glaring at Peval.

"Tulzik saw the address," Peval said, pointing at Tulzik.

"I'm no forger," Tulzik protested.

"How do *we* know that?" Peval demanded. "You might be an *expert* forger, for all we know."

"I'm not," Tulzik said calmly. "I'm just a country boy looking for the man who betrayed my sister."

Peval looked uncomfortable at that.

The Biologist asked, "Who are you, again? What was your name?"

"Tulzik Ambroz, from Emniln."

"So what are *you* doing here?"

"The Nine Families wanted me to come. Grandma Pilot had me brought here."

"Why?"

"I don't know, exactly. They knew you were coming, and they had some monkeyboys bring me here to meet you."

"You let them do that?"

"Have *you* ever tried arguing with four monkeyboys?"

The Biologist smiled unpleasantly. "You have a point," he said. "But why did they *want* you here?"

"I don't know," Tulzik lied.

"The Nine Families work with documents all the time!" Peval suggested. "They must have forgers. Maybe they're behind it. These six you killed might have been involved in an internal feud, and their own people set them up. After all, they knew who you were, but they didn't have any protective gear."

"*You* did, apparently," Tulzik said. "You were here when they died, but you're still alive."

"What?" Peval turned back. "No, I didn't bring any gear. I have immunities in my blood from when I worked for Dardem. I'm not using any special magic."

"Is that true?" Tulzik asked the Biologist.

"Probably," the exile said, with a shrug. "It's true I safeguarded my own people against most of my weapons."

"For situations like the one here today," Tulzik said.

"Exactly."

"How could the Nine Families not know you would fight back?"

"They set their own people up to be killed," Peval said. "That must be it!"

"If you didn't write the letter," Tulzik asked, looking at Peval, "what are *you* doing here?"

"I...I was..." Peval looked from Tulzik to the Biologist, then to the Guildsman.

"You said you were looking for *me*," Tulzik said. "Why?"

"I...the Ilm said you were here..."

"What does the Ilm have to do with anything?" Dardem asked.

"Why were you pursuing this man?" the Guildsman asked.

"I wasn't!"

"Yes, you were," Tulzik said. "You tried to kill me a few days ago. I fell in with the Nine Families trying to escape you. That sniffer you're carrying – the only place you couldn't track me was the water, so that's where I went. You were chasing me, trying to kill me."

Peval stared at him. His ability to devise quick lies had apparently reached its limit. Then he said, "I wasn't trying to kill you. I just wanted to talk to you about your sister."

"About Vika? The girl you killed?" Something was rustling nearby, but Tulzik did not look for the source; he kept his gaze focused on Vika's murderer. Peval was rattled, and Tulzik wanted to keep up the pressure. If he confessed to the murder, that should settle the matter for the Guild.

"I didn't kill her!" Peval insisted. "I didn't even know she was dead!"

"Of course you killed her. That's why I'm in Ragbaan in the first place. I came looking for you to avenge her."

Peval looked from Tulzik to the Guildsman, but could read nothing through the mask and goggles.

"I didn't kill anyone," Peval insisted. "Why would I want to kill her?"

"I would like to know that, too," said a new voice – a woman's voice, coming from above.

Tulzik looked up to see a huge creature, vaguely lizardlike and partly batlike with leathery wings and green scales, perched on part of the broken roof. He thought he had glimpsed its wing once before, atop the Red Museum; the rustling he had heard was the flapping of those wings as it settled into its present position.

Astride the creature's neck sat a naked woman, who was peering down through one of the gaping holes into the interior of the slaughterhouse. She had golden skin, and a magnificent cascade of curling black hair tumbled down her back but did nothing to obscure her voluptuous figure.

This, Tulzik guessed, must be the Sorceress. And however naked she might appear, she undoubtedly had formidable defenses protecting her.

CHAPTER 27

"Alsia!" the Biologist exclaimed.

"Dardem," she responded. Then she turned her attention back to Peval. "Who is this girl you supposedly murdered and why did you kill her?"

"I didn't kill anyone!"

"He poisoned my sister Vika," Tulzik called.

"And why would he do that, farmboy?" the Sorceress demanded.

"To test the weapon he intended to use on you," Tulzik replied.

"No!" Peval shouted. "No, I swear that's not true, Mistress."

"Alsia ter Bithuni," the Guildsman said, "*we* are questioning these people."

The Sorceress turned her attention to this new speaker. "If someone was plotting to kill me I believe that's *my* concern and not yours, Guildsman."

"There is no evidence of such a plot – " the Guildsman began.

"Of course there is," Tulzik interrupted. "I know the Biologist is a great magician, but I doubt he's good enough to hide every trace of his work. I think a careful analysis of Peval's genes will show that any woman he beds will die."

Peval went pale as he threw Tulzik a glance; then he stared up at the woman and her flying mount.

"Really?" the Sorceress exclaimed. She looked from Peval to the Biologist. "Clever, Dardem, clever! And you know my tastes, too – Peval is a pretty one. I probably *would* have invited him into my harem in another few days."

"I had nothing to do with it!" the Biologist protested, stepping back. "If this man *is* carrying some horrible poison, it's nothing *I* did!"

"*What?*" Peval turned on Dardem. "You lying, treacherous mutant!"

"Now, Peval, really, what's the point in dragging me into it?" Dardem said, hands spread. Tulzik noticed he still held the metal tubes. "You know I haven't seen you in years, not since I was sent into exile; how could I have done anything? No, Alsia, Peval did this one on his – "

He didn't finish the sentence, as Peval fired the sniffer weapon at the Biologist's chest at a range of no more than a few feet. There was a popping sound, and a hole appeared in Dardem's chest. Blood spurted, though to Tulzik it seemed as if there was something unnatural about that gush of red; he suspected that Dardem had modified himself somehow.

The Biologist looked down at the wound. "Peval, you idiot..." he began.

Then he collapsed, his knees buckling. His hands opened and the metal tubes tumbled to the ground. Whatever defenses he might have had, they had apparently not been sufficient to protect him from this. His head rolled forward, and he folded up.

The insects circling his head did not fall, though. Instead their buzzing suddenly increased in volume, and they swarmed forward, toward Peval.

"Oh, no," Peval had time to say before the first insect landed on his cheek. He tried to slap at it, but it buzzed away as two more plunged in. He slapped again. "No, please..." he said.

Then he began screaming, and Tulzik watched as his face began to turn first red, then black in growing splotches centered on each spot where an insect had landed. He clutched at his face, then fell to his knees.

A few feet in front of him, the Biologist, crumpled in a heap, had stopped moving.

Tulzik had thought he would take pleasure in seeing his sister's killer suffering, but instead he found himself wincing and wanting to look away. He forced himself to watch, but at the same time he called out to the Guildsman and the Sorceress, shouting to be heard over the screams, "Can't you do something?"

"Why should we?" the Sorceress called back. When he looked up at her Tulzik thought he caught a glimmer of something shining around her, like an immense bubble.

"I know you can't save either of them, but can't you at least give him a quicker death?"

"If you like," the Guildsman said. He fired his weapon at Peval;

there was a brief whistling, and the screaming abruptly stopped.

Then he pointed the weapon at Tulzik.

Tulzik raised his hands, his gaze focused on the Guildsman – but he still saw, as the Guildsman apparently did not, that the Biologist's stinging insects were still alive, and now that they had been deprived of their prey they were starting to fly long, looping paths, seeking new targets. None of them went anywhere near the Sorceress, he noticed; in fact, they seemed to be staying well away from her and her strange mount.

"This would seem to settle any questions about Dardem Karianthis' exile," the Guildsman said. "Or any threat Peval Salinzi might have posed. It still leaves *you* unexplained, though."

"I told you," Tulzik said. "They killed my sister."

"Your story is that Peval Salinzi poisoned your sister in Kalidar."

"Yes."

"Peval Salinzi has been here in Ragbaan all along. He has not had time to visit Kalidar."

One of the insects had discovered the Guildsman and landed on one of the straps holding on the Guildsman's mask. Tulzik watched it as it began crawling across the rubbery black material, seeking exposed skin.

He had to decide whether or not to warn the Guildsman.

The man was pointing a lethal weapon at him and accusing him of lying, and Tulzik had a witness that he was cooperating – the Sorceress was still sitting astride her flying mount, watching with interest. He could let the insect sting the Guildsman, and who would blame him? It was very tempting.

But on the other hand he had no desire to see an innocent man die horribly, and making enemies of the Starfarers' Guild was probably not a wise course. "One of the bugs is on your mask," he said.

Tulzik could not read any expression through the Guildsman's mask, but he did not see any sign that the other man believed him.

"Sorceress," he called, "can you do something about those little monsters?"

The Sorceress laughed. "Are you sure you want me to?"

"Yes, please," Tulzik said.

"Then hold your breath."

Tulzik could not imagine why that would be necessary when he was wearing the protective mask, but he was not about to argue with the woman said to be Ragbaan's finest gene-cutter, and one of the city's most powerful individuals. He took a deep breath and held it.

Even as he did, he wondered what she could do. She was stark naked; although she clearly had some sort of defenses in place, what equipment could she have that would deal with the insects? What weapons could she employ?

She leaned forward and whispered something, though Tulzik could not see who she might be talking to.

Then her scaly mount stretched out a neck that was much longer than Tulzik had realized, lowering its head down into the slaughterhouse, and coughed out a cloud of mist.

The insect had reached the edge of the mask and was making its way onto exposed skin, but was apparently taking its time about biting, or stinging, or whatever it did to deliver its load of toxin. The Guildsman had finally felt its presence; he stiffened, and the weapon in his hand wavered.

Then the mist reached him.

The insect fell away, tumbling from the Guildsman's neck. Other insects dropped out of the air – some simply fell as if invisible strings had been cut, while others swerved, staggered, and swooped before tumbling to the ground.

The Guildsman coughed. Then he coughed again, harder, and then again, and then the coughing turned into an uncontrollable fit. The weapon fell from his hand as he doubled over; one hand reached up and pulled the mask from his face to allow more air into his lungs. He stepped forward, trying to regain his balance.

"Look out for those things!" Tulzik called, letting out his breath as the Guildsman's foot fell mere inches from one of the metal tubes the Biologist had dropped.

With the goggles removed, Tulzik could see the still-coughing Guildsman's eyes widen as he stared at the shiny little cylinder he had almost crushed. He stepped back.

"I *told* you to hold your breath," the Sorceress called.

Tulzik had already let his breath out when he called the warning to the Guildsman, and now breathed in without feeling any ill effects. The mist had settled or dissipated and was no longer a threat.

"Thank you," he called up to the Sorceress.

"I want the bodies and whatever is in those tubes," she replied.

Tulzik shrugged. "I am not inclined to argue the point," he said.

The Guildsman who had been talking before was still too busy coughing to respond, but two more Guildsmen – or rather, a Guildsman and a Guildswoman – now stepped forward out of the shadows. "That may require discussion," the male replied.

"I just saved your companion's life," the Sorceress said. "What's more, these two were plotting to kill me."

"That has not been established," the Guildswoman said.

"It has been to *my* satisfaction," Alsia answered.

"You believe this Tulzik's story?"

"I believe that Peval turned on his employer when this Tulzik said the poison would show up in Peval's genes. That's certainly a good start on evidence, and I expect analyzing Peval's remains will confirm it."

"But he lied about Peval's whereabouts – "

"No, I did not," Tulzik insisted. "Peval made himself a doppelganger, and the Guild watched *that* for the entire time Peval was in Emniln and the other towns west of here."

"A doppelganger?" the unharmed Guildsman asked. "Then where is it?"

"Here," a new voice said.

Tulzik and the three Guildsmen turned to see Hrus crouching in the slaughterhouse door, his hand on the shoulder of Peval's doppelganger.

"I'm sorry we're late," Hrus said. "We seem to have missed all the excitement."

"What happened to my brother?" the doppelganger said. "Is he all right?"

"No, he isn't," Tulzik replied.

"Don't look," Hrus said, turning the doppelganger away.

"There *is* a doppelganger!" the Guildswoman exclaimed.

"I want *him*, too," the Sorceress said. "He's as pretty as the original – no, prettier. His nose isn't scarred. Comparing their genes should be interesting."

"There will be an investigation," a Guildsman said.

"There'll be more than that," a new voice said. Tulzik turned to see a man holding an arcgun walking up behind Hrus. He was not in the uniform of the Starfarers' Guild, but he did appear to be wearing a protective suit of some kind – a blue one, with a clear faceplate. "Six of our people are dead!"

"How did you know that?" the Guildswoman asked.

"We have our methods," the man in blue said.

"The rats told them," Tulzik said.

Even through the faceplate, Tulzik could see that the newcomer was annoyed. "Yes, the rats told us," he acknowledged, as Hrus grinned at Tulzik.

"We seem to have quite a body count here," Hrus remarked, looking over the interior of the slaughterhouse.

"They all belong to us," the man in blue announced.

"Oh, I don't think so," the Sorceress called down.

The man in blue looked up, startled; he had apparently not noticed the Sorceress and her bizarre mount before. "Dardem Karianthis owed us fifteen thousand *walu*!" he answered.

"Dardem Karianthis is dead," the Sorceress retorted.

"We are claiming his possessions and his remains to pay the debt!"

"What are you going to *do* with them? You don't have anyone who can study them safely."

"We'll manage."

"Wait a minute," Tulzik said. "The Biologist was killed by Peval Salinzi." Before the man in blue could respond, Tulzik continued, "Peval was working for the Sorceress."

"So he claimed," the Sorceress said. "*You* said he was really still working for Dardem, trying to assassinate me."

"He was, but still, he was your employee. He had been working for you as a gene–cutter."

"Yes. So?"

"Dardem Karianthis cannot pay his debt to the Nine Families because your employee killed him," Tulzik said. "That employee is also dead, so *you* are liable for the debt. *You* owe the Nine Families fifteen thousand *walu*."

"I do not!" the Sorceress protested. "Peval was not acting on my orders!"

"Of course, once you've paid that debt, the Nine Families have no further claim on any of the Biologist's effects," Tulzik continued. "They would all belong to you. Including the doppelganger."

For a moment, no one spoke. The Sorceress stared down at

Tulzik with a wry smile spreading across her face.

"Good for you," she said at last. She turned to one of the black-clad, goggled Guildsmen. "Does the Guild have any objection to that?"

The Guildsman hesitated before replying, "I would not think so."

"It would keep the peace in Ragbaan," Hrus remarked.

"Of course, the doppelganger may ask for his freedom," Tulzik pointed out.

"If he does, he'll have it," the Sorceress said. "I'm not stupid enough to defy the law that's at the heart of my business. If you could keep slaves against their will, any half-trained gene-cutter could make them."

"You'll pay us fifteen thousand *walu*?" the man in blue asked. Tulzik grimaced; the fellow seemed a little slow.

"Yes," the Sorceress replied.

"You get the Biologist and his assassin, then, and all their belongings, and the doppelganger – but we still take our own dead."

"Are you sure you want to touch them?" the Sorceress asked.

The man looked uneasily at the blood-soaked corpses. "Ah... perhaps not."

"I will be happy to return their remains to their families when I have completed my analysis and made certain they are safe to handle."

The man in the blue protective suit considered that for a moment, then said, "In that case, as the representative of the Nine Families, I accept your offer."

"Good! Now, where is that doppelganger?"

"Over here," Hrus called. "Crying."

"Of course," the Sorceress said, and Tulzik thought she sounded surprisingly compassionate. "He's just lost his entire family, hasn't he? I'll try to comfort him." She stroked her mount's neck, and the creature lifted its head, spread its wings, and leapt into the air, carrying itself and its passenger out of Tulzik's sight.

Tulzik turned to peer through the doorway where Hrus, the doppelganger, and the representative of the Nine Families had stood, but Hrus and the younger Peval were gone. Only the man in blue remained.

"It would appear you may have told the truth," one of the Guildsmen said, addressing Tulzik. "Nonetheless, we would still like to question you further."

"I'd be glad to answer your questions," Tulzik said, "but perhaps we could go somewhere more hospitable? This place was unpleasant enough even *before* it was littered with corpses."

"I think that can be arranged."

"If you would come this way?" the Guildswoman suggested.

Tulzik nodded and stepped toward her.

He heard movement behind him; he turned and found the four *baz* still there. He had forgotten all about them.

"We will accompany him," one of them said.

"They will accompany me," Tulzik told the Guildswoman.

"As you please," she said. She turned to lead the way.

Tulzik followed.

The *baz* accompanied him.

CHAPTER 28

It took all that night and half the next day for Tulzik to answer all the Guild's questions to their satisfaction, and for the Sorceress and her slaves and creatures to gather up the dead and transport them away. The Sorceress herself took the doppelganger in hand and escorted him back to the living part of the city.

What the Nine Families did Tulzik was not sure, but he glimpsed both *baz* and rats hurrying around the slaughterhouse.

The four *baz* who had guarded him in the slaughterhouse stayed with him throughout the Guild's interrogation, which began in the ruins near the slaughterhouse, then proceeded into a series of tunnels that Tulzik was fairly certain led back toward the inhabited areas. During one lull in the questioning Tulzik asked one of them, "Why are you still here?"

"Grandma's orders," the *baz* replied.

No further explanation was offered.

Tulzik tried to tell the truth – it was easier to keep consistent that way, and he had nothing he felt a need to hide. He told his story in absurd detail until finally the Guild ran out of questions and released him. Following his questioners' directions, he emerged from a tunnel to find himself under one of the High Piers, overlooking the Grand Avenue a little to the north of the Imperial Palace.

The *baz* emerged with him, but this, it seemed, finally ended their attendance on him. Without so much as a wave, the four hurried off to the northeast, heading home.

Tulzik watched them go, then looked around. He had lost track of time during his sojourn beneath the city, but judging by the position of the sun it was mid-afternoon, almost exactly a day after the Biologist and Peval had killed one another. He had been fed three meals of *drash* during his stay with the Guild, so he was not particularly hungry; he was desperately short on sleep, though. He considered finding an empty room somewhere and taking a nap, but decided against it. He wanted a real bed, and he wanted to be sure Hrus and Azl were alive and well.

He made his way through the tangled streets leading down the ridge and reached Grand Avenue without much difficulty. There he turned south and headed for the Palace.

As he walked, he looked at the city – the crowded streets, the mismatched buildings, the ruined towers, the horseless wagons and colored teklights, the airships drifting overhead, whirring little machines dashing underfoot, and brightly colored winged creatures fluttering from tower to tower. It was very different from Emniln, but it was beginning to feel familiar.

Still, his work here was done. Vika's killers were dead. Justice, or at least vengeance, had been served. He would be heading home soon. If he could find some way to raise the fare, he would take an airship to Zaraquan; if no money was to be had, he would just have to walk.

But first he needed to say farewell and thank you to Azl and Hrus, and he wanted to ask a few questions and clear up a few details. The Guild had asked hundreds of questions, but had not deigned to answer any.

He reached the palace without incident, hurrying past the dancers in the plaza, under the arched portico, through the ruined doors into the vestibule, past the map-sellers, and into the Great Hall, where the babble of voices echoed from the gilded galleries and the smell of cooked meat and fresh produce filled the air. He turned right and began weaving through the maze of merchants' stalls, past the yellow marble staircase and under the balconies, into the north arcade. He made his way past the first forty yards of people offering services and found the sign reading "Questions Answered & Things Found."

Azl was seated at the table, wearing a maroon blouse and black pants, and chatting with Hiji the Oracle. She looked up at Tulzik's approach.

"You owe us thirty-one *walu* and four *jit*," she said without preamble.

He stopped dead. "What?"

"Three *walu* a day, plus expenses. That was the deal."

"Oh, but I – "

"But nothing," Azl said. "Did you think we'd forgotten?"

"Not *forgotten*, but – "

"Not excused or forgiven or waived, either."

"But I don't have any money!" Tulzik exclaimed.

"Then you'll need to earn some."

"How am I supposed to do that?"

"If you were clever, you would have asked the Sorceress for a finder's fee for alerting her to the assassination plot. Alas, that you let that opportunity elude you."

"Perhaps you could still ask her," Hiji suggested.

Azl shook her head. "I think the moment has passed," she told Hiji. "He already cost her fifteen thousand *walu*. Going back for more now would only anger her."

"He what?" Hiji stared. "Fifteen *thousand*?"

"She got value for her money," Tulzik said.

"Did she?" Hiji asked. "You must tell me more."

"Another time," Azl said. "At our usual prices." She looked up at Tulzik. "Thirty–one *walu* and four *jit* – that's not so much."

"It's far more than I have."

"Perhaps your parents, or your uncle, might send you the necessary funds?"

"They might," Tulzik admitted.

Just then Azl turned to stare down the passage. She smiled. Tulzik followed her gaze and saw Hrus approaching. He wondered how Azl had spotted him so quickly when she had not even been looking in that direction.

Well, the two of them had always seemed to have some sort of supernatural communication. This was probably just more of the same.

For a moment, as Hrus made his way through the crowd, none of them spoke; then Hrus told Azl, "Grandma swears she didn't expect the Biologist to really show up."

Azl glanced at Tulzik. "I thought she liked him."

Hrus snorted. "Grandma never lets that interfere with business."

"Liked who?" Tulzik asked. "She didn't like the Biologist, did she?"

Azl said, "That's two questions. We can add them to your bill, I suppose."

"Never mind," Tulzik replied hastily.

"Has he agreed?" Hrus asked.

"Not yet," Azl answered.

Tulzik started to ask who they were speaking of and what he had not yet agreed to, but caught himself before the first word had entirely left his lips. Thirty-one *walu* were quite enough debt.

Hrus looked at him and said, "We offer an employee discount."

Tulzik blinked. "What?"

"You get that one free," Azl said, smiling. "If you want, you can work off what you owe us."

Tulzik looked from her to Hrus, then back. He started to ask why they would want to hire an ignorant country bumpkin, then stopped.

"You learn quickly," Azl said, guessing his thoughts. "Most people from out of town have far more trouble dealing with Ragbaan than you have. You have nerve – you faced Grandma and the Biologist and the Sorceress without quailing. You think fast. You recognize your mistakes and try to correct them, rather than denying them. You behave well – Scampers Too Fast to Be Seen was impressed with your manners. We have some jobs where we think you could be useful."

"We would credit your account with thirty *jit* a day," Hrus said. "Free room, but you buy your own food."

"You will abide by our agreement with Hiji and not warn off his customers," Azl added. "We have arrangements with other people, as well."

"At the very least, it should keep you entertained until your family sends the money to pay your bill," Hrus said.

That was true, and at the moment he had no better offers. "Employee discount," Tulzik said. "Just a discount?"

Azl and Hrus exchanged glances. "Fine," Azl said. "You get a dozen questions about recent events as a signing bonus."

"Fifteen."

"*You* owe *us* money, Tulzik Ambroz."

"A dozen, then." He held out a hand.

Hrus shook. "Welcome to the firm," he said. "Your first question?"

"What did Grandma Pilot tell you?"

Hrus grinned crookedly. "That would have been two or three *walu* right there," he said. "Come upstairs, and I'll tell you."

An hour later Tulzik sat back, popped another nut into his

mouth, and said, "So let me see whether I have this straight. When you asked why they sent six people and didn't provide them with the means to defend themselves against a master gene–cutter like the Biologist, Grandma *admitted* it was stupid?"

"She admitted the eager young volunteers were stupid, certainly," Hrus said. "Stupid enough that they had annoyed their superiors to the point of considering them expendable, stupid enough that they didn't realize just how much they had irritated people, and stupid enough that they didn't question the lack of defenses. But it wasn't really a deliberate attempt to get them killed; no one in the Nine Families really expected the Biologist to show up, and they definitely didn't have orders to try to capture him. Zara Fisher did that on her own, and you saw what happened. The six of them would have been more than enough to kill *you*, though."

"They thought so, anyway."

"I think so, too."

Tulzik grimaced. "So do I," he admitted. "But I wouldn't have made it easy."

"I'm sure you wouldn't," Hrus agreed. "But that's why they were there – to kill you once it was clear the Biologist wasn't coming. When he showed up after all – well, their orders didn't really cover that. Zara apparently decided they could handle him."

"Even if they didn't think the Biologist was going to show up, wouldn't it have made sense to be prepared?"

"Probably," Hrus admitted, "but the Nine Families didn't *have* any protective gear for them. They leave gene–cutting and protective suits and the like to the experts. They know the sea, and trade, and money, not biological magic. Grandma says the Divers have suits that might have worked, but nobody thought of it, and she isn't sure using those on land would be a good idea. Oragir Pilot got that one suit from the Antiquarians years ago and brought it along just in case – he'll probably get a promotion for thinking of that. If he'd thought to already have it on before Zara got herself killed, he'd *definitely* have been promoted by now."

Tulzik nodded. "I see."

"Grandma says she really did *hope* you'd live through all this somehow, but she didn't *expect* it."

"Nice of her."

"You don't live eight hundred years by being sentimental."

"I suppose not."

There were other questions to ask, but Tulzik was in no hurry. He was going to be living in Ragbaan, in the Imperial Palace, for some time. He had already learned that Azl had been the one who informed the Sorceress about the meeting at the slaughterhouse; the Starfarers' Guild had already been contacted by the Pilots. It had been Hrus who found the doppelganger and brought him to the slaughterhouse; he hadn't sent Azl because they assumed the original Peval had told his younger twin not to trust Tulzik or the woman who called herself Lizi Tamial. Just *how* Hrus had found the doppelganger he did not explain, beyond saying that he and Azl had a few trade secrets for locating people. Tulzik remembered how Azl had found him where the *baz* were holding him and guessed that those same secrets had been involved.

If he decided he really needed to know, Tulzik decided, there would be time to ask about that later. For now, he let the conversation turn from the recent confrontation to other, lighter subjects.

Later that evening, after a pleasant supper of ham and vegetables, Tulzik sat down to write a letter to his parents, describing the situation. He assured them that the two men responsible for Vika's death, Peval Salinzi and Dardem Karianthis, had both died horribly – while nothing could bring Vika back or make up for her loss, proper retribution had been taken. He did not go into much detail, but he assured them that while he had arranged for their deaths, he had not personally killed anyone. He explained about his debt to Hrus and Azl. He told them that they could send the money to pay his bill if they chose, but he did not mind staying in Ragbaan until he had earned it himself.

"Either way," he wrote, "it shouldn't be more than a few months before the bill is paid and I am free to return to Emniln. When that is achieved, I will be coming home."

He paused, lifting the pen from the paper and staring at the words on the page. Then he added, "Or perhaps not. You know, Mother, and Father, I think I like it here. I just might stay longer."

He signed it, "Your loving son, Tulzik." He put down the pen and started to fold the letter.

Then he stopped, flattened it out again, picked up the pen, and crossed out "longer." In its place, he wrote, "indefinitely."

A Traveler's Guide to Ragbaan

Welcome to Ragbaan!

As every traveler must surely know, Ragbaan is the greatest city upon the face of our world, the seat of civilization, the heart of our history. Its origins are lost in the mists of time, and it was already ancient in our earliest surviving records, but it has been a hub of commerce and home to a variety of peoples for at least ten thousand years, accumulating an astonishing range of streets and structures. As such, it can be perhaps a trifle daunting to a new arrival.

I, Arguin Arborsi, a native of the metropolis, have therefore taken it upon myself to write this little pamphlet, available for purchase for a mere four *jit*, as a beginner's guide to my magnificent homeland.

My services as a personal escort and advisor are also available to the cautious traveler at very reasonable rates. You can find me most afternoons at the Southgate gallery. If I am not present, leave a message at Sarago's Grill.

The South Gate, also known as Fimbir's Arch, is one of the traditional entrances to Ragbaan. It was erected by order of the usurper Fimbir Throat-Cutter during the Autumn Interregnum, in the 142nd year of the Theoretical Dynasty of the Fourth Empire, to commemorate his rise to power. Most of Fimbir's corpse was later hung from it as a warning to others who might challenge the Theoreticians.

While that bloody spectacle undoubtedly struck fear into many a heart in its day it is now merely a bit of local color, and what the astute traveler will find at the South Gate today is a commercial gallery offering a diverse selection of goods and services at bargain prices. Do try some of our local specialties – *sithis*, *drash*, roast tunnel rat, and grilled tower lizard are among the Ragbaan favorites rarely seen outside the city.

The South Gate has marked the southern limit of the city since the Thirty-Minute Plague brought down the Humble Federation, some six hundred years ago. The areas beyond were cleared of all structures as part of the failed attempt at quarantine, and indeed, stripped down almost to bedrock, leaving the land unfit for farming – but providing the children of Southgate with a very fine beach along the shore of Ragbaan Bay, and giving every traveler approaching from the south a clear view of the Arch and the city's skyline.

Passing through Fimbir's Arch you will find yourself at the southern end of Grand Avenue, the city's central axis. This ancient thoroughfare, paved some eight thousand years ago with a stonelike substance modern magicians have been unable to analyze or duplicate, extends twelve miles due north from the Arch, turns to the northeast at a plaza known by no fewer than thirty-one different names, and continues another four miles before ending abruptly at the ruins of the Alberam Borer.

The maker and purpose of the Borer, if they were ever known, have been lost in the mists of the past, but the frame of the great machine remains thrust diagonally up through the city, blocking Grand Avenue and several other streets. The local urchins will be happy, for a modest fee, to show you the safest trails up the side of the immense device and give you a tour of its mysterious rusting interior. (Be aware that being shown the route *out* may require an additional fee. The astute traveler will take careful note of landmarks on the way in.)

To the east of Grand Avenue the city extends down the gentle slope to Ragbaan Bay, and well out into the water. At times in the past the level of the Naris Sea has varied considerably, and the shoreline of Ragbaan Bay has receded or encroached accordingly; in fact, the whole bay appears to have gone dry for a few centuries during the Dry Years of long ago, and the entire seabed, from the Karvish Wrecks to Dagger Head, is covered with the ruins of that era's streets and structures – many of which still stand tall enough that their upper stories are above water, and can be used by our present population.

Do not attempt to visit any of the sunken towers on your own, though. All of them are the carefully-guarded property of the Nine Families, who control all of Ragbaan's water traffic.

And after all, you will find plenty to see on land!

To the west of Grand Avenue the land slopes upward, rising

above the heart of the city – but in the Warm Years the Bay rose as well, flooding much of Ragbaan. Grand Avenue itself was under almost a hundred feet of water! Even this could not kill our great city, though; our ancestors simply extended the city westward, over the hills, and built a new waterfront. You can see the remains of that era in the High Piers, some of the docks and wharves that lined that shoreline. These still stand, well over a mile west of the present–day coast, and hundreds of feet above sea level.

Of course, we can scarcely dock sea–going vessels at them up there, but we have put them to other uses, including docking our magnificent airships. These brightly–colored behemoths fill the skies of Ragbaan, and carry passengers for hundreds of miles in every direction.

Above the High Piers, another few miles to the west, the ridge crests in a jagged row of stony outcroppings known as the Peaks. The current inhabitants of our great city see no need to use any of the land beyond this natural boundary, but in olden times, when the population was larger, or the seas were higher, this additional space was filled with more of Ragbaan's grandeur. These abandoned districts, the Western Suburbs, now provide several square miles of ruins, should anyone be inclined to explore. Not all these ruins were built by humans, and even some that were are inexplicable to our modern sensibilities; a visit to the Western Suburbs can be intriguing, even baffling.

Further west of the Peaks, beyond even the ruins, lies the Crater. Legend has it that this was once a great port, where ships came down from the sky bringing immigrants and trade from other worlds, but at some point in the past – some historians place it at the fall of the Second Empire – this port was blasted out of existence by a great weapon, the likes of which our feeble modern magic cannot begin to approximate. That this knowledge was lost is all for the best, I would say! All that remains now is a great pit, miles across, where the soil and water are poisonous. The only entry into the Crater from the city is through Slaughterhouse Pass, at the end of the Old West Road; there are three exits on the western side, leading out onto the Ammerbal Plain.

And so you have the southern third of the metropolis, extending from Ragbaan Bay in the east to the Crater in the west, with Grand Avenue, the High Piers, and the Peaks dividing it. Fimbir's

Arch marks the southern end of this section, while the many-named plaza where Grand Avenue turns to the northeast is the northern end.

The area surrounding the plaza and extending down to the waterfront is known as the Tralast. This is the commercial heart of the city. It is here that you will find our centers of trade and industry, including the great market house known as the Imperial Palace.

This was the seat of government more than once, when Ragbaan ruled vast empires, but now it has been put to more practical use. Its grandiose halls are now filled with merchants and tradesmen of every kind, specializing in hard-to-find goods and services, transforming the ancient corridors of power into a veritable cornucopia of the arcane and exotic. Anything you wish to purchase that you cannot find at the South Gate you will find in the Imperial Palace, though of course it will be more expensive, and one cannot be as certain of the authenticity and quality as one would be in the shadow of Fimbir's Arch. Naturally, a market devoted to the uncommon will attract more than its share of charlatans and frauds.

Beneath the Tralast is a network of tunnels extending downward to well below sea level; the actual depth is unknown, since the lower levels are all flooded. These tunnels appear to have been built over several millennia, for a variety of purposes. Some are still used regularly as shortcuts, or as warehouses, or as meeting places, but many are abandoned and empty, and their full extent is unknown. Some tunnels may be found here and there throughout the metropolis, but the Tralast is home to by far the most complex, extensive, and mysterious network.

To the north and west of the Tralast you will find a patchwork of small communities in a maze of narrow streets – communities such as Dulsti, where the ancient secrets of producing *sithis* are passed down through the generations, or Vursei, where the cult of the Antiquarians gathers their artifacts and preaches their strange religion. These enclaves extend out past the northern end of the Peaks, along the highways to Pevigar, Shez, and the Mad Cities. There are also extensive ruins out to the northwest, just as there are west of the ridge.

To the north and east of the city's heart, beyond the Alberam Borer, along the northern shore of the Bay all the way to Dagger Head, and inland well into the Suvask Hills, humans are a minority. Visitors to this part of the city should proceed cautiously. The *baz* make their homes here, in a section called Monkeytown that extends from the Emerald Wall to Aberration Boulevard, and beneath these streets lies the core of Ragbaan's rat population. Neither group bears any ill will toward tourists, but cultural misunderstandings are common and can be extremely awkward.

Ah, but if you are from a less fortunate land than glorious Ragbaan, you may be unfamiliar with our non-human brethren. Ragbaan is inhabited by perhaps three million humans, the scholars tell us, but it is also home to several other intelligent species.

There are perhaps half a million *baz* – short, powerfully-built people with distinctive hairy arms. You will undoubtedly see many of them going about their business on the city streets; do not attempt to interact with them. If they are outside their own community, they are almost certainly carrying out tasks they have been hired to perform, and will actively resent any interruption in their employment.

There are untold millions of rats, both in their homeland in the northeast and scattered everywhere through the underground portions of the city. The true rats of Ragbaan are not to be confused with the animalistic tunnel rats found here and in other cities. The true rats are highly intelligent and thoroughly civilized, but due to difficulties in communication prefer to limit their interactions with their larger neighbors; you are unlikely to see any. If you do glimpse a rat, you can readily tell the true rats from their bestial kin – true rats will be clothed and probably carrying tools. Please respect these industrious citizens.

Do not be alarmed if you see rats roasted on skewers in the markets or restaurants; these are tunnel rats, mere vermin, despite their unfortunate resemblance to the true rats. Tunnel rat, properly seasoned, is a delicacy well worth trying, and there are professional hunters working beneath the Tralast to supply the city's markets.

Do not worry that a true rat might be disturbed by the sight of a human gnawing on his distant relative; the true rats are no fonder of wild tunnel rats than we are.

As for other species, there is the Ilm. This tall, white-skinned being with a feathery crest on its head is unique – and uniquely mysterious. No one knows where it came from, or how long it has lived in Ragbaan. It's possible the Ilm itself does not know.

There were the *tsaughth*. These squat, unpleasant creatures ruled Ragbaan briefly a few centuries back, and legend has it that a few may still lurk in the deeper tunnels and in the ruins of the city's uninhabited areas.

And there are the various artificial inhabitants – homunculi of all shapes and sizes, *kaua* built into innumerable structures, ghosts and spirits of various kinds, free-roaming machines, and so on. Ragbaan is blessed with the finest gene-cutters and roboticists in the world, and a variety of other remarkable magicians. If you see strange creatures lurking in alleyways or peering over rooftops, don't be alarmed – every gene-cutter and roboticist ensures that her creations have an unwillingness to harm humans built into them.

That is, every *present-day* gene-cutter and roboticist. Some remnants of older, less protective cultures still linger. It is very unlikely that any of these will trouble you, but they do exist.

One category of curiosity still roaming the streets is the *snaffer* – or *snarfer*, or *snuvver*, depending upon your dialect. These machines were built as assassins thousands of years ago, during the declining years of the Third Empire. Each was given the means to identify an individual target, which it would then hunt down and kill. It would then bring proof of its success to whoever it had been instructed to inform.

Not all the *snaffers* succeeded in locating their prey – their intended victims escaped, or died by other means before being caught. These machines had not been equipped with any understanding of failure, however, and perhaps twenty or thirty are still wandering the city in search of political enemies who have been dead for centuries. Some people find their futile hunts amusing; others worry that their old training may have become faulty, allowing them to misidentify unfortunate innocents as their quarry.

The odds that you might be mistaken for one of these ancient troublemakers are very low, I am sure, but if you would like to be *absolutely sure* of your safety, for a modest fee I, Arguin Arborsi, can provide protection against *snaffers* or other ancient machines.

My services as a tour guide are also available. I would be happy to show you my city, from the mysterious multi-level tunnels beneath the streets to the sunny heights of our remarkable towers. I can show you the strange and erotic dances of homunculi created purely to entertain, teach you how to coax answers from *kaua* that claim to hold the wisdom of bygone millennia, and introduce you to the city's elite, perhaps even arrange an audience with the Mayor. I can escort you to the sunken towers in the harbor, or the castles that guard the Peaks. Monuments to long-forgotten emperors, museums whose meaning has been utterly lost, temples of obscure cults – I know them all. Let me show them to you!

Let me show you Ragbaan!

PATRONS' PAGE

The following people were instrumental in seeing this book to publication:

Lemuel J. Bell Jr.
Norman R. Thallheimer
Melanie Fletcher
Christopher Turkel
Jake Kesinger
Alexis M. Allen
Simon Mark de Wolfe: *"The author writes on the page and opens a gateway to other worlds; it is up to us to fill in the colours."*
Ren Shore: *"My parents grew my imagination with comic books, Doc Savage, and science fiction for fertilizer."*
Dustin Sova: *"Thank you, Carol Asher, for introducing me to my favorite author."*
Brian Bilbro: *"Thanks for all of the adventures!"*